Gabriel watched Susan Carter embrace her daughters. The scene filled him with longing....

For all his talk about being willing to wait for a wife and family that would eventually come, the fact of the matter was simple: Gabriel Dawson was lonely.

Not the sort of loneliness that made people do irrational and potentially dangerous things. He instead suffered from the same affliction that plagued a lot of single people his age: the "no one to talk to at the end of the day" blues.

That just wasn't the sort of thing a single minister liked to broadcast, particularly given the matchmaking penchant of some of his parishioners.

FAITH ON THE LINE:
Two powerful families wage war on evil...and find love.

ADAM'S PROMISE—
Gail Gaymer Martin (LI #259, July 2004)

FINDING AMY—
Carol Steward (LI #263, August 2004)

GABRIEL'S DISCOVERY—
Felicia Mason (LI #267, September 2004)

REDEEMING TRAVIS—
Kate Welsh (LI #271, October 2004)

PETER'S RETURN—
Cynthia Cooke (LI #275, November 2004)

PROTECTING HOLLY—
Lynn Bulock (LI #279, December 2004)

Books by Felicia Mason

Love Inspired

Sweet Accord #197
Sweet Harmony #235
Gabriel's Discovery #267

Steeple Hill Trade

Sweet Devotion #5

FELICIA MASON

is a motivational speaker and award-winning author. She's a two-time winner of the Waldenbooks Best-Selling Multicultural Title Award, has received awards from *Romantic Times, Affaire de Coeur* and Midwest Fiction Writers, and won the Emma Award in 2001 for her work in the bestselling anthology *Della's House of Style. Glamour* magazine readers named her first novel, *For the Love of You,* one of their all-time favorite love stories, and her novel *Rhapsody* was made into a television film.

Felicia has been a writer as long as she can remember, and loves creating characters who seem as real as your best friends. A former Sunday school teacher, she makes her home in Virginia, where she enjoys quilting, reading, traveling and listening to all types of music. She can be reached at P.O. Box 1438, Dept. SH, Yorktown, VA 23692.

Gabriel's Discovery

Felicia Mason

Published by Steeple Hill Books™

Special thanks and acknowledgment are given to Felicia Mason for her contribution to the FAITH ON THE LINE series.

For my FAITH ON THE LINE editors and sister authors:
Carol, Cynthia, Diane, Gail, Kate, Krista, Lynn

STEEPLE HILL BOOKS

ISBN 0-373-87277-1

GABRIEL'S DISCOVERY

This edition published by arrangement with Steeple Hill Books.

www.SteepleHill.com

Printed in U.S.A.

To God belong wisdom and power; counsel and understanding are His…. He reveals the deep things of darkness and brings deep shadows into the light.

—*Job* 12:13 and 22

Cast of Characters

Susan Carter—The widowed single mom is busy running the Galilee Women's Shelter and raising twins. She doesn't have time for romance...until she meets the new pastor.

Gabriel Dawson—Good Shepherd's new pastor is tall, dark and handsome, setting the hearts of many female parishioners aflutter. But he only has eyes for one woman.

Hannah and Sarah Carter—Susan's six-year-old twins want a daddy, and they've found the perfect man for the job!

Evie—The battered woman in expensive clothes who'd arrived at the shelter one night brought more danger than anyone had expected.

Frank Montgomery—The mayor of Colorado Springs joins Gabriel in a city-wide prayer vigil to pray for peace in his troubled city.

Chapter One

Gabriel Dawson definitely had a way with the ladies.

From her vantage point standing near a booth selling warm kettle corn, Susan Carter watched the minister work the crowd. Every gray-haired matron at the annual Labor Day picnic in the park managed to find her way to Gabriel. And with good reason.

The Reverend Gabriel Dawson, M.Div., former marine and current pastor of Good Shepherd Christian Church, undoubtedly claimed a spot as one of Colorado Springs's most eligible bachelors.

Every one of those mamas and grandmamas fawning over him knew it, too. In the time since she'd started her vigil, Susan had spied more than one matron slip the minister a business card or a photo, undoubtedly with full dossiers printed in miniature listing the many and varied accomplishments of their single daughters, granddaughters and nieces.

For just a moment, Susan considered approaching him about participating in the fund-raiser for the women's shelter. The event could use a bachelor in the auction who would guarantee active and high bidding. Her friend and co-worker Jessica Mathers had already secured a number of impressive date packages for the gala that would benefit the Galilee Women's Shelter. If he'd agree to it, Gabriel Dawson sure would be an attractive addition.

She assessed him. Handsome didn't even come close to describing the man.

Tall, at least six-three, and muscular, Gabriel was a big man who inspired confidence just by looking at him. Though named for the archangel devoted to God, the penetrating black eyes and well-groomed shadow beard and mustache of *this* earthly Gabriel gave him dark good looks.

No, Susan decided. When she called on the good reverend to lend his support to her cause, it wouldn't be for a one-night gig enjoyed only by a single highest bidder. She wanted far more from him than a smile and to see that powerful physique decked out in black-tie.

But my, my, my what a sight *that* would be.

Suddenly a little warm, Susan fanned herself with one of the programs distributed at the picnic entrance. She had to remember to stay focused on the mission. Reverend Dawson couldn't be a date for the shelter's fund-raiser. That would never do because Susan wanted something more from him—she was in the market for a long-term commitment.

From the corner of his eye, Gabriel watched Susan Carter scoping him out. She'd been at it for a while now, and he was mighty curious about what she was thinking.

"And I just think it would be wonderful to have you over for dinner after church this Sunday, Pastor."

"Yes, that sounds lovely," he answered Mrs. Hardy with a pat to the elderly woman's hand. With most of his attention on Susan, Gabriel lent just half an ear to sweet Mrs. Hardy, a longtime member of the church.

"We eat at four o'clock," she said. "And my lovely granddaughter Samantha will be visiting that day from Denver. Won't that be nice? She's a doctor, you know. A pediatrician. She loves children."

The not-so-subtle hint and definite accent on that last part gave him pause.

With a sinking feeling, Gabriel turned his full attention to Mrs. Hardy. Had he just agreed to have dinner with her and her family, including someone named Samantha?

By necessity, in his nine months at Good Shepherd, he'd gotten rather adept at avoiding the obvious setups from his parishioners. It seemed they all wanted to see him walking down the aisle with a bride they could claim as first lady of the church. He wasn't the first pastor of color for the diverse congregation, but he was the first single one they'd ever had. His lack of a spouse apparently didn't sit well with some. They wanted to see their pastor happily married, and from the look of things the last few months, there existed a never-ending supply of would-be brides.

The only problem with the plans laid out for him by others was that Gabriel had no intention of getting married that way. He firmly and steadfastly believed that a wife and children were in his future, but it would be in God's time. He would be equally yoked with the woman the Lord designated for him, not one offered up like a sacrificial lamb or an item at the all-you-can-eat buffet.

To date, he'd been presented with a dizzying array of blondes, brunettes and redheads of all shapes, sizes and ethnic backgrounds, from athletic tomboys to full-figured models. Counted in the number were teachers and lawyers, a florist, an Olympic gymnast, even a best-selling romance author.

For Gabriel, though, what a woman did for a living and what her outer package looked like didn't matter nearly as much as her inside.

Did she have a one-on-one relationship with God? Was she a prayer warrior, someone who understood the power of prayer? Did she put her faith and her walk with the Lord above all else? Those things mattered to Gabriel.

Once before, he'd almost made the mistake of marrying to please others. The engagement to Mikki Metz had lasted all of six weeks before they both realized they were about to make a really big mistake.

No, siree, he thought as he nodded at Mrs. Hardy. He'd dodged bullets and land mines in the first Gulf War; surely he could dodge a few well-meaning matchmaking members of his congregation.

But first, it looked like he'd be having dinner at Mrs. Hardy's home on Sunday afternoon.

"You won't forget now, will you, Pastor Gabriel?"

He smiled at the dear old lady, who was all of four foot eleven. "I won't. I'll make a note of it in my appointment book."

She beamed up at him. "Wonderful. I'm sure you and

Samantha will have a lot to talk about. You have very much in common."

Gabriel doubted it, but kept that thought to himself as Mrs. Hardy bid him farewell for the afternoon.

Two more members of Good Shepherd, both of whom had single daughters, were making a beeline for him. Gabriel wasn't a coward by any stretch of the imagination, but today he decided retreat was, indeed, the better part of valor.

His gaze drifted to Susan Carter. Now, there stood a woman he could appreciate. Her bright smile and corkscrew curls appealed to him. Finding out why she seemed so interested in him today was preferable to sidestepping another offer of pot roast and apple pie.

Susan watched him duck and evade the latest salvos. As she turned to check on her girls, she smiled, first at the minister's efforts to get away from his members, then at the antics of her twins. They, along with several other children, ran around the church lawn chasing a multicolored wind sock held high and circled overhead by the church's youth minister.

She felt more than heard Gabriel approach.

"It's all your fault," he said softly. His voice, a rich tenor with just a smidgen of something southern lingering in the accent, washed over her, doing things it shouldn't...like making her wish she didn't have a bone to pick with him.

"I beg your pardon?"

Gabriel Dawson stood right next to her, almost crowding her personal space.

"It's your fault I now have a Sunday dinner engagement. You distracted me."

A part of Susan thrilled at his words. To make that claim, he had to have been watching her as closely as she watched him. But that, of course, was ridiculous. Susan knew the caliber of women who were after him—women who had a lot more going for them than being a single mother and the widow of a drug addict who didn't even have a home she could call her own.

Then she saw the teasing light in his eyes, the twitch of a grin at his mouth and she had to laugh in response.

"Well, if all it takes is somebody looking at you to get you distracted, Reverend, you might need a few lessons in how to focus."

"And are you teaching those classes?"

Susan blinked. Was he flirting with her?

Before she had the chance to decide, Hannah and Sarah ran up. Breathless, the twins tried to talk over each other.

"There's a juggler!"

"Can we go?"

"It's right over there."

"Ooh, look, he's starting!"

"Whoa, ladies," Susan said, putting an arm around the shoulders of each girl. They were decked out in identical sweatshirts, jeans and sneakers. "Did you forget something?"

The six-year-olds spared a moment to look up. "Hi, Pastor Gabriel," they said, their voices echoing off each other. "Can we go now, Mom? Pleeease."

Susan nodded and the twins jumped up and down.

"Hold hands," Susan called to their backs, the girls already heading across the lawn to a spot where a juggler on stilts had begun to perform in front of an excited crowd of children and teenagers.

Laughing, Gabriel watched Susan's daughters holding hands as they ran, long beaded braids flying behind. "Your daughters are a delight, Mrs. Carter."

"More like a handful," she said. "And why don't you call me Susan."

"I will," he said with a smile.

Susan spent a moment regretting that he wouldn't be one of the bachelors up for auction at the fund-raising gala the following weekend. Forget the fantasy dates Jessica had set up; she'd make a generous donation to her own cause just to watch this man smile.

"Only if you'll call me Gabriel."

"It's a deal," she said. "Though I'm not in the habit of calling clergy members by their first names."

"Then don't think of me as clergy."

She raised an eyebrow. "How am I supposed to accomplish that?" Like a game-show hostess displaying the grand prize for correctly answering the bonus-round question, she swept her hand in front of her. "Look at this. We're at your church's annual Labor Day picnic. The church is right over there with your name displayed—in rather *large* letters, I might say." The church with its stained glass windows was a centerpiece in the neighborhood.

Gabriel chuckled. "I had nothing to do with that sign."

A huge red-and-white banner welcomed members and friends to the church picnic. Gabriel's name was printed almost as big as the church's.

"Do you mind if we stroll that way? I want to keep an eye on the girls." She didn't wait for his answer, but started moving in the direction of the entertainer so she could see Hannah and Sarah.

"They're identical," Gabriel said. "How do you tell them apart?"

"I'm the mom, I'm supposed to."

"I bet you get that a lot with twins."

Susan's answer got interrupted.

"Hey, Pastor Gabriel. Wait!" The kettle corn vendor ran around his booth with a big bag of the sweetly flavored popcorn in hand. "Here you go. For you and your pretty lady."

Susan flushed and found herself grateful that her dark skin concealed most of the blush. Gabriel glanced at her and smiled, but he didn't correct the concessionaire.

He instead dug in his pocket for money, but the vendor shook his head.

"No charge, Pastor. We just want to thank you for letting us set up shop here this year. Business has been great all day. The missus and I are gonna come to one of your services this Sunday."

"Glad to hear it," Gabriel said, shaking the man's hand. "I'll look for you. And we're pleased to have you with us today." He nodded toward two couples who approached with money at the ready for kettle corn. "Looks like you have some more business headed your way." He lifted the bag of popcorn. "Thanks again."

"Anytime, Reverend. Nice to meet you, ma'am," the vendor said to Susan, who simply smiled.

Gabriel offered the bag to Susan. She opened her

mouth to ask him why he hadn't disabused the man of the notion that they were a couple, then decided that to call attention to it would only be...what? More embarrassing? So instead of saying anything, she accepted some of the treat he presented.

"Mmm. This is good." She looked back at the booth. The vendor waved and she waved back. "I'll have to remember to get some for the girls."

As they strolled across the lawn, several people called out to either Susan or Gabriel as they passed.

"You're quite a celebrity here," he said. "It seems like everyone knows you."

"Does that make you uncomfortable?"

He gave her an odd look, and Susan regretted the challenging tone she'd taken with him.

Then he smiled. "No. I like strong women."

Chapter Two

Susan hid a smile by taking another nibble of popcorn.

"I'm actually glad you came over," she said. "I wanted to speak with you about something."

"Hi there, Pastor Gabriel," said a man who touched the brim of his Denver Broncos cap in greeting as he passed. "Great picnic."

"Thanks, nice seeing you, John."

"You're the popular one," Susan observed.

Good Shepherd Christian Church's Labor Day picnic had grown into something of a tradition for members of the congregation as well as the community. The church stocked what seemed like an endless supply of hot dogs, hamburgers, chips and soft drinks. Picnic-goers could then purchase other treats, like kettle corn and cotton candy, or T-shirts and other mementos from vendors set up on two sides of the church's lawn. Entertainment and games claimed the other. From horseshoes to volleyball, the picnic included a little something for everyone.

The afternoon would close with a concert by a popular Christian recording artist. Most people would later make their way downtown for the city's big fireworks display.

"New preacher giving away free food," Gabriel said. "What's not to like?"

Susan chuckled. "The hard times will come later, huh?"

"Like death and taxes. So, you said you wanted to speak with me about something."

Enjoying the light moments with him, Susan found herself reluctant to end the easy companionship, but she had business to tend to, business that directly involved Reverend Dawson.

He *was* popular and bright. That's why she didn't understand why in all his outreach efforts to date, he hadn't stopped by or inquired about Galilee.

"You've been here almost a year now," she said.

Gabriel nodded. "Nine months."

"You've done a lot in the community. I've seen your name on several boards and you've started a couple of outreach ministries."

He glanced at her. "I'm hearing a 'but' coming."

Susan had the grace to smile. "But you've missed a big pocket of the community."

They'd reached the edge of the entertainment area where the juggler on stilts tossed six wooden pins in the air. Susan spotted her girls, who had somehow managed to creep to the front of the semicircle.

"And what pocket is that?"

"Women in need."

He looked at her then, wondering if he should read a dual message in her comment. "What, specifically, do you mean?"

"I'd like to show you our facility," she said. "Why don't you stop by the Galilee shelter and let me show you around?"

"You're the director there, right?"

Susan nodded.

"I'd be glad to put it in my book," he told her. "I'll have Karen schedule it. Maybe I'll stop by in a couple of months. What I've been trying to do first is get a feel for the larger community, some of the broader issues that have the biggest impact not only on members of Good Shepherd, but the people who live in the area that the church serves."

Susan bristled at his implication that abused women didn't rank very high on his priority or impact list.

That was the problem she had with him. Her goal today was to get him to commit to visiting the shelter. Once he saw for himself the work that was done there, she hoped he'd make a long-term commitment to the shelter's mission.

On several occasions, her director of development had tried to get an appointment with him, but either his secretary always brushed Jessica off or her calls went unanswered. So, as director of the women's shelter, Susan took matters in her own hands. She'd brought her girls to the picnic so they could have some fun, but her job today was to waylay the good reverend and make him see the error of his neglectful ways—at least where Galilee Women's Shelter was concerned.

"Reverend Dawson, I think you'll change your mind when you see what we're doing at Galilee."

"You're not going to stop until I say yes, are you."

"Now you're getting the idea," she said.

He smiled. "All right, then. I will come by."

Susan wanted to dance a jig. With the newest pastor in town also supporting the effort, maybe something could be done about the problems plaguing the city—in particular, areas near Good Shepherd.

She knew how to close a deal, too. "How about tomorrow morning?"

Gabriel laughed. "I have appointments all day."

She looked doubtful.

"Really. I do," he said.

"Then what about—"

"How about Wednesday?" he suggested. "Ten o'clock?"

Susan's smile for him was bright. She caught herself before she said *It's a date.* "I'll see you then."

Neither Susan nor Gabriel knew how much attention their stroll across the lawn of Good Shepherd garnered among onlookers. Jessica in particular noticed as her daughter Amy dashed ahead to catch some of the juggling act. Jessica nudged her fiancé, Sam Vance.

"I told you they were seeing each other. Susan plays things so close to the vest."

Sam looked in the direction she indicated. "There you go again, honey. Just because we're about to tie the knot doesn't mean everyone else is headed down the aisle, too. Knowing Susan, she's probably trying to talk him into being on the shelter's board of directors or giving a donation to Galilee. You *are* in the middle of a big fund-raising drive."

Jessica considered that. "You could be right," she

conceded. "But I doubt it," she muttered as she watched her pastor and her boss laugh together, sharing a bag of popcorn.

She eyed Sam as an idea began to form—a deliciously naughty idea. She'd have to work fast and get some help to pull it off, though. And she knew just who she could tap to make it happen.

Gabriel had big plans for the church he'd recently been called to pastor. Colorado Springs was a beautiful city with clean streets, fresh air and plenty of outdoor activities to keep people engaged in wholesome fun.

But since his arrival at Good Shepherd, a dark cloud had descended over the city. He'd been to three city council meetings as well as a citizen's watch session in his own gated neighborhood. The one question on everyone's minds was how to combat the effects of a crime and drug spree that seemed to have blanketed the city almost overnight.

Part of his mission was to create a better quality of life for his congregation. For Gabriel, spirituality was included in quality of life.

As he walked over to greet the recording artist who'd perform the afternoon concert, he thought about Susan Carter. If nothing else, she was persistent and dedicated. However, he seriously doubted that one little shelter could play a big role in revitalizing the city. He looked forward to seeing her again—even though he had no intention whatsoever of telling her why he'd *really* been ducking calls from her agency.

* * *

Her mission accomplished, Susan enjoyed the rest of the afternoon with the girls. As they headed across to the parking lot, she glanced down at the unusually quiet twins. One thing she'd definitely grown used to was their constant chatter. They talked about any—and everything—all the time. And the questions! Everything they saw, heard or even thought about came out in the form of questions. They kept Susan on her toes.

But now they walked in silence.

"All right," she said. "What's up? Didn't you guys have a good time? You were singing along during the concert."

"We had a good time," Hannah said, her voice slow and quiet.

"Yeah," Sarah agreed, equally as unenthusiastic.

"Then why the long faces and the silent treatment? I'm not used to that."

The girls looked at each other, then paused.

Concerned now, Susan stopped and stooped so she was eye level with her girls. "Hannah? Sarah?"

"Mommy," Sarah began. "You know how you're always telling us—"

"—to look for the signs that somebody's getting hurt?" Hannah finished.

Susan nodded. She'd be remiss as a mom and as the director of a women's shelter if her own children didn't know what to look out for. She didn't want them growing up the way she did, then as an adult making the same kinds of bad choices or living in an abusive relationship.

The girls both bit their bottom lips, mirror images of

each other. Susan tried to tamp down the panic she suddenly felt. If anyone had hurt her girls…

"Mommy?" Hannah's voice trembled.

Susan gathered both girls in her arms. "Whatever it is, it's going to be okay," she told them. "I promise."

Sarah was crying now. Seeing her sister cry made Hannah cry, too. Susan's heart was beating a thousand miles a minute. She held them too tight, but their distress freaked her out.

"Tell me what happened, girls. Please."

"It's Jasmine," Hannah said, choking back tears. Both girls clung to Susan as tightly as she held them.

Caught up in scenarios that ranged from someone inappropriately touching the girls to an all-out assault on one or both of them, Susan didn't hear the name.

What if someone at the picnic had tried to kidnap them? "Shh," she said, trying to calm herself as much as she did them. Few things rattled her twin dynamos, so this rated all the more frightening. "Tell Mommy what happened, okay?"

"It's Jasmine," Sarah repeated, pulling a long braid over her shoulder and sticking a purple bead in her mouth. "She's over there."

Susan turned in the direction that both girls pointed. "Jasmine? A classmate from school?"

The girls nodded.

Though still concerned, Susan wanted to weep in relief. She instead swallowed and took a deep, balancing breath. "What's wrong with Jasmine?"

"She has bruises on her arm," Hannah said.

"And she always says she just fell down," Sarah added.

Susan studied the little girl who quietly stood next to a tall, thin woman. "Is that her mother?" She hadn't recalled seeing the woman at any of the school's PTA meetings or parent-teacher nights.

"Uh-huh." The twins spoke and nodded in unison.

The woman was in her mid-thirties or maybe forties, tall, thin and tired-looking. Susan knew the look. She couldn't very well go up and confront the woman or the girl. But she did take a long look at the mother. Sadness or maybe weariness—possibly wariness?—ringed her eyes. Susan's gaze swept the area, looking for a possible threat to either the woman or the child.

"Do you ever talk to Jasmine's mom?" she asked Hannah and Sarah.

"Sometimes. But she falls down a lot, too."

Susan's eyes narrowed. She searched for a companion, but both the woman and the girl seemed rooted where they stood. Possibly waiting for someone?

"Mommy, can you help her?"

"Yes," Susan told her girls. "I'll see if anything's wrong and if it is, I'll try to help them both. I promise."

Chapter Three

From where he stood saying farewell to picnic-goers, Gabriel watched Susan Carter embrace her daughters. The scene filled him with a longing he'd, until now, managed to mostly ignore. For all his talk about being willing to wait for a wife and the family that would eventually come, the fact of the matter was simple: Gabriel Dawson was lonely.

Not the sort of loneliness that made people do irrational and potentially dangerous things, like meet an Internet chat buddy for the first time in a secluded location. He instead suffered from the same affliction that plagued a lot of single people his age: the "no one to talk to at the end of the day" blues.

That wasn't the sort of thing a single minister liked to broadcast, particularly given the matchmaking penchant of some of his parishioners. He led an active life, always had, but sometimes—like now, watching Susan and her daughters—he had to wonder if he filled his time with projects and people in an effort to escape what would otherwise be unbearable.

His sort of loneliness couldn't be cured with a pet, though he'd seriously considered adopting a dog from one of the city's animal rescue groups. Growing up, his family always had dogs in the house and yard, at least three. Gabriel came from a large, loud family. People were always underfoot and in his business. That's the sort of thing he missed. Though his brothers and sister lived all across the country now, they still remained as close as e-mail and phone calls, and two trips back to Carolina each year.

"This was a lot of fun, Pastor Gabriel. Thanks for keeping up the tradition."

Not given to long moments of introspection, Gabriel deliberately shifted so he didn't have to look straight at Susan and her daughters as he spoke to people.

"I'm glad you came," he told a man who was there with his wife and family. The wife looked disgruntled and the children tired.

It *had* been a long day.

"Are you going to the fireworks later?" Gabriel asked.

"We've had about all we can take for one day, Pastor," the woman said. "These guys have school tomorrow."

A chorus of "aw, Mom" followed that pronouncement as the family moved toward the parking lot.

Gabriel smiled. He'd expected to have trouble landing a pastorate the size of Good Shepherd because, at thirty-eight, he remained a single man—unusual, but not unheard of. Most congregations preferred that their leader come as a package: a lovely and devoted wife who would be expected to either sing in the choir or teach Sunday school, along with one, two or three perfect or near-perfect children rounding out the Christmas card picture. Though he didn't have that—yet—he'd been remarkably blessed. And he loved the people of Good Shepherd—even if he couldn't come right out and say that the thing congregations wanted for their pastors he also wanted for himself.

His gaze drifted back to Susan. She hugged the girls close to her and then appeared to wipe their eyes as she stood up.

"Pastor Gabriel!" A husky eleven-year-old tackled him in a bear hug.

"Tommy! You're going to knock the man down."

"He's fine, Mrs. Anderson," Gabriel said, giving the child a hug in return, the Down syndrome boy one of the most loving and gregarious members of the church.

"Did you have a good time today?"

"The best!"

"Gimme five, my man," Gabriel said, holding up his hand.

The two slapped palms and laughed at the ritual they shared.

"Thanks for everything, Pastor," Mrs. Anderson said. "Come on, Tommy. It's time to head home."

"Okay," the boy said, giving Gabriel yet another hug. "Had fun, Pastor Gabriel."

"Me, too."

The encounter left Gabriel smiling. Not two minutes ago he'd been standing here having a private pity party, only to have the reason for his being at Good Shepherd show itself moments later. It wasn't about him. It was about spreading the Gospel and being a good shepherd.

"Okay, Lord," he said with a chuckle after the two moved on. "I hear You."

Later that night, before turning in, Susan looked in on Hannah and Sarah. Their distress still weighed heavily on her.

Proud of her six-year-olds for having the courage to tell her their fears, Susan at the same time felt a sense of remorse over the impact her life work seemed to have on them. It was one thing for an adult to worry about issues like domestic violence, abuse, poverty and homelessness, and another issue entirely for two otherwise healthy, happy and secure children to spend their days constantly on the lookout for trouble.

Susan thanked the Lord that they were too young to remember their father. If they ever asked—and she could frankly say she didn't look forward to that possibility—she'd be honest with them.

For now, though, as far as the twins were concerned, Reggie Carter was merely a man they didn't know who smiled at them from the pages of a photo album. Photographs were all Susan had left of their father to share with Hannah and Sarah. Everything of value that she and her husband once owned had been hocked, traded or sold to support his drug habit. He'd been an all-star on his high school track team, but even the mementos of that brief glory period disappeared after he died. Susan always suspected his mother of clearing out their apartment before Susan had a chance to save anything for her daughters.

Now, as she looked in on the twins—both sleeping

peacefully in twin beds, their pink-and-purple bedroom a little girl's haven of comfort and toys—Susan fretted about how they were growing up.

Granted, the home she'd made for them was comfortable, filled with books, plants and country crafts that Susan either bought or made. "Cozy and inviting" is how her friend Tina described it. But Susan and her girls lived on Galilee Avenue, right next to the shelter that claimed so much of Susan's heart, soul and time. Right in the heart of the city's most drug- and gang-infested blocks.

The women who resided at Galilee on a long-term basis all struggled. Some still lived in fear of the husbands, boyfriends or other family members who beat or threatened them and their children.

Was this any place to raise her own?

She'd negotiated into her compensation package the apartment located above the Galilee Foundation's office.

Grateful for a home, Susan still wondered if maybe it was time to move away to one of the city's better neighborhoods. She'd diligently saved money from the first opportunity she'd been given. Interest rates weren't too bad. Maybe the time had come to start looking at homes. She had halfway decent credit, though the time with Reggie and the debt that he'd racked up and she wound up being responsible for would in all likelihood count against her.

She'd like to find a place where she wouldn't have to worry if the girls played out front, someplace that had a backyard, room for a dog to run and maybe for Susan to plant a garden, some flowers and vegetables.

Unable to resist, she tiptoed into the room again and placed a kiss on each girl's forehead.

"Thank You, Lord, for giving them to me," she whispered. "Thank You for keeping them healthy."

The prayer of thanksgiving, a frequent one, always crossed her heart and her lips when she gazed at her daughters. At the time of her pregnancy, Reggie had been using drugs a lot. She had worried for the entire nine months that he may have passed on something to her that she in turn might transmit to the babies. That hadn't been the case, and Susan remained ever so grateful.

These children, her precious, precious gifts from God, brought joy to her each day. Susan didn't know what she'd do if harm ever befell them.

That thought made her think of Jessica and her daughter Amy. "Thanks for bringing Amy back, too," she added to the casual prayer.

With a final look at Hannah and Sarah, Susan slipped from the room and sought her own rest.

By Wednesday, her mind still on doing right by her girls, Susan decided to take a look through the real estate ads in the *Colorado Springs Sentinel*. A headline on the front page caught her attention before she could turn to the inside section. The mayor and police spokesman provided an update on the crime wave and the city's effort to stamp out what one source in the story said were the signs of an organized crime group seemingly overnight claiming a chokehold on Colorado Springs. The mayor refuted that theory, though.

"That's the problem," Susan said, tapping the newspaper with her pen.

"Talking to yourself again, boss?"

Susan looked up to see Jessica standing in front of her desk, a Cheshire-cat smile on her face.

"No," Susan said. "And what are you up to?"

"Oh, nothing. Just a few last-minute things before I leave."

"You shouldn't even be here today," Susan said. "Your wedding is on Saturday. That's just a few days away, you know."

Jessica waved a hand. "With all I've been through, the wedding is going to be the easy part."

It had been an incredibly stressful few weeks for Jessica. Recovering from surgery and dashing to New Mexico with Sam to reclaim her kidnapped daughter had just about done Jessica in. Now, however, all seemed right in her world. No one deserved happiness more than Jessica, Susan thought.

She came around her desk to give Jessica a hug. "You're going to be a beautiful bride, and this time, the happily-ever-after will be for a lifetime."

Jessica's eyes misted as the two women hugged again. Then, seeming to pull herself together, Jessica picked up the newspaper. "This thing is turning the entire city upside down."

Returning to her desk, Susan hit a few keys on her computer. "It's also affecting us," she said. "Our intake numbers are through the roof. If it keeps up like this, we're going to have to find another building for long-term shelter."

"Another building? But where? How? I'm scrambling as it is trying to bring new money in. And how in the world would we pay for something like that?"

Good questions, Susan thought. She'd been asking herself similar ones since they'd gone from accepting two or three women a month to that many each week. Not everyone needed long-term shelter, but even so, they were just about at capacity at Galilee.

"I don't know," Susan said. "The Lord always opens a window when He closes a door."

"I'm expecting the auction to bring in about one hundred grand," Jessica said, citing their optimistically high goal. "But that money, no matter what we get from the gala, is already earmarked for operating expenses and the emergency houses, not new capital outlay."

Jessica wasn't saying anything that Susan didn't already know. "I'm working on a few leads," Susan said. "If we can just get some more buy-in from a few key players, I think some of those closed doors will spring open."

The director of development didn't look too convinced, but Susan had other things on her mind. Like how to convince the pastor of Good Shepherd, the church closest to the shelter and therefore the one that should have the greatest interest in helping the neighborhood, to understand that he could be instrumental in turning things around.

Gabriel arrived promptly at nine forty-five for his ten o'clock appointment with Susan. He didn't like admitting that he'd spent a great deal of the last two days thinking about her.

When he walked into the Galilee Women's Shelter, though, he got the first surprise of the morning. He wasn't exactly sure what he'd been expecting, but the cheery reception area, with its ficus trees and spider plants, looked more like a well-appointed physician's office than his image of a battered women's shelter. After checking in with the receptionist, he took a seat and fingered the leaves on the ficus. Real. Not plastic.

Somehow that made a difference.

A quilt on the wall arrested his attention. He got up to take a closer look. The scene depicted on the fabric illustrated a door closing on a woman, but a window near her opening with light and sunshine pouring through. Women waited for her on the other side, hands extended in welcome. The window portion of the quilt featured light and vibrant-colored fabrics—golds, blues, reds—while the life the woman was leaving was depicted in dreary browns and dark streaky blues and grays.

The artist who'd created the piece had put a lot of time and effort into it.

Bible verses in a flowery script ringed the border of the quilt. Gabriel tilted his head to read the one on the left.

"It says, 'Come unto me all ye that labor and are weary and I will give you rest.'"

He turned. Susan Carter stood there looking like sunshine on a cloudy day. A flowing gold pantsuit flattered her. He extended a hand in greeting.

"Good morning."

"Prompt."

"That's the marine in me."

Susan cocked her head. "I didn't know you were a marine."

He nodded. "Two tours."

Susan filed that information away. It might come in handy somewhere down the road.

Gabriel faced the quilt. "This is phenomenal."

"Thank you. We like it a lot. I thought we'd begin by giving you an overview of what it is we do here. I'll show you around the business office here, then we'll go next door to the shelter. Can I get you a cup of coffee to start?"

"Thanks," he said. "I'd like that."

Susan directed a comment to the receptionist. "We'll be in my office, then walking through. I have my phone if anything comes up."

Susan turned a smile on Gabriel. "Ready?"

He nodded. With another look at the quilt, Gabriel turned to follow her.

Just then, a woman burst through the front doors.

"Help me! Help me!" she screamed. "He's got a gun!"

Chapter Four

Susan reached for the woman's hand to drag her to safety, but Gabriel was already there, shielding both Susan and the hysterical woman.

Blocking the door, he stood sentinel.

"Let me deal with this. It's what we do here," Susan said, trying to push him out of the way.

Gabriel, however, was an immovable force. "You don't deflect bullets."

"Neither do you."

Without looking over her shoulder to confirm it, Susan knew that Christine had activated the alarm notifying security.

"He took my pipe," the woman said. Her dirty blond hair caked with grease and dirt looked as if it hadn't been washed in months.

A man approached. He eyed Gabriel and tried to peer over his shoulder. He didn't look enraged and he didn't have a visible firearm, but he held a baseball bat in his hand and bounced it off his thigh.

"May I help you?"

"My woman. She came this way."

"I'm not your woman," the woman called from within.

"She took some things that belong to me."

Gabriel eyed the bat in his hand. "What are you going to do with that?"

The man looked down, then grinned at Gabriel. "Me and the boys were just gonna go play some ball."

"Then I'm sure you don't want to keep them waiting," Gabriel said. "I used to hit a few in my day. Where do you play?"

A security guard in a brown uniform came up behind the man. Gabriel saw him, but not a muscle or eyelash revealed it. Instead, he continued to look directly at the man in front of him. The man looked him up and down suspiciously and again tried to peer over Gabriel's shoulder.

"You a cop?"

"No," Gabriel said.

The man flexed and took a step forward. Gabriel did likewise, and the aggressor paused, taking full stock of Gabriel. Though he wasn't muscle-bound like a bodybuilder, it was clear that Gabriel didn't miss any workouts.

"Is it worth it?" Gabriel asked.

"Worth what?" the man said, his voice gruff and irritated.

"Whatever your dispute is with her, is it worth going to jail over?"

"Jail?" His eyes narrowed. "Thought you said you wasn't a cop."

"I'm not. I'm Reverend Gabriel Dawson, pastor at Good Shepherd Christian Church."

The man smirked. "What's a preacher gonna do, take me out with a Bible?" But the smirk faded when Gabriel took another step forward. The man took in the size and strength of the preacher.

Gabriel shrugged. "It's not about taking somebody out. It's about doing the right thing."

"But she took…"

Gabriel nodded over his shoulder. "You can leave, or we can escort you downtown."

For the first time, the man looked over his shoulder. The security guard stood there. And a Colorado Springs Police squad car was headed down the street.

The man swore. "Tell her I want my stuff."

Gabriel nodded.

With another look at Gabriel and the guard, the man loped off, disappearing between houses a few doors down.

The police car continued on down Galilee Avenue. For a moment, Gabriel looked surprised, then he chuckled and sent up a silent "Thank you." The cruiser was just on routine patrol.

"Hey there," the guard said, sheathing his own billy club as he approached. "You really a preacher or you here about the job? We could use a man like you on board. That was smooth." He stuck out his hand. "Solomon's the name. Edgar Solomon."

"Nice to meet you," Gabriel said. "And, yes, I'm really a pastor."

"Too bad," Solomon said. Then he flushed. "I didn't mean it like that."

Gabriel laughed. "I know."

The two headed for the door.

"All clear, Christine," Solomon told the receptionist. "I'll tell Ace to keep watch on the back perimeter just in case. And I'll leave a note for Lambert and the night shift."

"Thanks, Solomon. Reverend Dawson, Ms. Carter is waiting for you in her office. Right this way, please."

Gabriel shook the guard's hand and then followed Christine.

"I'm sorry you had to get in the middle of that," she said a little later as she poured him a cup of coffee. She refilled her own mug and placed the carafe back on the burner.

"Does that happen all the time?"

She shrugged. "It's not unheard of. We've seen Janie before, though. She and her man get into it and she runs down here."

"Can't you help her?"

Susan sighed, shaking her head. "It's the drugs. She's a crack addict. I've talked to her several times. She's even spent a few nights at our emergency shelter."

Gabriel looked confused. "I thought *this* was the shelter."

Susan motioned for him to sit. "The shelter next door is primarily a long-term transitional facility. Women and children stay there up to nine months, until they can get their lives back in balance. We have emergency houses, but we keep those locations secret.

"People know we're here," she said. "Word has gotten out that you have to be drug-free to stay here. For some, that's a really big problem. Janie refuses to go to a rehab center. We can't treat addictions at Galilee."

"So what will happen to her now?"

Susan sighed again. "She'll go home. They'll get high and they'll forget for a while why they were angry at each other."

Settling in his seat, Gabriel balanced the coffee mug on the chair arm.

"What happens to the women who stay next door? After they leave?" he clarified.

Susan smiled. "That's what I wanted to see you about, Reverend Dawson."

He took a sip of the coffee, held the mug up in silent salute and smiled. "I thought you were going to call me Gabriel."

Flustered at both the smile that sent her insides tumbling and at the way her normally open office suddenly seemed crowded, filled with nothing but Gabriel's presence, Susan smiled back over the edge of her cup.

"That's right," she said. "Gabriel."

Gabriel couldn't truthfully say what he'd expected to see at the Galilee Women's Shelter. He'd had some vague notion of the place being sterile, unwelcoming, much like an unemployment or public assistance office. What he saw surprised him.

Plenty of lush green plants and framed children's artwork decorated the walls and halls. Susan explained that the shelter's business and intake divisions, as well as staff offices, were here. Next door consisted of the living areas and lounge and kitchen spaces of the transitional housing for women and children.

That's where Gabriel got the biggest surprise of the morning.

As Susan gave him the grand tour, Gabriel found himself struck by two things: the identical quilt in the lounge of the actual shelter, and the number of women he recognized as he walked with Susan through the first-floor common area of the facility. A couple of them called him by name.

"Hi, Reverend Dawson. Did you come to check up on us?" a woman asked.

Before he embarrassed himself by admitting he didn't know her name, she supplied it.

"Mary Hill," she said. "I've been to a couple of services at Good Shepherd."

Gabriel nodded, remembering now. "And how are your daughters?"

"Just fine, Reverend. They're just fine now that we're here."

He shook her hand. "I hope to see you on Sunday."

"You will. Church is one thing we try not to miss. Other than Galilee, it's the only good thing in our lives these days."

At her words, Gabriel felt a need to pause, to provide her with encouragement. "Do you mind if we pray?"

The woman shook her head. She motioned for another woman to join them. "This is Nancy," she said. "She just got here. She's going to come with me on Sunday."

Gabriel prayed with the two women, thanking God for getting them to a safe harbor, a place of refuge. He prayed for infinite mercy and sustained grace. When he finished, he warmly shook each woman's hand, offering a "God bless you."

Susan didn't say anything about the impromptu prayer meeting as they moved on.

"Upstairs are the bedrooms. We can accommodate up to a dozen women for six to nine months each. There's space for another six, but only for short-term stays, no more than eight weeks."

"This place is huge," he said as he passed by yet another woman who looked vaguely familiar to him. "What was this building before you moved in?"

"A drug-infested eyesore," Susan said. "But if you mean originally, it was a mansion, a single-family home that belonged to a prominent businessman. He'd had a falling-out with his family and left no heirs. Over time, the property changed hands, the neighborhood changed characteristics, and before long, this grand old house became nothing more than another blight on the block.

"When the Galilee Foundation purchased it from the city, it was with the provision that we assume all debt and residential responsibilities."

"Residential? I thought you said it was abandoned."

"Abandoned by its owners. But not by the homeless and the drug-addicted, not to mention truants, who'd claimed it as their own. There was a lot of tiptoeing around issues back then."

"Have you always worked with the shelter?"

She gave him an odd little look, something that in such a fleeting moment gave him no time to dissect.

"You could say that," she said.

Gabriel sensed there was more to the story, but Susan

didn't elaborate as they paused in the lounge, at yet another wall quilt.

"This work is spectacular," he said, taking a step closer to inspect the stitching.

"You know something about quilting?"

He glanced over his shoulder at her. "Enough to know when I'm looking at fine craftsmanship."

Susan smiled but didn't say anything.

"I wonder if this artist takes commissions," Gabriel mused. "It would be nice to have a wall art quilt hanging in the vestibule or maybe in the fellowship hall."

"That could probably be arranged," Susan said.

Something in her tone, a dry note, made him look at her. "What?"

"Nothing," Susan said. "Those pieces don't come cheap."

"I wouldn't expect them to."

"Come on," Susan prompted. "I'll show you the play areas for children."

Half an hour later, they finished the tour of the shelter. Gabriel had remained quiet through most of it, only asking for clarification on a point now and then.

Then he looked speculative. "May I ask you a question?"

"Sure."

"What's the likelihood of a single congregation having multiple cases of domestic violence?"

Susan considered the question for a minute, understanding that he was trying to come to grips with what he was seeing. "It depends on a number of things," she said. "The size of the church. The backgrounds and situations of the people who attend. Statistics show that young boys who witness physical violence against their mothers are likely to grow up to be abusers, and girls who are exposed to domestic violence as children run the risk of later becoming involved with an abusive partner."

"So the cycle never ends."

"We work to educate here," Susan told him. "To reduce the odds. As far as a single church's ratio of domestic violence cases, the probability gets higher, the more people you have in a congregation."

Gabriel looked troubled. "But you can't tell by looking?"

Susan shook her head. "That's one of the challenges we face—the perception that you can just look at someone and tell if that person is being abused or is an abuser. Unfortunately, it doesn't work like that. Domestic violence doesn't know income, economic, racial or cultural boundaries. And domestic violence doesn't just mean physical violence. It can take many forms."

Gabriel had seen no less than five women he recognized from Good Shepherd. Unless he'd completely missed his mark, Good Shepherd was having a domestic violence problem. And if what Susan said was true, there was no way for him to know if a church member or couple was in trouble unless something was said or a couple came in for counseling.

Was he so out of touch with his membership that he hadn't even realized that?

As if reading his mind, Susan said, "It helps when local leaders can see firsthand the work we do here. I especially wanted you, as the new pastor of Good Shepherd, to be on board with our mission and goals."

"I'm seeing your mission," he said. "What are those goals?"

"You're just seeing a part of the big picture, Reverend. I'd like to show you the rest on another day."

He hedged. "I have quite a busy schedule."

"Too busy to make a connection with a neglected part of the community? To meet the people who for too long have had a blind eye turned to their suffering?"

"I sense of note of censure," he said.

Susan shrugged. "I think it's deserved," she said, pulling no punches.

He raised a brow, reminded that beautiful roses had deadly thorns.

"Pardon me for being so blunt," Susan said. "But there is a need here in this community, the very community served by Galilee, yet despite today, we haven't been able to get an audience with anyone from Good Shepherd."

"I'm here now."

"Only because I corralled you."

He tucked his hands in the pockets of his slacks. "You have an interesting approach, Mrs. Carter. I thought the idea was to garner my cooperation."

"It was. And is," she said. "The frustration is a result of what it took to get your attention."

Gabriel looked at her in a new light. Had she flirted with him at the picnic just to get him to agree to visit her shelter?

Chapter Five

"That's why I wanted you to visit Galilee, Reverend Dawson. It's one thing for people to make a financial commitment to a nameless, faceless charity or cause. It's something else entirely when you can make the personal connection. When you can look into the eyes of someone who needs help or talk to someone who has been helped."

Gabriel considered what she had said. This time he didn't mistake the censure in her voice. It was a quiet but definitive reproach. "What have I done that makes you so hot under the collar?"

There was a time to be coy and a time to be blunt.

Folding her arms across her chest, Susan stared him down. "It's not what you've done, Reverend. It's what you *haven't* done."

Since he'd been called to Good Shepherd, Gabriel's focus had been on getting to know community leaders, assessing the congregation's many needs, and encouraging members to take part in the whole church, existing programs as well as ones he proposed. In addition, he had to stay a step ahead of all the matchmakers who filled the pews. He had a vision for the church, one that he'd promised to implement when he'd been hired as pastor. So he didn't take too kindly to Susan Carter's assessment of him as a slacker.

He leaned back in his chair, steepled his hands and met her direct gaze. "What is it, Mrs. Carter, that you see I'm not doing?"

Rising, Susan came around her desk and faced him. "For starters, don't you think it's odd that so many of your members or regular visitors call the Galilee Women's Shelter home? You asked me about the odds, but you didn't ask the next obvious question."

"Which is what?" He folded his arms. Then, recognizing the defensive gesture for what it was, he carefully placed his arms along the chair rests.

"Have you given any thought to how you and Good Shepherd might reach out to those women and others in need?"

"I take it you have a proposition?"

"Not a proposition, Reverend. A reality check."

He shifted in his seat, bristled at her characterization. "My feet are firmly planted on a solid foundation, Mrs. Carter."

"Let me show you the community. Let me show you what we're fighting every single day."

She leaned over and pulled from a stack of file folders a single thick file. Handing it to him, she said, "That's just the last two weeks of articles from the local newspapers, *The Gazette* and the *Colorado Springs Sentinel,* as well as the *Denver Post* and the *Rocky Mountain News.* Street crimes, domestic violence calls to police—up. Drugs and crimes that can be directly attributed to drugs—up. The problems here in Colorado Springs have the potential to spill into other areas. Containment is what city officials like Mayor Montgomery are after."

Gabriel flipped through some of the clippings. He'd read many of the same stories and had seen television news reports, yet he hadn't connected the dots in quite the same way as Susan.

"What's the trickle-down effect of this?" he asked, holding up the folder.

"The woman who ran in here earlier," Susan said. "That's trickle-down. An increased number of women and children seeking shelter. More and more children and teens left alone, fending for themselves, they find solace in the very thing that's destroying this community."

"Drugs?" he asked.

Susan nodded. "And gangs, where they find the family or the bonding they don't have at home."

He glanced at more of the newspaper articles before closing the folder and placing it on her desk.

"Let me show you the human effect."

He nodded once. "All right."

When he left the shelter after almost two hours, Gabriel had a handful of handouts featuring statistics, demographics. But he hadn't seen these statistics. Susan was right. He hadn't been out in the trenches.

That would change tomorrow afternoon.

Susan wasn't sure she'd gotten through to him, but she knew one thing for certain: he'd gotten through to her. She chided herself for getting distracted by his eyes, the color of dark chocolate and so penetrating that she wondered if anything ever got past him.

She thought herself prepared to impartially lead Reverend Gabriel Dawson on a tour of the Galilee Avenue area the next day. She'd dressed carefully—for both the minister's benefit and to acknowledge that they'd be doing a lot of walking—in a pair of blue pants, a cream twinset rimmed in blue, and comfortable flats.

She'd expected him to show up in one of his designer-looking suits, clothing that would immediately peg him an outsider in the neighborhood, as maybe a cop or a government worker. Susan's mouth dropped open when he stepped into the reception area.

"Gorgeous, isn't he?" Jessica said.

Susan started, dragging her gaze off the minister, who stood chatting with Christine at the front desk. "I...He—" She cleared her throat and started again. "We're going on a walk around the neighborhood." As if to prove her words, she snatched up a stack of the shelter's brochures.

Jessica grinned at her.

"What?" Susan snapped.

"Oh, nothing," Jessica said. Susan's sudden ill-temper made her smile.

"And why are you even here?"

"Just dropping this off for you, boss."

Susan rolled her eyes at the "boss" label. Though she was, she always viewed herself as more of a battlefield coordinator.

"Enjoy your date."

"It's not a date," Susan said. "I'm just showing him what we do."

"Whatever you say," Jessica said with a smirk.

"Good morning, Reverend," Susan called out, approaching him.

"Hello there. Good to see you again."

His eyes took in her appearance and he smiled. Susan was grateful she'd spent a little extra time on her makeup this morning. Not, she told herself for the umpteenth time, that that had *anything* to do with Gabriel Dawson.

Liar, liar. Pants on fire. The line the twins used when they played a game came to her and Susan's mouth quirked up in an involuntary smile.

"Have fun," Jessica called.

Gabriel lifted an eyebrow but didn't say anything.

The day was just right for this sort of outing. The city had been blessed with a week or two of Indian summer and people were out and about, taking advantage of the warmer days. Before long, chilly temperatures and then out-and-out cold would descend on the city. For now, however, they could enjoy the reprieve.

"This is one of my favorite things to do," Susan said.

"Walk?"

She nodded. "There's nothing like fresh air. That's one of the reasons I love Colorado so much. Of course, I've never been anywhere else but here, but I'm glad this is home. I wouldn't trade it for anything."

"I'm starting to feel the same way," he said. "I've been here for three years now, and wonder what took me so long to make my way to this part of God's country."

Susan directed their path. "We'll head up Galilee, then turn down some of the side streets." He fell into step beside her, walking on the street side of the walk. "Three years? I thought you'd just arrived in Colorado Springs a few months ago."

"I am new to this city, but I've been in Colorado since I got out of the Marines."

"What brought you here?"

He glanced at her and smiled. "The lure of fresh air. That and snow."

"Well, we get a lot of that. So you should be thrilled."

"Tell me about how you got started working at the shelter."

Susan looked up at him, wondering if she should tell the whole story, wondering how or if he'd judge her if he knew. A moment later, she realized she couldn't be anything except totally honest. Not only did she pride herself on being a woman of integrity, but also he needed to know that she knew what she was talking about.

She handed him one of the brochures. It featured a woman and child embracing as they shared a book together. "We'll be passing these out today," she said. "Not too long ago, I could have been that woman on the cover."

For just a moment he looked surprised. "What do you mean?"

"Exactly what you think," she said. "My husband got caught up in drugs. Even before that, he had a temper. He could get really ugly when he was angry or thought he'd been slighted in the least bit. I was the outlet for his anger."

Gabriel's mouth tightened. "You're still together?"

"No," she said. It could have been a trick of the light, but Susan thought she saw his jaw loosen a bit when she said that. "He died a few years ago. He OD'd."

"So that's when you took up the crusade to save other women?"

"I've never thought of my work as a crusade, but I suppose it is," she said. "And to answer your question, no. That came a long time later. After the healing. After living in the shelter. After rededicating myself to the Lord and getting my life together."

Not comfortable being the focus of their conversation, she deftly turned the tables. "You were in the military."

Gabriel nodded. "Marines."

"*Semper fi* and all that." She glanced up at him. "What does that mean anyway?"

"It's short for *semper fidelis*, always faithful."

Susan smiled. "Really? I like that. It works on a couple of levels, including a faith-based one. So how'd a big, strapping marine end up as a minister in Colorado Springs?"

"Being faithful to my calling," Gabriel said. "I've always ministered to people whether I was ordained or not. But accepting the call to ministry in this way enabled me to put my own faith on the line for a higher cause."

"And people shooting at you in a war isn't a higher cause?"

The edges of his mouth curved up. "Yes, but..."

She waved a hand in dismissal. "Just messing with you, Rev." They paused in front of a house, all of its first-floor windows boarded over. "It's been a real tragedy to see what's happening to our city. It's turning into something like the 'killing fields' you probably encountered overseas."

"What happened?"

Susan didn't know if he was asking about the house they stood before or the decline of the city she loved, but the answer in either case was, unfortunately, the same. "Drugs. Too many people indifferent until it's way too late. Neighborhoods don't decay overnight. But one day someone in the city looks up and says, 'Hey, how did this happen?' It seems like an overnight transformation only because no one notices the slow decline. We all just woke up one morning and our community had been taken over."

"But it wasn't overnight?"

She shook her head. "Hardly. My husband got caught up in what was probably the first wave of this epidemic. He killed himself by overdosing on cocaine."

He reached for her hand. "I'm sorry for your loss."

"There's nothing to be sorry about. Reggie..." She paused before she said *got what he deserved,* the bitter words swirling in her head surprising her. After all this time she had thought she'd put the experience with him behind her. She had thought she'd let go of all the anger.

But how could she really? Everything she was today, from her position as director of the Galilee Women's Shelter to the woman standing here on this street corner with Gabriel Dawson, was a direct result of what Reggie had put her through. If it hadn't been for the way he'd forced her to grow up, Susan knew she could very well *be* one of the people she was trying to reach out to.

"Reggie was a man who let his compulsions get the best of him," she ended up saying.

"You miss him?"

She glanced up at Gabriel. "Not the way you think." And because that sounded so cold, she added, "Our marriage was over long before he died. He'd been on a path toward destruction for a while, a long while. His death, like so many others, was a direct result of readily available drugs on the street. But if it hadn't been cocaine, he'd have found some other way to self-destruct. Reggie was just like that."

She walked up the steps leading to the porch at the house and tucked three of the brochures in the mail slot on the front door.

"It doesn't look like anyone lives here," Gabriel observed.

The house had the stillness of decay and neglect that said it had been abandoned for some time. Dead leaves, spiderwebs and debris including potato chip bags and mangled beer cans jammed the corners, mixing with peeling paint chips.

"You'd be surprised, Reverend," Susan said.

She bent to the mail slot and hollered through. "Hello to the house. I dropped some information about Galilee Women's Shelter in your front door."

When she turned to go, Gabriel paused.

"What's wrong?" Susan asked him.

"I thought I heard something."

As if she were guiding along one of the twins, Susan took his hand. "Come on. You probably did. People coming to see what I put in there."

Gabriel remained silent as they descended the steps and continued their walk. But he looked back at the house.

"Is there a lot of that?" he eventually asked.

"A lot of what?"

"People living in abandoned homes?"

"In certain parts of the city, yes."

"And this is one of those parts." It was a statement, not a question.

"Welcome to the hidden and forgotten underside of Colorado Springs. This would be the part not in the tourism brochures."

A couple of people sitting on a stoop called out to Susan. She waved, then spotted one of the pillars of the neighborhood sitting on her front porch. Susan motioned for Gabriel to follow. They stepped carefully around an area of buckled sidewalk.

"How are things with you, Mrs. Turner?" Susan called in greeting.

The frail-looking woman sat on a plaid sofa that had seen better days, but looked as comfortable as the woman holding court. "'Bout as well as can be expected for an eighty-year-old blind lady."

Susan smiled. "You may not have your sight, but you know everything that happens on this block."

"That's the truth," the woman said. "Who you have with you today?"

Gabriel looked startled.

Mrs. Turner smiled. "My eyes don't work, son. There's nothing wrong with my nose and my ears. You smell good. Come on up here. This your beau, Susan?"

She blushed, not that Mrs. Turner could see it, but

Susan had a feeling the elderly woman knew anyway. She quickly made the introductions. "Nothing like that. This is Reverend Gabriel Dawson, the new pastor at Good Shepherd. Reverend, this is Mrs. Mattie Turner."

"A preacher, huh?" Mrs. Turner said. "That's a lot better than what you had before, God rest his soul." She turned unseeing eyes toward Gabriel. "I used to go to Good Shepherd. It's nice meeting you, Reverend."

Gabriel took her hands in his. Contrary to her appearance, Mrs. Turner's grip was strong and sure. Susan got a kick out of again seeing his surprise.

"Well, you're a tall one, aren't you."

"Yes, ma'am. Six foot three. It's a pleasure to meet you, too. You said you used to be a member of Good Shepherd. I'd like to invite you back. We have some innovative programs for members of all ages. I think you might enjoy it."

"He's a charmer, isn't he," Mrs. Turner said to Susan.

She agreed, but had no intention whatsoever of admitting that. Susan made a noncommittal sound.

"I'll think about it," the elderly woman said. "Don't get around as well as I used to."

She invited them to sit, then she started telling them about her "great-grands."

There was no point in rushing Mrs. Turner. When she had a point to make, she made it—even if it took an hour or all day. Susan settled into one of the straight-back kitchen chairs that had been hauled to the porch for the sole purpose of this kind of entertaining.

In addition to squiring the handsome preacher around the neighborhood, Susan's walk had another purpose.

By knocking on doors, she hoped to find the twins' classmate's house. Hannah and Sarah thought Jasmine lived in this block, but they weren't sure. Jasmine, the girls said, wasn't allowed to have company.

Susan had in her pocket an invitation to a tea party. Granted, there'd been no tea party actually scheduled, but it would be easy to round up a few little girls for an outing. With the twins and Jessica's daughter Amy, they'd have a full complement. But before she could invite Jasmine and her mother to a fact-finding tea, she had to find them, period.

And if anyone existed in this neighborhood who knew everyone, it was Mrs. Mattie Turner.

"So, what are you two out doing today?" the elderly woman finally asked.

"Mrs. Carter is showing me the neighborhood."

Mrs. Turner chuckled. "Trolling for lost souls on both ends now, huh?"

Gabriel smiled. "Something like that."

"How has your hip been doing?" Susan asked.

"Supposed to be just like new," Mrs. Turner said. "Those doctors just gave me a tune-up and said I'm good for another one hundred thousand miles."

Susan turned to Gabriel. "You wouldn't know it to see her moving down the street, but Mrs. Turner had hip replacement surgery a while ago."

"Slowed me down, it did," Mrs. Turner said.

They all chatted for a few more minutes about the weather and how Gabriel was getting along at Good Shepherd. Then, when she couldn't think of a way to finesse her question into the conversation, Susan figured she'd just blurt it out. "While we're out, I'm trying to find Jasmine Shaw. She's in the girls' class and I have an invitation for her. But we're not sure about the address. Hannah and Sarah think she lives somewhere around here."

"Shaw?" Mrs. Turner said, stroking her arm. "Shaw. Let me see. Well, years ago, there used to be a Shaw family lived around the block, over on Madison in the first block. But I think they're all gone now."

Susan tried to hide her disappointment.

"But wait a minute," Mrs. Turner said, shifting in her seat. "There was a grandson. Trifling sort, from what I recall. Don't know if he's still around or if that's the right one. It's the only Shaw I can think of."

Susan patted the woman's hand. "I'll check there."

"I hope I'll see you on Sunday, Mrs. Turner," said Gabriel. "We have two services. One at eight and one at eleven. And we have a van that can pick you up."

Mrs. Turner nodded. "Do tell. I didn't know about that. I'm an early riser, Reverend. I'll think about taking you up on that eight-o'clock invitation."

"You said you used to attend Good Shepherd, but stopped. May I ask why?"

"Simple enough," Mrs. Turner said. "Those sermons were deadly. Preacher put me to sleep. I can sleep at home."

Gabriel laughed. "Well, I promise to keep you awake for the duration."

The woman nodded. "Maybe I'll see you there."

Susan kissed her cheek and stepped back so Gabriel could say his own farewell. He instead took Mrs. Turner's hands in his. It wasn't until she heard Mrs. Turner say "Amen" that Susan realized he'd been quietly praying with her.

"He's a good one, Susan," Mrs. Turner called out as they headed down her front steps. "Keep this one."

Susan's face flamed.

"So," Gabriel said. He fell into step beside Susan, who set a brisk pace toward Madison Street. "What's more embarrassing for you? Having her think we're a couple or you being associated with a minister?"

Chapter Six

Stunned at the question, Susan almost stumbled over the uneven sidewalk. Before she knew it, Gabriel's arm was under hers, steadying her.

The first impression she got was of strength, like that of a bulwark. The second was that it felt good to let someone else bear her weight. For so long, Susan had had to fend for herself. So many people depended on her—the twins, the women and children who called Galilee shelter home, the handful of employees and army of volunteers who carried out and made possible the mission of Galilee. They all looked to Susan for guidance, for strength. Not until just now did she realize what a heavy burden it could all be. Heavy, but not unbearable or unwanted.

Regaining her balance, she edged away from him before she could get used to leaning on his strength.

"I… Thank you. I…" She clamped her mouth shut until coherent thoughts decided to come out again. "I'm not embarrassed," she finally said.

Gabriel looked at her askance, and Susan decided the expression didn't need to be interpreted.

"Come on," she said. "We're headed this way."

Two houses away from Mrs. Turner's residence, they turned and headed down a short block until they came to Madison.

"Are we looking for something or someone in particular?"

Susan bit her lower lip. "Sort of."

They did the same thing on this street that they'd done on the others. Talked to people who were outside on porches or stoops, knocked on doors introducing themselves and leaving brochures about the shelter.

"Do you do this often?"

"About three times a year. Sometimes four. We go to different neighborhoods."

"And you just do blind calls like this? Walking up to houses and telling people about the shelter?"

Susan nodded.

"Incredible," he said.

"It's not so incredible. This is just one small part of the city. It's too important to overlook. Many of the residents in this neighborhood won't see fliers or posters at work or hear presentations at a luncheon. They might see an ad in the newspaper, but we can't afford to run ads all the time. What money we get goes directly to services."

"That's not it," Gabriel said, as they climbed a set of stairs to the last house on the right side of the street. "Look at how much ground we've covered today. If church members took the gospel to the street in this way, think of all the good we could do for the community."

Not seeing a bell, Susan knocked on the front door. A moment later, they heard a man's gruff voice saying,

"Get rid of whoever it is." A television blared in the background.

The door opened a sliver, just enough for a woman's eye and mouth to appear behind a chain lock.

Bingo!

"Hi. My name's Susan Carter and this is Gabriel Dawson. We're just walking through the neighborhood today, letting people know about some services that are available."

"Why is the door still open, Alice?" a man hollered.

"We don't want any," the woman said.

Susan jammed her foot in the door before the woman could close it. She winced as it bit into her shoe.

"Galilee Shelter," Susan said softly. "It's free and help is available twenty-four hours a day." She tried to slip a brochure to the woman, but Alice shook her head. She glanced down at Susan's shoe obstructing the door. That's when Susan saw the black eye the woman had been trying to conceal from view.

Susan gave the phone number, but couldn't be sure the woman had heard it. Removing her foot, Susan stepped back. The door closed.

Sighing heavily, Susan pinched the bridge of her nose. She wouldn't cry, she told herself. But every time she faced this situation she felt as if a piece of herself were being battered again.

"That's who we were looking for, isn't it."

She nodded but didn't say anything. Gabriel took her hand in his. Still standing on the front porch he began to pray.

"Father, there's a need here on Madison Street today.

You know the situation. You know how much she can bear. Lord, we pray that Your protection and Your grace will be with all those who need it under this roof. Let the doors and the windows of Your sheltering grace open wide for them, we beseech You, Father, in Your son's name. Amen."

Susan murmured an "amen." When Gabriel squeezed her hand, she looked up, this time not trying to hide her tears.

"I just hate to see them like that."

Gabriel led the way down the steps. "Do you see that a lot?" Before Susan could answer, he said, "I guess you do. How did you get in this line of work?"

She glanced over at him. Susan wasn't shy about telling her own story, she did so in public presentations all the time. She just didn't normally tell it in this type of up-close-and-personal setting. But for Gabriel Dawson to understand just how important it was that the Galilee shelter and the church work together, he needed to know the extent of her commitment not just to her job, but to her calling.

"That woman back there, she has a daughter. A girl the same age as my twins. Take away the years, take away these clothes," she said, indicating her color-coordinated outfit, "and what you have is Alice, except her name was Susan and she had two toddlers."

"It's hard for me to believe you were really an abused woman. You seem to have it all so together."

"Yes, Reverend Dawson. I was. And the reason I seem to 'have it all together,' as you say, is because God is good. His grace sustained me when I didn't think I could put one foot in front of the other. It was His mercy that kept me when I wanted to just let go, when all I wanted to do was curl up and die."

She didn't know what kind of response she'd expected from him, but her mouth dropped open when he reached for her hand.

He placed a kiss there. "God knows where and how to place His helpers."

They headed in silence back toward the shelter's administrative office. They'd walked a good five-mile circuit of the area that serviced not only Galilee Women's Shelter, but Good Shepherd Christian Church as well. Gabriel silently seethed. The petite woman next to him had no business traversing these mean streets by herself.

"You said you do this several times a year. I hope you don't do it by yourself."

"Do what?"

"Walk around out here without an escort."

Susan chuckled. "This is twenty-first-century Colorado, Reverend. It's not the Old West with a bad guy lurking around every rock."

Gabriel looked around at the people on the street corners, at the shadows in doorways. He moved closer to Susan as he eyed a guy across the street who could very well have a concealed weapon under his bulky coat. It was still fairly warm, not cold enough to warrant that type of outerwear yet.

"Could have fooled me," he said. "In many ways, our society today is worse than it was in the nineteenth century when gunslingers wore their weapons for all to see. They're still with us, those gunslingers. The weapons of choice have changed and the stakes are higher."

"I disagree with you there," Susan said. "The stakes and goals remain the same now. They're the same ones our forefathers faced one hundred years, two hundred years ago—life and liberty in a free society."

With the shelter in sight about a block away, Susan got down to the business of the afternoon. "I wanted you to see what we're up against," she said. "This neighborhood once thrived. It could do that again. But it takes more than one person's effort or, in the case of the shelter, more than one organization's effort, to turn this community around. We need the support of leaders in the community, Pastor Dawson."

"I thought we agreed you'd call me Gabriel."

She nodded. "Gabriel."

Though they couldn't see Good Shepherd from where they stood, the church was a mainstay in the community, a beacon for all of the people it served. "Your focus since arriving at Good Shepherd has, at least from this view, been on the north and west boundaries of the church, in areas of the city that thrive. This little pocket on the eastern side needs some looking after, too. The people we met today aren't just potential or actual victims of domestic violence or some other crime, they're souls waiting to hear the Word."

"You've given me a lot to think about."

As comments went, it wasn't exactly what she'd been hoping for. Susan bit back a sigh and her sweeping gesture encompassed the neighborhood. "If it's money for the church you're looking for," she said, "you're not going to find a lot of it here. Ten percent of nothing is still nothing, but that doesn't mean that these people should be ignored because their tithe envelopes don't contain big checks."

He regarded her for a moment, his gaze locked on her like a heat-seeking missile. Susan shifted uneasily under the force of that stare and realized just how formidable he would be as a marine facing a hostile combatant. He could just look at the enemy with those eyes the color of midnight, and surrender would be inevitable.

"My ministry isn't about money," he said, the words coming out tightly controlled. "If you've gotten that impression, maybe you need to spend a little more time at Good Shepherd."

Susan sucked in her breath. She tried to count to ten before she spoke, but only got to three before she let him have it. "You might think you're the new sheriff, riding into town on your high horse, but let me tell you something," she said. "For a lot of people who don't have it, money sure is the answer to their problems. If you spent a month or even a week living the way a lot of hard-working Americans live, you'd know that."

Gabriel held up his hands, surrendering. "I apologize," he said. "I was out of line." He shifted a bit, seemed to take a deep breath and said, "I gather you're upset with me. And it didn't just start now. What, besides what I just said, did I do?"

Susan blinked. Whatever she'd been expecting—and she couldn't frankly say what—that definitely wasn't it. A moment later she realized why and how he'd thrown her for such a loop. It was the honesty. In his gaze. In his bearing. In the zealous way he faced confrontation.

She liked that, preferred it over subterfuge, of which she'd gotten plenty while married to Reggie. Angry words didn't have to translate into physical violence.

She couldn't afford to antagonize him, not while she courted his support for the shelter. Not while she found herself captivated by his gaze. She wondered what he did for fun, just to relax, and had to admit to herself that she'd like to find out.

She opened her mouth to say something, changed her mind and then folded her arms across her chest. She didn't like being dishonest—with herself or anyone else.

Her suddenly conflicting feelings about the pastor of Good Shepherd were enough to drive her to distraction. She needed to focus on the mission. And her mission consisted of a single thing: the women and children at Galilee. They depended on her directly and indirectly to court the sponsors who would bring in the money to keep the shelter not only operating in the black, but thriving as a viable resource in the community. To that end, she needed his support.

"Reverend Dawson…Gabriel, I have to tell you, I've been a little piqued at the way you seem to have avoided the east side of Good Shepherd since you arrived here. You've made a concerted effort to court city officials, state politicians, even the media—"

"I didn't know my actions were being so closely observed."

Susan snorted. "The spotlight has been on you from the day you agreed to be pastor at Good Shepherd.

You're the first single pastor the church has ever had, also probably the youngest. And gorgeous to boot."

He grinned at that.

She held up a hand. "I'm not flirting with you, Reverend. Just telling it like it is."

"By all means, continue."

"Everyone wants to know how you're going to handle the myriad personalities of the church's leading families—whether you're going to just end up paying lip service or really going to make a change."

"Are you challenging me, Susan Carter?"

"Not at all, Pastor Gabriel. I'm just telling you that the curtain has gone up on act two. You've been here almost nine months now, so the first act has ended and everyone's back from intermission now, waiting to see how you're going to follow up on that opening act."

"Thank you," Gabriel told her.

"For what?"

"For being honest."

He'd surprised her yet again. Susan punched in the access code and he held the door open for her. "You're welcome."

"And thanks again for the tour," he said. "It's been a real eye-opener. I'll be in touch."

Part of her wanted to apologize for jumping down his throat. The other part was glad she'd said what she had. Not many people, except maybe Mayor Montgomery and his wife, Liza, would confront him like that. Gabriel Dawson didn't look like the sort of man who took well to people being in his face quite that way.

Then again, Susan thought, he'd paused to pray at

the doorstep of a woman in trouble and with an elderly woman.

She watched from the doorway as he made his way to his car, a luxurious late-model town car that somehow didn't quite seem to fit his image. Everything about Gabriel Dawson said rough-and-tumble—she half expected him to own an SUV, one of the really big, rugged ones—but he could also be subdued when the mood struck.

He waved as he drove off, and Susan returned to her office fretting that she'd driven him away instead of inspiring him to take up the shelter's cause.

Gabriel returned to his church office in a reflective mood. A number of conflicting thoughts raced through him. Overlaying them all was surprise that he'd found out as much as he did about Susan Carter—and that he wanted to know more.

Of all the people he'd met since accepting the job at Good Shepherd, Susan Carter was the one he most wanted to get to know better. He couldn't just pursue her—that would be unseemly.

As pastor, he had both a professional standard and a personal benchmark to live up to, as well as a tone to set. Too many clergy members in recent years had given the ministry a black eye. Gabriel had no intention of adding to the perception by chasing a pretty congregant.

Susan had, however, provided him with the perfect excuse to get to know her better.

Except now that he'd spent an afternoon seeing the world through her eyes, he realized he'd been more than curious about her. His interest was also personal, no doubt about it.

And instead of his curiosity being satisfied, he wanted to know more, to see her again. But the shelter director had both raised the stakes and turned the tables on him. She was clearly pitching the shelter as an outreach ministry for the church, a pet project the membership could sponsor—similar to the school the congregation had adopted.

He didn't really have a problem with that. What really irritated him was that Susan had accused him of being insensitive to the needs of the community. That charge didn't sit well with Gabriel. From the moment he'd arrived he'd been working nonstop in laying the groundwork for Good Shepherd to take the forefront in civic activism.

If Susan thought he was ignoring the community, it stood to reason that other people may have come to the same erroneous conclusion.

He buzzed the church secretary. "Karen, I'm headed to my three-o'clock appointment. Call me if anything comes up."

"Will do, Pastor Gabriel. Is there anything you'd like me to do to follow up on your meeting with Mrs. Carter?"

Gabriel thought about all the ways he'd like to respond. Topping the list was sending Susan Carter a dozen or so roses. But since that would have nothing to do with the church—and even if it did, would be way over the line—he simply said, "No, thanks. I have it covered."

He glanced at his watch and realized he had time to

make a personal call before leaving for the ministerial council meeting. He reached again for the phone on his desk, then changed his mind, instead pulling his cell phone from his belt loop and Susan's business card from his pocket.

Chapter Seven

The last person Susan expected to call her was Gabriel Dawson, yet that's who Christine said was waiting on line two. She gave her office a quick perusal to determine if he'd left something behind. When she didn't see anything, she wondered if he'd already made up his mind about Good Shepherd's contribution and commitment to the shelter.

"This is Susan," she answered. "Reverend Dawson?"

"Hello there. Yes, it's me. But Gabriel Dawson is calling. Not *Reverend* Gabriel Dawson."

Susan lifted a brow and settled back in her chair. Maybe the vibes she'd been getting about him weren't just one-sided. She decided to play along for a moment.

"Did you want to speak with Susan Carter, the director of Galilee Women's Shelter?"

"Actually, no. I'd really like to speak with the other Susan Carter."

She smiled, enjoying the game. "I see. Well, let me check her availability." A moment later, she added,

"You're in luck, Gabriel. She's in. To what do I owe the pleasure of this call?"

"I hope you don't think it's forward of me, Susan, but I was calling to ask you out. Maybe to dinner tomorrow night?"

Susan's eyes widened. He didn't waste any time. She wanted to say yes. Gabriel Dawson intrigued her. But all of the reasons to say no came bubbling up.

"Thank you," she told him. "But I can't." She didn't owe him any explanations, but for some reason she felt inclined to give him one. "I can't get child care arranged that fast for a Friday night."

"Then how about if I take three pretty ladies to dinner?"

Her mouth dropped open and Susan was glad they weren't on one of those video-phone lines. She sat up, clasping the receiver in both hands. "Excuse me?"

"I'd like to take you and the twins to dinner."

"Why?" The question, a favorite of her daughters, popped out before she could catch it.

"Because I'd like to get to know you better. A lot better. And I know how close you are to Hannah and Sarah. If it'll make you more comfortable having them with us, I'd like that, too."

Susan didn't know what to say. Most men weren't interested in package deals, and definitely not when it was a package of three. Yet Gabriel not only wanted to include the girls, he seemed to understand her dilemma without her giving name to it. Finding a last-minute sitter on Friday night would be difficult, and expensive. It was one thing to have the girls in the shelter's child-care center during the day, and quite another to foist them off on someone so she could go out partying with a preacher.

That, too, gave her pause. A preacher!

Mrs. Turner had been right about Gabriel being a far cry from Reggie. *My husband was a drug addict and now a preacher wants to date me.* The very thought boggled her brain.

"That doesn't have anything to do with you," Gabriel said. "And, yes, I would like to go out on a date with you."

Belatedly Susan realized she'd voiced her thoughts about Reggie. She slapped a hand over her mouth. "Oh my. Did I say that out loud?"

Gabriel chuckled. "You did. But if you thought you were scaring me away today, I should let you know, I'm not a man who backs down from a challenge or one who is afraid of the dark."

There had been many dark moments in Susan's life. But she walked in the light now. And just like with the quilts she'd stitched for the shelter, an open window and door was available. Did she dare walk through?

"Pastor Gabriel, I'm just not sure..."

"This is just Gabriel," he said. "Who you were then doesn't matter to me. It's the woman you are now that I'd like to have dinner with. And, tell you what, we'll do something fun. The girls will enjoy it and so will you."

"Fun like what?"

"We'll go skating."

Susan's answering smile was big, though she knew he couldn't see it. She thought about the offer for a moment. What could it hurt? Besides, the twins had been pestering her about going skating for a while now.

"I think the three of us will enjoy spending an evening with you."

* * *

With the date made for the following evening, Susan found it difficult to focus on work the rest of the afternoon. She had a pile of it in front of her, though, and if she put it off, she'd be in trouble in no time flat. As the shelter foundation's development director, Jessica's job was to scout and secure funding. Susan needed to go over some employment applications and review the campaign Jessica had proposed.

A series of small fund-raisers had been planned, but Galilee's biggest function by far would be the bachelor auction.

Though she was getting married Saturday and heading out on her honeymoon, Jessica had made sure everything was ready to roll and insisted on getting back in time to make the gala.

"Bless her heart," Susan said aloud. She wasn't at all sure she'd rush back from her own honeymoon to preside over a work event.

She glanced at the brochure advertising the gala and smiled. They were really going to pull this off.

Leaning back, Susan studied the "bachelors"—Travis Vance, Jake Montgomery, and a long list of good sports willing to give up an evening for a good cause. Each guy had come up with ideas for their date or had had Jessica suggest one. The highest bidder at the live auction would win the evening with the bachelor.

It was too bad Sam was getting married. He'd have been a great draw. But Susan couldn't find a bit of fault with the so-called celebrity dates—a few of whom actually were local celebrities. Travis was offering box seats and a catered meal at a Broncos game in Denver. Susan wouldn't mind claiming that one herself. The limousine ride from Colorado Springs up to Denver would be fabulous.

Even the adventure package, white-water rafting, skydiving and bungee jumping, looked interesting. Not that she had any compulsion to jump off a cliff attached to nothing but a giant rubber band. Different strokes and all that. No doubt that date package would go for a pretty penny, especially considering that the bachelor was the host of the city's premier extreme-sports program.

She opened the computer file and took a look at Jessica's estimates on how much each package should bring in.

"This is going to be great," Susan muttered as she worked through the spreadsheet.

Knowing the week would fly by between now and the night of the auction, she then made fast work of reviewing the short stack of reading material on her desk. For once she wouldn't take work home over the weekend. A date with Gabriel Friday night, Jessica's wedding on Saturday, and then a full Sunday would leave little time anyway.

As she turned her attention to the files of new long-term residents at the shelter, Susan felt a moment of pride. They'd helped a lot of women and children in the time since Susan had taken over the reins as director.

Right along with the shelter, Susan herself had come a long way. Whether it was time to consider dating was something else entirely.

She'd been too busy raising the girls and making a living to miss male companionship. Besides, after Reggie, she'd vowed to be alone forever rather than open herself to that kind of heartache and trouble again.

After thinking about it some more, she reached for the phone with every intention of calling Gabriel and canceling their date. Then she sat back, wondering. Did she owe it to herself just to try a date? Would it kill her?

No. It wouldn't. The problem, Susan feared, was that she might enjoy it too much.

The business of the ministerial council swirled around Gabriel, his mind on the fact that he had not only asked Susan Carter out on a date, but also arranged to have a family date that included her daughters.

He wasn't quite sure from where that inspiration had sprung, but it had been just right. Maybe he'd sensed her reluctance and wanted to reassure her. More than likely, though, he wanted to protect himself.

Gabriel had dated before, had even gotten serious with a woman, but he'd never felt the sort of tug that kept drawing him toward Susan Carter. She appealed to him on so many different levels.

This line of thinking couldn't be constructive, not when so many other issues were before him. Like the ministerial council's business…

When his turn to address the group came up, Gabriel laid out his plan for a citywide prayer vigil.

"We can do something to take back our streets, our neighborhoods and our city," he told the gathered brethren.

"It's always the new guy who has the energy," one of the ministers said on a laugh.

"Well, we need not only energy, but support from the members of our congregations," Gabriel said. "As a community of faith, we can't afford to sit back and let whatever may come, come. We have the ability and the power to do something about this."

If anyone questioned his fervor, they probably chalked it up to the righteous indignation of a minister new in town who wanted to make a name for himself.

But Gabriel's next words put even that supposition to rest. "As men of God, are we going to sit behind our stained-glass windows waiting for the authority to do something?" He held up his Bible. "Ladies and gentlemen, we already have the authority. Our marching orders are plainly laid out. 'Take the gospel to all the lands.'"

Around the room, heads bobbed in agreement.

"Pastor Gabriel, I'm so glad you could come."

Shaking hands with Frank Montgomery, Colorado Springs's mayor, Gabriel was reminded of a drill sergeant he'd encountered years ago. Frank Montgomery was a stocky man with a ruddy complexion, as if he ate a lot and stayed out in the sun longer than he should. Gabriel might come to the conclusion he spent all of his time on a golf course, but since he'd been at Good Shepherd, Gabriel had gotten to know—and respect—the mayor. A devoted family man, the mayor had a gruff exterior that belied what at the core was a solid commitment to do what was best for the people of the city.

"Thank you for seeing me on such short notice." Even as Gabriel spoke, Susan's words came back to him, and he wondered if the mayor who had a city of more than 360,000 residents to look after was more accessible to his constituents than the pastor of a medium-size church was to his congregation.

After enjoying a cup of coffee and a few pleasantries, the men got down to the business of the meeting.

"So, what you're proposing," the mayor said, "is a citywide prayer vigil."

Gabriel sat forward. "I realize there are church-state issues..."

Frank held a hand up, staving off that concern. "We've done this sort of thing before. I mean, council members taking part in rallies and marches."

"Something has to be done about the things going on in the city," Gabriel said. "Just yesterday I went door-to-door along the southeast border of the church. Some of the things I saw there..." He just shook his head.

"The Galilee Women's Shelter is over there," the mayor said. "They do good work. My wife's a volunteer. Every time I turn around, she's headed out to do something for either the shelter or one of the women she's met there."

"The director, Susan Carter, showed me around," Gabriel said.

"Now, there's a fine example of what this city needs more of," Frank boomed. "A woman who isn't afraid of hard work and knows how to get a job done. If I could clone her and my wife, maybe have about twenty-five copies of each one of them, this city could be wrestled into shape in no time at all."

Gabriel smiled at the mental image of a line of Susans and Lizas marching through the streets. "What's the root cause?" Gabriel asked. "I've been in places before where drugs and poverty and crime took over, but it was never so fast or so all-consuming."

Frank got up from his desk and began pacing the area between the desk and Gabriel's chair.

"We've been working on that, Pastor Gabriel. I'm not at liberty to say some things right now. But as a God-fearing man, I can say this—the people of Colorado Springs who pray should be on their knees twenty-four hours a day. We're battling something big here."

"Then a prayer vigil *is* in order," Gabriel said.

The mayor nodded, then came over and clasped Gabriel's shoulder. "Indeed, Pastor. Indeed. You get the people and I'll get the necessary permits."

The two men settled on a date. Gabriel promised to get the word out in the faith community and to the other pastors. Because of the short notice, participation might be limited to the membership of Good Shepherd and a few neighboring congregations, but if all of Good Shepherd's members turned out, that alone would be more than a thousand people.

Since she hadn't gone out on a date since the girls were old enough to know what one was, Susan hadn't quite known how to broach the topic with them. The twins were six. And two precocious six-year-olds meant double the trouble, and double the chance that she couldn't get anything by them anyway. In the end she had just decided on the direct approach. Before they'd left for school that morning, she had told them she had a surprise for that night.

Just what that special surprise might be had been the nonstop subject of speculation from the moment the girls burst into the apartment fifteen minutes ago.

"So, we're going out for pizza?" Hannah guessed.

"No, I think the surprise is that we get to go to the movies. My pick this time," Sarah said.

The two bounded onto Susan's bed, watching as she stood in front of her closet, hands on hips, surveying her wardrobe.

"Naw," Hannah surmised, pink braids swaying as she swung around to watch Susan riffle through the closet. "Looks like we're gonna have to change clothes."

"Mo-o-om!" The whine duet sounded. "Do we hafta go to another one of those talks?"

Chuckling, Susan turned and held up a pair of bootleg flare jeans and a tunic with a handkerchief hem. "You're both wrong. Do you like this?"

"It depends," Hannah said.

"Yeah," Sarah agreed. "It depends on where we're going."

Susan put the outfit back in the closet, knelt on the floor and propped her elbows on the hope chest at the foot of her bed. The twins both settled on their stomachs and faced her.

"You guys remember Pastor Gabriel, right?"

The girls nodded. "He gave us popcorn at the picnic," Sarah said.

Susan nodded, remembering the moment after the juggler's act when they'd run up and Gabriel had offered them some of the sweet kettle corn.

"Well, he's invited us out tonight."

The twins shared a look.

"Whaddya mean?" Hannah asked.

"Well, he called and asked if we'd like to go skating with him."

That news yielded another conspiratorial look between the girls. Susan could only wonder if they communicated telepathically.

"So, like, is this a date or something?" Sarah said.

"One where he kisses you at the end?" Hannah added for clarification.

Good question, Susan wanted to say. Instead, she told them what she knew. "It's an outing. He invited the three of us."

The twins considered that for a moment, then Sarah asked, "Tonight?"

Susan nodded.

"Can we all dress alike?"

Susan's smile grew broad. "What a great idea."

When Gabriel pulled up to the curb in front of the brownstone next to the shelter at five-thirty, three identically dressed Carter women stood waiting to meet him. Each wore black jeans, black ankle boots, and had a black-and-dun pashmina draped dramatically over her shoulders. Susan held a small tote bag that looked like the repository for gloves and hats.

"Wow. I've never been on a date with triplets before," he said. "How do I tell you three apart?"

The twins giggled. Hannah poked Sarah. "I told you it was a date," she whispered loud enough for the hard of hearing to receive and translate clearly.

"I'm going to be the envy of the skating arena," he said as he escorted Susan, Hannah and Sarah to the waiting SUV.

"What happened to the town car?" Susan asked.

"That's the official pastor-mobile. It came with the job. This is my personal vehicle."

The girls hopped in and immediately started exclaiming about how high up they were. "We'll be able to see everything!" Hannah announced.

"Yeah," Sarah said. "Not like in our car."

Susan made sure they were both strapped in, then she turned. Gabriel was there, holding the front door open for her. "Thank you," she murmured as he assisted her up.

"You do look fabulous."

"Thank you, Pas…Gabriel."

Susan didn't have to worry about coming up with witty conversation on the drive to Chapel Hills Mall. The twins talked nonstop: about school and their teachers, about their Sunday school lesson, about what they could see from high in the SUV that they couldn't see in their mother's sedan.

At one point, Gabriel glanced at Susan. "Do they ever take a breath?"

She just laughed. "You're the one who suggested a triple play."

"We tried on four different outfits before we decided on this one," Hannah said.

Gabriel lifted an eyebrow and said, "Oh, *really?*"

"Mommy said black is flattering, especially with gold."

"Well, I think I'm going to agree with your mom," Gabriel said. "The three of you are absolutely stunning."

Gabriel suggested dinner first, so the foursome headed toward the food court.

"Wise choice," Susan said. "Otherwise, we'd be here for an hour trying to figure out which restaurant. We have a system on who gets to pick videos and meals when we go out."

Not surprisingly, the twins chose burgers, fries and milk shakes. Gabriel and Susan opted for entrees from a Greek restaurant in the food court. Lively music and laughter from the skating rink encouraged them to eat fast. Twice Susan had to tell the girls not to scarf down their food. The girls finished eating before the grown-ups and begged to go watch the skaters already on the ice.

"Don't set a foot on that rink," Susan said. "You can stand along the outer rim."

Holding hands, Hannah and Sarah raced off to get a close-up.

"Hannah in pink beads, Sarah in purple," Gabriel said, as if committing to memory a way to tell the identical girls apart.

"Mmm-hmm."

"Don't they ever get tired of the same colors?"

Susan laughed. "You should see their bedroom. It's a pink and purple explosion."

Gabriel took Susan's hand in his. "Having fun?"

She nodded, but eyed the ice rink with a bit of apprehension. "I'm in a wedding tomorrow," she said. "You know, the one where you're officiating. I'm the maid of honor. If I break my leg out there and can't stand up with Jessica, she's going to have your head."

He smiled. "Then I'll be extra careful to hold you close so you won't fall."

Susan blinked and looked up, meeting his gaze. "Are you flirting with me?"

"And if I say yes, what'll you do?"

She smiled. "I don't know. I think I'll just enjoy it."

His answering smile was broad. "Then, yes. I'm flirting with you."

A few feet away, the twins watched their mom make goo-goo eyes with Pastor Gabriel.

"He's cute," Hannah said.

"Yeah," Sarah agreed. "You think he likes Mom?"

"Duh, Sarah. Look at them."

With growing speculation in their young eyes, the two watched Gabriel help Susan put on her skates.

"Are you thinking what I'm thinking?" Sarah asked her twin.

"Starts with a *D* and ends with a *Y*?" Hannah asked.

"Uh-huh." The twins grinned and gave each other a high-five.

Chapter Eight

Gabriel kept his word. On the ice he never let Susan go. It felt wonderful to be watched over and protected by such capable hands.

By the end of the evening, the twins were wiped out. Both were asleep in their seats by the time Gabriel pulled up in front of the redbrick building next door to the Galilee Women's Shelter.

"Did you forget your briefcase or something?" Gabriel asked, surprised that Susan directed him to the shelter instead of to her home.

"Nope," Susan said, digging out her key.

"You live here?"

She looked at him. "Yes. You have a problem with that?"

For just a moment, he looked stunned. For Susan, a little of the joy of the evening vanished in that instant. She opened her mouth to explain that she and the girls lived in a large apartment above the shelter's administrative offices. But she changed her mind. She didn't owe him any explanations.

Like many who were nurtured in need and in at-risk areas, she was sensitive to any perceived slight. And she'd heard censure and scorn in his voice a minute ago. She went out of her way to be nice to people and expected the same in return.

"Thank you for treating me and the girls."

He got out and came around to open the passenger door for her. When she tried to hop down and brush by him, he caught her. "Susan."

Defiant eyes flashed up at him. "What?"

"What just happened here?"

"Nothing, Pastor Gabriel. Nothing at all."

He sighed. "We're back to that 'Pastor' business, so I know something's wrong. All we did was pull up in front of the shelter and…" He paused. "That's it, isn't it? You think I care if you live at Galilee?"

"I don't live *at* Galilee." Susan yanked her arm free from his light hold and moved to open the back door. "And I don't care what you think," she told him.

If she hadn't already been feeling guilty about bringing the girls up in this environment, she might not have jumped to the defensive so quickly.

He caught her hand as she reached out to tug open the door. "I think you do." He placed a kiss in her hand. "I'm interested in you, Susan Carter."

Susan had dated exactly three guys before she met Reggie and let him whisk her out of poverty and into what she thought would be a happily-ever-after. Two of the three didn't count, because she'd been out with them just a couple of times before their intentions and her reluctance became abundantly clear. Reggie was the first to come by with some cash and dash and a touch of class.

The bottom line was that, despite the fact she'd been married and was the mother of two, Susan didn't know a lot about the nuances of dating. All of her focus and energy went to her work and raising her daughters.

"I don't understand."

"I asked you and the girls out because I wanted to spend some time with you. To get to know you."

Susan knew she had an outgoing personality. People always told her she was bubbly and friendly and made them feel at ease. Her hairstyle of springy corkscrew curls contributed to the effect. The outer package had nothing to do with the inner woman, though. Susan hid, sometimes even from herself, self-esteem and worth issues. Intellectually, she knew that the things Reggie used to say about her weren't true, but it would take more than a couple of years on her own to wipe away the residual caution she'd learned over time.

"Why?" Susan asked him.

He gazed into her eyes. "Because you're the first woman who has come along in a long, long time who intrigues me."

He was going to kiss her. Susan just knew it. She wanted to kiss him, too. But it was too soon for that. Wasn't it?

His head lowered.

"Mommy?"

Susan jumped back and licked her lips. "Yes, Sarah?"

"Are we home yet?"

"Yessiree," Susan said, wiping her hands on her jeans. She stepped away, taking a moment to clear her head. "Wake up, Hannah," she coaxed the other girl.

A minute later, the girls emerged, both wiping their eyes. Gabriel lifted each one to the ground and, with a girl holding each hand, started toward the front of the Galilee shelter building.

"Over here," Susan said.

He turned. Susan led the way to the brownstone next door. "We live in an apartment above the offices," she told him, feeling a little silly about her earlier reaction and behavior.

She punched in a security code and then unlocked a side door, one Gabriel wouldn't have noticed on his two previous visits.

"Thanks for a fun evening," she said.

Hannah and Sarah gave him big twin hugs. "Yeah, we had fun."

"I can skate backward!" Sarah said.

"And you did a terrific job at it," he told her.

"Can we go again?" Hannah asked. "Tomorrow?"

"Girls!"

Gabriel chuckled. "Your mom has a big day tomorrow. Maybe some other time, all right?"

The twins nodded.

"You guys go upstairs," said Susan. "I'll be along in a minute."

The girls ran up the steps, but not before Gabriel and Susan overheard "Now he's gonna kiss her."

Susan put a hand over her face. "This is why I don't go out."

"I'm glad to hear it."

"You're glad to hear I have no social life?"

He nodded. "It means I have a better shot of sweeping you off your feet."

Before Susan could respond to that, Gabriel kissed her on the cheek and murmured, "Good night, Susan Carter. I enjoyed our evening. Sweet dreams."

She stood right there, too astounded to move. She watched him walk back to the SUV. At the curb, he turned and waved.

Susan put a hand on her cheek where he'd kissed her and let her fingers drift to her mouth. "Sweet dreams, indeed."

Jessica Mathers and Sam Vance were getting married at Glen Eyrie, a spiritual retreat nestled in the hills. After all Jessica and her daughter had been through in the past month, the last thing she or Sam wanted was a production of a wedding. Small and intimate with family and just a few close co-workers and friends was the order of the day.

"You look beautiful, Jessi," Susan told the bride after Jessica's parents left the bridal suite. As maid-of-honor, Susan took seriously her duties to keep the bride calm today.

Jessica placed one hand on her stomach and one on her forehead. "Please tell that to the butterflies dancing in my stomach and the drummer who has taken up residence in my head."

Smiling, Susan reached for a small zippered bag. "The butterflies are normal. The headache is because you haven't eaten anything all day."

"I'm too nervous to eat."

"Uh-huh," Susan said as she opened a package of cheese and peanut butter crackers. She handed one to Jessica. "Eat it. Now."

Jessica nibbled on the cracker. "Where's Amy?"

"Right next door," Susan assured her. "She's getting a touch of makeup."

Jessica looked alarmed. "Makeup? She's just a baby."

"And babies want to be glamorous, too," Susan said. "A stroke of lip gloss and a little glitter in her hair."

Jessica smiled and tears gathered in her eyes. "Thank you for everything. I don't know how I would have made it through the last few weeks without your prayers and love."

"That's what friends are for," Susan said as the two women hugged. "It's about that time. You ready?"

Jessica nodded.

"But not until you eat one more cracker."

"I'm going to show up at the altar smelling like peanut butter. What will Sam think when he kisses me?"

"That he's the luckiest man in the world."

Jessica's eyes misted. The two women shared another hug.

As they moved apart, Jessica ran her hands over the brocade suit she'd decided to wear.

"Let's make sure we didn't forget anything," Susan said. "Something old."

"The groom," Jessica said on a laugh. But she touched a cameo pin on the suit jacket. "This is old. It was Sam's grandmother's."

"Check," Susan said. "Something new is your dress and all that pretty lingerie. Something borrowed?"

Jessica lifted a foot to show off her shoes. Decorative filigree clips on the otherwise plain cream-colored pumps jazzed up the shoes and added a touch of elegance. "Borrowed from your overflowing stash of shoe accessories."

Susan grinned. "And something blue?"

Jessica waved a fine linen hankie edged in a pale blue lace.

"Then you, my friend, are ready to get married."

"I saw Pastor Gabriel," Jessica said. "He looks scrumptious in that tailored suit."

Susan refused to rise to the bait, but she couldn't stop the smile that started to blossom at the edges of her mouth. "I'm telling Sam you're checking out other guys on the day you're supposed to commit forever to him."

"You think you're slick," Jessica said. "But I think there's more going on with you and the reverend than you're letting on."

Susan cleared her throat, then adjusted the pillbox hat and veil on Jessica's head. "Then you'd be wrong." She glanced at the door. "What *is* keeping them?"

"Aha! I knew there was something you're not telling me. You're practically glowing."

"It's that new shimmering foundation and blush I got. Where is everybody? It's time for you to march down the aisle and claim your destiny."

"And what about yours?" Jessica asked.

A moment later, a knock sounded at the door.

"Whew," Susan murmured as she went to let in Amy. "Saved by the bell."

A few minutes later, as Sam and Jessica exchanged the sacred vows pledging eternal love, Susan covertly watched Gabriel. He *was* handsome in that suit. More than handsome, actually.

Despite the disaster of her own marriage and her unfortunate choice in a husband, Susan loved weddings. For a brief moment she let herself fantasize about what it might be like to stand at an altar next to Gabriel—or someone like him, she amended before the fantasy got too far out of control.

"Susan?"

She blinked.

"The ring," Gabriel prompted.

His smile was indulgent. Susan felt heat rise in her cheeks as she handed over the band for Sam that she'd been entrusted with. Gabriel's gaze lingered on her for a moment as he took the ring, joining it with the one he'd accepted from the best man. Susan swallowed, grateful that he wasn't able to read her thoughts.

Before what would have been the close of the ceremony, Gabriel asked the bride and groom and their daughter to kneel for prayer and for the witnesses to the nuptials to bow their heads. The minister then prayed for the family as they began their lives together.

"Now may the grace of the heavens, the peace and protection of the Holy Spirit, and gift of eternal life in Christ Jesus rest, rule and abide with you as you walk confidently in His truth and in His love."

Gabriel's benediction and blessing left more than one person nodding in agreement or reaching for a tissue to dab at moist eyes. A lot of prayers had been sent Jessica and Sam's way. They and Amy had overcome a kidnapping, grueling physical rehabilitation following an accident, and trial by fire to find true love.

"I now pronounce you man and wife," Gabriel said. "Sam, you may kiss your bride."

As the happy couple kissed, Susan's gaze slid to Gabriel. Her breath caught when she realized he was looking at her, instead of at the bride and groom. A small thrill raced through her.

Then, the guests were applauding as Sam lifted Amy in one arm and clasped Jessica's hand in his free one. "Whoo-hoo!" he yelled out, to the delight of all. "I've got the two best girls in town."

The reception, like the wedding, was an intimate affair. They dined from a buffet of hors d'oeuvres in a small parlor off a courtyard. Calla lilies graced the table.

Sam's sister Lucia nibbled on a cream puff and indicated the flowers. "Where in the world did you get these?"

Jessica had carried a single calla lily with trailing ribbons to the altar. "Sam had them flown in just for me."

Lucia laughed. "My brother, the indulgent, reluctant hero."

Sam walked up, Amy at his side. "Hey, no maligning the groom."

"Hi, Auntie Lucia," Amy said.

Lucia bent down to the girl and her hair, usually in a ponytail, fell forward. Absently, she pushed it out of the way. "Hello there, new niece of mine. Would you like a piece of wedding cake?"

Amy nodded. Lucia glanced up at Jessica for the okay. When Jessica nodded, Lucia took the girl's hand and led her to the table where cake was being served.

"Did I tell you how much I love you?" Sam asked with a gentle smile.

"Not in about five minutes," Jessica told him.

"Then I'm overdue, Mrs. Vance." The two shared a kiss.

"See, the honeymoon is supposed to start after the reception," Susan said, approaching with Gabriel.

"Thank you for everything, Pastor," Sam said.

"Anytime. I wish the two of you much happiness. You deserve it."

"So does someone else I know," Jessica said.

Susan gave her what she hoped was a pointed look, but Jessica just laughed.

"Are you going away on a honeymoon?" Gabriel asked.

Clasping hands, Jessica and Sam nodded. "My parents are going to keep Amy tonight," Jessica said. "Then the three of us are headed to Breckenridge for a couple of days."

Susan shook her head. "I tried to get her to stay longer. Work will be here when you get back, no matter if you stay out a day or a week."

Sam kissed Jessica's hand. "She's dedicated. That's one of the things I love about her."

"And I have a ton of last-minute details to take care of before the bachelor auction."

Jessica cast a sly glance at Gabriel. The two men cleared their throats.

"I'm glad I got out of *that* one," Sam said. "You can't very well auction off a married man."

Susan reached for a stuffed olive and a napkin and caught a look between Gabriel and Jessica, but dismissed it. "Well, Jessica has done a great job putting everything together," she said. "Pastor Gabriel, I hope you'll be able to attend the gala. It's a fund-raiser for the shelter. I'd offer you a free ticket, but that would defeat the purpose of raising funds. It's next Saturday."

He took a sip of punch. "I'll, uh, check my schedule."

Susan smiled. "All right, I understand. That's a polite way of saying no. We're going to have a great time, though."

Sam grunted, but didn't out-and-out dispute that notion.

Laughing, Jessica tucked her arm in her groom's. "There are some people we need to say hello to."

The gentlemen shook hands, and Susan watched the bride and groom head off together. "If ever two people deserved happiness, it's those two."

"What about you?" Gabriel said. "Don't you think you deserve happiness?"

Chapter Nine

Hours later, Susan was still thinking about his question—and the answer she'd given him: happiness was a utopian myth, an illusion perpetuated by advertising agencies in conjunction with Hollywood.

"Contentment," she'd told him. "The best people could hope for was to be content with their lot in life, or their circumstances. They had to rely on faith to see them through tough times. But happiness, well, that was a state that could never truly be attained because it didn't exist."

He didn't challenge her on the statement, but he'd given her such a sad look that even now, as Susan stood before the mirror in her bathroom taking off the day's makeup, she wished she could return to that moment with Gabriel and answer in a different way.

Her thinking, she knew, wouldn't change, but she wished she could rephrase her answer, so that he didn't respond by giving her a look as if he pitied her. If he'd grown up the way she had, he'd understand her perspective.

There were few things Susan didn't like in life. People lying to her topped the list. Being treated like a second-class citizen or someone on which charity and pity should be heaped was another.

She didn't have a lot of letters after her name signifying degrees and academic achievement. She did claim a good head on her shoulders, compassion for her fellow man, a strong work ethic and plenty of love to share for children, her own and others. What she didn't need was a highfalutin, designer-suit-wearing preacher looking at her as if she needed tending to.

About fifteen minutes after Susan got the girls settled for the night, the telephone rang. She'd just gotten comfortable on the sofa to do half an hour of hand quilting on a small wall hanging before giving the twins a lights-out call. Reluctantly, she set the quilting hoop aside and reached for the cordless telephone.

"Hello?"

"Mrs. Carter? This is Lambert."

Susan gripped the receiver. The shelter's security captain wouldn't be calling unless there was a problem next door or at one of the emergency houses.

"What's happened?"

"You need to get over here. We need your help."

"Where are you?" Susan asked him.

"Next door."

It wasn't the first time she'd been called back to the shelter late at night. If the overnight staffer couldn't watch the girls, she had to roust them up and take them with her. She wouldn't leave them here alone, even if she were only next door.

"What's the situation?" she asked. Lambert managed a team of guards who patrolled the perimeter of the Galilee grounds here and at the undisclosed locations around the clock.

"Mrs. Montgomery is here. She asked if you'd come down."

"Mrs. Montgomery?" Susan was already up and moving toward her bedroom to slip on a pair of jeans. "Can you put her on the line?"

"Uh, I don't think that's possible, ma'am." His next words were muffled, as if he'd placed his hand over the receiver to answer someone else nearby. "Mrs. Carter, the police are outside."

"I'm on my way."

She got the twins settled with Kim, a longtime volunteer, then hustled to find Liza.

The scene that greeted Susan was unfortunately like so many others: a battered woman in need of care.

She reached for and snapped on a pair of rubber gloves. "What happened?"

"Oh, Susan. It's just awful," Liza Montgomery said. While her husband ran the city as mayor, Liza spent her days and many evenings doing charitable work at Vance Memorial Hospital and at Galilee. If her children were to be believed, she also spent a lot of time "interfering" in their love lives.

As far as Susan was concerned, Liza was a Godsend. She was already trying to get the new woman to settle on a sofa, but she'd only stand.

"We can take care of you a little better if you'd have a seat," Susan said.

The woman was tall. The cut of both her auburn hair

and her suit were expensive despite the grass and dirt stains. A tear in the fabric of the suit jacket went from right shoulder to elbow. The woman's lip was bleeding and her hands were scraped as if she'd been clawing at something—or someone. She had no shoes, and her taupe hose, which matched her blouse, were filled with runs and a hole in the toe.

In short, this was no homeless person who'd just gotten into an altercation on the street.

"What's your name?" Susan asked.

In response, the woman just closed her eyes. When she swayed, they managed to get her onto the sofa.

Susan looked at Liza, who shrugged. "She wouldn't tell me either."

"My name is Susan Carter," she said. "You're at Galilee Women's Shelter. You're safe. Do you understand?"

The woman, looking dazed, just stared at Susan.

Susan bit back a sigh. This was always the hard part. Truth be told, every part of the work she, the staff and volunteers did at the shelter was the hard part. Sometimes women who sought refuge weren't willing to go through the process necessary to end the relationships that left them in danger. This shelter was a long-term facility, housing women and children who were in transition and on the road to new lives. Sometimes angry husbands or boyfriends showed up at the front or back doors demanding entrance. Hence the need for guards.

In cases like this one, though, after emergency intake here, they'd get the woman to a safe house, one of Galilee's homes in undisclosed areas of the city.

"Mrs. Carter?" Lambert said from the door.

"Yes?"

"The officer wants to speak with you."

The woman let out a squeal and quickly averted her face.

"It's all right," Liza told her, trying to comfort the woman. "He's not here to take you away."

The woman swallowed and kept a steady gaze on Liza as the cop entered the room.

"We got a call about someone needing assistance," the police officer said.

Liza looked up and a smile broke across her round face. "Oh, Brendan," she said, greeting him. "I'm so glad it's you."

Brendan Montgomery took in the situation. His aunt, who claimed more causes than anybody he knew and somehow managed to squeeze thirty-two hours of work in every twenty-four-hour day, and Susan Carter hovered over an injured woman.

"I wish Dispatch had said it was you two."

Liza glanced over her shoulder. "What's that supposed to mean?" Before he could answer, she went on. "Susan, you remember my nephew, Brendan, right? His mother is Fiona from the Stagecoach Café."

Distracted, Susan greeted him over her shoulder and turned all her attention to the woman. Susan wasn't medically trained, but she knew the basics and how to determine if someone needed to go to the hospital. This woman did—she held her side as if maybe a couple of ribs were busted.

"Brendan, will you hand me that towel?"

He passed along a hand towel and watched them

clean the woman's face and hands. Both Susan and his aunt were wearing plastic gloves. Whatever the situation, the woman was in good hands with these two ministering to her.

"We need to get you to the Emergency Room," Susan told the woman. "It's not far from here."

"No. I'm fine."

The first words from the woman surprised them. Not the actual words, since many battered women claimed to be "just fine." It was the quality and lilt of her voice that was striking. She bore a slight though undetermined accent.

Susan was gentle, but firm with her. "You're not fine. You need medical attention that we can't give you here. You could have a concussion."

"No hospital." The woman's eyes filled with tears. "Please."

Susan and Liza shared a look.

"Aunt Liza, is there something I need to know about?" Brendan asked. "And I mean 'know about' in an official capacity?"

"Not at all," Liza said, but she didn't meet her nephew's gaze.

There was little he could do without witnessing an assault on a person. In these cases, if the victim refused treatment, he'd typically refer her to an agency like the Galilee shelter. He and other officers routinely carried brochures detailing ways to get assistance for domestic violence. At the moment, there was nothing for him to do.

"Call me if you need to. My shift ends at midnight, but call me anytime."

"Thank you, Brendan," Liza said.

"I'll let myself out."

"Will you let us at least take a look at your bruises?" Susan asked.

The woman nodded. Susan and Liza then did what they could and got her to a room on the first floor. It was small but clean and cheerily decorated. Several pillows were propped at the headboard of the twin bed, which was covered in a blue and yellow quilt.

A knock sounded at the partially closed door.

"Yes?"

"Mrs. Carter, a Reverend Dawson is here."

Susan blinked, confused. "Gabriel Dawson?"

"I called Pastor Gabriel," Liza said.

Susan glanced up. "Why?"

After getting the woman comfortable, Liza took a seat and pulled the chair close to the bedside. Taking the woman's hand in hers, Liza stroked it in a calming manner. "I found her at the church. She'd collapsed at the side door, the entrance to his study. I thought he might know who she is."

Susan accepted that explanation, though her mind raced in different directions. This was just another example of Gabriel Dawson's failure to tend to the individual needs of his congregation. Not only were they showing up at the shelter, now they were apparently flinging themselves at his very doorstep seeking solace.

The woman's condition alarmed Susan. If she'd simply been mugged, which might explain the rip on her sleeve and the condition of her hands, surely she'd *want* to talk to the police and go to a medical facility to get checked out. But the woman had averted her face when the officer arrived, and flat-out refused treatment other than the basic care Susan and Liza could offer.

In Susan's estimation, that left few possible explanations for what had happened to her.

Susan's anger level rose. Good Shepherd needed a proactive pastor instead of one who spent his time wining and dining big shots.

"Not, I suppose," she mumbled to herself, "that he'd be drinking wine."

"What was that, dear?" Liza said.

Susan shook her head. "Nothing."

Seeing as how the woman had no identification on her and refused even to speak, there was little they could do until Gabriel could provide some details.

While they waited for Lambert to escort the minister to the back, Susan and Liza tried to get her to eat something or to sip a bit of broth. That also was refused.

"I'm okay," the woman said, the two words slow and tentative.

"I know you are," Liza said. "But would you humor an old lady and take just a sip or two? After that, I'll sit with you while you sleep."

Tears filled the woman's eyes. "Thank you," she said, and for the first time she seemed to relax. A moment later she closed her eyes and was asleep.

"You go see Pastor Gabriel," Liza told Susan. "We'll be all right here."

With a final look at the sleeping woman, Susan said a silent prayer and closed the door.

When she greeted Gabriel, the first thing she noticed

was that he looked like a cleric doing rounds at the hospital. He'd donned the official minister's collar—the white band on a black shirt. He also held a small Bible. Apparently, Susan wasn't the only one who had her evenings interrupted on a regular basis.

She explained the situation to him and didn't hold back her opinion that he was indirectly responsible. Susan recognized, at least on some level, that Gabriel didn't cause the problems city residents faced. But in her book, he sure could be a better part of the solution.

"She was found at the church, right outside your office door, almost as if she were trying to run to you for help."

"Thank you for alerting me," he said. "Is she all right?"

"One of our volunteers is with her. We don't know her name, but she's resting quietly right now. Would you mind taking a look so we can at least know who she is."

"Not at all," he said. "By the way, nice jeans."

Susan looked down. His comment defused her anger. Her face flamed. In her hustle to get out of the house, she'd put on a pair that featured a large smiley face on the right thigh and a matching one on a rear pocket.

She gave him a saucy smile—part apology, part acceptance—but didn't comment.

Liza looked up when Susan softly knocked at the door. "She hasn't stirred," she told Susan. "Hello, Pastor. Thanks for coming."

"Not a problem."

Liza motioned for him to take a look, to see if he could identify the woman.

Gabriel shook his head. "I've never seen her before. She's not a member at Good Shepherd. At least not one I've met."

"I was afraid of that," Susan said.

The three went out to the hallway.

"She looked as if she was dressed for a meeting," Liza said. "Or a business dinner."

"That's the part that doesn't fit," Susan said. "Something about her is familiar, but I just can't put my finger on it."

Whimpering came from inside the room. Liza rushed back in to find the woman shaking her head, murmuring something, then, "No, please. No."

"It's all right," Liza said as if she were comforting a small child. "It'll all work out okay." She began to hum a hymn as she stroked the woman's hair.

Susan closed the door. No matter how hard she worked, it was never enough. Never enough time or money or resources.

"This is what we do here, Pastor Gabriel. We take in people who can't seek refuge at church."

He raised a hand. "What makes you think she was seeking refuge?"

"She was knocking on your door."

"We don't know that."

Susan rolled her eyes.

"Besides," he said, "we don't live in an age where we can just keep the doors of the church open twenty-four/seven for anyone who wants sanctuary or a quiet place to worship."

"Humph," Susan grunted.

"Well, that's articulate."

She narrowed her eyes at him. "I was trying *not* to say how if some of the ministers in this town paid more attention to the people in their flocks and those neighboring their churches, there might not be a need for women or anyone else to seek shelter behind stained-glass windows."

"There are several things wrong with your logic," Gabriel countered. "First of all—"

"Susan!"

They were halfway down the hall toward the reception area when Susan heard her name, turned and saw Kim, the shelter's overnight staff person, hustling forward. She'd agreed to keep an eye out on the twins, who'd claimed a bed in the child-care center. Kim had started off at Galilee as a volunteer and Susan's trust in her was absolute.

"There's a woman and girl at the back door," she said.

"It's going to be one of those nights," Susan said.

"Looks like it," Kim said.

"Come on," Susan told Gabriel. "Save your argument for later. Right now, we might need a hand. And you'll see some more of what goes on around here on a regular basis."

When they got to the back entrance, Susan saw Alice Shaw and Jasmine, the twins' classmate. Both were in a pitiful state. Next to her, she heard Gabriel suck in his breath and mutter something unintelligible.

Jasmine, in raggedy pajamas, was crying and the woman looked as if she might collapse at any moment. She had a black eye and her left arm was in a sling. She clutched one of the shelter brochures in that hand, and Jasmine in her right.

"He's asleep," she said, glancing over her shoulder just in case.

Gabriel stepped forward to help her inside.

"I don't have any money."

Susan opened her arms to the woman. "You don't need any money. Welcome to Galilee."

Since Alice and her daughter lived so near the shelter, Susan quickly made arrangements to get them safe housing in one of the emergency homes a distance away. "I'll tend to your eye just as soon as we get to the house, all right?"

Alice nodded. Kim led them to a quiet room where Susan knew she'd give Jasmine a doll or a teddy bear.

"Would you drive us?" Susan asked Gabriel.

He didn't hesitate. "Just tell me where."

"I have to ask for your discretion, Pastor Gabriel." She caught a flash of irritation in his eyes, and then apologized. "The welfare of the women—"

"I know," he said. "I've just never seen anything like this."

She touched his arm. "It takes a while to get used to."

While he got Alice and her daughter into his car, Susan checked in on the twins. She didn't tell them that their classmate was nearby. "Mommy has to go to work. You guys gonna be all right?"

"Uh-huh," Hannah said sleepily. They were in a bed together.

"Kim gave us a cookie. She baked 'em," Sarah reported.

Susan smiled. "Well, you guys get some sleep. I'll be back in a flash. Kim's here for you. And Mrs. Montgomery is here, too. She's right down the hall. Call me if you need anything."

The twins murmured goodnight. Susan kissed their foreheads and then tiptoed from the room.

Kim handed her two tote bags, both filled with toiletries and other things Alice and her daughter would need. "They're waiting for you out front."

After a few questions Susan needed to get answered to process Alice and Jasmine, the ride to the safe house was silent. It took almost thirty minutes to get to the home. The two-story brick house was nestled on a well-maintained and landscaped lot on a tree-lined street.

"Pull into the driveway and go to the back," Susan said.

"This isn't what I expected," Gabriel observed.

She glanced at him, and then at Alice who huddled in the back seat of the town car with Jasmine close at her side. "Good. That's the way we like it."

Two cars were already in the back. The fenced-in yard kept prying eyes away. A picnic table and swing set were visible in the darkness under a large tree.

"Would you like to come in?" Susan asked him.

Gabriel opened his mouth, then closed it. "I'll wait for you here."

"All right." He helped Alice and Jasmine out of the car and to the back door.

Susan punched in an access code and let them into the home. "It won't take me long," she said.

A light came on in the kitchen.

As the door shut, Gabriel heard Susan say, "You'll be able to stay here up to two weeks."

Gabriel went back to the luxurious car and got behind the wheel, his chest heaving with pent-up emotion.

Chapter Ten

Forty minutes had passed since she'd escorted the woman into the house. Susan appeared on the deck, stood at the door for a moment, then came down the steps. Gabriel was waiting. He opened the door for her and Susan slipped inside.

"Are they okay?"

"As okay as they'll be tonight. Hot shower, clean bed, something to eat." She rubbed her temples. "Thanks for driving us. It would have taken longer if I had to do their intake once we arrived here."

"May I ask you a question?"

She leaned her head back on the smooth leather. "That sounds like the preface to something that's going to make me angry."

"I hope not."

"Go ahead. What's your question?"

"How can you all afford this house? I looked at this neighborhood when I was in the market for a home."

"God looks out for us," she said. "That's the best answer I can give you. We have three safe houses as well as the transition home that's a long-term facility. That one next to the administrative office houses the largest number of women. Plus we have the child-care center there."

She looked out her window toward the darkened backyard. "This house came to us by way of a foreclosure sale," she said. "We desperately needed a new place, a location in this part of the city, and the next thing you know, this home was available. One of the members of our board of directors bought it for next to nothing considering the neighborhood, and turned the deed over to the Galilee Foundation."

Gabriel was quiet for a while, then he looked at her. "You do a lot of good work, Susan Carter."

For some reason uncomfortable with his praise, she fiddled with the smiley patch on her jeans.

Gabriel started the car, then, with one hand, pulled off the cleric's collar and rolled his neck. "Want to get a bite to eat?"

"It's been a long day. I don't think..." She looked at him, felt more than saw the weariness in him and understood that he needed to process all that he'd seen tonight. Galilee's work could be overwhelming to someone not used to it. "That sounds like a great idea."

They found a waffle house open twenty-four hours. Gabriel ordered an omelette and waffles. Susan asked for cinnamon toast and tea.

"I didn't mean to lash out at you back there," she said. "We've been under a lot of stress. Our numbers are way up, in terms of the women and children referred to us. We can directly track the escalation of tension in the city to our own intake. It puts a strain on resources. That's why the gala coming up next week is so important. It's our biggest fund-raiser of the year."

"No wonder you and Jessica are so excited about it."

"That, and the fact it should be a lot of fun." She told him some of the fantasy dates Jessica had set up.

"May I make an observation?"

"Oh dear," Susan said, holding up a hand. "That sounds like the preface to something that will really make me angry. Let me get my 'mad' on first." She gave him a fierce scowl, then grinned. "Okay. I got the anger all out. What's your question?"

Gabriel laughed. "You're a riot." The warmth of his smile echoed in his voice.

"You're not so bad yourself, Rev."

The air between them stilled. Susan's breath caught. For a moment, neither said anything as their gazes met and locked.

In his dark eyes she saw gentleness, understanding and promises. That's what shook her to the core. His eyes seemed to probe her, promising things she dared not even hope for.

A part of Susan reveled in his admiration. The other part wondered how and when the subtle shift had occurred. Sure, she could joke around and call him "Rev," but at some point during the last few days, the tone between them had changed. She saw him not as the pastor of Good Shepherd or even as a potential donor or supporter of the shelter. For the first time in a long time, Susan looked at a man and saw just that—a man.

And her interest was piqued. *This,* suddenly, was personal.

Wordlessly, she stared across the table at him, her heart suddenly pounding as confusing emotions tumbled in her.

"I…"

Their server arrived and topped off Gabriel's coffee and placed a container of hot water near Susan's cup. "Here's another tea bag for you," she told Susan.

"Thank you," Susan said, grateful for a break in the exquisite tension between them.

When the waitress left, Susan added sugar to her tea and chanced a quick look at Gabriel. "What was your question?" For a moment he looked confused, then he shook his head. "It was about the auction," he said. "I was going to say it seems a little, well, odd that given the business you're in, Galilee's fund-raiser would be an event that auctioned off men."

With a nod, Susan conceded the point. "That's something the board talked about for a while before we gave Jessica the okay to proceed. Some of our clients are afraid of men, all men, not just the ones who've abused them. In the counseling sessions that we hold, we try to teach them about healthy relationships between men and women."

She took a sip of tea before continuing. "Given the demographics and the goals we're trying to reach with this event, a bachelor auction seemed a good choice. Believe me, the board went around and around on possible events. There's been a lot of publicity, so we're hoping not just for a good turnout via ticket sales, but a lot of interest in the dates."

"Matchmaking, are you?"

Susan smiled. "Not at all. But with the reaction from some of the guys when Jessi first approached them about participating, you'd think they assumed *you* would be standing there at the gala with marriage licenses and an organist." A yawn slipped out before Susan could contain it. "Ooh, excuse me."

"I'm sorry," Gabriel said. He motioned for their server. "I'm keeping you up."

"You're the one who has to be in the pulpit at oh-eight-hundred hours. I can sleep at least that late or until the girls wake me up."

"So I'll see you in service tomorrow?" After a quick glance at his watch, he clarified. "Today."

Susan leaned back, a slow smile curving her mouth. "You bet, Rev."

When the alarm went off the next morning, all Susan wanted to do was nestle under the covers to sleep for another two or three hours. Sorely tempted to skip Sunday school, she pressed the snooze button on the clock.

Two minutes later, though, her natural alarm went off—the twins bounded into her room and onto her bed.

"Get up, Mommy."

"We fixed breakfast."

Susan pulled the pillow over her head. "Ugh."

The girls giggled. "Hey, we're supposed to do that," Hannah said.

Their words registered with a still-groggy Susan. She lifted the pillow and her head to peer at the girls. "You didn't turn the stove on, did you?"

Sarah gave her a look that reminded Susan so much of her own mother that she had to smile.

"No. We made cereal and grapes and orange juice."

"Come on, Mom," Hannah said. "Your flakes are getting soggy."

Susan let them tug her from the bed.

As she passed by the dresser, she got a good look at herself in the bureau mirror. She groaned. It would take at least an hour to repair the damage of a very late night.

But less than an hour later, Susan and the girls were out the door and headed to Good Shepherd. As always, Susan paused to stare at the large stained-glass window. The scene of Jesus with His flock always filled her with a sense of both wonder and peace. The many colors reminded her of a quilt. A thought crossed her mind. Would it be presumptuous of her to give Gabriel a Christmas present?

She and the girls had always baked cookies for the former pastor and his wife for the holiday. But for this year she had another idea. She was almost done with the wall hanging project and that would be a Christmas present for Jessica and Sam. If she started soon, she could design and create a quilt based on the window.

With a final glance at the stained-glass panes, Susan wondered what a quilted, smaller version would look like hanging in Gabriel's office.

When Gabriel entered the sanctuary in his robe, Susan noticed just how handsome he really was. Regal, even. As he made his way into the pulpit, she could easily discern his military background in the way he carried himself. She'd never really noticed before—or maybe, she conceded, she'd never really seen him before. Glancing around, Susan tried to assess if anyone else, namely the church's large number of single women, might be dating the minister.

Not that she was, of course.

Mentally chastising herself for her wayward thoughts, Susan cleared her throat and tried to focus on the service.

For the first time in a while, Gabriel spoke before the congregation without a prepared sermon. He had an index card with a few notes on it, but the message he'd delivered to those who attended the eight-o'clock service was one from the heart, just like this one would be.

After the children were dismissed to disperse for Children's Church, he faced the adult parishioners.

"I've spent this past week in a training camp," he said. "I've learned some things about this community that I didn't know. And I've made a personal commitment to help make a difference. I'd like you to search your hearts and do the same."

He then talked about his meeting with the mayor and the community-wide prayer vigil that was planned for the following week. "We want to get the word out that we're serious about taking back our streets," he said.

A smile quirked Susan's mouth. He caught her eye and returned the smile with a slight nod.

"As a church, it's important not only that we make a unified statement—something we can accomplish with a candlelight prayer vigil—but, more importantly, that we step up to the bat as individuals and each take a turn for the team." He then shared with the congregation his experience in going door-to-door with Susan Carter.

Susan was astonished. She hadn't expected him to mention her or the shelter in his pastoral remarks.

"Mrs. Carter, as many of you know, is the director of the Galilee Women's Shelter. Won't you stand, please."

Suddenly glad she'd spent a few extra minutes with makeup concealing the circles under her eyes from lack of sleep, Susan rose to a smattering of applause. When Gabriel nodded and smiled at her, she took her seat.

"Mrs. Carter doesn't know this, but we've been busy in the church office this week. I've run the staff ragged trying to set up a program for Tuesday night. In place of our regular auxiliary meeting, we're going to have a Volunteer Fair."

He outlined the basics of the fair, then said, "I believe in walking my talk. So right now I'm telling you I'm going to do what I can for the Galilee Foundation."

Susan's mouth dropped open.

She got a nudge from the woman sitting in the pew next to her. "Wow. You really made an impression on him."

Susan stared at the woman. "Apparently," she said, but her attention was on the man at the pulpit.

She'd been regretting how she'd jumped all over him, not once, but twice—and that wasn't even like her.

But it had worked.

It had really worked.

Her hands in her lap, Susan sat back in the pew and thanked God.

"As you leave today," Gabriel said, "please pick up one of the fliers about the Volunteer Fair. We'll hold it in the fellowship hall Tuesday evening. We have three speakers lined up already, and hope to have at least two more. Each person is a member here at Good Shepherd who volunteers somewhere in the community. They'll tell you a little about what they do. We'll have some refreshments for you as well as some folks who'll be happy to claim as little as an hour a week of your time to make a difference.

"No one is too young or too old," he said.

Following a song from the choir, Gabriel preached from the New Testament, sharing examples from the Gospel of how Jesus eschewed hanging out in the temple for mingling with the common people.

"Church folk see each other every Sunday. We worship as a body. But how do you spread the Gospel of the Good News on the other six days of the week? Are you too holy to help your fellow man? Do you think yourself better than Jesus? He didn't run from the woman at the well. He gave her peace."

He stepped forward and lifted the edge of his robe to make another illustration. "When that woman of strong faith simply touched the hem of his garment, believing she'd find healing and grace and mercy just by touching his clothing, He didn't snatch up his cloak up and say, 'Don't put your grubby hands on me.'"

Understanding the analogies, people in the congregation laughed.

"The Lord said, 'Come unto me all ye that labor and I will give you rest.' We may not be able to provide eternal rest and peace to our fellow man, but we can make the way easier. We can open our hearts and our doors and give of our time and our talents and our money to make the way lighter for someone else."

Gabriel was on fire for his cause, not just Galilee shelter and its operating foundation, but on the whole issue of being a part of and helping the community. Once he made his mind up about something, he wasted no time at all taking action.

Susan Carter grinned through the entire sermon.

The new Mr. and Mrs. Samuel Vance walked up to greet Gabriel after the service.

"Well, I certainly didn't expect to see the two of you today," Gabriel said.

"Sam and I didn't want to miss the opportunity to attend our first church service as a married couple. We're going to go pick up Amy, then head to Breckenridge."

"Great sermon, Pastor Gabriel," Sam said. Just then, someone hailed him. "I'll be right back, honey."

Jessica watched him thread his way toward the man, then turned to Gabriel. "Thank you for everything yesterday. The service was beautiful."

"So was the bride," Gabriel said gallantly. Jessica glanced around, her actions almost furtive. "But that's not what you wanted to see me about," he added.

"Not exactly. Do you have a moment?"

Gabriel led her into an alcove away from prying eyes and listening ears.

Susan chatted with a few people who had questions about the Volunteer Fair, and opportunities to assist at the shelter. She couldn't answer questions about the former since she knew just as much as they did, but she gladly let people know how they could assist Galilee. Then she waited in line with other parishioners to greet the minister. She wanted to thank him for supporting the shelter's efforts in such a public way.

"I'm impressed," she said when she finally reached him. "You don't waste any time."

He took her hands in his, just as he had with everyone else. Susan wondered if all the others who shared a few words with him felt the same quiver of warmth, almost a ripple of excitement at just being near him. Maybe that explained his popularity with the membership. He was young and dynamic, and inspired confidence with both his bearing and his words.

Yeah, she told herself. *That's it.* His larger-than-life presence and nothing else.

"Don't be impressed," he said. "I'm ashamed to admit how blinded I've been."

He still held her hand, and Susan looked down at the joining. After a moment, he seemed to realize he was clasping her hand longer than politeness warranted, but when he released her, she missed his warmth. She looked up and into his eyes and for a moment, forgot about the need for oxygen.

"I..."

It was easy to get lost in the way he turned that oh-so-focused gaze on her. Susan resisted the urge to lick her lips or convulsively swallow. None of her inner turmoil showed on the outside, though. She presented herself as the cool, calm and collected director of a nonprofit help agency.

It almost worked, too.

"I— I'm glad to have your support," she managed to squeak out.

Every time her gaze met his, her heart did a little flip. Maybe, she told herself, she was coming down with an early fall flu.

The sound of his voice affected her, too. The deep and soothing tenor seemed to take control, expelling her fears and doubts.

Susan cleared her throat, trying to banish from her mind these thoughts about the minister. Despite her attraction to him—and the intent she could have sworn she'd read in his eyes last night—Susan wasn't in the market for a man, even one as accomplished and handsome as he. And she doubted that the good reverend, an obvious up-and-comer in the city, had his eye set on a woman with the sort of baggage she carried.

"I didn't mean to spring anything on you," he said. "Once I make up my mind about something, there's no need to delay."

She thought about how he'd called and asked her and the girls out. He'd wasted no time then, either. "You are a man of action."

"I believe in going for what I want."

Susan's eyes widened, and she wondered if he'd meant for her to interpret that the way she had. Before she could make up her mind, she saw people approaching.

"Would you have lunch with me tomorrow?" Gabriel asked quickly.

Her attention riveted back on him. "I beg your pardon?"

"Lunch," he repeated, as if that explained everything.

"I'll give you some more details about the Volunteer Fair and we can decide the shelter's involvement."

"Lunch?"

He grinned at her, seemingly amused by how dazed she appeared. "I'll pick you up at twelve-thirty?"

Susan nodded.

Leaning forward as he did with each parishioner, but whispering in her ear, he said, "It's a date, then. I'm looking forward to it."

Susan was pretty sure he didn't make lunch dates with all the members of Good Shepherd. A multitude of confusing emotions swirled within her as she headed to collect the girls.

Not too long after they were headed home, Hannah said, "Mommy?"

Susan glanced in the rearview mirror at the girls who were buckled into the back seat. She didn't bother to answer, since she knew one or both would immediately launch into whatever topic was on their minds.

"We have a question," Hannah said.

"Yeah," Sarah said.

Susan lifted her brow, waiting.

"When can we get a daddy?"

Chapter Eleven

Susan was so stunned she almost ran a stop sign. With her foot firmly on the brake, she turned around and looked at the twins. Even used to the way their minds took leaps and jumps and the many questions they asked on a regular basis, she had to admit this one had come out of left field.

Then an image of Gabriel laughing with the girls at the ice arena rose in her mind. Had that prompted their thinking?

"What makes you guys ask that?"

"Amy just got a new daddy," Sarah said, a plaintive note in her voice.

"And in Sunday school today," Hannah said, "we talked about how mommies and daddies have to set an example for their kids."

"And then we told Mrs. Henderson we didn't have a daddy because he went to heaven."

Susan doubted it, but she wasn't there at the end of her husband's life. He could very well have made a profession of faith.

With one exception, she'd always been honest with the twins about their father. There was nothing she could do for Reggie now, except continue to not malign him in front of the girls—something she was vigilant about.

"What did Mrs. Henderson say then?"

"That not everybody has a mommy and daddy."

Susan had been deluding herself that the topic of a father would never come up because they hadn't broached it so far or because they didn't care one way or the other. They'd watched her prepare for Jessica's wedding and knew how excited Amy was about it. Maybe Susan should have anticipated that that would trigger this discussion.

But this wasn't a conversation she wanted to have with the girls on the road. Her plan for the afternoon was to go home and cook a nice dinner, but she spotted one of the twins' favorite pizza places up the road.

"How about we talk about this over dinner?"

Twin indifferent "okays" drifted over from the back seat. When she pulled into Pizza Palace, the girls' enthusiasm level cranked way up. They let out whoops of delight, already chattering about what kinds of toppings they'd get on their pizza.

By the time they were served their food and drinks and had settled down a bit, Susan approached the topic again. "So, tell me some more about your Sunday school lesson."

"Mostly it was about how kids can help each other," Hannah said.

"Yeah," Sarah added around a mouthful of pizza. She started to say something else, but Susan gave her the mommy-eye. Sarah finished chewing and swallowing before she continued. "Like when we told you about Jasmine."

Susan felt a twinge of guilt over not disclosing to the twins that their friend and her mother had, indeed, been in trouble. She didn't bend confidentiality rules, even for her own children.

"We were kind of thinking…" Sarah started.

"Since Pastor Gabriel took us skating…" Hannah picked up the trail, her voice hopeful.

"That, you know…" Sarah finished, a grin on her face as she twirled her straw.

Knowing exactly where this train was headed and not at all liking the direction, Susan aimed to apply the brakes. "Guys, just because Pastor Gabriel treated us to an evening doesn't mean anything else is going to come of it."

Hope flickered out of two sets of identical brown eyes. Susan felt like a heel for dimming the light in those eyes, but she was realistic and needed the girls to be as well.

"But—" Hannah started.

"But nothing," Susan told her. "He showed us a kindness and that's all there was to it." Her piece said, she lifted a slice of thin-crust pizza piled high with green peppers and extra pepperoni and took a healthy bite.

The twins glanced at each other.

"But he's never taken anyone else out skating and to dinner at the mall."

They'd caught her with her mouth full, so it was a moment before Susan could ask the question she'd have blurted out if she hadn't had those few extra chewing moments to gather her thoughts.

It was bad enough that her own flights of fancy had drifted into *what-if* with Gabriel Dawson. She couldn't have the girls following her down the same path. She'd once had her own heart trounced by a smooth-talking operator—one who talked a good game. And Reggie had nothing on Gabriel. Through seminary and other ministerial training, Gabriel had probably been taught how to persuade people, how to make a convincing argument.

But he walks his talk, a small voice said inside her.

Susan ignored that thought, and banished from her head an image of the handsome minister and those unfathomable dark eyes.

She took a breath to steady herself, afraid she already knew the answer before she asked the question. "How do you know that he's never taken members of the church out?"

"We asked," Hannah reported.

"And everybody said no," Sarah finished.

Susan's stomach lurched. "Everybody? Like who?"

They proceeded to name several of the children in their Sunday school class.

Susan stifled a groan. If those kids talked half as much as her own did, before the end of the day at least a quarter of the membership would know that Pastor Gabriel had been out with Susan and her twins. Among the things Susan truly disliked, right next to people lying to her, was being the subject of gossip. She'd gotten enough of that growing up poor and in the projects. Then came the whole business with Reggie and her own stint at Galilee shelter.

When she'd been named director at Galilee, the newspaper and one of the local television stations ate up the fact that a former client at the shelter had triumphantly returned to lead it. She'd worked hard to get where she was today and knew it was by God's grace alone that she and the twins were healthy, comfortable and had a semblance of financial security—thanks in part to a benefactor Susan liked to refer to as her fairy godmother.

No, she decided, looking at the twins and wondering what sort of damage control she might be able to do; she'd never liked people pointing and whispering about her. Which is what would probably go on after Gabriel's glowing praise of her in the service and the girls' conversations with their friends in Sunday school.

Susan encouraged the public spotlight to shine on Galilee, not on herself. It was okay when the attention was on the work of the shelter and foundation.

"So everything is cool?" Hannah asked. They obviously weren't too sure what to make of the expressions that crossed their mom's face.

Susan blinked, pulled her thoughts back to the moment.

There was nothing she could do about what people might or might not say about her relationship, such as it was, with Gabriel, so she endeavored not to stress over it.

"Everything's copacetic."

The twins frowned. "What's cope at septic?"

"Down the toilet," Hannah translated with an air of superiority.

Susan laughed out loud at that. With a three-minute

advantage as oldest, Hannah assumed the role of gifted know-it-all. "Copacetic—" Susan spelled the word for them "—means everything is A-okay."

She lifted her cup and the girls followed suit. "To fun," Susan said. Grinning, the twins tipped their plastic tumblers to hers.

To Gabriel's astonishment, he found himself nervous about the meeting with Susan. Though he'd called it a meeting to discuss the shelter's involvement in the Volunteer Fair, he couldn't help thinking of it as a date.

Maybe if this went well he'd ask her out on a real date—one minus the girls. The twins were a delight, something that surprised him, since he spent little time with children other than his nieces and nephews on infrequent visits back home. But he'd like some one-on-one time with Susan. Time that didn't involve work or family.

She'd had her secretary call his to say she'd have to meet him at the restaurant because she had another appointment right after.

As he pulled into the parking lot at the Stagecoach Café, Gabriel couldn't help wondering if Susan's later appointment was a real one or a phantom engagement set up so she wouldn't have to spend too much time with him. It was a tactic his sister used to use with dates she didn't like. She always had an out set up in advance—a telephone call, a hair appointment or a church meeting. Anything that would give her a legitimate excuse out of a bad date if she didn't like the guy or the situation.

He pressed the remote and locked the doors of the

town car and strode toward the entrance of the restaurant. Every time he came here, the big red building made him smile. It so very much looked like a relic of the Old West. Yet, extensive renovations inside and out ensured the café was truly a twenty-first-century establishment with a nineteenth-century ambience.

Gabriel entered the eatery and passed by the small wooden bar area. He caught a glimpse of himself in the mirror backing the bar and felt overdressed in his dark suit and tie.

"Pastor Gabriel!" Fiona Montgomery, the owner of the Stagecoach Café, greeted him. "What a delight to see you."

Fiona was responsible for the makeover at the café and usually spent her time either in the office or mingling with the guests. Today her red hair was pulled into a ponytail secured with a red handkerchief that matched the red-checked cloths on each table. Her cheeks were rosy and her eyes sparkled with what could best be described as a touch of mischief.

"Hello there. You're playing hostess today?"

"Just for a moment. Your lady friend is already here," she said, slipping her arm through his and guiding him through tables. "I thought you'd like a bit of privacy, so I've put you over here."

"Fiona, that wasn't necessary. We're just having a meeting."

"Meeting? Is that what they call it these days?" she said with a mischievous grin.

Gabriel wanted to groan, but he held on to the self-assured bearing that had served him well in the military.

"I missed service yesterday, but I heard all about it."

For just a moment Gabriel regretted choosing the Stagecoach Café. Fiona baked the best apple pie in town, but she was also a world-class gossip. He wondered what she'd heard and just what she'd passed along.

When they arrived at the table, Susan rose, extending her hand for Gabriel to shake.

He could have kissed her for that.

Fiona frowned at the formality. "But I thought—"

"What's good today?" Susan asked before Fiona got out the rest of what she'd been poised to ask.

The restaurateur's face broke into a wide smile. "Well, everything's good. As always." She leaned forward. "But I'd order the special today. It's fabulous, if I say so myself."

Laughing, Fiona passed them off to their server. "An appetizer is on the house for this table."

"Fiona, that's not necessary."

She placed a hand on Gabriel's back and leaned forward so just Susan and Gabriel could hear. "My treat. For your…meeting." She winked and sashayed off, greeting customers at the nearby tables.

"This is why most pastors arrive in town with a wife and family in tow."

"To avoid public embarrassment?" Susan asked.

"To avoid the matchmaking schemes of a well-meaning membership. It'll be all over town that we're having lunch together here." He glanced at the secluded alcove into which Fiona had tucked them. "Here in this cozy corner."

"I don't mind being seen with you."

She said the words so casually that Gabriel gave her a sharp glance. Was that his opening?

Not sure, he decided to take it rather than miss the opportunity.

"If that's the case," he said. "Would you like to go on a real date with me? Just the two of us."

"You're moving fast, Rev."

"Not really," he said. "I'm a man of action. When I know what I want, I usually go for it."

Susan reached for her water glass with hands that he noted trembled just a bit, then she took a sip.

"Nothing ventured, nothing gained," he said.

"You make a date sound like a dare."

"I suppose some people might view it that way," he told her.

"But you don't."

Gabriel shook his head.

Susan ordered the day's green special, a smoked salmon Caesar salad, while Gabriel went with the Pioneer Pie, a buffalo stew topped with puff pastry and mashed potatoes. Fiona's food was filling and hearty—just like the pioneers would have wanted it.

When their meals arrived they ate in silence for a bit and then talked about the Tuesday evening Volunteer Fair.

Gabriel pulled a small leather-bound notebook from his suit jacket. "We have someone from Galilee on the program." He flipped through a few pages and checked a name. "Patricia Streeter. Do you know her?"

Susan nodded. "She's in the air force and is one of our longtime volunteers."

"She's one of the speakers the Volunteer Center lined up for us."

"You'll be pleased. Tricia is one of our best."

The conversation eventually drifted into the subject they'd been discussing last week. Something Susan had said still nagged at Gabriel. He didn't at all agree with her charge that he spent more time wooing bigwigs than he did on his congregation.

"An effective leader has to be able to see the big picture," he said. "To know the enemy's strengths and weaknesses."

"True," Susan said, pushing around a last bit of salmon. "But an effective leader also has to know the capabilities of his—or her—ground troops before launching a full-scale campaign," she said. "It would be foolish to go into a battle not knowing exactly—or at least to the best guess based on the intelligence you've gathered—just what lies ahead."

He gave her an odd look. Susan Carter was even sharper than he'd thought, and his first assessment had not been a stingy one.

Gabriel more than merely sensed, he *knew* that she sat there trying to warn him off. They were no longer talking about his approach to civic affairs. But he had done his homework—thoroughly, as a matter of fact.

He grinned.

"What?"

"I was just thinking that you're something of an enigma."

"Me?" Susan said, looking surprised. "I'm an open book."

"Really?" he said, leaning forward, steepling his hands.

Susan tried not to squirm under that intense gaze, the very one that seemed to melt all her defenses.

"Then tell me why I make you so nervous."

She opened her mouth to deny the charge, then snapped it shut. He watched her, wondering if she felt the connection between them and was merely fighting it. He'd just—deliberately?—changed the tenor of their lunch conversation. Yes, he conceded to himself, he'd intentionally shifted the tone to the personal.

He waited while she formulated an answer, expecting a half truth since it was taking her a while to respond to his very simple question.

"I don't know what you want," Susan finally said.

"What if I said what I want is you—to get to know you better?"

Her already wide eyes widened even more. She carefully placed her napkin at the side of her plate. "I think…I think that that scares me."

"Why?"

She licked dry lips, and in that moment Gabriel wished he could read her thoughts.

"Because I don't understand where you're coming from," she said. "I don't get it. There are a lot of women after you."

"That's not a positive," he said dryly. "Trust me."

Susan stared at her bread plate for a moment, then raised her gaze and met his head-on. "That's what frightens me the most," she said. "I do trust you."

Gabriel spent the rest of the afternoon thinking about their conversation, about what it meant and why he'd insisted on pressing her. He didn't have an answer except that the moment seemed to call for it. Something about Susan Carter addressed a need deep inside him—a need to connect with another human being who understood exactly where he was coming from. And he knew she did—whether she admitted it or not.

Maybe that's what scared her, he thought as he paced the terrace at his home. Though the church offered a parish house, Gabriel preferred his own residence, one that wasn't tied to the church or to the job of leading its membership.

His unobstructed view of Pikes Peak always inspired in him a sense of wonder. He started humming "Great Is Thy Faithfulness," then wondered at the choice of hymn, which had come unbidden to mind.

He'd stopped home after lunch with Susan to pick up a file he needed for a meeting later in the day. The Volunteer Fair would take place the next day and there was still plenty to do. But his thoughts were of nothing but Susan Carter, particularly what she'd said about a commander leading troops.

He snatched up the phone and called on an old friend, someone he could always turn to. Most people didn't think much about where a minister might go for help. Preachers had emotional needs just like everyone else.

Gabriel was glad he'd maintained ties with his seminary professor and mentor, Geoffrey Phillips, an Old Testament scholar whose research and publications focused on the poetry books of the Bible—Proverbs, Psalms, Ecclesiastes and Song of Solomon. Considering romance was what he wanted to talk with Geoffrey about, it seemed appropriate.

"So what you're telling me," Reverend Phillips said, after Gabriel had explained, "is that she's got you turned every which way but loose."

Gabriel let out a bark of laughter. "I see nothing has changed with you, my old friend."

"Watch that 'old' business," Geoffrey said. "Just because a body is turning sixty is no reason for insult."

Knowing he teased, Gabriel smiled. Then, sobering, he said, "I've never felt this way before."

"Even with Mikki? You were going to marry her."

"That was a mistake from the get-go," Gabriel said. "Both of us knew it and we should have listened to you."

"And so it's different with Susan?"

The indignation he felt about her unfair challenges came back. "She thinks I don't care about the community.

Everything I've done since arriving at Good Shepherd has been geared toward improving the quality of life for the members of my church."

"Then why are you on the phone telling me instead of showing your lady friend? It sounds to me that the problem is not so much what she said, Gabriel. You've taken criticism before."

"Yes, but…"

Geoffrey talked over the objection. "I think the issue is that her criticism of you is all mixed up in how you feel about the woman herself, not the work she represents. It's hard to take criticism from people we love."

Chapter Twelve

He had protested, but Geoffrey had just chuckled.

"Whatever you say, Gabriel."

His mentor's words still echoed in Gabriel's head all the next day as he visited with homebound members and walked his chaplaincy rounds at Vance Memorial Hospital. He grabbed a light dinner on the run, and ate at his desk at church. Now, as he watched people fill the seats in the fellowship hall, Gabriel tried to focus on the evening instead of the implications of what his mentor had said.

He managed to do just that, until Susan entered the hall. Though she'd walked in with four other women, including Mrs. Montgomery, his attention zoomed right to her.

Deliberately, Gabriel turned away, sought out his notes. He needed to focus on something other than the reality staring him in the face.

Since the rally had been called so hastily, Gabriel hadn't been able to predict how many people might actually attend.

"I can't believe the turnout," his secretary Karen said as she placed glasses and a pitcher of ice water on the table where the speakers would sit.

"I was just thinking the same thing," Gabriel answered as he did a quick head count.

He was surprised and pleased to see more than one hundred people, including children, filling the chairs in the fellowship hall. Neither Gabriel nor the maintenance man who had done the setup had believed they would need more than twenty-five chairs, and some of those, they'd figured, would be taken up by purses and sweaters. When it had become evident that the evening would be well attended, they'd hastily hauled out more chairs.

"The room looks good," Gabriel told the maintenance man. "Thanks for putting the effort in on short notice."

"Not a problem, Pastor Gabriel. If you don't mind, I'm going to stick around for the program. I've been thinking about doing a little something. I'm pretty sure I have a spare hour or two in every week."

Gabriel clapped him on the back. "Excellent. You're more than welcome."

Eight tables ringed the chairs that faced the front of the fellowship hall. Representatives from six different nonprofit agencies had arrived early to set up their booths or table displays. Two of the tables were reserved for the Volunteer Center, the city department that coordinated volunteer activities throughout Colorado Springs. Agencies that had openings for volunteer help registered with the center, and people looking to give an hour or more to the community could find a match through the center's database.

Mayor Montgomery walked up and shook Gabriel's hand, then Karen's. "The wife said I needed to be here," he said.

"Glad to have you," Gabriel told him. "Would you like to say a few words of welcome?"

"Why not?" the mayor said, nudging Gabriel. "May as well start trolling for a few votes."

Joining her husband, Liza Montgomery pinched him on the side. "I cannot believe you just said that. We're members of this church and support all of its activities."

The mayor looked genuinely contrite. "It was just a little joke, right, Pastor Gabriel?"

Gabriel had no intention of getting in the middle of what looked like the makings of an argument between the Montgomerys. "It's good to see you both, no matter the circumstances."

Liza gave him an assessing look. "Always the diplomat. I like that in you."

Since Gabriel didn't know what, if anything, he was supposed to say in response, he asked about the welfare of the woman who'd been brought to the shelter on Saturday night.

"She's doing much better, at least physically. I'm a little worried, though. She still hasn't told us her name."

"Maybe she can't remember it," Gabriel said.

Liza rolled her eyes and shook her head. "Amnesia? Don't tell me you buy into that. Besides, she knows where she is, what day it is. This morning while I was over at Galilee, she even helped out with the meals. She definitely knows her way around a kitchen."

"I'll stop by and visit with her before the week ends."

Liza motioned for two of the women who'd entered with her to come forward. "Pastor, I'd like you to meet a couple of ladies from Galilee. You've met one of them. They've decided they'd like to help as well."

"Hello again, Pastor," one of the women said.

Gabriel remembered her as Mary Hill, who had been at the shelter during his first visit there.

"It's good to see you both," Gabriel said in greeting. "Thank you for coming."

"I don't have much," Mary said. "But time is free, right?"

He nodded, and in that moment, as he looked those two women in their eyes, Gabriel realized that there was so much more at stake. Here stood two women, essentially homeless and living in a shelter for battered women, yet they'd come forward to help the less fortunate.

Gabriel was humbled in their presence, and he realized that that was what Susan had been riding him about. Not his level of commitment, but rather the scope and depth of his net. Everyone had something to offer the world at large—no matter whether that offering came in the form of a corporate donation, a bill in the state legislature, or an hour of a battered woman's time.

Following Gabriel's welcoming prayer and comments, the mayor reiterated Gabriel's admonition to ask lots of questions of the volunteers who'd come out to talk about their own experiences.

Major Patricia Streeter was by far the most eloquent. In her uniform, she talked from the heart. "When I first joined the military, I took a solemn oath to defend my country and its ideals. As a volunteer in Colorado Springs,

I signed on for a tougher job, but one that has rewarded me far more than I've ever been able to give back."

She shared her experiences as a volunteer and how she'd learned from one of the women, an older one, to carry herself tall and proud.

After asking Susan to stand and wave, and pointing out the table where interested people could get more information about Galilee, Tricia took her seat next to Susan.

Susan clasped her hand and squeezed it. "Good job!" she whispered.

"Thanks," Tricia said. "I was nervous."

"But you know all of these people."

As Gabriel introduced the next speaker, Tricia whispered, "That's why I was nervous."

In all, the crowd heard from a representative of the food bank, a youth ice-hockey league, a seniors respite-care center that used animals as comfort visitors, a hospice serving mentally challenged young adults, a self-improvement workshop for at-risk populations, and the Galilee shelter. Two delegates from the Volunteer Center briefly explained about all the other opportunities available in the city.

People then mingled, enjoyed refreshments and signed up for or got more information on volunteer positions that they found intriguing.

"Congratulations, Pastor," Susan said during the reception.

"I thought we'd gotten beyond that 'Pastor' business."

"All right, *Rev*."

He smiled.

"Seriously, though," Susan continued. She balanced

a small glass of red punch and two cookies in one hand. "You not only pulled this off in less time than it would take most people to decide what to do, you have what's looking like some serious commitments here."

"Thanks to you."

"Me?"

"Yes, you. If you hadn't goaded me, I never would have thought of this."

"I don't goad."

He leaned forward. "All right, then, you argue persuasively."

Susan gave an unladylike harrumph.

"Where are the girls?"

"Over there playing with the dogs. What a hit they were with the crowd! I didn't even know that program existed."

The speaker from the hospice center brought a Lab and a chow mix to demonstrate how the animals worked with senior citizens. They, along with a rabbit, had drawn the attention of most of the young folks.

"You never answered my question yesterday," Gabriel said.

Susan nibbled on a cookie. "Which question was that?"

"The one where I was begging you to go out with me again. Just the two of us."

"I..." She made the mistake of looking into his eyes. "You can be quite persuasive." Susan didn't at all care for the husky timbre of her own voice. This was, after all, the preacher...and they were both at church.

"Does that mean okay?"

She nodded. "But I don't recall any begging."

He smiled, and Susan got the distinct feeling that more might be at stake here than just a date with Gabriel.

"Saturday night?"

She started to nod, then shook her head. "No. I can't do this."

At her words, he looked as crestfallen as if she'd taken away his favorite toy or kicked him out of the playground sandbox. She reached out and touched his arm. "I meant, not Saturday."

At just that moment, Fiona Montgomery swooped in. She looked from Susan's hand to Gabriel's expression and clapped her hands. "I knew it! I'm so happy. Pastor Gabriel, you sly fox, you."

Susan dropped her hand as if she'd been scalded.

Fiona wrapped her arms around Susan in an exuberant hug. "I'm so happy for you. You deserve the very best."

"Mrs. Montgomery," Susan and Gabriel said at the same time, though Susan's voice was a bit muffled given that she was being smothered in Fiona's amble bosom. "It's not at all what you think."

Fiona let Susan go long enough to clasp one of their hands in each of hers. "All right," she stage-whispered. "This will be just between us. If you ever need anything—like that little private alcove at the Stagecoach Café to meet—you just let me know. Whatever I can do to advance the cause of true romance..."

Susan sent Gabriel an imploring look. Though she said not a word, he got the message loud and clear: change the subject. Now.

"Mrs. Montgomery," he said, "I hope you're here tonight because you're thinking of volunteering. Or maybe you have an opportunity available at the restaurant."

"I'm here because Liza made me come," Fiona confessed. "And I don't use volunteers. What I need is a cook and two waitresses. I already had one opening, then Shelley—" she turned to Susan "—you remember her, right? She was dating that Rochelle boy before he decided to be a cowboy and just plumb up and left home and went on the circuit. Well, anyway, she quit to go chasing after him. Heard he was down in—"

"Mrs. Montgomery?" Susan said, before Fiona launched into a half-hour description of what she'd heard the couple was doing. She indicated Liza Montgomery. "I think your sister-in-law is calling you."

Fiona looked around. "Oh, did I go running off again? You know how I can get. Well," she said, patting both their hands, "you just give me the word."

When Fiona finally departed, Susan turned to Gabriel. "I'll go out with you on one condition."

"What's that?"

"You get me far away from prying eyes."

The next morning, Susan looked in on the Galilee shelter's mystery guest. She found the woman in the kitchen, pulling a dozen cookies out of one of the large ovens.

"Hi."

The woman glanced up and smiled.

"How are you feeling?"

"Much better. Thank you." She transferred the rack to a cooling stand, turned off the oven and removed the thick protective mitt from her hand.

"Do you have a minute to talk?"

The woman nodded. Without being rude, Susan assessed the woman's bruises in an attempt to see if she should insist on a hospital visit. A slight bruising near her eye looked as if she'd evaded a direct hit. The bruise was just starting to fade a bit, but Susan knew it would take a full two weeks to completely clear and heal. The clean and pressed but plain cotton shirt and chinos from the shelter's clothes closet were a far cry from the very expensive suit the woman had been found in.

The lounge was empty, though the large-screen television was on. Susan muted the sound and invited the woman to have a seat on one of the two sofas.

"It's been a few days since you were brought here," Susan said. "Do you remember what happened Saturday night?"

The woman clasped her hands in her lap. Instead of answering directly, she stared at her hands and nodded.

"What's your name?"

When the woman remained silent, Susan bit back a sigh.

"We need to call you something besides 'hey, you.'"

That got her a smile in return.

"A couple of the kids have started calling me Cookie."

"But that's not your name."

The woman shook her head. "No, it's not."

Susan, a woman of infinite patience, just waited. Eventually she got what she wanted.

"You can call me Evie," the woman said. She folded her hands together. "I can't...it's just too complicated."

"I realize this has been a traumatic time for you, but we do have some rules here," Susan said, her voice gentle. Her heart went out to women like Evie. It wasn't in Susan's nature to not give where giving was possible, to not aid where aid was needed. She couldn't, however, put the other residents in jeopardy.

"This house is a transitional one, for women and children who are moving toward independence," Susan explained. "You were brought here by one of our volunteers, Mrs. Montgomery. You remember her, right?"

Evie nodded. "I can pay my own way," she said. Then her face crumpled. "If I use my credit cards, though, he'll know. I just can't…" Tears welled in her eyes. "My purse. He took my purse."

Susan took her hand. "It'll all work out," she said. And she hoped that was, indeed, true.

"I don't want to be a burden to anyone."

"You're not," Susan said. "But I need you to answer a few questions."

When Evie finally nodded, Susan continued. "Are you in trouble with the law?"

"No. Not the way you think."

That answer didn't ease Susan's disquiet about Evie. Something more was going on here. And for some reason, Evie still looked familiar to her. Given the number of faces she'd seen come and go through her life and work, that was understandable. But still…

Susan completed the interview with Evie and let the woman get back to her baking, which she seemed to enjoy. As Susan headed outside to return to her office in the administration building, her cell phone trilled. Lost in thought about Evie, she absently answered.

"This is Susan Carter."

"Hi, Susan," Christine said. "Reverend Dawson is here for you."

She stopped in her tracks, her gaze whipping to the curb in front of the building. There sat the town car. The pastor-mobile. So, Susan thought, he was here on church business.

"Tell him I'll be right there."

Instead of coming through the front as she'd planned, Susan went around to the rear entrance. She needed the time to get her approach together. Cool and calm, which, according to the way her heart was suddenly pounding, she couldn't claim to be. Precise and professional? She could always pull that off, no matter the situation. It was a simple matter of putting her game face on, presenting to the world the accomplished director of the shelter.

But when she came face-to-face with Gabriel, neither strategy worked.

He held out a small arrangement of colorful flowers, pinks and reds and yellows, in a small, round, glass bowl. "A little something to brighten your desk."

She met the smile and the flowers he offered with a grin as wide as her face. "You continue to surprise me."

"Good," he said.

Aware of the receptionist listening to their every word, Susan beckoned him forward. "Come on," she invited. "We can talk in my office."

Gabriel nodded, then turned toward Christine. "It's good seeing you again."

"You, too," the young woman said.

Susan glanced around Gabriel. She'd never heard that dreamy quality in Christine's voice—almost a purr. She then had to tamp down a streak of territorial jealousy.

That gave her a jolt. She had no reason to harbor any jealous feelings.

Liar, liar, pants on fire.

When they reached her office, Susan took a deep, steadying breath and closed the door before facing him with a bright smile. "To what do I owe the pleasure of this visit?"

"I've been giving some more thought to what I might be able to do here."

"You're serious?"

He gave her a quizzical look. "Of course I'm serious."

Susan folded her arms, testing him. "And if I weren't the director here?"

"I'd still be serious. About my commitment to the work done here...and to you."

The corner of her mouth tilted up. "Thank you for the flowers." She'd placed them on her desk, near the computer monitor.

Gabriel kept her off-kilter. She wondered if she had a similar effect on him.

She motioned for him to take a seat. She went behind her desk and settled in her chair, needing the distance of the desk between them for her own peace of mind, if nothing else. Everything about Gabriel was a distraction. From the way he wore a suit—today a three-piece charcoal pinstripe—to the scent of his aftershave or cologne. She got a whiff of something woodsy and rugged, the scent reminding her that he was more than the pastor at Good Shepherd Christian Church. He was first a man.

"I met with the woman who was brought in Saturday night."

"How is she doing?"

"Better," Susan said. "She's up and about and has been helping out in the kitchen. I'd been concerned that she might have a couple of bruised or cracked ribs, but she's not showing any outward signs of pain." She moved the day's newspaper out of the way, then glanced back at it, frowning.

"What's wrong?"

She shook her head. "I don't know. I just get the feeling I've met her before somewhere. I can't place it, though, and it's driving me nuts."

"That's why you need an evening alone with me, to clear your head."

Susan's laugh rang through the office. "You don't give up, do you." She didn't add that an evening alone with him would hardly clear her head—more likely, an evening with him would completely scramble it.

"You agreed to go out, but not Saturday night."

"That's the gala."

He touched his forefinger to his mouth. "That's right."

"How about lunch instead?" Susan said. She reached for her PDA. "Tomorrow? I can take some extra time if we go after one."

"Deal."

"But not to the Stagecoach Café," they said at the same time.

After their chuckles died down, the air between them stilled again. Susan's breath caught and the hair on her arms rose. The room was charged with an electricity that seemed to spark only when she was near Gabriel.

She cleared her throat and rose. Gabriel stood as well. "Is it all right if I visit with Evie for a moment?"

"Not at all," Susan said, then shook her head. "I mean, that'll be fine. The residents are allowed to have guests in the lounge. And they can come and go at will."

At her office door, he reached a hand out and touched her below the chin. "I'm looking forward to our afternoon together."

At that moment, Susan decided to get an oxygen tank for her office. She seemed to need a boost every time he got close.

Gabriel couldn't say what got into him each time he was near Susan Carter. He just wanted to fold her in his arms and never let her go, to protect her. Of late, it seemed he couldn't go a whole day without one of her smiles. From that wildly curly hair to her wide eyes and full mouth—

He stumbled on the walkway toward the shelter.

Slow down, he coached himself.

It was one thing to be infatuated with a woman, and quite another to be more than halfway in love. But Gabriel couldn't deny it, not to himself, the one person he'd never lied to.

Geoffrey was right. Gabriel had fallen in love with Susan Carter.

How that had happened, he wasn't quite sure, especially since their actual one-on-one time together had been limited. He'd admired her work and her style from afar from the moment he'd met her several months ago.

He knew that to Susan—and outside observers like Fiona Montgomery—it might seem as if he were running full-speed ahead in his pursuit of her. But the fact was, he'd been enchanted with Susan from the first.

She still kept up her guard around him, though. Gabriel attributed that to his role as a minister. She seemed to have a hang-up with him being a preacher.

He'd have to show her what he was like as simply a man.

Chapter Thirteen

Evie was a little more forthcoming with Gabriel present than she had been with Susan, but not by much.

After taking a call, Susan had joined him. She watched as Gabriel talked to Evie and decided that if he hadn't gone into the ministry, Gabriel would have been a good therapist. Pastors were in a sense therapists, anyway. They listened to the problems of their members and dispensed wisdom or guidance depending on the situation. Sometimes, just like a good therapist, they referred people to other resources that might help.

Susan didn't know what Evie's situation was, but she did sense that the woman was being less than forthcoming even in the answers she willingly provided.

"Thank you for inquiring about my welfare, Reverend Dawson," Evie said. "Your concern and Mrs. Carter's has been a—" she paused, met their gazes for a moment and then gave a small, graceful almost-shrug of her shoulders "—I suppose you would use the word 'blessing.' Authentic kindness from strangers is not something I'm accustomed to."

"Is there someone we can contact for you?" Gabriel asked. "A pastor, or maybe a rabbi or priest?"

Evie laughed, the sound melodic as if she once used to laugh a lot. "We only appear in church during the season," she said, "and this go-round..." She abruptly stopped and looked away, as if realizing she'd said far too much.

Gabriel deftly probed, but got no further information out of Evie on that line of thought. He shared a glance with Susan, who shrugged.

"How about instead of talking about the past," Gabriel said, "we look toward the future and what you'd like to do when you leave Galilee. Do you have a high school diploma?"

Evie nodded.

"A college degree?"

She nodded again.

"In what area?" Gabriel asked.

"Nothing that will be helpful in the job market, I'm afraid. I'm thirty-five years old and have no marketable skills. It's pathetic and my own fault." She put her head down, and the heavy mass of her hair fell forward.

"That's not true," Susan said. "You have skills. You walked into that kitchen and produced food and cookies that everyone has been raving about."

She raised her head and pushed her hair back from her eyes. "Knowing how to bake a cookie is hardly a marketable skill."

"Tell that to the founder of all those cookie franchises in the malls," Susan said. Gabriel caught her eye and tilted his head just so. Susan had a feeling their thoughts ran on parallel tracks.

"Tell you what, Evie," Gabriel said. "I'll ask around, see if I can pull a few strings on your behalf."

"Please don't go to any trouble," Evie said. "I've already caused enough disruption here."

"You haven't been a disruption," Susan assured her. "And we'll work it out so you have somewhere to stay until you're back on your feet."

Tears gathered in Evie's eyes. "Thank you," she murmured.

Gabriel asked whether she minded if he prayed. Evie glanced from Gabriel to Susan, who nodded, then Evie rose, took their hands in hers and bowed her head.

"You're right," Gabriel said a little while later, as he and Susan made their way back to Susan's office. "There's something awfully familiar about her. The more she talked—"

"In that very cultured and sometimes formal lilt," Susan interjected.

"—the more I realized that something about her danced just off the edge of my consciousness."

"But you're still going to approach Fiona Montgomery about getting her a job at the Stagecoach Café?"

His eyes expressed his surprise. "How'd you know that's what I was thinking?"

Susan waggled her fingers from her head to his. "Same wavelength, Rev. Same wavelength."

"Great minds and all that?"

She smiled. "Yeah. Something like that."

Susan let him into her office, then retreated for a moment and returned carrying two steaming mugs. After handing one to him, she opened her fist and let sugar packets and little creamer tubs fall to the desktop. "I wasn't sure how you take your coffee."

After they doctored their cups of brew, Susan leaned on the edge of her desk. "And what was that business about the season?"

"The first thing I'd guess is football season."

Susan nodded. "Or hockey. It's September. There's also fall, a new season in nature, or the start of the new school year."

"But the start of fall or even school is no reason to suddenly decide to go to church."

Susan's eye fell on the newspaper she'd pushed aside earlier. She put her coffee mug down and reached for that day's edition of the *Colorado Springs Sentinel.*

"What is it?" Gabriel asked.

Her gaze met his and in a voice that was almost a whisper, she said, "I think I know where I've seen Evie."

Susan's cell phone rang before Gabriel had a chance to ask her where. She peeked at the number, then held a finger up to him. "Excuse me, I need to take this call."

He rose, taking his mug with him, and stepped into the hallway to give her some privacy.

He took time to admire the various paintings that adorned the walls—some obviously works of art by five- or six-year-olds with more artistic exuberance than talent, and others that were clearly done by a painter of some skill. Then he paused in front of the wall quilt.

"This is truly remarkable," he said.

"Susan's quite a quilter."

He turned. Liza Montgomery stood at the door

watching him. His surprise over her words must have shown on his face because she smiled. "Susan did this?"

Liza nodded.

Gabriel placed the mug on a coffee table and peered at the quilt, then pointed toward the hallway. "That Susan?"

Amused, Liza joined him at the large wall hanging. "Its twin is hanging next door."

"Yes," he said. "I've seen it. I thought they were done by an artist commissioned for the work."

"They were," Liza said.

Gabriel stared at the quilt—the many shades of blue and gray that made up the window before passing through to the light, the details in flowers and vines and rays of sunshine.

"We're going to have one of her quilts for sale under a silent auction Saturday night. It should fetch quite a bit."

"I don't know much about quilting, but I know a bit about art. That," he said, indicating the wall hanging, "takes a lot of time and patience to accomplish. She's a very talented woman."

Liza studied her pastor, then the quilt. "Yes, she is," she said, her voice carrying a speculative note. "Would you like to see the other one again?"

"Yes," he said.

Liza beckoned for him to follow.

Back next door for the second time that evening, Gabriel was shown the quilt. Liza held it up so he could see the back of the much larger work. This one covered a good portion of the wall.

"Hey, Pastor Gabriel," a woman said. "I thought that was your voice."

Gabriel and Liza turned. One of the members of Good Shepherd who was also a shelter resident stood there. "Hello."

Liza made introductions, just in case Gabriel didn't recall the woman's name.

"What are you doing here?" Betty asked. "Following up on that sermon on Sunday about volunteerism?"

"Actually, I was making my rounds. I was thinking I might start a prayer group and Bible study here."

"Really? That would be so cool," Betty said. "Marie and I were just saying the other day that we can't always get to some of the programs held at the church. Hold on for a second. I'll go get her. She's new."

Before Gabriel knew it, the room was filled with five women, four of them shelter residents and all with Bibles in hand. He glanced at the expectant faces of the women gathered around. "Who said church had to be held behind stained-glass windows? The Lord said where two or three are gathered in His name," he said.

"That's right," Betty agreed.

"And with you, Pastor, we've got six," Mary Hill added. She held her Bible high. "Let's have some church up in here!"

And for the next forty-five minutes, that's just what they did. Gabriel, thinking about the quilts Susan had made for the shelter as well as the many lonesome and dark roads the shelter's residents traveled in their lives, led a lesson from the twelfth chapter of Job. " 'He reveals the deep things of darkness and brings deep shadows into the light,'" Gabriel read. "I see that applied here at Galilee. In your lives. In my life. In the quilts that hang here."

"But what's the purpose of shining a spotlight on something bad?" one of the women asked.

"Think about it," Gabriel said. "If you're in a dark place and light is suddenly drawn to a corner, what happens?"

"Roaches run," someone else said.

That earned chuckles from some of the women and a shudder from Liza.

"And what else?" Gabriel prodded.

"You can see?" Betty said, obviously not sure if that was the answer he was looking for.

"Exactly," Gabriel said.

Betty beamed under the praise. "That dark corner isn't so scary anymore," she said. "And maybe the only thing really there was shadow, but you didn't know it was just a shadow because it loomed so large."

Gabriel nodded. "Well put."

Betty got a high-five from the woman sitting next to her. Gabriel smiled, wondering why it hadn't crossed his mind to take a ministry like this out of Good Shepherd to meet the people where they lived, rather than waiting for them to come to the sanctuary.

He had Susan to thank for this new way of thinking.

He closed the session with a song and a promise to come back to lead another Bible study.

Liza, who was working her volunteer shift, saw him to the door. "I'm so very glad you stopped by, Pastor Gabriel. It's been really good for the ladies."

"And for me," he said.

"Are you and Susan done with your business? Would you like me to take you back to her office?"

He hadn't even thought about Susan. It was like that

when he was preaching or teaching; his total focus was on the Word. He shook his head. "We were just finishing up."

After saying farewell to Liza, Gabriel sat for a moment in his car, contemplating what he knew about Susan Carter. It amounted to quite a bit now. And the more he discovered, the deeper he fell for her.

Leaning forward, he started the car, and when he glanced up he saw the curtain move at the window of what he guessed was Susan's office. He smiled.

If nothing else, he'd grabbed Susan Carter's attention.

The next afternoon proved the perfect autumn day. Snow might be falling in the high country, but the temperature in Colorado Springs was mild, warm actually, hovering in the high sixties—just right for an afternoon stroll through Old Colorado City.

The street, the city's oldest historic district, had been converted into a trendy tree-lined oasis with neat little shops, galleries and cafés, and plenty of benches along the promenade for strollers to take a break, enjoy an ice cream or just watch the world go by.

After a filling lunch at a barbecue place on Twenty-fourth Street, Gabriel and Susan decided to do all three. He'd shed his suits for a turtleneck and slacks, and looked right at home on the avenue. Knowing the middle of her day would be spent with Gabriel, Susan had dressed carefully that morning, even waiting until she got the girls up and off to school before she finished getting ready.

"I can't remember the last time I did this," she said.

"Sat on a park bench?"

"No," she said, sending him a sassy smile. "Ate an ice cream without having to referee over who got the larger scoop."

"Raising twins must be a handful."

He didn't add, *by yourself*, but Susan sensed that's what he meant.

"It is," she said. "But I wouldn't trade it for the world. How does that old saying go? 'Wouldn't take nothing for my journey.' That's how I feel about all I've been through. I'm who I am today, a better person, because of all the struggles I've survived, and I count in that being a better mom."

"I admire you."

"Why?" she asked, looking genuinely amazed. "Half the time I'm barely holding it together."

"It doesn't show," he told her. "I think you underestimate yourself."

"That's not what my employees say," Susan said with a smile. "To hear them tell the story, I'm like the pharaoh ordering bricks made without straw. They say I outfly any superhero."

"You juggle a lot," he said. "*And* you find time to create beautiful art."

She gave him a sidelong glance. "Who spilled the beans about the quilts?"

The corner of his mouth edged up. "Liza Montgomery. I don't think she knew it was supposed to be a state secret."

"It's not. I just…" She shrugged.

He leaned forward, his elbows resting on his thighs

as he licked his ice cream cone. "I find your modesty enchanting."

Susan shifted on the bench, not comfortable with the spotlight on her. She wondered how to move the conversation in another direction.

Gabriel gave her the opening when they had finished their treats. He tossed their trash in a receptacle and held out a hand for her. It was a natural thing to lace her fingers with his. West Colorado Avenue offered lots of distractions, and since neither Susan nor Gabriel were in a hurry to return to work, they strolled along the thoroughfare.

Outside a shop displaying snow globes of every conceivable size and shape, Gabriel paused. Susan looked back at him, a smile edging along the corners of her mouth. "Did you want to go in here?"

"No," Gabriel said.

"That one might look good on your desk," she said, pointing to a gaudy globe. With its orange, purple and green polka dots and overlay of spiderweb gauze, it didn't stand a chance of gracing anyone's desk, except as a gag gift.

"Susan."

Something in his tone made her pause, the teasing words she'd been about to say lost. Gabriel gazed into her eyes, and Susan knew what he wanted. She wanted it too.

"I'm going to kiss you," he said, giving her plenty of time to object.

"I know."

She stepped closer. He lifted a hand to the curls framing her face and tugged on one of the corkscrews. He smiled, but his gaze never left hers.

"I've wanted to do this for a long time," he said.

"Tug on my hair?"

He rubbed his thumb along the edge of her mouth. It was all Susan could do to stand there, enjoying his touch. She shushed the little voice that said, You shouldn't be flirting with your preacher!

"Preachers are people too," she said.

His eyes narrowed and darkened. "That's right," he said. "They are."

And then his mouth covered hers.

Susan gave herself to the moment, reveling first at the touch of his mouth on hers, then at the joy that flooded her spirit. It was as if blinders had suddenly been removed from her eyes and the long-lost key to her heart located. Gabriel Dawson had had it in his possession all along, and she'd never suspected…had never even imagined.

"Susan?"

She blinked, trying to get herself centered, oriented. The feat may have been possible if she weren't feeling like the heroine in a romance novel—swept away and captivated by a dashing hero. Except this wasn't fiction, it was her real life.

She saw the concern in his eyes and realized she must have looked as dazed as she felt. "I…I'm fine," she said, only realizing too late that that's not what he'd asked her. *Had* he asked her something?

How was a woman supposed to think after being kissed like that? Right in the middle of West Colorado Avenue on a gorgeous fall day.

She stared up at him.

"Are you all right?" he asked.

Not trusting her voice, or what she might actually blurt out if she spoke, Susan simply nodded.

"Would you like to walk some more?" Gabriel asked.

"Yes," she said and hoped her voice didn't give her thoughts away. Trying to figure out how she'd managed to get blindsided by so many overwhelming emotions, Susan suddenly wanted to know everything she could about Gabriel.

How, she wondered, could she fall in love with someone she barely knew?

Love? In love with Gabriel?

Hot on the heels of that thought came the sobering realization that she'd *married* Reggie knowing less about him than she currently knew about Gabriel. And she hadn't felt for Reggie a fraction of what she now felt toward Gabriel. That made her a little sad. With Reggie, she hadn't truly been in love; rather, she had loved the attention from him, and the opportunity to escape the housing project where she had lived with her mother and the poverty that besieged them.

The impetuous decision to marry Reggie had ended up costing her far more than inconvenience. He'd almost broken her spirit.

With Gabriel, she felt complemented, not conquered.

"You're awfully quiet," he said. "I hope you didn't take offense."

Susan's heart swelled and she blinked back sudden tears. But not before he saw.

He reached out a finger to capture a tear, but pulled his hand back a moment before it came in contact with her soft skin. "Susan, I'm sorry I kissed you. I didn't mean to upset you."

She pressed a finger across his lips. "I'm not upset. Don't be sorry. I'm not."

Then she stood on tiptoe and pressed a quick, playful smooch on his lips.

It was Gabriel's turn to look shell-shocked. His expression heartened Susan. Clearly she wasn't the only one affected by the growing tenderness between them.

Leaving Gabriel on the sidewalk, Susan ducked into the nearest shop. Was it just last week that she had been thinking she wanted a long-term commitment from Gabriel on support for the shelter? Maybe her subconscious had known all along that what she *really* wanted was a personal long-term commitment with him.

"Hi there, Susan," Polly, the shop manager, greeted her.

"Hello."

"Come for some fabric?"

The quilt shop was one Susan liked to visit when she splurged on exquisite fabric. When Gabriel had suggested Old Colorado City for lunch, Susan had hoped she'd get a chance to stop in the store.

"I'm thinking about a new project," she told the woman.

The door tinkled when Gabriel entered.

"Good afternoon," Polly said, greeting him. "May I help you?"

Susan saw him look around the shop, at the bolts of multicolored fabric, at the notions and fat-quarters of fabric piled high in baskets, at sample quilts on the walls and hanging from the ceiling. She wondered what was going through his head.

"I'm with her," he said.

The woman smiled. "Well, enjoy your browsing. Susan, I'm in the back room. Holler if you want me to cut for you."

"Will do, Polly."

Gabriel fingered a display of vibrant blue, red and yellow batiks. "So this is where you get the material to create your art."

"One of the places. The city has quite a few quilt shops."

With him so near, she wasn't able to concentrate on why she'd wanted to come to the store. She couldn't even bring up a mental picture of the stained-glass windows at the church. Her entire being seemed suffused with the thought and joy of that kiss they'd shared on the sidewalk.

Spying a display of sewing machines, Gabriel went over to it. "My grandmother used to have an old Singer machine. She made lots of clothes with that...Good grief!"

Alarmed, Susan went to his side. "What's wrong?"

"Do you see how much that costs?"

She laughed. "Yes. It's not your grandma's sewing machine."

"Obviously." Looking flabbergasted, he peered at a couple of other price tags on the state-of-the-art machines. "This is like the down payment on a house!"

"That's why I don't have one of those. That's top-of-the-line. Come on," she said. "I'll show you something pretty."

She led him to a fabric wall. She wanted to see if anything grabbed him. She could recreate the stained-glass window at Good Shepherd, but wanted to see how his tastes ran, since she'd need fabric for borders and the back of the quilt. She could always come back later to pick coordinating material.

The plan didn't work, though, because Gabriel seemed more interested in talking to her than looking at hundreds of bolts of fabric.

"You never did tell me who you think Evie might be."

"Oh," Susan said, that topic distracting even her attention from her favorite pastime. Leaning over a clearance pile so her voice didn't carry, she told him, "Remember I said she looked familiar but I couldn't place it?"

He nodded.

"It was the newspaper. I'd seen her in the newspaper. I think she's really Yvette Duncan."

"That doesn't ring any bells."

"Does the name *Bill* Duncan click with you?"

"Bill Duncan? The fiber optics and telecommunications guy?"

Susan nodded.

Gabriel frowned. "But he's a multimillionaire. And he's running for the U.S. Senate. I saw him on CNN the other day. He's a strong contender and seems to have some solid ideas about the economy and California's trade programs."

Susan folded her arms and looked up at him. "And because he's a rich Senate candidate, that makes it okay that he beats up his wife?"

"Of course not." Gabriel peered at her. "But are you sure the woman at the shelter is his wife?"

"As sure as her photo in the newspaper. It's in profile, but I'm positive it's her."

"That would explain her comment about 'the season.' She must have meant the campaign season when candidates go to churches to rustle votes."

Nodding, Susan agreed.

"So now what?" he asked.

"We wait. What happens next is Evie's call."

Chapter Fourteen

"Why can't we go?" Hannah asked.

The twins were on Susan's bed, watching her get dressed for Saturday night's fund-raising gala.

"We've been over this before, girls," Susan said as she slipped an elaborate sequined cocktail dress over her head. The purple beading shimmered in the light. "This is an event for grown-ups. Besides, I thought you guys were excited about going to Mrs. Jackson's house and spending some time with Amy."

"Yeah," Sarah said. "But going with you would be more fun."

Susan smiled. They were probably right. Susan and Jessica had arranged for Eleanor Jackson, Amy's new baby-sitter, to watch the three girls for the evening.

"Tell you what," Susan said. "How about if we have our own dress-up night next week?"

The twins looked at each other. "We can wear your makeup?"

"And your shoes?"

Susan chuckled. "We'll talk about it." She put the finishing touches on her makeup, carefully checking her lipstick before dropping the tube in a small beaded bag. As she took a final look in the full-length mirror on the closet door, Susan wished Gabriel could see her now.

There was no sense thinking about that, though. He wasn't going to the gala. And in the time since their Thursday date she'd managed to convince herself that her burgeoning feelings could be chalked up to not enough male companionship in her life. It had been a long time since she'd been on a date or been the focus of anyone's attention the way Gabriel had been focusing on her.

And his kiss!

Susan cleared her throat, glanced at the girls and then forced her mind to concentrate on reality-based thoughts. Like making this night a success for the shelter.

"You look like the queen," Sarah said.

"Yeah," Hannah agreed. "All you need is a crown on your head."

"Thank you, ladies." She opened her handbag to make sure the index cards with her comments for the evening were tucked safely inside. "You guys ready? Mrs. Jackson will be here in just a moment."

The twins scrambled from the bed. Hannah slung a pink backpack over her shoulder and Sarah grabbed her purple one. Susan stepped into her shoes, straightened the comforter and followed the girls. Sam and Jessica arrived at the same time as the baby-sitter and Amy. Sam would drive to The Broadmoor Hotel, giving Susan and Jessica the opportunity to fine-tune any last-minute details.

After plenty of hugs and kisses all around, the adults headed to the hotel.

"You guys doing all right?" Sam asked when the women fell silent after a while.

Jessica rubbed her hands together. "Just a little nervous. We have a lot riding on this night."

"It'll be perfect," Susan said. "Everything that can be done is done. All we can do now is wait to see if our bachelors bring in the high bids we anticipate."

Jessica turned to face Susan. "So are you going to bid on anyone?"

Susan laughed. "Hardly. Remember, this is a fundraiser. I'm sure I won't be able to afford anything."

"That quilt of yours will probably go for a pretty penny," Sam said as he turned into the drive.

"I hope so," Susan said, then added, "Look!"

She pointed toward the grand hotel nestled in the foothills of Cheyenne Mountain. The resort property combined Old World and new elegance in a captivating mix that never failed to dazzle guests and residents.

The hotel shimmered a golden pink in the early twilight. The mountain backdrop highlighted The Broadmoor, casting a glow that both welcomed and enchanted visitors.

"It's beautiful," Jessica said.

"I'm glad we're holding the gala here."

Minutes later they were in the ballroom. By the time Susan got up to make her welcoming comments, the ballroom was filled and people spilled onto the terraces. It seemed that all of Colorado Springs' elite had turned out for the event. Susan recognized officials from the city and the state legislature as well.

"Thank you all for joining us this evening," she said. "Eat a lot, drink a lot, and please give a lot. Your bids this evening will ensure that women and children right here in Colorado Springs get the emergency and long-term shelter they need."

She introduced the mayor, who made a few remarks, then promised that the bachelor auction would begin promptly at nine.

From across the room, a man in an elegantly casual black suit that might loosely be called a tuxedo, stood watching her. *"Bella,"* he murmured.

"What's that?" the man standing next to him said.

"She's very beautiful."

Alistair Barclay looked around, the drink in his hand sloshing over the rim of the crystal tumbler. "Which one? Lots of eye candy walking around tonight." At that moment, a tall blonde joined them, her hair swept up in a 1940s-style roll and her formal dress, also a throwback to the period, hugged her lush figure.

Alessandro's gaze raked over her. "Hello."

"Hi, honey," the woman said, giving him a little finger wave. "You're a cutie."

Alistair scowled, his bushy eyebrows forming a thick line across his forehead. "Hey."

The woman giggled and snuggled close, tucking her arm in his. "Alistair, you know you're the only one I'm interested in." But when he downed the rest of his drink, she winked at Alessandro, who gave her a slow, appreciative grin.

"Make yourself scarce," Alistair told her, pinching her behind. "I need to talk."

"Okay, honey." She wiggled away, giving the dark man with wavy hair a final glance.

"Susan, this is fabulous!"

Susan turned to greet her best friend, Tina, with a big hug. "I'm so glad you made it. I thought you'd miss the big night."

"I told you I'd be here," Tina said.

"So," Susan said, holding her friend at arm's length and gesturing so Tina could do a little spin to show off her slinky white dress. "How was the seminar?"

Tina pulled a face. "Two hundred copy editors together for a week in Durango, Colorado. How do you think it was?"

Because Susan knew her friend loved her job at the *Sentinel* and had been looking forward to the copy editors' conference for a good six months, she just grinned. "From the glow you're sporting, I'd say more than journalism was going on down in Durango."

"I wish," Tina said, taking a sip from a glass of punch. She leaned forward, lowering her voice. "But *he* sure could give me a glow. Who is that? Talk about tall, dark and delicious."

Susan's gaze followed her friend's until she spotted the man who had turned more than one head since his arrival. "That's Alessandro Donato, our Italian playboy."

Tina's eyes lowered in speculation. "Italian playboy? Tell me more."

"Actually, I shouldn't say that. Someone else called

him that this evening. There's a rumor going around that he's a count."

"Ooh, girl," Tina said. "For the record, if he's one of the guys up for auction tonight, I'm telling you now, I'll take out a second mortgage on my condo to pay for my winning bid."

Susan laughed. "You're a mess, Tina. And lucky for your condo, he's not one of the bachelors. I just met him tonight myself. He's Lidia Vance's nephew."

"Hmm," Tina said. "She looks like Sophia Loren. Must be an excellent gene pool in that family."

Chuckling, Susan said, "Come on. I'll introduce you. But after that, you're on your own."

Susan and Tina weren't the only two people watching Alessandro Donato that night.

"Do you see what I see?" Sam asked his brother Travis.

"Yeah, and I'm not liking it one bit."

Though Travis had left the Colorado Springs Police Department where Sam was a detective, Travis kept his law enforcement ties current and was now a security expert. The brothers had been looking into the recent crime wave and Travis had formulated a theory—one that he had yet to voice, but that was starting to seem a lot more plausible now.

Jessica walked up, joining her husband and new brother-in-law. "What are you two looking so serious about?"

"I was just noting the unsavory company that scoundrel Alessandro is keeping."

Jessica's gaze swept the ballroom until she spotted Alessandro. "He's just talking to Mr. Barclay."

Travis grunted. Sam's eyes narrowed.

"You know, it must be a cop thing. You two don't trust anyone, even your own cousin."

"And with good reason," Sam said. "Why is he always slinking about?"

Jessica laughed. "You call it slinking. Every woman in this room calls it something else."

"Hey," Travis said. "You're still a newlywed. Is your wife's eye straying already, Sam?"

Sam snaked an arm around Jessica's waist. "Not if I can help it." The two shared a kiss.

Travis's gaze slid away from the newlyweds and back toward Alessandro in time to see the younger man shake hands with Barclay. He wondered what deal had just been struck between them.

"You've turned quite a few heads tonight. But we haven't met." For an opening line, it was bold and just a little flirtatious. Colleen Montgomery had become a reporter because she had an insatiable curiosity. That curiosity had been piqued by the dashing man in black with the faint European accent. He'd been working the room with a casualness that she recognized as calculated. She wanted to know why. He put her in mind of Cary Grant in *To Catch a Thief* or George Clooney in *Ocean's Eleven*—tall, dark and dangerous.

Since she'd already asked around and found out his name, all that remained was introducing herself to him.

"Hello, *cara,*" he said, taking her hand. "Had I

known how many beautiful women grace the fine city of Colorado Springs, I would have paid my dear aunt a visit much sooner."

He smiled at her, and Colleen caught her breath. Talk about magnetism. Suddenly feeling out of her league—way out—she lifted a hand to run it through her hair. At the last moment, she remembered the hair-style her mother had convinced her to put it in for this night. For once, Colleen was grateful she'd listened to her mother.

"Who is your aunt?" Colleen said, though she already knew the answer.

"Lidia. Lidia Vance. Do you know her?"

"Yes." But Colleen was having trouble concentrating as she listened to that voice. She wondered what her own name might sound like in that distinctly European accent.

"Would you care to dance?" he asked. Several people were already on the dance floor. The music had been lively, but now the band played an American standard, maybe Cole Porter or Gershwin.

"I don't believe that's possible," her brother Jake interrupted before Colleen could say yea or nay. "My little sister promised this dance to me."

Jake then started half dragging her away. "My name is Colleen," she called back to Alessandro.

He blew her a kiss. "Until another time, Colleen."

Despite the manhandling from her brother, Colleen thought she might melt right there on the floor. Her name on his lips sounded even better than she'd thought it might.

Jake pulled her forward, clasped a strong arm at her waist and whirled her away from where Alessandro stood.

"What'd you do that for?"

"You're swimming with the sharks, little sister. I'm just rescuing you before you get a limb chewed off."

"I am not a child," Colleen said. But a childlike pout spoiled the delivery.

"No," he said. "Even a child would know not to play with fire like that."

"I can handle myself," Colleen said. "I'm all grown up. And I'm a journalist. I was merely investigating a hunch."

"Uh-huh," Jake said.

"You can't baby me forever," she said. "You and Adam act like I can't take care of myself."

She thought he was just overreacting—as usual. But the laugh lines at his blue eyes, the ones that always crinkled in amusement at most everything she did, weren't in evidence.

Jake was a bit of a playboy himself, so maybe he did know something about Alessandro. Takes one to know one. She looked up at her brother. At six foot two, he was taller than Alessandro. She knew women found him attractive, though for the life of her Colleen didn't see it.

"Don't you have a date or someone you can go harass instead of me?"

"As a matter of fact, I do," Jake said. "I see my assistant Holly over there. I need to have a word with her."

"Good," Colleen said, disengaging from her brother's arms. Before she could turn to search the crowd for

Alessandro, another man took her hand and led her right back on the dance floor. "Daddy! Come on, guys. This is too much."

"Shush, and dance with your old man."

By five minutes to nine, the crowd was well wined and dined. Excitement buzzed in the air. Susan hoped it was a portent of good things to come.

Jessica had outdone herself in securing the bachelors. In addition to doing her own petitioning, she'd convinced board members to call in favors with their friends and business acquaintances. As a result, fifteen of the region's most eligible bachelors stood ready to be auctioned off to the highest bidder. Each man, sometimes with Jessica's assistance, had set up a fantasy date for a special lady—the bidder with the biggest number on a check made out to the Galilee Shelter Foundation.

"It's show time," Susan told Jessica. The two squeezed hands, then Susan stepped into the middle of a semicircle the men had made. They were dressed in everything from tuxedoes to outfits that clearly indicated how their fantasy date would be spent.

"Are you all right in all that?" Susan asked the adventure sports reporter for one of the local television stations. He was outfitted in full ski apparel, including a parka, gloves and boots. A pair of skis were propped up near the entrance to the stage.

He gave her the thumbs-up sign, but clearly looked overheated.

Susan snagged the attention of a hotel employee.

"Would you get him a glass of ice water, please? We don't want anybody passing out."

"He'll be fine," one of the other bachelors called out. "He's just going for that pity bid. He wants the ladies to feel sorry for him so his bidding will be fast and furious."

Susan grinned. "That's the kind of thinking I like."

She turned, holding out her hands and making eye contact with each man. "I just want to thank all of you for giving of your time tonight and for arranging the dates. I think this will be a lot of fun, and I hope we raise a lot of money as well."

Someone let out a "whoo-hoo" and the men applauded.

Out on the stage, they could hear the evening's auctioneer getting the crowd revved. Priscilla Patterson, the lead anchorwoman for the WFOL evening news, had volunteered to emcee the evening.

"Well, this is it," Susan said. "I'm going to go get a good spot to watch."

"And will you put in a bid for me?" the city's assistant fire chief said. Rex Brown would give even Denzel a run for the money in the handsome division. That his job was to run into burning buildings and rescue people only added to his appeal. But he was seriously worried that no one would bid on him.

"Don't worry. You're going to get lots of bids," Susan said, patting his arm.

"You two owe me big for doing this," Travis Vance said before Susan could escape.

She laughed and patted his cheek. "You'll be fine, too, Travis," she said. "And who knows, you just might end up with someone who knocks you off your feet."

"I doubt it," Travis muttered.

"Cheer up," Jessica said, tucking her arm in his. "At the very least, you'll get away from AdVance for two nights. Tonight and the evening of your date."

"And what if it's with someone who is, er, not exactly a...well, not pretty."

Jessica poked him in the side. Susan laughed. "I'm sure her personality will dazzle you," Susan said. "Thanks for doing this, Travis."

"For you, Susan, anything."

"Oh, but I get a hard way to go?" Jessica intoned.

He nodded. "You're family now, so yeah."

Susan saw Jessica's eyes mist. She knew how much it meant to her friend to be welcomed into the Vance family. As Jessica hugged Travis, Susan headed back out to the ballroom where she would enjoy the evening from the floor.

The first few closing bids had her worried. Dinner, dancing and a limo ride with a local actor who had a couple of walk-on roles on two sitcoms only went for two thousand dollars. Front-row seats and backstage passes to a rock concert with a radio station personality fetched four thousand, and a wine festival date only garnered thirty-five hundred.

She and Jessica had been through the figures so many times, Susan knew exactly what they needed to reach their goal for the evening. She didn't count the silent auction items like her quilt, since the live bachelor auction would bring in the most money. Each bachelor would have to average a closing bid of six thousand for them to reach the figure the shelter needed.

"Ladies," the auctioneer said, "I think you need to pack your weekend bags with something warm and toasty for this next date. May I introduce you to WFOL's own Brian Boxley!" The sports reporter sauntered out, the skis over his shoulder, a pair of dark sunglasses on. The crowd went wild.

So did the bidding.

The ski weekend went for eight thousand four hundred dollars to a tanned, athletic woman who looked like she spent a lot of time on the slopes. She tucked her arm through Brian's and the two headed to the station where final bids were being processed.

Susan grinned and turned to Liza Montgomery, who'd found her and now stood at her side. "Now, that's more like it."

"I was getting a little worried, too," Liza confessed.

After a few more bachelors, Priscilla paused to read from a list of volunteers who had either helped put the gala together or who gave of their time to the shelter.

"We'd also like to recognize some people who have put in more than a thousand hours of volunteer time," she said. She then called off several names, including that of Liza Montgomery, who waved from where she stood next to Susan and Holly Vance.

Backstage, Jake Montgomery's brows lifted. He knew about his mother's extensive involvement at Galilee, but he had had no idea that his executive assistant Holly Vance volunteered with them as well. He'd been working with Holly for two years and had had no clue.

Maybe he needed to spend a little more time on his people skills.

"Hey, Rex. You're up next," Jake called.

The two men slapped palms, and the assistant fire chief went to stand at the curtain to wait for his cue to head out.

"This next date," Priscilla said, "is one I think I'm going to have to bid on myself." The anchorwoman leaned forward, lowering her voice as if conspiring with the women in the audience. "I saw this guy backstage and decided he could put out a fire at my house anytime he wants. I might set one myself just to get him to come on over.

"How does an afternoon at Garden of the Gods sound to you?"

A couple of the women in front, who were actively bidding, sort of shrugged.

"Yeah," Priscilla said. "That was my thought, too. I can go there anytime, right? But, ladies, what about an afternoon at Garden of the Gods, followed by a picnic lunch for two, then a romantic ride through the city with this fabulous bachelor."

The assistant fire chief made his entrance. The bidding went much higher than anticipated, mostly due to Rex's mugging and smiling. Susan, pleased, finally relaxed.

She mingled some more, chatting up potential bidders, encouraging them to have fun. The night was going well—very, very well.

As the bachelors were auctioned she tried not to think about what the entire process represented—couples pairing off for fun evenings. These dates were way out of her own price range. The most she had by way of disposable income was a couple of hundred dollars, and any spare cash she had always went for the girls—rarely for herself. Susan knew the value of a dollar and wished she were in a position to be able to do something frivolous like bid on a fantasy date.

Priscilla's introduction of the next bachelor caught her attention. "This next bachelor isn't in your program. He's a late addition that I think you'll all find just heavenly."

Susan snagged a strawberry dipped in chocolate and turned to see what was going on.

"Our next bachelor calls his date Best of Colorado Springs. And I can tell you, I'd sure like to call this one mine. It includes a ride on the Cripple Creek and Victor Narrow Gauge Railroad, a tour of Seven Falls, which is just lovely at night, and then dinner and the theater. Does this guy know how to set up a date or what?"

Cheers went up. "Who is it?" someone called out.

"I'm getting to that part," Priscilla said, laughing. "But there's another little part of this date you all aren't going to be able to resist. This very special bachelor wants you to feel special, too. So before your date, you'll get to spend an afternoon being pampered at the Lily Pond Spa. Manicure, pedicure, facial and massage."

Priscilla pointed to a tuxedoed older man in the crowd. "Excuse me. My purse is right over there. Could you pull out my credit card and bid on this for me?"

The crowd laughed; even Susan chuckled, though she wondered about the evening's mystery man. Getting Priscilla Patterson had been perfect for this evening. Susan would have to think of a special way to thank her for her efforts.

Susan lifted the strawberry to her mouth to take another nibble, careful not to drip any of the juice on her dress.

"Ladies and gentleman," Priscilla said, "let's give a warm applause and hefty bids to our next bachelor—the Reverend Gabriel Dawson."

Chapter Fifteen

Strawberry juice spurted in every direction. Susan quickly wiped her mouth.

Gabriel! What was he doing up there?

"Ah, I see that Dr. Samantha Hardy is interested in dating a minister," Priscilla said as she called out the opening bid. "Don't be shy, ladies."

Susan didn't even want to address the shot of jealousy that hit her. She'd heard the older Mrs. Hardy bragging at church about her granddaughter the pediatrician.

Before she could register that the baby doctor was serious in her intent, other bids were being called out and cheerfully accepted by Priscilla. Apparently, quite a few people realized just what a catch Gabriel was.

"Who'd have thought a minister would fetch so much?"

"Indeed," Susan muttered, wondering just when he'd agreed to *be* one of the bachelors. She'd gotten the distinct impression—from him, no less—that he wouldn't be able to attend the gala and had no desire to, even if he were available.

And now, instead of being at home writing a sermon

on a Saturday night like a minister should be doing, he was standing on stage managing to look shy and scrumptious and sexy in a white Nehru-cut tuxedo. Unlike the other bachelors, Gabriel didn't make any boasts and declined to comment when Priscilla offered him the microphone.

When the bidding finally slowed, Priscilla looked out over the crowd. "Whew, ladies. You have been fast and furious." She called out the last high bid. "Going once, going twice. Reverend Gabriel Dawson, for nine thousand six hundred dollars, you're headed out with none other than Susan Carter."

"What?" Susan shrieked.

The audience cheered. Susan whirled around, shaking her head. "There has to be a mistake. I didn't bid anything."

"Yes, you did, dear," Liza said. "The bids were on your behalf."

Ninety-six hundred dollars. Where in the world was she going to get that kind of cash? A moment later, Liza's words registered. "Come again?"

Jessica ran up to her then. "I hope you're not mad."

Susan eyed her so-called friends. "What's going on?"

Liza gave her a little push forward. "Go claim your date and then we'll tell you."

To cheers and catcalls, Susan walked to the stage. Priscilla handed her the microphone.

"I had nothing to do with this," she said. The crowd laughed. "Really," Susan insisted. "I think I've been set up."

"Are you upset about it?" Gabriel asked.

She turned and looked into his eyes, saw there affection and something else. Then she gazed out over the audience, saw Liza smiling. Jessica gave her the thumbs-up sign. Fiona Montgomery was grinning from ear to ear.

"Not in the least," Susan said.

Gabriel kissed her on the cheek and looped his arm so she could tuck hers inside. Together, they exited the stage to applause from all of the onlookers.

"I knew there was something between them," Susan heard someone say.

"It's always the quiet ones."

Backstage, she turned to Gabriel. "You've just ruined my reputation."

He smiled. "I guess I'll just have to make up for it by making sure you have a terrific fantasy date."

"Now all I have to do is figure out how to pay for this joke someone's played on me." Susan eyed him. "Is that part about the Lily Pond Spa for real?"

Gabriel nodded.

"When he suggested it, I thought that was a fabulous idea," Jessica said as she and Liza approached. "Please tell me you're not mad."

"I'm just trying to figure out where I'm going to get nine thousand-some dollars and how many years it's going to take me to pay it off," Susan said. "Maybe payroll deduction or something."

"That's not necessary," Liza said. "This night, the fantasy date with Pastor Gabriel, it's my gift to you. I'm so proud of everything you've done, Susan. Everything you've become. You never take time for you. So when

Jessica approached me about doing this for you, I couldn't resist this time."

"This time?"

Liza blushed a bit, then glanced at first Gabriel then Jessica. "Well, let's just put it this way. A certain benefactor is pleased to see that things have turned out so well."

Dawning came slowly for Susan. Her glance roved among the three people. Both Jessica and Gabriel were relatively new on the scene. But Liza Montgomery had been there all along.

Liza had been there when Susan was a battered woman with two little kids and no future. She had been around when Susan got a mysterious package containing diapers, formula and other items she needed for the girls along with an envelope with a cashier's check made out in her name. And she had been in the picture when "scholarship" money appeared out of nowhere, allowing Susan to get an education.

"It was you," Susan said, admiration and awe in her voice. "You were my fairy godmother all those years ago."

Liza laughed. "Well, I've never thought of myself in quite that way, but yes. It was me."

Susan clasped Liza's hands. "Why? How? Thank you. Oh!" Overwhelmed, she hugged Liza, not minding the tears that streaked down her face.

Jessica beamed. "I told you it would be okay," she told Gabriel.

Susan and Liza clung to each other. "Why?" Susan asked. "Why me?"

"Because," Liza said, wiping a tear from Susan's face. "Because in you I saw so much potential. So much promise. All you needed was a helping hand. You've done all the hard work. All I did was plant a seed."

"Oh, Liza." She faced Gabriel. "But how did you get involved?"

"Jessica asked if I'd participate. I told her only if you were the guaranteed winner of my date."

Jessica took a look around, then consulted the list she held. "Travis," she said, calling him over. "Looks like you're up soon."

"And *you,*" Susan said, pointing to Jessica.

Gabriel took her free hand.

Seeing the intimate gesture, Jessica grinned. "I knew I was on target."

The two women hugged. "Thank you, Jessi," Susan said.

"Just have fun," Jessica said. "And who knows," she added on a whisper for Susan's ears only. "Maybe a wedding will come out of this."

Susan gave her a mock warning look.

"Come on," Liza said. "I need to get that bidding paperwork done. And since it's so close, I'll make it an even ten. By the way, the board of directors decided that you're getting a day off next Thursday just for this."

A little overwhelmed, Susan just shook her head.

Then, still holding Gabriel's hand, she followed Liza to the auction checkout station.

At the break before the last five bachelors were presented, Susan checked the index cards with her notes. She didn't want to forget anyone as she made her remarks.

"It has been one spectacular evening. Here I

thought all the surprises had been arranged for you all, and I end up with one of my own," she said. "But I'd like to again thank each of you for your generosity and your commitment to the Galilee Women's Shelter. We have another five dates to auction off, but let's give a hand now to all of the bachelors and their dates."

Priscilla, who'd exited the stage, came back and whispered something in Susan's ear.

"You're kidding."

Priscilla shook her head.

To the audience, Susan said, "We've fielded several inquiries this evening about what we do at Galilee and how individuals and corporations can contribute. I'm pleased to say that before Priscilla returns, Mr. Alistair Barclay would like to make an announcement."

Travis and Sam both stopped talking. As one, they turned toward the stage.

Mayor Montgomery frowned. He'd seen Barclay eyeing Colleen. Barclay never lacked for the company of a beautiful women. His money was a magnet that always attracted a bevy of them. Colleen had been busy chatting up Barclay and Alessandro. Both men, sophisticated in their tastes, were way out of his little girl's league. At least Barclay had come by his money honestly. The same couldn't be said for that louse Alessandro.

If he had to choose between them, Frank preferred Barclay, the stable, if a little scuzzy-looking, businessman.

Alistair Barclay didn't seem to care what people said about him. He was a rich but tasteless tycoon who had more money than he knew what to do with. But there remained about him the air of a used-car salesman, something just a little sleazy.

But the real issue wasn't his appearance. Frank didn't want to see his daughter hurt—by either man.

Barclay had made a fortune in Great Britain via a chain of worldwide luxury hotels, and he lived the life of a man accustomed to wealth and its attendant privileges.

That Alessandro, though—something about that one just rubbed Frank the wrong way. He'd almost requested that a cop circulate the room to make sure Alessandro wasn't pocketing jewels while he roamed.

Barclay approached the stage. Instead of wearing a tux like most of the men present, he wore a black pinstripe suit that looked like a relic from Al Capone's days as an American gangster. His date's dress was also reminiscent of a bygone era. Maybe they had another engagement that evening.

"Too bad he doesn't use some of his money to get a decent rug," Sam said. The comb-over effect was in full force with Barclay. What little hair he had always seemed plastered in place with an industrial-strength hair spray.

Barclay shook Susan's hand and then turned to the audience.

"I have listened this grand evening to people speak of the fine work done by this lady and the people at the Galilee shelter." He placed a hand over his heart. "I have been touched. I have been moved to do something. As you know, my life has been blessed and I have always believed that you must, must give back."

His gray eyes danced with delight as he turned to

Susan. He took her hand. "To you and the Galilee shelter, Mrs. Carter, I make a pledge tonight. Whatever you raise this evening, I will personally match, dollar for dollar."

Susan clutched *her* heart. "Oh my!"

Spontaneous and loud applause ripped through the ballroom.

A little later, Susan stood with Gabriel, accepting well-wishes. Half of the people wanted to know how they, too, could help out the shelter.

"Apparently, Mr. Barclay's gesture has spawned a considerable amount of like-minded generosity."

"It's human nature," Gabriel said. "People want to be on the winning team."

Shaking her head, Susan said, "I still can't believe he did that. We're going to be able to do so much."

"Hey, Susan," someone said as they passed by. "Enjoy your date."

The wink that followed concerned her. No one believed she'd had nothing to do with the bid for Pastor Gabriel. "We're going to be all the gossip tomorrow in service."

"Does that bother you?" he asked.

Susan glanced up at him. She started to deny it, to say no. Then she shrugged. "A little."

"Because it's me?"

Did his voice really hint at a vulnerability? She looked at him more closely. "No, Gabriel. Because I don't want you to be the butt of any jokes or the subject of gossip."

He cocked his head. "Why?"

Suddenly flustered, Susan waved a hand, dismissing the words that had revealed more about her feelings toward him than she'd intended. "Because you're the pastor."

"Tonight I'm just a bachelor."

Her gaze met his and Susan lost herself in the moment. He was just a man. That he'd made a commitment to God to lead others to Christ didn't mean he had let go of the things that other men might want: companionship, love. But what about a ready-made family?

She cleared her throat, tried to lighten the mood. "All right, Bachelor Dawson. When do I get to go do this spa thing?"

He grinned. "Something tells me that's what you're interested in. There's more to the date than that."

"Yeah. But that's the part that has me really jazzed."

Gabriel just chuckled.

Susan tuned in to what Priscilla was saying about Travis. Despite his grousing, he'd set up his own date without Jessica's assistance. His lucky lady would share box seats and a catered dinner with him at a Denver Broncos game. If he had to do this thing, he'd said, he may as well enjoy the activity.

He need not have worried about what his date looked like. A stunning brunette in a form-fitting, red fishtail gown claimed his arm. Susan's attention was drawn away then by well-wishers and a potential donor who wanted to get some more information about the shelter.

When she glanced back at the stage, Jake Montgomery was strutting off with his date, a model friend of his who Susan suspected he may have set up to be the winner. Given the way the woman looked at him, though, Jake might be in for more than he bargained for in that hot-air balloon date he'd agreed to.

Jake caught up with Holly near a table filled with sweet confections. "I didn't know you volunteered at the shelter."

Holly looked up at her boss. "There's a lot you don't know about me."

He gave her a funny look. "Apparently."

"Sounds like you're going to have fun on your date. I've always wanted to ride in a hot-air balloon."

"Well, maybe we could—"

"There you are, Jake, honey. I paid too much money for you to have you chatting up some other gal."

Jake introduced Holly to the woman who'd placed the highest bid for him. Holly had met her before, but apparently the woman didn't remember. That was one of her problems. No one ever remembered anything about her.

The last bachelor of the evening was a popular wide receiver with the Denver Broncos. His fantasy date was billed as An Enchanted Mystery Evening, and he promised an airplane ride no longer than an hour to an undisclosed location. The possibilities were intriguing and the buzz in the audience indicated just that.

"Ten thousand," Susan predicted. She'd made a circuit of the ballroom and once again stood near Liza Montgomery and Gabriel.

"I think eleven, maybe twelve," the older woman guessed. "Do you know where he's taking his date?"

Susan nodded. She leaned over and whispered in Liza's ear.

"Ooh. Do you think Frank would mind if I put in the winning bid?"

The two women grinned. Susan knew Frank and Liza were still too much in love for Liza to even consider going out with another man.

The football star took the microphone from Priscilla and made his own pitch. "Ladies, I'm just a good ole boy from Tennessee who likes to have a good time. I like my dates to have a good time, too. Since the preacher is giving his lady a day at the spa, I thought I'd better make my date happy as well." He reached inside his suit jacket. "And to make sure you are, I'm tossing in this little thing."

"What is it?" Priscilla asked. He handed her a small envelope. The anchorwoman peeked inside. "Oh, ladies. This is a *very* generous gift certificate to my favorite jeweler."

"Where we're going," the football player said, "the lady on this date might want a little something sparkly to go with her fancy dress."

The bidding went through the roof.

Chapter Sixteen

The week following the gala was a busy one. Gabriel returned to Galilee to lead a Bible study and Evie started working at the Stagecoach Café.

"I can't thank you enough for your assistance on my behalf," she told them.

Since it was clearly out that they were seeing each other, Susan and Gabriel had come to the café for a quick lunch—and there was Evie.

"This is just my third day, but it feels good to be earning my own money. I can't stay long. I'm on my break."

"How are you feeling, Evie?" Susan asked.

Evie touched the bruise that was still evident despite the careful application of makeup. "Much better. Thank you." She glanced left and right. "After all you've done, I just feel I need to be honest with you."

Susan and Gabriel exchanged a look.

"My name isn't really Evie."

Susan smiled. "We sort of figured that out."

Evie flushed. "My name is Yvette. Yvette Duncan. Evie is a nickname I had as a child."

"You were right," Gabriel told Susan.

"Right about what?" Yvette asked. "You knew who I was all along?"

"Not at the beginning," Susan said.

"Susan kept saying you looked familiar," Gabriel added. "I thought so too, but we couldn't place the where or why."

"Then I remembered," Susan said. "I saw a photo of you in the newspaper. It was in profile and half chopped off, but I recognized you."

Yvette's brow creased. "Then you know my husband is Bill Duncan?"

Susan and Gabriel nodded. Yvette sighed. "A lot of people say what happens in a politician's life has no impact on the public job he or she does. I disagree with that. Bill has a lot of people fooled, but his true colors will show one day. I just hope not too many other people have to pay the price I've paid with him."

Susan touched her hand. "You're from California. What were you doing here?"

"Bill had a security conference at the Air Force base. I was with him as the dutiful and beloved candidate's wife." She glanced to either side again as if expecting her husband to jump out of the shadows.

"An interview didn't go well," she continued. "I made a suggestion about what we could do better the next time that line of questioning came up." She touched her face near her eye. "He didn't take too well to the idea." Yvette sighed. "This is all so complicated. I don't want to go home, but I can't stay here forever. I have a life in California and a good mind to run for the very office Bill wants."

"Take it one day at a time," Susan said. "And remember that you aren't alone. You're never alone. You have our support, and you always have God's."

Yvette nodded and blinked back tears. "Thank you so much. For everything. I'd better get back to work."

They watched as she made her way to the back and disappeared through the kitchen doors.

Susan put her arms on the table and stared at the closed doors, behind which Fiona and her staff created the meals that got raves all over town.

"Yvette Duncan is the picture of domestic violence that people don't normally see," Susan said. "Few people want to believe that well-to-do or wealthy women have the same issues as everyone else who suffers from abuse."

Gabriel took her hand. "I'm glad you do the work you do."

Susan smiled. "Thanks," she said, appreciating his praise. "That means a lot."

What none of them saw was the man who'd been watching their exchange. When the double doors closed behind Yvette, the man put a twenty-dollar bill on the table to cover his meal, then slid from his seat.

The next night, more than three hundred people turned out for the candlelight vigil sponsored by Good Shepherd Christian Church. Couples with children in tow showed up, as did many members of area churches whose lives had somehow been affected by the crime wave.

"I've seen candlelight vigils before," Gabriel told Mayor Montgomery as they prepared to open the service. "I was hoping we'd have fifty or so people out here. This is truly heartwarming."

Frank nodded. "The good people of Colorado Springs know how to band together," he said. "That's why I love this town." He clapped Gabriel on the back. "Ready?"

Gabriel picked up a small, leather-bound Bible and followed Frank to the podium and stage set up on the church lawn. The state legislators whose districts included Colorado Springs were there, as was hotel magnate Alistair Barclay, who glad-handed people and boasted about his contribution to the battered women's shelter.

After the mayor's welcome, Gabriel stated the purpose of the vigil. "When we come together as a community we have power. One person alone can't battle this storm, but a united front against crime, against domestic violence, against the cancer that has been eating at our neighborhoods, can make a difference. You're making a difference just by being here tonight."

Colleen worked the crowd, getting comments from residents that would go into a *Sentinel* story about the vigil and its purpose.

When the candles were lit, silence fell over the group.

"Mommy, it looks like lightning bugs all over," a child said.

Chuckles came in response.

Then, after a full minute of silence, Gabriel led the crowd in a prayer for the well-being of the city.

Later, as the last participants left and the twins ran around the lawn, Susan, Gabriel and a couple of church members picked up bulletins and paper candle-holders that had been dropped on the ground.

Susan and Gabriel reached for the same cola can. They smiled, then Gabriel picked it up and deposited it in a large green trash bag.

"I promise that picking up trash won't be a part of our fantasy date on Thursday."

"Hmm, I was beginning to wonder about that."

"I want you to have a good time," Gabriel said.

Something in his voice arrested her attention. Susan paused, looked up at him. "I'm not too sure what's happening here, Gabriel, but I want you to know this. If I'm with you, I'm having a good time. Whether we're walking the streets of a blighted neighborhood, ice-skating at the mall or picking up soda cans."

"You don't know how happy that makes me to hear you say that." He leaned forward.

Susan closed her eyes, anticipating the kiss—and almost got knocked over when the twins came racing by.

"Whoa," Gabriel said, reaching for her arm to steady her.

"Hannah! Sarah!"

The girls came to halt. "Yes, ma'am?"

"Is there a reason you two are running around like chickens with their heads cut off?"

The girls giggled. "Sorry, Mom."

"Come on," Susan said. "It's time to head home."

Grabbing each other's hands, the twins dashed across the grass toward the parking lot.

"I'm sorry about that," Susan said.

Gabriel just smiled. "I'll see you Thursday."

Susan nodded. Her fantasy date day would begin at noon with her appointment at the spa.

"Until then."

* * *

For Susan those two days seemed to take a week to arrive. The plan was that Jessica and Sam would keep the girls while Susan was out being first pampered at the Lily Pond spa, and then romanced by Gabriel. Still a little uneasy about being the pastor's girlfriend, Susan wasn't exactly buying Jessica's story that Gabriel was all too willing to be a bachelor once he'd been assured that Susan's bid would be the highest.

Susan planned to ask him about that. She'd had two opportunities to do so since the gala, but had chickened out each time.

It was one thing to fantasize about someone like Gabriel whisking her off her feet and straight into a fairy-tale romance, and something else completely when she opened her eyes and faced the reality of her life. Gabriel was a highly educated man who lived in one of the gated communities Susan could only dream about.

If he were truly in the market for a wife—not, she told herself, that she'd been harboring any true illusions along that line—he'd seek a partner from the legion of professional women who surrounded him. Women like the accomplished Dr. Hardy.

The widow of an abusive drug addict who lived next door to a battered women's shelter and had two kids didn't rank very high when compared to successful physicians and lawyers, women who would not only look like a minister's wife, but effortlessly slip into the role.

She parked in front of the Lily Pond and stared at the

front entrance of the spa. The facade gave one the illusion of walking through a grotto toward a waterfall.

She walked through and came face-to-face with that waterfall, a two-story oasis of flowers and greenery. Ahead she spotted the retreat's centerpiece lily pond.

Soothing music that seemed to include nature sounds in the background greeted her at the reception desk. Susan had never been to a spa before, and she glanced around, trying not to feel intimidated by the obvious luxury everywhere her eye landed.

This was the sort of place where rich women came every week to get pampered and petted. For Susan, it was a once-in-a-lifetime visit and she wanted to savor every moment and detail.

Soft cushions in muted creams and tans were piled high on a comfy-looking sofa.

She ran a hand along the lightly textured surface of the semicircular reception desk. The soft texturing was repeated on the walls.

"Hello. You must be Susan," a hostess said in greeting.

Susan turned to face the woman, who wore a uniform of khaki slacks and a cream polo shirt with the Lily Pond logo. "Yes. I'm Susan."

"I'm a Susan, too. But most people call me Suzy. Won't you follow me? I'll show you where you can put your things and then you can change."

In a locker room, Susan stashed her purse, shoes and clothes and changed into a to-die-for plush robe. She checked the label, then giggled. "One hundred percent

Egyptian cotton." She loved the feel of the rich fabric on her bare skin.

"Right this way," Suzy said, appearing again, seemingly out of nowhere, just as Susan slipped her feet into a pair of flip-flops that had been with the robe. Suzy gave her a tour of the facilities. "We'd like you to drink plenty of water. Your masseuse today will be Annette. Your manicurist will be Elena..."

Susan heard the words but didn't register any of the names of the technicians who would give her a facial, manicure and the like. She was too busy feeling like Cinderella. Gabriel had been right, she'd been looking forward to this more than any other aspect of her fantasy date.

Less than thirty minutes later she was on a massage table getting every last worry rubbed and stroked away, including ones she hadn't even realized she'd had. She thought her body might just melt into the table.

"Did I die and go to Heaven?"

The technician chuckled. "I get that a lot. Is this your first massage?"

"Umm," Susan said, slowly drifting off.

Before long, she heard her name being called. "Mrs. Carter?"

Susan didn't want the dream to fade away. In it, she'd been drifting on a cloud, sipping ambrosia.

"Mrs. Carter?"

"Huh?"

"It's time for your manicure and pedicure."

Susan lifted her head, glanced around. "It wasn't a dream."

"No, ma'am. You're still at the Lily Pond. Let me help you down."

By the time Susan floated out of the Lily Pond spa she truly felt like a princess. All she wanted to do was go home, sprawl on the sofa and stay there forever.

But her fantasy date was only just beginning. Her dress for dinner hung on the closet door, but for the afternoon tours she dressed in slacks, an embroidered vest and a light turtleneck.

When Gabriel arrived, he too was in casual wear.

"Have you ever been on the gold-rush mining tour?"

Susan shook her head. "I think it's one of those attractions that you just never get to because you live here. It's always on the one-of-these-days list. But every time there's an opportunity to do something new, we never pick it."

"Then we'll get to experience it together for the first time."

She looked at him, wondering if this was a real date or just an elaborate gesture on Liza's part, and with Jessica's coordinating, to get her out.

"Gabriel?"

He took his eyes off the road for a bit. "Yes?"

What Susan wanted to ask him was who was paying for the date part. Was Liza Montgomery also picking up the tab for the spa package, the tours, the dinner and show? She couldn't think of a graceful way to ask—is this real or just a public service on your part?

"The spa was fabulous," she said instead.

He grinned. "So what, exactly, happens in the Lily Pond?"

Susan held out her hand so he could see the nail polish. "My hands haven't been this soft in I don't know how long." She inspected her nails. "I rarely wear nail color, and never red. It's a little bold."

"It looks great."

She told him about the massage and the other services. "And guess what?" she said, practically bouncing in her seat.

He smiled at her enthusiasm. "What?"

"They let me keep the robe! And..." she said, waving her hands. "And I got a bag of goodies, some of the products they used, including an eye mask."

"Hmm, sounds like I'm going to have a rough time competing with that spa."

Susan glanced at him and grinned. "I think so, too."

The Cripple Creek and Victor Narrow Gauge Railroad was a scenic adventure into Colorado's days gone by. More than 800 million dollars in gold had been mined in the Cripple Creek area during Colorado's gold rush. In an old steam engine complete with pillaring smoke, the narrated railroad tour took Susan, Gabriel and other visitors along the route that gold miners used.

"I didn't think to bring a camera," Susan said.

"Neither did I." But wearing miners' hats, they had their picture taken at one of the stops on the route.

At Seven Falls, they gazed dubiously at the long stairway leading up the mountainside.

"Steps or elevator?" Gabriel asked.

"If I climb all those steps, I'm going to need another massage to get all the kinks out."

Laughing, Gabriel led her to the mountain elevator that blasted them up through fourteen stories of granite to the Eagle's Nest lookout.

"The girls would love this," Susan said when they arrived, taking in the view from every direction.

"We'll have to bring them one afternoon."

Susan glanced at him and nodded, then looked out at the landscape again. "This is awesome. God truly created a work of art."

Gabriel agreed. But his gaze was on Susan, not the spectacular view of plains and trees.

Later, they sat across from each other at one of Colorado Springs' best restaurants, adjacent to the theater where they were to see an eight-o'clock performance. Candlelight flickered between them. Dinner dishes had been cleared and they were waiting for dessert and coffee to arrive.

"This day has been the best," Susan said. "Just the best. Enough for three dates. Thank you."

"It's been fun spending it with you."

"I'm glad Liza set it up," Susan said as she reached for her water goblet.

Gabriel stayed her hand. "Liza didn't do this," he said.

Susan's gaze met his steady one, though her voice wasn't controlled when she asked him, "What do you mean?"

"When Jessica first approached me about being a bachelor in the auction, I declined. I didn't think it was appropriate."

"What changed your mind?"

"A few weeks later she came back," Gabriel said,

smoothing the immaculate white linen tablecloth. "By that time, I think there was some matchmaking afoot."

Susan had never shied away from anything in her life. But now that the situation was about her, things were a little different. She felt tongue-tied.

"The proposal had changed," Gabriel said. "She wanted to know if I would set up a date just for you."

"Just for me?"

He nodded. "She and Liza Montgomery wanted to do something nice for you."

She relaxed a bit, sat back in her chair. This part made sense. It was just Jessi and Liza deciding she had been working too hard and needed a day to play. "So they arranged for the spa, the tours, this?"

He shook his head. "I did that."

Susan's mouth dropped open.

"Why are you looking so shocked?" he asked.

"You…*you* set all this up? *You're* paying for it?" She put her hand over her mouth. "That sounds callous, I know. But…"

He reached for her hands, clasped them in his. "Yes, Susan. Each bachelor set up and financed his own date. But this one, knowing you'd be the only woman who'd win, I created it especially for you."

"Why?"

"Here we are," their server said, interrupting with two very large slices of berry-covered cheesecake. He placed the desserts in front of them, added forks and then offered additional berry sauce.

Susan tasted the cheesecake, which was rich and delicious, but her mind was on what Gabriel had said. He'd set all of this up…just for her?

She put her fork down.

"What's wrong?"

"This picture is wrong," Susan told him.

"What do you mean?"

"I don't get the game, Gabriel. And I don't like being the object of jokes."

He carefully placed his own fork on the dessert plate and regarded her. "What are you talking about?"

"This," Susan said, hoping she would be able to explain.

Until Gabriel Dawson had come along, upsetting her equilibrium, Susan had thought she had a liberal dose of self-esteem. Dealing with Gabriel had somehow managed to get her insides all twisted. He made her confront things she'd rather keep buried. The main thing being her fear that she couldn't trust her own judgment. After all, Reggie too had wined and dined her. He'd made her feel like a cherished queen, only to turn the tables just when Susan let down her guard and opened her heart.

She couldn't take that chance again. Too much was at stake. Not just her own heart—which she didn't think could withstand another fracture. She had the girls to think about.

When Reggie was alive, the girls had been too young to know what was happening. Now, however, was a different story.

"I don't understand any of this," she told Gabriel. "I don't get the why? You. Me. I just don't get it."

Though he'd never given her any reason to doubt that his words and actions weren't true, Susan had a healthy respect for self-preservation. Gabriel had too many things in common with her late husband. They were both good-looking men who knew how to use words and promises to woo and entice. Susan couldn't afford to make the same mistake twice.

"What's there to understand?" he said. "I enjoy spending time with you."

"But why?"

For a moment, he looked confused. "Because I like you."

"Why?"

His eyes narrowed. "Susan, what's going on here?"

She blinked, trying not to get emotional, fearing that she'd been played for a fool—again. "That's what I'm trying to figure out."

Gabriel found himself at a loss to figure out just where the evening had gone off track. They'd had a nice time all afternoon and throughout dinner. Then, out of nowhere, Susan starting shutting him out.

He'd feared that he was moving too fast, sweeping both of them up in the vortex of his own emotions. Throughout his life, Gabriel had always relied on the quiet conviction of the Holy Spirit that he felt within. Some people heard from God through prayer or meditation or even in the voices of other people. For Gabriel, it had always been a quiet knowing, a sureness that guided his actions.

The moment he'd met Susan Carter, he'd felt a connection with her, one that had been stronger and surer than anything he'd ever experienced. Doubting himself for the first time, he'd hesitated in taking any steps toward getting to know her. Maybe he'd waited too long.

"You're seeing someone else?"

Too late he realized he'd blurted out the question.

"What?"

Susan shook her head and held up her hands.

"Wait. Just wait," she said. "We need to start all over. At the very beginning. Because frankly, I think I'm missing something."

"Me, too," Gabriel said.

Susan pushed the cheesecake plate away, folded her arms. "All right, you go first."

Chapter Seventeen

"I was going to say, ladies first."

She leveled a gaze at him. Gabriel realized it was a look normally reserved for the twins, and had to smile.

Maybe his waiting to seriously approach her had been for the best. Time merely cemented his feelings. Now all he had to do was make Susan realize he was serious. "These last few weeks with you have been terrific," he said.

"But?"

He leaned forward. "There is no 'but,' Susan. There never has been. When I arrived in Colorado Springs, I came here with a mission to build Good Shepherd into a church that was a beacon in the community. After meeting with the various boards and committees, I knew the plan I had was a solid one. There was one piece missing, though."

"What?"

"You."

"Excuse me?"

He shook his head. "Not you specifically at the time. I mean…a wife."

Susan's eyebrows lifted high.

Gabriel waved a hand, trying to clear the air and his thoughts. "Let me explain. Most ministers arrive at a pastorate with families. Being a single man, I counted myself blessed to have been called to Good Shepherd. Members gave me about a month to get settled, then the matchmaking started in earnest. Susan, you just don't know. I've been propositioned in ways that would make your hair stand on end."

She lifted a springy curl. "It already does."

Gabriel smiled and felt the tension between them dissipate a bit. "Even as the parade of women kept getting longer, I was only interested in one. And she was someone who didn't seem to like me very much."

Susan waited.

"That would be you," he said.

"It's not that I didn't like you. What I didn't like was the way you were ignoring the community most affected by Good Shepherd. The sphere of the church's influence was neglected while you were off chasing city council members and state legislators."

He knew where she was coming from this time, so the barb didn't hurt the way it had before.

"Susan, if you must know the truth, I *was* avoiding you. Whenever my secretary gave me a message from you or someone at Galilee, I would conveniently put it in a to-be-done pile—a pile that never got answered or addressed."

It was Susan's turn to look confused. "Why? What did I ever do to you?"

"It wasn't what you'd done," Gabriel said. "It was

what I felt toward you. I believe there are rules. Boundaries shouldn't be crossed between a minister and parishioner, especially a single minister and his single, female members."

"If boundaries aren't crossed sometimes, how is someone like you, a single pastor, ever supposed to find a mate?" She looked away for a moment, then, blushing, quickly added, "Hypothetically, of course."

Gabriel sighed. "That's why many ministers marry while they're still in seminary or shortly after graduation. When a pastorate comes along, they have a wife and possibly children. It's different for associate ministers of a church. The boundaries, at least in my estimation, aren't as stringent for them because they aren't in the senior leadership position." He met her gaze. "With you, I wanted to cross those lines."

"You never said anything. You never even gave any indication that you knew I existed."

"Trust me," he said, his tone sardonic, "I knew."

He could tell she was digesting his words. Susan was a smart woman, and Gabriel's new fear was that she would take the next mental leap and realize just what he had on his mind. He'd had months to think about all of the what-ifs. For Susan, this was all new.

"So tonight—" she began, then shook her head. "The night of the gala, I mean. So that was what—a public declaration?"

She'd made the leap.

"Do you mind terribly?"

Susan frowned. "That depends," she said, drawing out the word. "I'm starting to feel like a marionette in some sort of drama you're orchestrating. When do I get some say in this?"

Her cautious tone was far from the loving one he'd hoped for, or even the playful one that delighted him. Gabriel closed his eyes for a moment. This wasn't going at all the way he'd planned.

"I'm a big-picture man, Susan. Whether it's the church, my own life or even my military career, everything is like a chess match where I think three, four or five moves ahead."

One of those arched eyebrows lifted and he saw steam gathering.

"So now I'm a pawn in your little chess game of life. Is that it?" Susan plucked her napkin from her lap and dropped it on top of her uneaten cheesecake. "I'm ready to go."

A line had been crossed and she'd shifted from cautious to caustic. He reached for her hand. "You don't understand. I'm not making myself clear."

"Oh, you're making yourself pretty clear, Pastor Gabriel." She put her elbows on the table and held out one hand. "First," she said throwing out her thumb. "You're looking at forty and beginning to wonder how long you can play the single-minister role before people start wondering about you. So you start scouting for a suitable pawn to play. Second," she said, lifting her index finger. "You spot a civic-minded widow in the congregation. 'Ooh,' you say, 'she'll be desperate,' so you saunter on over and put into play your little scheme that includes cozying up to the widow's pet cause. Third," her middle finger shot out, ticking off the next charge against him "—oh, look, the widow comes with two little kids. Twins at that. Perfect for the picture Christmas card to send to all the church members."

She threw the words at him like stones, her nostrils flaring with fury. "And fourth, you set up this elaborate date thinking I come so cheap that I'll just fall slobbering into your lap because you pay me a little attention."

Susan stood up, snatched her small evening bag from the table. "Well, let me tell you something, Pastor Gabriel. There will be no fifth move in your chess game, 'cause this little chess piece is declaring checkmate on you."

Gabriel rose. "Susan, that's not it. You're blowing this way out of proportion."

She eyed him with disdain. "You know what, Gabriel? You're worse than my late husband. He might have been a liar, a cheater, a wife beater and a drug addict, but at least he was honest about what he wanted from me. You're a sneak, and in my book, that makes you worse."

Gabriel glanced at the couple at the next table who'd looked up with curiosity. "Susan, please."

"Don't bother," she said. "I can see myself home. I've been surviving all these years without you. I think I can manage one more night." Susan wound her way through tables and toward the entrance of the restaurant. Gabriel moved to follow.

The waiter appeared, blocking his exit. "Sir, is something wrong?"

Gabriel bit back words of frustration. Then he reached into his suit jacket and pulled out a billfold and credit card. "Nothing's wrong. I'd like to settle this," he said, handing over the credit card. "Quickly."

* * *

Outside, there wasn't a cab in sight. Susan seethed with anger and humiliation. How could she have been so blind? The manipulation was so evident now.

Truth be told, she was angrier at herself than at Gabriel. She'd up and done it again—fallen for a sweet-talker. Despite her mental objections and all evidence she tried to put forth to the contrary, she'd fallen hard for Gabriel Dawson. But at least she'd found out the truth before she'd done something stupid—like tell him how she felt.

Tears sprang to her eyes and she dashed them away. This perfect, perfect day, a day fit for a princess, had been a carefully orchestrated scheme. And she'd played her part like an Oscar-winning actress.

"A taxi, madam?"

"Yes, please," Susan said.

The doorman spoke into a small microphone, and Susan saw the lights of a cab glow down the street. But by the time it reached the curb and she'd stepped forward, so had Gabriel.

"That won't be necessary," Gabriel told the doorman, who was reaching for the back door to open it for Susan.

"I told you I can see myself home."

"I know you can," Gabriel said. "But since I brought you here, I'd like to make sure you get safely home."

He waved the cab on and handed the valet a ticket to retrieve his town car.

"I'm very angry with you," Susan said.

"I know."

"And disappointed. A minister shouldn't use people the way you've used me."

Gabriel opened his mouth to argue the point, then thought better of it. "Will you give me another chance to explain?"

"I've heard everything I needed to hear, Gabriel. I just want to go home."

The ride back to her apartment was a silent one. Gabriel tried to explain, to talk, but Susan kept her face averted, staring out the passenger window.

When he pulled in front of the brownstone, Susan didn't hesitate. As soon as the car came to a halt, she had the door open.

"On behalf of the Galilee Shelter and Foundation, I'd like to thank you for your generous support of our endeavors, Reverend Dawson."

"Susan," he said.

She refused to run, but she didn't break her stride on the way to her door. She heard his car door shut and the sound of his shoes on the pavement behind her.

"Susan."

She didn't turn around, but in the still of the night, she heard him pause. The only sound carrying on the air was the faint twang of live country music from The Longhorn Saloon, a few blocks down the street.

She punched in the access code, then ran upstairs.

How this perfect day had twisted into this sorry state she didn't quite know. The only thing Susan was sure of was that she needed a good cry. Upstairs, the apartment was as still as the evening, deserted and desolated just like Susan felt. Jessica and Sam had the girls for the evening, so she couldn't even divert her attention and misery.

She toed off her shoes and sat on the sofa. A moment later, she reached for a quilted pillow, one she'd made to coordinate with the slipcovers.

"What a fool you've been, Susan Carter," she muttered.

Wrapping her arms around the pillow, she tucked her feet under her. A moment later, the first tear fell. Then another. And soon, all their cousins and friends joined in.

All the way to his house in the hills, Gabriel berated himself for the way he'd handled the evening.

He had to think of a way to make it up to her, to make her realize that no matter how badly he'd botched the explaining, *she* was the light in his life.

Susan wouldn't take his calls the next day and sent the flowers he had delivered straightaway to the shelter's community lounge.

When Jessica and Liza showed up in her office to get the juicy details of the fantasy date, Susan was all business, instead reviewing the financials from the gala.

Jessica glanced at Liza. "I think something bad happened."

"I'm getting the same impression," Liza said. "Susan?"

"I'd rather not talk about it."

She got her wish, too. Both women backed off, apparently realizing that it wouldn't do to press her. Their consideration only made Susan feel worse. When Jessica left for the day, Susan stopped by her office and left a note apologizing for acting like a baby. “I’ll explain on Monday,” she wrote.

By the time she called it a day, she was exhausted—not from doing shelter work, but from actively not thinking about Gabriel.

She made spaghetti and meatballs for the girls for dinner and had just dried the last dish when the doorbell rang.

“We’ll get it!”

“No, you won’t,” Susan told the girls. “What did I tell you two about answering the door?” As she pressed the intercom, she heard her pager go off. “Will you grab my purse?” she asked Hannah. Then, into the intercom, she said, “Who is it?”

“It’s me, Susan. Gabriel. I’d like to speak with you.”

“You did all your talking last night,” she said.

Hannah handed Susan her purse. Susan unclipped the pager from the strap and then glanced at the number. One of the emergency shelter houses.

She didn’t realize she’d buzzed the door open until a knock sounded on the other side. Susan yelped and clutched her throat.

“May I come in, please?”

She opened the door to Gabriel.

“I’m sorry,” he said.

“Hi, Pastor Gabriel!” the twins said, their voices, as usual, echoing off each other.

“Hey there, ladies.”

“We got paper dolls today. Mom says we can make more clothes. She’s gonna show us how.”

"Is that a fact?"

She glared at him. "Have a seat," Susan said, being cordial in front of the girls. "Excuse me for a moment while I answer this call." She stepped into the dining area, close enough to keep an eye on the girls, but far enough away that her telephone conversation would be private.

Gabriel sat on the middle cushion of the sofa. Hannah and Sarah immediately claimed his sides, each vying to show him something in either a coloring book or sticker binder.

"See, I'm gonna put this dress on my lady," Hannah said. "It's pink like my beads."

"And I'm gonna give mine a fur coat. Mrs. Montgomery has a fur coat. She let us feel it last year."

"When I grow up, I'm not gonna wear fur," Hannah declared.

"Why is that?" Gabriel asked.

"I'm gonna save all the little animals, not wear them."

That statement sparked a dispute between the girls. Gabriel didn't know whether to referee or take a side in the argument.

He was about to point out to them that grown-ups disagreed on the same points, when Susan reappeared. She looked shaken.

He rose. "Is something wrong?"

Her gaze met his, and he knew that whatever it was, it was bad. "What happened?"

Susan glanced at the girls and shook her head. "I have to go to a site. There's a family...They..." She pressed a hand to her mouth. "Girls, come on. Mommy needs to go to work. I'm going to have to take you next door. Miss Tricia's on duty and she'll watch you."

"Aw, Mom. We were just gonna dress the dolls."

"Can't we just stay here this time?"

"Susan," Gabriel said, touching her arm. "Let me help. What can I do? Do you want me to go with you?"

She shook her head. "I...I just need to get myself together. It's really bad, Gabriel," she said, loud enough for only him to hear. "Three children."

He glanced over his shoulders at the twins. "Then I'll stay here and watch the girls. That way their evening won't be disrupted."

She opened her mouth to protest, to say he knew not the first thing about baby-sitting two active six-year-olds. Her pager went off again. It was the same number, but this time with a 9-1-1 code following the number.

"All right," she said, making up her mind. There could be worse things than leaving her children in the care of their pastor. "I'll leave my numbers with you in case you need me. And Tricia is right next door. Kim will be coming in later."

Gabriel took her hand, squeezed it tight, then bowed his head. The prayer was quick and to the point.

"Be safe," he told her.

Susan nodded. She grabbed her purse and briefcase. "Girls, Pastor Gabriel is going to stay with you while I go to work, okay?"

"Yippee!"

"You can cut out the dresses," Sarah said, directing him.

Susan kissed each girl, then, with a final glance at them, ran out the door.

* * *

Several hours later, she wearily let herself back in the apartment. The sight that greeted her made her smile.

A half-filled bowl of popcorn was on the coffee table, kernels spilled onto the table surface and the floor. A mountain of clippings, testament to failed paper doll dresses, was to the side of the popcorn bowl.

The television was on with the sound down. And on the sofa sat Gabriel, fast asleep with a girl tucked under each arm. Hannah was softly snoring.

"Gabriel," she said quietly so as not to wake the twins.

His eyes popped open. "Hey. What time is it?"

"After midnight," Susan said as she picked up some of the popcorn.

Gabriel carefully disengaged himself from the girls. Neither one stirred.

"So who wore whom out first?"

"I think it was a tie," he said. "Did you know that paper dolls must have at least as many clothes as real people?"

Susan smiled. "Thanks for doing this. I'm sure you had better things to do on a Friday night than baby-sit."

"I had a great time," he said. "We even created some costumes like Bible characters may have worn. So, what happened with you?"

Susan sighed. "Do you mind if I put them to bed and then start a pot of coffee first?"

"I'll help. Point me in the direction of the coffee."

Twenty minutes later, both girls were tucked in their beds after murmuring sleepy good-nights, first to Gabriel, then their mom. Fresh java dripped from the coffeemaker, and Susan pulled down a couple of mugs and set them on the kitchen table.

"It apparently started as a domestic dispute. A nasty custody battle."

"Those can get ugly sometimes when people take out their frustrations on their children rather than confront the source of their problems."

"Well, this," Susan said, "was a tragedy all around. The family lives right across the street from one of our safe houses. With all the shouting going on and then when all the police started arriving, the women there freaked, thinking someone's husband had found them. It'll be all over the news in the morning. A SWAT team ended up coming."

She told him the rest of the evening's events, leaving out none of the details.

"I don't know how you do it," Gabriel said when she finished.

"Do what?"

"How you can handle being around and a part of so much violence."

"I learned how to compartmentalize my life," Susan confessed. "When I walk into this apartment, I'm Susan and Mom. Nothing else. When I go downstairs to work, I become the person who has to deal with the day-to-day operation of running a shelter."

"You seem very hands-on," Gabriel said.

"I am. I do more of the day-in, day-out stuff than a lot of my counterparts in other cities." She shrugged. "Because I've been there, where my clients are, I generally have an idea of what they may need or want, and the main thing is someone who understands without passing judgment."

They drank their coffee and nibbled on cookies Gabriel had found and put on a plate on the table.

"Thank you for looking after the girls." She leaned forward, inspecting his ears.

Gabriel touched his right ear with his hand. "What?"

"I was just checking to see if they talked your ears off."

He chuckled. "Almost. But we had a great time."

"I hope they weren't too much of a bother."

He reached for her hand. "No bother at all. And neither is asking for a little help now and then."

"That doesn't come easy for me," Susan said. "I've learned how to fend for myself."

"Sometimes two can make the load easier," he said, his voice quiet.

Susan looked at him over the rim of the mug she held in her other hand, wondering if the meaning she was attaching to his words was the right one.

After what she'd witnessed tonight, her argument with Gabriel seemed superficial. Her feelings hadn't changed. What had changed was the way she perceived them—and him.

"I need to tell you something else that happened tonight," Gabriel said. He was looking a little sheepish, and Susan detected a blush.

"Oh my," she said, putting her cup on the table. "I'm afraid to ask."

"I promised them we'd all go out to play miniature golf tomorrow."

"We, as in you, Hannah and Sarah?"

He shook his head. "No, Susan. We, as in you, me, Hannah and Sarah."

Susan wasn't sure how she felt about that. "The family date thing was cute while we were sort of seeing each other. But I don't think it's a good idea anymore. And I don't want the girls thinking you taking them out is a habit."

"Good habits are the ones you want to keep. And repeat."

She clasped her hands together and took a deep breath. "Gabriel, I'm going to try to say this without getting emotional. I don't like or appreciate being used. What you said yesterday hurt me a lot."

"Susan, I wasn't making myself clear."

She held up a hand. "Let me finish, please. My life work is about helping people. Most of what I do involves people's lives falling apart. So I have to be replenished often. Worship, personal and at church, is a part of that rejuvenation. I quilt to help me relax. I garden so I can thrust my hands into the warm soil and then see life form from the seeds I plant and nurture."

Taking a deep breath, she met his gaze. "Then along comes a storm that rips apart all I've done, that destroys my confidence in who and what I am. I can't operate on a half-empty well, Gabriel. I know things will grow again, that it'll be all right, by and by. But for the now, it hurts. You trampled my emotional garden yesterday, Gabriel. Just like a flower bed that gets blown around or ripped up in a storm, it's going to take me a bit to recover."

Chapter Eighteen

Her words haunted him. Though she seemed to accept that he was truly contrite and hadn't intentionally hurt her, seeing the sadness in her eyes disturbed Gabriel. He hoped that part of it was what she'd experienced that evening in the city.

After she'd locked her door behind him, Gabriel had sat in the SUV for a long time. He had to figure out a way to show her that his intentions were honorable and his love for her real.

For love her he did. With every fiber of his being.

In the last few weeks with Susan he'd discovered a lot, about himself, about his motivations and about the community he now called home. But the main thing he'd discovered was what resided in his heart. He wanted Susan at his side forever and always, and for the twins to eventually want to call him Dad.

Besides learning how to cut out and dress up paper dolls, one other good thing to come out of the evening was that Susan hadn't refused him the promise he'd made to the girls. He'd learned to care for them. They were inquisitive and precocious. Gabriel didn't know what qualities Hannah and Sarah had inherited from their father, but he definitely knew what they'd gotten from Susan.

The next day, Gabriel arrived at eleven for the miniature golf date. Since the twins had nothing but great things to say about his paper doll-making skills, and he seemed to know how to handle himself around kids, Susan thought about just sending the girls on without her.

They didn't take to that idea at all. So she dressed in jeans and a corded sweater and trumped downstairs with them.

"Mommy wasn't going to come," Hannah reported as soon as her seat belt was locked.

Gabriel looked in the rearview mirror of the SUV and then at Susan.

"We think you had a fight," Sarah said.

"We didn't have a fight," Susan answered.

Gabriel started the truck. "While we were having fun last night, your mom had a rough evening helping people."

"Is everybody all right?" Sarah asked.

"Yes, sweetie," Susan said, but instead of turning toward the girls, she looked out her window.

Gabriel had seen the morning news and knew everything wasn't all right. After hostage negotiators got the three children out of the house, the man shot his estranged wife and then killed himself. The woman survived, but was in critical condition and not expected to make it. Gabriel reached for Susan's hand. She didn't pull away.

Not realizing the gravity of the situation, and seeing their mom and the pastor holding hands, the twins grinned at each other. Gabriel caught the exchange in his rearview mirror.

By the middle of their miniature golf game, Gabriel had Susan laughing and the girls giggling at his antics as he tried to get his ball into a gorilla's mouth.

"Try it from this side, Pastor Gabriel," Hannah said.

He considered her suggestion. "Oh, you definitely want me to miss this shot, don't you."

Hannah nodded and stumbled over laughing when he tried it and missed.

"We're winning!" Sarah said, jumping up and down.

"The next round is mine," Gabriel promised. He scooped a twin under each arm and they marched to the next hole.

"This is fun," Susan said while the girls were deciding how best to navigate their balls through a giraffe's legs. "I'm glad I decided to come."

"Would you really have sent them with me alone?"

Susan's gaze met his. She nodded. "Yes."

A lump formed in Gabriel's throat and he blinked back a rush of moisture in his eyes. "Thank you."

Susan placed her hands on top of each other and leaned on her club. "For what?"

"For trusting me with them."

"I never distrusted you, Gabriel. The things I said the other night—that was anger and fear talking. I'm sorry."

"You don't need to apologize," he said. "I was rushing you."

"Your turn, Mommy," Sarah called out.

"All right."

"So does this mean you're my girlfriend again?"

Laughing, Susan nudged him aside with her golf club. "Step aside, preacher man. It's time for some championship golf."

Susan lined up her ball and did an exaggerated hip swivel that made the girls giggle.

Gabriel watched the three of them and realized he more than liked the Carter women. He'd fallen head over heels, crazy in love with all three of them.

After some creative score keeping, Hannah and Sarah were declared the victors. "Losers buy the winners ice cream," Hannah announced.

The three women looked up at him. "Hey, weren't you on my team?" he asked Susan. "You're one of the losers, too."

"Not when it comes to treating for ice cream."

Gabriel smiled, shaking his head. "There's a sucker born every minute."

They each got scoops with waffle cones and claimed a table near the course. Hannah and Sarah enthusiastically put a dent in their cones, while Sarah looked at Gabriel.

"Hannah and I have talked it over," she started.

"And we decided that we want you to be our daddy," Hannah finished.

Gabriel almost choked on his ice cream. Susan looked mortified.

"Girls," she said, while slapping Gabriel on the back. "It doesn't work that way."

"Yes, it does," Hannah said. "We saw it on TV at Amy's house."

Susan could only wonder what they'd been watching. She winced when she glanced at Gabriel. "I'm sorry about that. They've gotten this notion in their heads…"

"It's all right," Gabriel said.

Inside he was rejoicing. It was all he could do not to jump up and do a dance. He'd almost choked on the waffle cone because the girls were the one thing he hadn't been sure about. He enjoyed spending time with them. Until just now, though, he hadn't known if his feelings for them were reciprocated.

Susan got up to toss away the napkins and other trash.

"So, how about it?" Hannah asked Gabriel.

He leaned forward and whispered, "I'm working on it, ladies. I'm working on it."

Hannah and Sarah beamed.

When they got back to the apartment, the girls gave Gabriel huge hugs, then ran upstairs, leaving Susan alone with him at the bottom of the stairs.

"Thanks for a fun afternoon," she told him. "I needed this."

"Thank you for letting me back in."

She knew what he meant and offered him a shy smile. "What happens now?"

He took her hands in his. "I think this is the part where I start begging for another date."

She shook her head, sending corkscrew curls bouncing. "No begging."

"Then how about if I just ask. Tomorrow? A quiet supper after church?"

"Quiet? With Hannah and Sarah around? I don't think so."

"Maybe I'll find a sitter."

Susan chuckled. He had no idea just how tough that task could be at times. "Tell you what, Rev."

He grinned at the nickname, knowing that if she was back to calling him "Rev," she had well and truly forgiven him.

"You find a sitter," she said, adding, "one I approve of—and I'll have a quiet supper with you."

"Deal."

He said it so quickly that Susan narrowed her eyes. Had he just set her up? She punched him in the arm. "You had a baby-sitter already lined up, didn't you."

He nodded, but had the grace to blush.

Sometimes though, unforeseen circumstances sabotage the best-laid plans. In Gabriel's case, it was well-meaning members of Good Shepherd.

Not realizing that Gabriel and Susan had mended fences, Liza waylaid him in the fellowship hall, invited him to dinner at her home and wouldn't take no for an answer.

Gabriel finally got in that he had plans for dinner, but Liza still looked concerned.

"I hope whatever happened Thursday night is resolved."

He nodded but didn't provide any details.

Looking worried, Liza finally set off to find her husband.

In the fellowship hall, Tricia Streeter caught up with Susan. The Air Force officer wore her dress uniform.

"Do you have a moment?" Tricia asked.

"Sure," Susan said. "I'm sorry you missed the gala. We have a plaque for you. Longtime volunteers were honored."

"Thanks, Jessica told me and I picked it up when I did my service the other night. But that's what I wanted to talk with you about. My hours at Galilee."

Susan touched Tricia's arm. "Is everything all right?"

"I've been assigned to a case that's taking a lot of time," Tricia said. She indicated her uniform. "I'm headed to work right now."

"Of course," Susan said. "Don't worry about it."

"I feel terrible about this," Tricia told her. "You guys give me an award for showing up all the time and the next thing I say is I can't come anymore for a while."

"Work is your priority," Susan said. "I understand that. Don't worry. Just let us know when you're ready to come back and the volunteer coordinator will put you back in the schedule."

Tricia nodded. "And Susan? I know you're a prayer warrior. Would you pray for some friends of mine? There's a murder involved in the case I've just taken over. And my friend's wife and daughter..." She shook her head. "They need prayer now. Life without him isn't going to be the same."

"I will," Susan said. "What are their names?"

Tricia told her and the two women prayed together right there. When Susan finished, Tricia hugged her.

"I'd better go." With her Bible in hand, Tricia headed for a side door.

"Tricia?"

The officer turned back toward Susan.

"I'll be keeping you in my prayers, too."

Tricia smiled and mouthed, *Thank you.*

Gabriel had planned to dazzle Susan with his culinary skills. He had everything all ready at his house. The table was set on the terrace. Steaks were marinating in the fridge. All he had to do was drop the girls off at Sam and Jessica's, get home to toss a salad and set up his special surprise, then pick up Susan.

The only problem was Mrs. Hardy. The elderly woman insisted he come by to see her granddaughter, who was visiting.

No amount of explaining or evading worked with her.

When he finally freed himself after two pieces of German chocolate cake, his pager went off. A situation at Vance Memorial Hospital required his services as chaplain.

Gabriel looked at his watch, sighed and called Susan.

"I have a problem," he said.

"What's up?"

He explained, and Susan seemed to take it all right. "You forget," she said. "I understand because my work calls me away, too."

"I'll make it up to you," he promised. "How about lunch tomorrow?"

"I have a pretty busy day. Can we make it someplace fast?"

"Willing to brave the Stagecoach Café again?"

"That'll be fine," Susan said. "But that's not the makeup date."

"What do you mean?"

"I want a dinner that Gabriel has prepared, not Fiona."

"It's a deal." As he walked into the hospital, his Bible in one hand, his communion kit in the other, Gabriel was smiling.

The next day Susan was glad she'd agreed to the café. She'd done some research and now had some data to drop off for Yvette, who had been able to secure herself a house to rent after getting access to some of her independent financial resources.

Instead of Galilee giving her a donation, Yvette had written a substantial check out to the shelter to say thank you for the care they'd given her.

She was seriously contemplating a run for public office, but knew her personal struggle as well as any potential candidacy would be a long, uphill climb.

Though offered the cozy little nook, Susan and Gabriel opted for a table out in the open where service was faster. She spied a television crew setting up near the bar.

"What's going on over there?" she asked the hostess who seated them.

"It's CNN," the hostess said. "They're doing a piece about the Stagecoach Café in a travel segment on the best food in the West."

"Cool," Susan said.

"Fiona must be pleased," Gabriel noted, as the cameraman hoisted the camera to his shoulder and a reporter dabbed her nose with a powder puff.

"She's beside herself. She's in the back putting on the

finishing touches of her camera makeup. Yvette will be your server. She'll be right with you."

On Yvette's recommendation, they both ordered the roasted pork green chili, the day's special, then watched the television production crew for a bit. Susan sat back.

"What's wrong, Rev? You're not sporting that 'all is well in my world' look of yours."

His mouth tipped up in a smile. "I didn't know I had such a look to sport."

"You do. And I can tell something's up. Spill it."

Gabriel, dressed in a charcoal-gray suit with a red-and-gray print tie, slipped his hand in his jacket pocket. "This isn't at all how I'd planned to do this."

"Do what?" Susan asked.

He opened his palm and placed a small velvet box on the table.

"What is that?"

"I think you know," he said. "But why don't you open it and find out?"

Susan reached for the box, her hand unsteady, her gaze lifting and falling between Gabriel and the jeweler's box.

"Gabriel?"

"Open it."

Almost in slow motion, she lifted the lid. A large emerald-cut diamond winked at her. She quickly closed the box. "Oh. Oh." She looked as if she might pass out.

Gabriel leaned forward, clasped her hand. "Breathe, honey, breathe."

"I am." Susan took a deep, steadying breath. She looked up at him. Looked down at the ring box. "I…"

He took both her hands in his and rubbed them. "Okay now?"

She nodded. "But—"

"Let me do this properly," he said. His thumb grazed her hand as he spoke. "All my life I've been searching for you. All my life I've known that the Lord would lead me to the woman He meant for me to be with. In the military, I got the opportunity to travel all over the globe. I met a lot of women, but not a single one of them ever moved me the way you do."

"Gabriel."

"I've never been a dad before, but I'm an uncle. I'd like to learn more, a lot more, about being a father to Hannah and Sarah. They're beautiful girls and I'd be honored to be their stepfather.

"I wanted to do this yesterday, in a romantic way. I had it all set up, too. The romantic music. The fire burning. But that didn't work out. When I woke up this morning, I realized that the place doesn't make a difference. It's what's in here," he said, touching his heart, "that does. And what's in my heart is a love for you and the girls that's so big I can't contain it."

He looked at the ring box, then opened it, pulled out the solitaire and offered it to her. "Susan Carter, would you do me the honor of marrying me?"

She just sat there, staring at him. Gabriel, already nervous, began to sweat. If she turned him down, he didn't know what he'd do.

The ring. Maybe she hated the ring.

"I didn't know what kind of stone or setting you'd prefer," he said, talking fast, trying to get all the words out. "So I got something that I thought was pretty. You hate it, don't you. The jeweler said we can exchange it. We can get something else."

She shook her head. Gabriel's gut clenched.

He closed his eyes, hoping, praying. "Please, don't say no." When he looked at her again, all of his heart was evident in his eyes.

"Gabriel." Her voice was very, very small. He almost didn't hear her. "I don't want you to exchange the ring."

His shoulders slumped and he bowed his head. In his growing misery, all Gabriel heard was "I don't want you..."

"I don't want to exchange it, because I want *this* one."

He looked up. Blinked. "What did you say?"

"I want this ring. Yes, Gabriel. I'll marry you."

His face split into a wide grin. "You will?"

She nodded.

A warm glow spread through him where moments ago only a cold emptiness had resided. Then he was up and out of his seat and hugging her.

"Here you go," Yvette said, arriving at their table with two bowls of Fiona's spectacular chili. "Hot and delicious." They looked at her. Susan and Gabriel both started laughing; tears of joy streaked down Susan's face.

"What's wrong?" Yvette asked, looking confused.

"What's wrong is that a woman shouldn't leave her husband right when he needs her most," an angry voice said from behind.

Yvette whirled around, the tray in her hand slipping.

Gabriel moved to catch it. He got most of it, but condiments and one of the bowls of chili crashed to the floor. Heads turned their way. He looked up and saw a man approaching them.

"B-Bill? Wh-what are you doing here?"

She backed up, but the table was a barrier behind her.

Susan moved in front of Yvette, using her own body as a shield for the vulnerable woman.

"Did you really think you could run away from me?"

"How did you find me?" She cast accusing eyes at Susan. "You said you wouldn't tell him where I was."

"We didn't."

"Get out of my way," the man snarled at Susan.

"I think you should leave," Susan said.

"Susan, let me handle this," Gabriel said. He'd righted the tray and placed it on the table, scooping up Susan's ring and depositing it in his pocket as he went.

"What's going on here?" Fiona said, hustling to the table and casting a worried eye toward the camera crew. She motioned for a busboy to get the mess on the floor cleared away. "Pastor Gabriel, who is this man?"

Someone at a nearby table said, "That looks like Bill Duncan."

Fiona turned. "Bill who?"

"Yvette, I'm not in the mood to play games. And I can't believe you're actually waiting tables in a restaurant. You're an embarrassment." Bill looked over Susan's shoulder at his wife, then down at Susan. "Get out of my way, lady."

"I think you should leave," Susan and Fiona said at the same time.

What came next happened so fast that the only person who saw it all was the CNN cameraman who'd moved in close to capture the altercation on videotape.

Bill shoved Susan aside and grabbed Yvette's arm. Susan hit the edge of the table and stumbled. She landed hard on the floor. Fiona screamed.

"You're coming home with me," Bill told Yvette.

"I'm not going anywhere with you. Let me go." Yvette struggled to free herself.

Bill backhanded her.

Diners gasped; some screamed and scuttled from their tables.

Bill never saw Gabriel coming.

One moment, Bill had Yvette by the hair and was trying to drag her away from the table. The next, he was whirling around, dragging Yvette with him, trying to find his balance and recover from the blow that had come out of nowhere.

Enraged and swearing, he lurched toward Gabriel with a right hook. Yvette shrieked, tried to yank free of his grasp. Instead of connecting with Gabriel, Bill caught her on the jaw. She crumpled to the floor.

Gabriel tackled him low and both men crashed to the floor, knocking over chairs and banging into a table. Dishes smashed around them, but neither man noticed that or the hollering going on around them.

Bill was no match for Gabriel, who had might and rage and military combat experience on his side.

Police sirens could be heard above the melee in the restaurant.

Once Gabriel had Bill completely subdued, a couple

of men helped him up. Gabriel yanked Bill off the floor and shoved him into a chair.

"Don't you ever lay a hand on my wife or yours!"

A group of men surrounded Bill in case he got any ideas about trying to escape or go after anyone else.

Gabriel rolled his shoulders, then shook his hands out. His suit was covered in food and bits of glass. He cast around, looking for Susan. He spotted the two women in a corner, huddled together on the floor. Susan had Yvette in her arms.

He dashed to her side. "Susan, are you all right?"

"Uh-huh."

"Yvette?"

Susan rocked the other woman. "Ambulance. We need an ambulance, Gabriel."

A moment later, police officers poured into the restaurant.

"This is a disaster," Fiona wailed, her arms waving in the air. "Just a disaster. That man. He just came busting in here like a crazy person."

The television crew that had been in the Stagecoach Café to shoot a feature about the restaurant's great food and atmosphere instead got a barroom brawl reminiscent of the true stagecoach days.

"Do you know who he is?" the reporter asked her, while police officers questioned Gabriel and other patrons.

Dazed at the destruction of a portion of her restaurant, Fiona looked around. "Somebody said he's Bill Duncan. But I don't know a Bill Duncan. He attacked Yvette. She's one of my best workers."

The reporter's jaw dropped. "Bill Duncan from California?" she asked. "The Senate candidate?"

Fiona shrugged. "I don't know."

"That's him," one of the diners standing nearby piped up. "I recognized him from the newspaper and was gonna ask for an autograph when I saw him come in. But he went over there and hit that woman. Who knew he was a wife beater?"

The reporter and cameraman looked at each other. The cameraman hotfooted it to where the police were and the reporter grabbed her cell phone. "Dave, you're not going to believe what we just got. The truck's outside, we can get a live feed to you in less than ten."

A little while later, after the police and the local news crews left, Susan turned to Gabriel.

"My ring!" She rushed to the table where they'd been sitting. It had already been cleared and reset. She pushed flatware and glasses aside, picked up the salt and pepper shakers as if the diamond might be hiding underneath. "It's gone."

"Susan."

She spun around, anguish in her eyes. "It's gone, Gabriel. My ring."

He stuck his hand in his pocket and held out his palm. "This one?"

Susan looked at it, then up at him. He slipped the ring on her finger and she slipped her arms around his neck.

"So, are you still willing to marry a guy who gets in fights in restaurants?"

In answer, she kissed him.

* * *

They'd both eventually made it back to work, but Susan had invited Gabriel to have dinner with her and the girls that night. "You know," Gabriel said after the meal as he helped Susan clear their dishes. "I've been thinking maybe we shouldn't eat at the Stagecoach Café anymore."

Susan laughed. "Well, I was thinking we should have Fiona cater our wedding reception."

Gabriel put a plate in the dishwasher, then wrapped his hands around Susan's waist. "You're really going to marry me?"

She nodded.

"I am a well and truly blessed man."

They shared a kiss.

A scream of distress from the living room broke them apart. Susan dropped the dish towel and went running, Gabriel on her heels.

She looked around for an intruder, an injury. "What's wrong? Hannah? Sarah?"

The girls were standing in front of the television. Pointing, staring, lips trembling, Sarah hopped from one foot to the other. "Mommy! No!" She ran to the television, put her hand over the image as if to make it stop.

Susan and Gabriel caught enough to know it was footage of Susan falling to the floor and Gabriel tackling Bill Duncan.

"Police in Colorado Springs say that Duncan's wife, thirty-five-year-old Yvette Duncan, had escaped an abusive marriage and was living and working in Colorado Springs. The telecommunications magnate has been placed under arrest and granted no bail."

Susan went to the girls and gathered them in her arms as she knelt on the floor.

They touched her face. "Are you all right?" asked Sarah. "That man hit you."

"I'm fine, babies. Mommy's fine. And so is the other lady. Thanks to Gabriel." She held a hand out to him. "He rescued us."

Fiona was on the television now with other witnesses, explaining what had happened. The last footage showed Bill Duncan in handcuffs, being led to a squad car. "This very likely spells the end of Bill Duncan's political aspirations," the anchor said.

Gabriel shut off the television.

"You saved Mommy?" Hannah asked.

"I did what I could," he told the girls. He reached out a hand to caress the edge of Susan's face. "I love your mother very much."

"Girls, there's something we want to tell you."

Hannah and Sarah warily eyed Susan and Gabriel. Sarah swiped at her eyes. "What?"

"Gabriel asked me to marry him today and I said yes."

The twins shared a glance.

"Does that mean you marry us, too?" Hannah said.

Gabriel smiled. "You betcha. I wouldn't have it any other way." He took Susan's hand in his. "I love the Carter women very, very much. Would you, Hannah, and you, Sarah, mind if I married you and your mom?"

The girls disengaged from Susan and tackled Gabriel. It was a good thing he was already on the floor, because they all landed in a heap, the girls planting kisses on his face.

Laughing, Gabriel looked up to Susan. "Does this mean yes?"

She chuckled at the picture they made. "I think so."

Gabriel struggled up, righting the twins.

They shared another of those looks they used to communicate.

"What's wrong?" Susan asked.

"Well," Hannah said. "We were wondering..."

"If now that you're gonna marry us, we still hafta call you Pastor Gabriel," finished Sarah.

Gabriel smiled. "Why don't you just drop the Pastor part and call me Gabriel?"

The girls frowned. Hannah whispered something in her sister's ear. Sarah shook her head. Then she cupped her hand at her twin's ear and whispered something back.

Gabriel looked to Susan for the translation, but Susan just shrugged.

"We talked it over," Hannah said.

"And we decided that we don't want to call you Gabriel."

"All right," he said. "What would you prefer?"

The twins shared another glance. Then together exclaimed, "We want to call you Daddy!"

For the second time, tears misted Gabriel's eyes. What a day it had been. But he thanked the Lord for bringing into his life three beautiful women. He wiped at his eyes.

"Uh-oh. Mommy, we made him cry."

Susan hugged the girls close. "I think it's all right. Isn't it, Gabriel?"

He nodded. "You three have made me the happiest man alive."

Hannah and Sarah clearly weren't quite sure. "So it's okay?"

"Yes," he said, hugging each girl. "It's more than all right with me."

"Yippee!" Hannah and Sarah said. "We're getting a daddy!"

Epilogue

Susan and Gabriel stood before a packed congregation at Good Shepherd Christian Church.

Among their guests were women from the Galilee shelter, and Yvette Duncan, who'd found incredible support in Colorado Springs and back home in California. From jail where he awaited trial, Bill had agreed to a divorce.

Susan had walked down the aisle alone and joined Gabriel at the altar. Standing nearby, Hannah and Sarah, dressed in identical white lace dresses, held miniature bouquets that matched their mom's. Instead of braids, the girls' hair had been curled in ringlets, Hannah's pulled back with a pink headband and Sarah's with a purple one.

Gabriel had already figured out how to tell them apart, and no longer had to rely on the color-coded method.

The Reverend Geoffrey Phillips cleared his throat and looked out over the bridal party. "Who gives this woman in holy matrimony?"

"We do!" twin voices yelled out.

The wedding guests laughed. Hannah and Sarah turned around to see what was so funny.

Sitting with the Vance family, Alessandro Donato spotted Colleen Montgomery with her parents. He winked at her. She blushed and turned away.

"Girls," Susan whispered, a smile at her own mouth. "Face this way."

"Why's everybody laughing?" They settled down then and looked up at the minister who was marrying their mom and new dad.

Chuckling, Gabriel nodded to Geoffrey. "Next question."

Geoffrey proceeded with the service uniting Susan and Gabriel.

"Do you promise to love, honor and cherish this woman?"

"I do," Gabriel said. "I certainly do."

* * * * *

Dear Reader,

Thank you for spending a while with Pastor Gabriel, Susan and the members and friends who make up the FAITH ON THE LINE community in Colorado Springs. It's been a pleasure being a part of the wonderful team that brought this project to fruition.

When trouble besets you on every side, remember that God is there to shed light on the dark places. In Him you'll discover peace and truth and joy everlasting.

Blessings to you,

Felicia Mason

Travis Vance gets a second chance with an old flame when they team up to investigate murder, missing planes and drugs in
REDEEMING TRAVIS
coming only to Love Inspired in October 2004.

And now for a sneak preview, please turn the page.

"Believe me, Travis, I understand that the kiss was nothing but a diversionary tactic. I wasn't born yesterday. I meant, what are you doing here?"

His eyes narrowed. "Where exactly is *here*?"

"The middle of my investigation. You just blew my chance for that Hispanic guy's license number. I'd have known who he is by six tonight if you hadn't gotten in my way. Maybe even where he was headed if I'd had the chance to follow him."

A muscle in his jaw flexed but he maintained his smart-alecky air. "Maybe I just happened along."

Tricia propped her sore hand on her hip. "Why don't I believe you? You almost gave me away."

He smirked. That was the only description that fit his insolent, slightly crooked grin. "I believe it was you who ran into me. You really ought to watch where you are going, Ms. Streeter."

"That's Major Streeter, AFOSI. Air Force Office of Special Investigations, in case you don't know. Now answer me," she demanded. "What are you doing here? You followed someone. Which of them was it and why?"

"I'm doing a little legwork on behalf of my brother and a friend. That's all you need to know and all I'm saying. It's a free country. And before you try to dissuade me the way you did Sam, I'll save you the trouble. I don't have a boss to order me off a case I've decided to pursue."

She knew he was referring to the fact Sam Vance, Travis's younger brother, a Colorado Springs police detective, had been ordered off the investigation into the murder of AFOSI Major Ian Kelly. Ian's body had been moved clear across Colorado Springs from Peterson Air Force Base and dumped behind the Chapel Hills Mall, but AFOSI DNA evidence proved his murder had taken place on the base, so the Air Force had claimed jurisdiction. Sam Vance had quietly turned over everything he'd already compiled, but he hadn't been happy.

It was an awkward situation for Tricia, since she attended the same church as the Vances. But she kept getting mental pictures of Ian laughing with his wife and daughters earlier in the summer at a backyard barbecue. He'd deserved so much more than to be executed for just doing his job. She was going to make whoever killed him pay. And no one, not even the former love of her life, was going to get in her way.

She stepped back and stretched to her full five feet nine inches. "You really don't want to take on the United States Air Force, Travis. AdVance might be an elite name in corporate security and antiterrorism circles, but compared to the might of the United States government, you're small potatoes. And you'll lose. Big time."

She turned smartly and stalked away. The general was not going to be happy about this when he saw her report. And frankly, she couldn't wait to watch the fallout.

Travis watched Patricia stride off. If he'd asked anyone at school to describe her, they'd have said amiable, shy and maybe even a little guarded. He'd found her appealingly mysterious but vulnerable. And what the air of mystery and timidity hadn't done to draw him, her long auburn tresses, short straight nose and wide golden-brown eyes had.

Now he found himself absolutely bowled over by all the changes in her. In his mind, she'd stayed the quiet girl of barely twenty who'd broken his heart. Now he knew she'd gone on—without him. She'd changed so much. She had curves where there'd been none to speak of. Her exceptional hair was now cropped short in what could only be called a non-style. But the biggest change of all was that the quiet, self-contained young woman he'd known had disappeared and become open, candid about her intentions and nearly volatile. He rubbed his stomach. Maybe "nearly" was a bit too hopeful. The young woman who'd brought out his every protective instinct was gone and in her place was a warrior in her own right.

Remembering that old Patty and the one personality quirk that had probably foreshadowed all the changes he saw, he listened for the sound of her car. Sure enough, the familiar six-second heavy rev of an engine reached his ears. Ah, the sound of Patty Perturbed. He grinned, wondering if she still drove with the same edgy recklessness as she had in college.

Travis caught himself smiling and scowled. Unfortunately, he had a whole lot more to wonder about than her driving. Like, if he'd lost his mind when he'd touched her—when that same electric spark he remembered so well from college had shot through him once again. Like, why matching wits with Patricia Streeter had felt so good.

What was it about her?

In those few moments with her in his arms, he'd felt more alive than he had in years. It was as if that first touch had reawakened all the feelings he'd once had for her. As if all those feelings had been hiding deep inside his frozen heart.

He took a breath and huffed it out in an explosive burst. Why had he been so angry when he'd realized who it was he held in his arms? Could all that latent anger be a sign that he hadn't really gone on with his life when he'd married?

THE BALFOUR BRIDES

A proud, powerful dynasty...

Scandal has rocked the core of the infamous Balfour family.

Its glittering, gorgeous daughters are in disgrace.

Banished from the Balfour mansion, they're sent to the boldest, most magnificent men in the world to be wedded, bedded...and tamed!

And so begins a scandalous saga of dazzling glamour and passionate surrender.

Each month, Harlequin Presents® is delighted to bring you an exciting new installment from THE BALFOUR BRIDES. You won't want to miss out!

MIA AND THE POWERFUL GREEK—
Michelle Reid

KAT AND THE DARE-DEVIL SPANIARD—
Sharon Kendrick

EMILY AND THE NOTORIOUS PRINCE—
India Grey

SOPHIE AND THE SCORCHING SICILIAN—
Kim Lawrence

ZOE AND THE TORMENTED TYCOON—
Kate Hewitt

ANNIE AND THE RED-HOT ITALIAN—
Carole Mortimer

BELLA AND THE MERCILESS SHEIKH—
Sarah Morgan

OLIVIA AND THE BILLIONAIRE CATTLE KING—
Margaret Way

Eight volumes to collect and treasure!

Kat stared up into icy black eyes which were skating over her with undisguised disapproval.

"You!" she accused, though her knees had turned to jelly and her heart was thundering so loudly that she felt quite faint. But what woman in the world wouldn't feel the same if confronted with that spectacular physique, clad in close-fitting black jeans and a soft white silk shirt—even if his handsome face was so cold that it might have been sculpted from some glittering piece of dark marble? "Carlos Guerrero!" she breathed.

"Who were you expecting?" challenged Carlos silkily. "It *is* my boat, after all."

Sharon Kendrick

KAT AND THE DARE-DEVIL SPANIARD

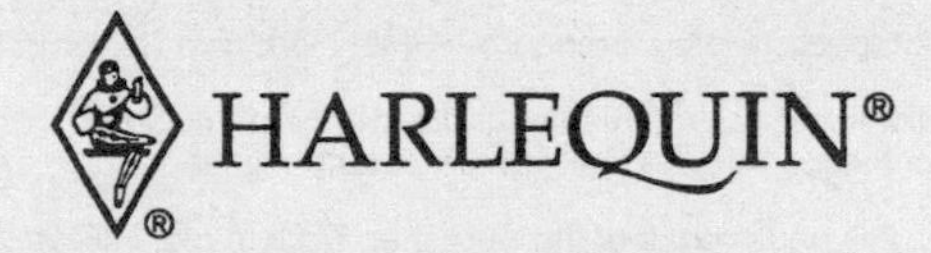

TORONTO • NEW YORK • LONDON
AMSTERDAM • PARIS • SYDNEY • HAMBURG
STOCKHOLM • ATHENS • TOKYO • MILAN • MADRID
PRAGUE • WARSAW • BUDAPEST • AUCKLAND

Special thanks and acknowledgment are given to Sharon Kendrick for her contribution to The Balfour Brides miniseries.

ISBN-13: 978-0-373-12940-9

KAT AND THE DARE-DEVIL SPANIARD

First North American Publication 2010.

This edition published by arrangement with Harlequin Books S.A.

For questions and comments about the quality of this book please contact us at Customer_eCare@Harlequin.ca.

www.eHarlequin.com

Printed in U.S.A.

To my Uncle Aidan—a great thinker, wit and musician—who could charm the birds from the trees. A great man all-round. I miss you.

All about the author...
Sharon Kendrick

When I was told off as a child for making up stories, little did I know that one day I'd earn my living by writing them!

To the horror of my parents I left school at sixteen and did a bewildering variety of jobs: I was a London DJ (in the now-trendy Primrose Hill), a decorator and a singer. After that I became a cook, a photographer and eventually, a nurse. I waitressed in the South of France, drove an ambulance in Australia, saw lots of beautiful sights but could never settle down. Everywhere I went I felt like a square peg—until one day I started writing again and then everything just fell into place. I felt like Cinderella must have done when the glass slipper fit!

Today, I have the best job in the world—writing passionate romances for Harlequin® Books. I like writing stories which are sexy and fast-paced, yet packed full of emotion, stories that readers will identify with, laugh and cry along with.

My interests are many and varied: chocolate and music, fresh flowers and bubble baths, films and cooking—and trying to keep my home from looking as if someone's burgled it! Simple pleasures—you can't beat them!

I live in Winchester, (one of the most stunning cities in the world—but don't take my word for it, come see for yourself!) and regularly visit London and Paris. Oh, and I love hearing from my readers all over the world...so I think it's over to you!

With warmest wishes,

Sharon Kendrick

www.sharonkendrick.com

CHAPTER ONE

EVEN the brilliant Mediterranean sunshine couldn't lighten her mood.

With a stab of frustration, Kat pushed the spill of dark hair away from her eyes and leaned back against the soft leather seat of the limousine. A week had passed, but the memories of that night were still vivid. A night when accusations—and counter-accusations—had spun through the air like the blade of a helicopter. And another guilty family secret had reared its ugly head.

If only…

If only it hadn't happened at the glittering Balfour Charity Ball—where half the world's press had been camped outside, waiting for an almighty scoop. Briefly, Kat closed her eyes. Bet they couldn't believe their luck.

Last year's ball had been bad enough—when she had made a humiliating fool of herself in front of the arrogant Spaniard, Carlos Guerrero—but at least nobody except her father had witnessed it. This time had been worse—with her twin sisters announcing the news that their beloved sister Zoe had been sired by another man and was not a true Balfour after all.

Scenting blood—the paparazzi had been baying around the fabulous family mansion for days—and once again the Balfour name had been splashed all over the papers. Those words Kat had become so used to, whenever her family's name was mentioned, were once again the hot topic of the day. Words that still had the power to wound, no matter how many times she'd heard them.

Scandal.

Shame.

Secrets.

And the truth was that, yes, the Balfours were brimming with all of those things—and more. But just because they were rich, didn't mean they were impervious to pain or hurt. Prick them, and they bled—just like everybody else. Nobody saw *that*, of course, and nobody ever would—well, certainly not in Kat's case. She allowed herself a grim smile. Because the moment you showed hurt, you made yourself vulnerable—and vulnerability was the most dangerous thing of all. Didn't she know that better than anyone?

She stared out of the car window, reminding herself how she'd coped with the latest indignity. The same way that she always coped. She'd cut loose and run from the family estate. Not far, it was true—only as far as London—where she had booked into a hotel, using a fake name and a vast pair of sunglasses to hide behind.

Until her father had rung her yesterday morning offering her an 'opportunity.'

Why had she felt a momentary wave of suspicion? Was it because that although Oscar was her true blood father, he had never been close to her heart in the same way as her beloved stepfather, Victor? Kat blinked back the tears which sprang to her eyes and replaced them with the defiant expression she had perfected. She wasn't going to think about her stepfather, or the past. She just *wasn't.* Because that way lay madness and regret and all those other painful emotions which she fought like crazy to keep at bay.

Nonetheless, her voice had been wary as she'd replied, 'What kind of opportunity, Daddy?'

There had been a pause. Had she imagined the unfamiliar steely quality which had entered his voice? 'The kind of opportunity which should be seized,' he said flatly. 'Didn't you tell me at the ball the other night that you were bored with your life, Kat?'

Had she said that? In a moment of weakness, had she been stupid enough to let on to the patriarch of the Balfour clan that a stream of loneliness as deep as a river seemed to be coursing through her veins?

'Did I?'

'Indeed you did. So why not grab at the opportunity for a change of scene and a change of air. How does a boat trip round the Mediterranean sound?'

It sounded exactly what she needed. Some good sea air and the chance to escape. And even though her father had tantalisingly refused to give her any more details, Kat knew it would be a treat. Because despite the impatience Oscar occasionally felt towards his daughters, deep down he loved nothing more than to lavish life's extravagances on them.

Which was why she was now reclining in the back of a luxury limousine, heading for the glamorous port of Antibes, while outside the brilliant Provençal sun beat down on all the wealthy holidaymakers. The glittering sea was shaded brilliant colours of cobalt and azure and the port was crammed with the biggest motor yachts you would find anywhere in the world. But that was the south of France for you—all glamour and glitz and buckets of money.

With a slickness perfected by years of practice, Kat pushed away her troubled thoughts as the limo slid to a halt next to a line of beautiful, bobbing yachts.

'There it is, miss,' said the driver, pointing to the biggest boat of all—where a couple of white-uniformed crew members were moving purposefully around the deck.

Suddenly, her mood was forgotten as Kat stared up at the most amazing-looking yacht she'd ever seen. With its long, aerodynamic shape and pointed prow, it rose up out of the water like some dazzling seabird. She could see a polished wooden deck and the turquoise glimmer of a swimming pool—as well as the ultimate convenience of a helicopter pad.

'Oh, wow,' she said, lips softening into a smile. Since babyhood, she had mixed in exalted and rich circles and knew that superyachts cost a fortune to own and maintain—but this magnificent vessel really was in a league of its own. It was…*spectacular.* Tourists were standing taking photographs of it and briefly Kat wondered who the owner could possibly be—and why her father had tantalisingly refused to tell her.

The name gave few clues. Painted in dark, curving letters along the side were the words *Corazón Frío.* Behind her dark glasses, Kat's eyes narrowed. Meaning *what*, precisely?

She was certainly no linguist—but even she could recognise that the language was Spanish. Her heart skipped an erratic beat. As was the only man who had ever slapped her down and humiliated her in public.

And who had haunted her dreams ever since. A man with a hard, lean body and wild black hair and the coldest eyes she had ever seen.

Shaking away a memory even more unsettling than the uproar at last week's ball, Kat stepped out onto the quayside and couldn't help noticing that people had stopped to look at her.

But then, people always did. If you dazzled them with the externals, then they never really looked beyond to see the real person underneath. Clothes could be the armour that shielded you—that stopped people from getting too close. And it was better that way. Much better.

She was wearing a teeny pair of shorn-off denim shorts and a shrunken white T-shirt which gave the occasional glimpse of a flat midriff tanned the colour of pale caramel. Shiny black hair cascaded down over her shoulders and all the way down her back—and her Balfour blue eyes were hidden behind a pair of enormous shades. She knew exactly what kind of uniform to wear on this kind of rich and privileged yachting trip—and she had abided to it by the letter. You dressed down, but you wore as many status symbols as possible.

'Bring my bags, will you?' Kat said to the driver, before making her way towards the gangplank. Teetering a little on a pair of the season's most fashionable espadrilles, she saw a fair-haired man in uniform approaching her and she smiled.

'Hello. You're probably expecting me. I'm Kat Balfour,' she said.

'Yeah.' The man nodded, squinting his pale blue eyes at her, a small diamond glinting at his ear lobe. 'I thought you must be.'

Kat looked around. 'Any of the other guests here yet?'

'Nope.'

'And my…host?' How crazy it sounded not to even know him—or her—by name! Why hadn't she insisted her father tell her? *Because you were too busy trying to ingratiate yourself with him,* whispered the candidly cruel voice of her conscience. *Knowing that he was in an odd sort of mood and terrified that he might put a stop to your allowance—and then where would you be?* She could see the man looking at her quizzically and realised it would look faintly ridiculous if she had to ask him who his employer was! 'Has my host arrived yet?'

The man shook his head. 'Not yet.'

'Perhaps you'd like to take my luggage?' she suggested pointedly.

'Or you could do it yourself?'

Kat stared at him in disbelief. 'I beg your pardon?'

'I'm the engineer,' he said with a shrug. 'Not a baggage handler.'

Somehow she kept her smile fixed to her face. No point in getting into an argument with a deck-hand but she would certainly speak to his boss about his attitude. He would learn soon enough that *nobody* spoke to a Balfour like that. 'Then perhaps you could show me to my cabin,' she said coolly.

'My pleasure.' The man smiled. 'Follow me.'

Kat hadn't carried her own bags since she'd been expelled from her last school. These were heavy and they were cumbersome—and on the too-high shoes she was wearing, it wasn't the easiest task in the world to walk across the gleaming deck with any degree of grace.

If that was bad, then it suddenly began to get worse because just then they arrived at her cabin—and Kat looked around in disbelief. It had been ages since she'd stayed on a yacht, but in the past she had always been given the best and most prestigious accommodation available. Something near the deck, where you could climb out of bed and wander straight outside in the morning and be confronted by the ever-moving splendour of the sea. Or somewhere a little farther down towards the centre of the vessel—which meant that you were in the most stable part of the boat and buffeted from the possibility of too much movement.

But *this*.

Kat looked around. It was *tiny*. A cramped little bunk and barely any wardrobe space. No pictures on the walls and, even worse, *no porthole*! And someone had actually left a drab-looking piece of clothing hanging on the back of the door! She dropped her bags to the ground and turned to the man. 'Listen—'

'The name's Mike,' he interrupted. 'Mike Price.'

She wanted to tell him that his name was of no interest to her and that by the time the day was out he would be looking for a new job, but right then there were more pressing matters on her mind than the man's crass inefficiency and overinflated sense of his own importance. Kat took in a deep breath. 'I think there's been some sort of mistake,' she said crisply.

'How come?'

'This cabin is much too small.'

'It's the one you've been assigned.' He shrugged his shoulders. 'Better take it up with the boss.'

Kat gritted her teeth. If only she knew who the boss was! But by now she knew she couldn't possibly lose face by asking this unhelpful man. 'I don't think you understand—'

'No, I don't think *you* understand,' interrupted the engineer brusquely. 'The boss likes his staff to put up and shut up—that's why he pays them so well.'

'But I'm not a member of staff,' she protested. 'I'm a *guest* here.'

The man's eyes narrowed and then he laughed—as if she'd made some weird kind of joke. 'I don't think so. Or at least, that's not what I've been told.'

Kat felt the first tremor of apprehension. 'What are you talking about?'

Jerking his head in the direction of the garment which had caught her attention when she'd first walked in, Mike reached out and plucked it from the hook before handing it to her.

Kat looked at it blankly. 'What's this?'

'What's it look like?'

It took her a moment to realise—since it wasn't an item of clothing she was familiar with. 'An…an *apron*?' Momentarily, Kat's fingers tightened around the heavy fabric before she pushed it back at him, her heart beating wildly. 'What the hell is going on?'

Mike frowned. 'I think you'd better follow me.'

What could she do, other than what he suggested? Start unpacking all her expensive clothes and attempt to start storing them away in that rabbit's hutch of a room? Or maybe she should do what her gut instinct was telling her—which was to get off the wretched boat and forget about the whole idea of a holiday at sea.

She began to follow him through a maze of wood-lined corridors until at last he threw open a set of double doors and Kat quietly breathed a sigh of relief. Now *this* was more like it.

The room in which she now stood was the polar opposite of the poky cabin she'd just been shown. This had the enormous dimensions she was used to—a grand dining salon set out on almost palatial lines. Inlaid lights twinkled from the ceiling, but these were eclipsed by the blaze of natural light which flooded in through sliding French windows which opened up on to the deck itself.

There was a dining table which would have comfortably seated twelve people—though Kat noticed that only two places had been laid and used. Various open bottles were lined along the gleaming surface and candle wax had dripped all over a bone-china plate. At its centre was a beautiful blue-glass platter of exotic fruits and next to it sat a crystal goblet of flat champagne along with a carelessly abandoned chocolate wrapper.

Kat's lips pursed into a disapproving circle—wondering why on earth a member of staff hadn't bothered to clear it away. 'What a disgusting mess,' she observed quietly.

'Isn't it?' agreed Mike, laughing. 'The boss sure likes to party when he parties!'

So at least she now knew that the 'boss' was a man. And an untidy man, by the look of things. With a sudden smooth purring of powerful engines, the boat began to move—and Kat's eyes widened in surprise. But before she could register her inexplicable panic that they were setting sail so soon, something happened to wipe every thought clean from her mind.

The first was the sight of a bikini top—a flimsy little excuse for a garment in a shimmering gold material which was lying in a discarded heap on the polished oak floor. It was a blatant symbol of decadence and sex and, for a couple of seconds, the blood rushed hotly into her cheeks before she allowed herself to concentrate on the second.

Because the second was a photo of a man.

Kat's heart thundered as she stared at it—recognition hit her like a short sharp slap to the face.

The man in the photo must have been barely out of his teens, yet already his face was sombre and hardened by experience. Black eyes stared defiantly straight into the lens of the camera, and his sensual lips curved an expression which was undeniably formidable.

He was wearing a lavishly embroidered glittering jacket, skintight trousers and some kind of dark and formal hat. It was an image which was unfamiliar and yet instantly recognisable—and it took a few moments for Kat to realise that this was the traditional garb of the bullfighter. But that realisation seemed barely relevant in the light of the horror which was slowly beginning to dawn on her.

That she was staring at a likeness of the young Carlos Guerrero.

Trying to conceal the shaking of her hands, she turned to Mike.

'Whose boat is this?' she croaked.

Mike's blond head was jerked in the direction of the photo, and he smiled. 'His.'

'C-Carlos?' Even saying his name sent shivers down her spine—just as the memory of his harsh words lancing through her still had the power to wound. 'Carlos Guerrero?'

'Sure. Who else?' Mike's expression grew even more curious. 'You didn't know?'

Of course she didn't know! If she had known, then she would never have set foot on the damned vessel—why, she wouldn't have gone within a million miles of it! But there was no way she was going to enlighten this smirking engineer about her misgivings, or the reason for them. She needed to assert her authority and get onto dry land again.

'I think there's been some kind of mix-up,' she said, her smooth tone belying the fast beating of her heart and sudden sense of urgency. 'And I'd like to go ashore. Please.'

'I'm afraid that won't be possible.'

Kat's eyes narrowed. 'What are you talking about?'

'Well, Carlos told me that a new domestic was arriving—and that her name was Kat Balfour.'

One word reverberated around the room and she repeated it, just in case she had misheard it. 'Domestic?' she repeated incredulously.

'Sure. You're Kat Balfour and there's six hungry crew on board.' He smiled. 'And we need someone to clean up after us and make our meals, don't we?'

It was so outrageous a statement to make that for a moment Kat thought he must be having some kind of—extremely unfunny—joke at her expense. As if she was some kind of lowly deck-hand who was about to wait on a load of crew members! But one look at his face told her he was deadly serious. What the *hell* was going on?

'Get me off this wretched boat!' she said, as a sudden wave of panic washed over her. 'And I mean *immediately*!'

Again, he shrugged. 'Sorry, no can do. You'll have to take that up with the boss—I don't have the authority to clear it and we've left shore now. But I wouldn't advise you to try asking him any favours without clearing up this mess first. He'll be here later.'

Carlos Guerrero was coming *here*? Well, of course he was—if it was his boat. Kat blinked, feeling as if she had fallen into the middle of a raging sea, without any way of keeping herself afloat. And then another—equally shocking—thought occurred to her. Her father had arranged this trip for her. And if so—then *why*? Nothing seemed to make sense.

Yet none of that mattered—not now. She could take that up with him some other time. The most important thing was to get away. To run. To escape before…

Before the man who had made her senses scream with longing put in an appearance.

Staring out of the windows to see that the port of Antibes was now just an array of glittering masts and boats in the distance, Kat realised she was trapped. Well and truly trapped—unless she could make this man Mike free her.

'Now listen to me, *Mike*,' she said, emphasising a cut-crystal accent which usually got her exactly what she wanted. 'Are you going to let me go, or not?'

'Sorry, love. No can do. More than my job's worth.'

'Right. Well, then, let me tell *you* something—and you'd better listen carefully. I am *not* your domestic and I am *not* going to cook or clean up for you and your fellow crew members. And what is more, I am certainly not going to clean up the mess left behind by your slob of a boss and his…his…*girl*friend. Do you understand?'

Mike shrugged. 'Loud and clear. Do what you like—I sure wouldn't want to be in your shoes when you tell Carlos that.' He glanced at his watch. 'I'd better get back to the captain. I'll leave you to calm down, and then you can come and find me and I'll show you the galley.'

And without another word, he turned and left, leaving Kat staring after him—shocked and stunned—her heart now racing with a fear which she hadn't felt in a long time. The one which she shoved deep down inside her, whenever it reared its dark and threatening head. That terrible tearing sensation of a hostile situation taking over and rendering her helpless….

Well, she wasn't helpless. And neither was she going to 'calm down' and acquaint herself with a galley she had no intention of ever using! Presumably she was stuck here until Carlos and the owner of the gold bikini top returned. A hot little curl of something which felt like *jealousy* began to unfurl inside her and Kat willed it to go away. She wasn't jealous of any poor unfortunate woman whose bikini top must have been removed by the arrogant Spaniard. Why, she…she *pitied* her—

and what was more, she would have him arrested for kidnap when he finally *did* show his haughty face!

Pulling her cellphone from her bag, she desperately tried to get a connection—but for some reason, it refused to work. Even angrier now, and unable to bear the thought of just sitting there, Kat decided to explore the boat. And it didn't take her long to discover that her first impressions had been spot on. It wasn't just big, it was absolutely vast—and no expense had been spared during its outlay.

There was a cinema, a library and a well-stocked wine cellar—as well as an enormous sitting room which spread out onto the deck area. And she counted five luxury guest suites which even had their own elevator to connect them to the decks. This was wealth on a scale that far outweighed even her father's and briefly Kat found herself wondering how the Spaniard had made his money. Surely not through bullfighting?

By now she was feeling very hungry. It seemed a long time since her flight into France this morning and she never ate the disgusting food they served on scheduled flights. She needed to eat something, but was loath to go down into the galley in case she bumped into any of the other crew. Because wouldn't that seem like some silent admission of defeat?

Instead, she went back into the dining room and looked around to see what was left from the remains of the meal on the table. Not a lot. She ate a banana, two pomegranates and some rich, dark chocolate. And then, more out of defiance than desire, opened a bottle of wine whose label she recognised as being one of the world's finest and poured herself a large glassful.

Never a big drinker, the bouquet and depth of the claret was wasted on her, but at least the wine made her feel better. And more than a little rebellious. Her feelings of disbelief that this should actually be happening to her began increasingly to be replaced with a sense of fury. Just you *wait*, Carlos Guerrero, she vowed silently as she finished off the glass of costly wine and poured herself a second, before flopping down on a wide, squashy sofa which was heaped with cushions and staring out of the windows.

Watching the frilly white tips of the waves as the yacht powered its way over the sapphire sea, Kat was almost halfway through the bottle when she heard a sound which made her heart miss a beat. And then begin to accelerate with excitement.

It was the sound of a rich man's toy. The distinctive whirr-whirr chopping sound from overhead which could mean only one thing—a helicopter! And whoever was flying it would surely take pity on her and whisk her away from this luxurious prison.

Slamming the glass down on the table, Kat lurched to her feet. She would throw herself on the pilot's mercy. Inform him—or her—that she was being held here against her will and that she wished to be taken to the nearest police station.

But her rush to reach the deck and the helicopter pad

seemed blighted—probably due to the amount of alcohol she'd drunk and her high-heeled espadrilles. To her horror, Kat slithered on the wooden floor and ended up sitting slam on her bottom. And by the time she had scrambled to her feet and got her bearings and worked out which of the many doors would give her access to the helicopter pad, she heard the heartbreaking sound of accelerating propellers. Which could only mean one thing. Please, please don't leave without me catching you, she prayed, even as she heard the loud rush of air which indicated that the craft was indeed now heading skywards.

With a small whimper she flung open one of the doors and hurled herself through it—only to be brought up short by a solid object as she cannoned into it.

A very solid object indeed.

'*Buenas tardes, querida,*' came a deeply accented voice which trickled over her senses like thick, dark honey.

And to her horror, Kat found herself staring up into the forbidding features of Carlos Guerrero.

CHAPTER TWO

KAT stared up into icy black eyes which were skating over her with undisguised disapproval. *'You!'* she accused, though her knees had turned to jelly and her heart was thundering so loudly that she felt quite faint. But what woman in the world wouldn't feel the same if confronted with that spectacular physique, clad in close-fitting black jeans and a soft white silk shirt—even if his handsome face was so cold that it might have been sculpted from some glittering piece of dark marble? 'Carlos Guerrero!' she breathed.

'Who were you expecting?' challenged Carlos silkily. 'It *is* my boat after all.'

Trying like mad to control the writhing tumult of her feelings, Kat glared at him. 'I thought…I thought I was in the middle of a nightmare, but it turns out it's true.'

'You mean you don't want to be here?' he mocked, his black eyes piercing into her like twin lasers.

Instinctively she stepped away. Away from the raw, masculine scent of him, and the heat which emanated from his powerful body. Away from the dangerous sizzle of sexuality which surrounded him like a dark and sensual aura and made her want to run her fingers through his riotous black curls.

'I'd rather be anywhere but here—with you,' she said. And yet didn't her words carry a hollow ring to them, because how could she protest at his presence when already she could sense his irresistible magnetism? The kind that made women—and her especially—make complete fools of themselves. Well, not this time—that was for sure. *'Anywhere,'* she finished bitterly.

'I can assure you that the feeling is entirely mutual, *querida.*'

'Then let me go,' she breathed. 'Send for the helicopter and let it take me away.'

'No,' he negated harshly. 'I cannot and I will not.'

Kat looked at him in alarm. 'But you can't keep me here against my will!'

'Can't I?' A slow and mocking smile curved the edges of his lips. 'Aren't you even a little bit curious about why you're here—or did you think I was just longing for a little of your exclusive company?'

'Of course not,' she snapped. 'Any more than I'm longing for yours!'

'Good. Because, believe me—you were never going to be my number-one choice of sailing companion.'

Eyes narrowing, Carlos began to study her. She was beautiful, he conceded reluctantly. Even more beautiful than he remembered. Black hair tumbled like wild, dark silk over her shoulders, and her eyes were the most astonishing shade of blue he'd ever seen, framed by outrageously long, curling black lashes. Her lips were as pink as crushed rose petals—and her body was positively sinful.

Unfashionably curvy, she had the kind of legs which seemed to go on for ever—a fact emphasised by the tiny pair of denim shorts she wore, along with a pair of high-heeled espadrilles which showcased her painted toenails. Luscious-looking breasts were thrusting towards him as if crying out for him to cup them in the palms of his hands—their fullness set off perfectly by the simple white T-shirt which stretched tightly over them. So that they looked like two ripe peaches which had been smothered in cream…

But she left him cold. Completely cold. Her type always did. She was a predatory type of modern woman who flagrantly used her sexuality like a bitch in heat. Who saw what she wanted and then just went right out and took it. His mind took him back to the extravagant ball her family had thrown last year—when she had approached him with all the subtlety of a cheap *prostituta*, and his mouth hardened with remembered contempt.

¡Maldición! It was a pity he was forced to accommodate such a woman as this on the sanctuary of his beloved yacht—but he owed her father. Owed him more than he could ever say. And perhaps it would be amusing to snap this spoiled little madam from out of the privileged bubble in which she seemed to exist.

'Have you qu-quite finished?' questioned Kat in a voice which was shaking with rage and humiliation—for she had never been stared at like that before. She attracted attention, yes—but no man had ever had the temerity to study her as if she was being slowly stripped naked by a pair of contemptuous eyes. *And aren't you shaking for another reason?* questioned a taunting voice in her head. Aren't you shaking because you actually *like* him looking at you like that? Aren't your breasts tingling after his insolent scrutiny—and isn't there a kind of soft, aching pool where the denim is rubbing against the fork of your thighs?

'Finished?' echoed Carlos. 'Why, *querida*—I haven't even started.'

Kat's heart thumped, but she was damned if she would show even a trace of nerves. This man was nothing to her. *Nothing.* Fearlessly, she lifted her chin and iced him a look. 'Would you mind telling me what the hell is going on?'

Black eyes regarded her. 'You don't know anything?'

'Would I be asking if I did?' But then Kat remembered her father's strange reticence to disclose any details about her proposed boat trip, and now as she stared into the hard, cold face of the Spaniard her misgivings began to grow. 'This is something…something which has been cooked up between you and my father, isn't it?'

'Bravo,' he mocked softly, curious to see how she would react.

Kat's hands curled into two fists by the sides of her bare thighs. 'Well, I want to speak to him. Now!'

'Didn't anyone ever teach you to say *please*?'

'I don't really think that you're in a position to give me a lesson in manners when you're the one keeping me prisoner! I want some sort of explanation about why I've been…*kidnapped* by some wretched brute of a man like you!'

Carlos saw the icy blue fire of defiance spitting from her eyes and he felt a sudden rush of blood heating his veins. Oh, but he was going to enjoy taming her. To teach her that she could not just waltz through life, relying on her blindingly beautiful looks and her limitless bank account, taking exactly what she wanted, without a thought as to what the consequences might be.

'Just lose the hysteria—'

'But I—'

'I said *lose it,*' he snapped. 'And come with me.' He walked straight past her into the still-untidy cabin, his eyes narrowing with anger as he registered that she hadn't lifted a finger to clear anything away as he had expressly instructed she do. But he would deal with that. Later. Turning to face her, he pulled a cream envelope from the back pocket of his jeans and handed it to her. 'From your father,' he said.

Snatching the envelope from him, Kat was trembling as she ripped it open and withdrew a large sheet of paper, her eyes scanning over it quickly as she recognised her father's handwriting. *My dearest Kat,* it began.

It was the most bizarre document she had ever seen.

Words flew off the page as if determined to grab her attention and she read them in rapidly mounting disbelief.

Words such as *powerful, proud and loyal*—and they were written in Latin too. *Validus, Superbus quod Fidelis.*

Kat's head was spinning as she read on.

These are the words of our family motto, which for many years used to guide the Balfours. But something else used to guide us too—a set of principles which were known in the family as the rules.

Kat's frown deepened. What on earth was her father going on about? The letter continued.

Of late, these principles have become wilfully neglected and our name has become a laughing stock—both at home and abroad. In many ways, I blame myself. The example I have set to my children over the years has been a poor one, but I am determined that my daughters will not replicate my chequered lifestyle.

Then came the paragraph which made Kat's blood run cold.

Which is why I am cutting off your allowance, Kat, and forcing you to earn your keep for the first time in your life. It will also ensure that you embrace the concept of the word commitment*—*

which is rule 6: run away from your problems once and you will run for ever.

You have spent your whole life running from your problems, Kat, but it is time that you learned to look them in the face. By facing problems, you defeat them. Running away is what cowards do, not Balfours. You need to figure out a direction for your life, instead of just drifting aimlessly. A little hard work might help focus your mind.

This is why I have arranged for you to work your passage on the yacht of Carlos Guerrero. He is a man I know and trust to set you on the right path. He is the only man I have ever seen stand up to you, and you cannot run away while you are at sea! Forgive me for what must seem like an extreme measure, my dearest Kat, but I am confident that one day you will be grateful that I took it.

Your loving father, Oscar

Kat's manicured nails dug into the expensive cream velour paper and it took a moment or two for her to compose herself enough to risk looking Carlos in the face. And when she did, it only increased her ire, for his black eyes were glittering with what looked like *pleasure*, and a smile of satisfaction was curving his lips.

'You knew about this!' she accused.

'Of course I did.'

'Rules? *Rules*,' she spluttered. 'It's outrageous.'

'I quite agree,' he said unexpectedly, and then his

accented voice grew harsh. 'Completely outrageous that a woman of twenty-two has never done an honest day's work in her life!'

Kat swallowed. 'That's none of your business!'

'Oh, but it is, *querida*. Your father has made it my business by electing me as the poor unfortunate who has been forced to employ you—because I doubt that anyone else would!'

'I can't *believe* that Daddy would willingly subject me to…'

The black eyes challenged her. 'To *what, exactamente*?'

'To be holed up with a man who's world famous for his womanising!'

For a moment, Carlos didn't respond. The slur was an oft-repeated one which infuriated the hell out of him, and it was made by the press and the public at large simply because women had a terrible tendency to fall in love with him. And then to talk about it to whoever would listen—the way women always loved to talk when their hearts were smitten. But if he could have a euro for every woman he was supposed to have slept with, then his already-generous bank accounts would be overflowing.

He stared at the stunning brunette—almost marvelling at her gall and wondering how she, of all people, had the nerve to level such an accusation at him.

'But I'm extremely picky where women are concerned—you of all people should know that,' he drawled. 'After all, I turned *you* down, didn't I, *querida*?

Even though you were pretty much begging me to make love to you.'

Kat flushed. Of all the most hateful…*hateful* things he could have said.

But it was true, wasn't it? That was the painful reality of it. She *had* thrown herself at him. Behaved in a way which had been completely foreign to her. Because despite her worldly appearance and air of sophistication, Kat was a disaster where men were concerned.

Sometimes her sisters teased her about her lack of boyfriends and Kat had often wondered if she would ever experience the kind of overwhelming emotional and sexual desire which other women spoke of. And yet she wasn't even sure she wanted to—because getting close to people meant that you could get hurt.

So she hid behind her outrageous outfits, presenting a fashionable, brittle exterior to the world—terrified that somebody would find her out and see through to the gaping insecurities inside. And it had always been easy, because she had never really felt stirred by a man. Not until last year's ball….

The dress she had worn had been pretty daring—even by her standards. Carefully constructed in scarlet satin, the low-cut bodice had left her breasts half bare and the thigh-high slashes of the skirt showed off her long legs as she walked. Precious gems had sparkled in her hair—with the famous Balfour Brilliant winking in a provocative diamond teardrop between her breasts.

Kat remembered descending the stairs into the grand

ballroom, aware that all eyes had turned to watch her, but she had felt oblivious to their interest…as if she was half asleep, like a person in a dream.

And then she had seen him. Standing out among the hundreds of other guests like a bright planet in a clear night sky. Her heart had begun to thunder powerfully with some kind of ancient recognition and in that single moment she had understood what all the fuss was about. Why women fell in love at first sight. And why it could happen without reason, or warning.

Carlos Guerrero.

He had been wearing a formal suit—the stark black clothes exquisitely tailored to emphasise every hard sinew of his impressive physique and his long, lean legs and narrow hips. His black hair had been longer than the other men's in the ballroom—and wilder too. Yes, that was the best way to describe what Carlos Guerrero had looked like that night—there was a sense that beneath the immaculate exterior, he was untamed. Proud, dangerous and sexy—he seemed more alive than anyone else she'd ever set eyes on, and just looking at him sparked a longing as old as time.

The only problem was that he was with a woman—a serene-looking woman who barely wore a scrap of make-up—but then, she didn't really need to. Not when you were as naturally beautiful as that. Kat remembered her dismay as she'd stared at his partner's soft, even features and the elegant chignon of her hair. Her gown was a fluid fall of cream, quietly emphasising a stunning figure, and two luminous pearl studs gleaming at her ears were her only adornment.

Kat had suddenly felt like an overdressed Christmas tree in comparison—yet that didn't stop her wanting the man with a hunger which made her feel positively weak.

But he had refused to play ball—his black eyes had been cold, his manner dismissive, when she was introduced to him. Carlos Guerrero was his name, and she remembered thinking that it was the most gorgeous name in the world.

Kat did everything to get him to notice her—but because she'd never had to try with a man before, she tried too hard. Much too hard. Every time she thought he was watching her, she had played up to it like mad. Tipping her head back and giggling. Letting her eyes close in dreamy surrender. Yet she might as well have been trying to get a reaction from a stone for all the good it did. Until at last, when his lovely partner had disappeared in the direction of the cloakrooms, Kat had spotted him going out onto the terrace. And shamelessly she had followed him.

The moon had been full, the night thick with the scent of jasmine and honeysuckle, and there was an air of promise bubbling within her—a sense that, in that moment, anything was possible if only she had the courage to reach out and take it. Overladen with unfamiliar longing, Kat had walked towards him.

'Hello,' she said softly.

His black eyes had narrowed and he had nodded his

head in a kind of resigned recognition. 'You're the woman who's been flirting with me so outrageously all evening,' he said slowly.

'H-have I?' Thankfully, the darkness had hidden her sudden rise in colour. But hadn't her sisters told her that it was an equal world now and that women could approach men these days, if they really wanted to? 'I wondered, would you...would you like to dance?' she had asked, her careless tone disguising the fierce pounding of her heart but she could feel the tightening of her breasts as she moved a little closer.

She would remember the look on his face for as long as she lived. Something which looked uncomfortably like anger and which quickly grew into cold contempt as he briefly stared down at the large diamond which glittered between the scrap of scarlet satin straining over her bust.

'Do you always behave like such a tramp, *querida*?' he bit out with soft derision. 'So that you flaunt your wares like a trader in the marketplace? Or do you only want a man when he is with someone else?'

Cringing beneath the icy disdain in the Spaniard's eyes, Kat barely noticed the figure who had now appeared in the doorway and who stood watching them.

'B-but—'

Putting his mouth to her ear so that only she could hear, she would never forget his contemptuous words.

'You are dressed like a hooker and you are behaving like a hooker!' he had hissed. 'So why don't you go and cover yourself up, and then take the time to learn a few lessons on the correct way to conduct yourself in public.'

After this blistering attack, he had sauntered back into the ballroom—past her father, who had silently been observing them—and returned to the beautiful woman in cream. Where, according to her sisters, he had tenderly wrapped her in a soft shawl and had taken her off into the night—leaving Kat alone with her shame and her disbelief that she could have behaved in such a way. That she could have been so *predatory.*

Her sisters had also taken great delight in informing her that not only was the man a famous ex-bullfighter, but that he could have his pick of the most gorgeous women in the world. Which had only made her feel worse.

And that had been the last time she'd seen Carlos Guerrero.

Until now.

Painful memories cleared and Kat realised that the Spaniard was watching her and that she was still holding the letter from her father which had put her in this man's power.

So forget the terrible way you behaved and the cruel way he rebuffed you. That's all in the past now. Why not appeal to his sense of logic instead? Forcing a smile, she turned to him. 'Look, Carlos, you can't want this any more than I do,' she urged.

Carlos considered her words. When her father had asked him to employ her, his first instinct had been to bat the suggestion away. Because he wasn't into playing mentor. Particularly not to spoiled little rich girls who lived their lives like greedy children let loose in a candy store.

So why the hell *hadn't* he refused this challenge?

Because Oscar Balfour had been good to him, had helped him set up the property business which had made him a very wealthy man indeed. For there had been a time when nobody wanted to know the angry young Spaniard battling to make a new life for himself. When Carlos had been nothing but an ex-matador who had spent every penny he'd earned, Oscar had taken a risk by giving him a sizeable loan. Had trusted him at a time when few others had—and a man never forgot something like that.

No, he could not have turned down Oscar's request—no matter how unwanted the suggestion had been.

'Since you ask—no, I don't want this at all. I have much better things to do with my time than playing nursemaid to a spoiled brat,' he said coolly. 'But my wishes are irrelevant. Your father asked for my help, and so I'm giving it. I owe him.' He shrugged. 'And it wasn't exactly onerous to employ you on my boat. I'm always looking for an extra pair of hands.'

Kat shook her head. 'You want money?' she questioned desperately. 'I can write you a cheque if you set me free.'

For a moment Carlos shook his head, appalled by the sheer impudence of her offer. Did she think that he could be bought, or that money could buy her out of any tight corner? He guessed she did—for hadn't it been lavished on her during all her life? Suddenly, he found himself remembering the unalloyed poverty of his early years. Of the way his mother had spent every waking hour cleaning for the rich—her careworn hands red and cracked, her eyes dark from lack of sleep. And Carlos felt another wave of contempt for this girl who had always had things so easy.

'You forget that buying your way out is no longer an option since your father has cut off your allowance,' he drawled.

'But I have money I can access!' she declared. 'Jewels I can sell!'

'Just not when you're in the middle of the Mediterranean, hmm?' he countered sarcastically.

And suddenly the reality of the situation hit her. Him. And her—stuck in a boat whose dimensions seemed to be diminishing by the second. 'I'm...I'm sure we can come to *some* sort of agreement,' she said wildly.

'I don't think so.' The black eyes narrowed and he glanced over to the tight, white T-shirt and the tops of her bare brown thighs which were so graphically showcased in the tiny pair of shorts. 'Unless you're offering payment in kind, of course?' he added insultingly, his voice soft. 'You're certainly dressed as if you are.'

It took Kat a moment for his words to register, and when she realised exactly what he meant she felt a strange, burning fury—and a renewed sense of rebellion.

How could she bear to be trapped on board with such a powerfully attractive man as this—especially when he had made his contempt for her so apparent? Expected to cook and clear up after him like a servant! Heart now pounding with anticipation of what she was about to do, Kat gave him one final glare of defiance.

'Maybe you're used to paying for sex!' she retorted, and had the brief satisfaction of seeing his lips tighten in anger. 'And maybe you're used to calling all the shots. But not this time. I won't be kept prisoner here by you, Señor Guerrero!'

Without warning, she ran across the salon and out onto the deck, tearing off her espadrilles before scrambling up the side of the guard-rail. At least it was as wide as a small ledge. Wide enough to dive from.

For a few seconds, Kat experienced a moment of wild exhilaration as she stared down into the dark sapphire of the sea, before taking a deep, deep breath. And then, with the sound of Carlos Guerrero's furious shouts ringing in her ears, she plunged into the blue water beneath.

CHAPTER THREE

THE shock of impact and the cold temporarily winded her, but Kat was a good swimmer—when she'd lived in Sri Lanka, she'd spent so much time in the water that they used to call her Little Fish. But the trouble was that swimming in pools or striking out from a beach was quite different to swimming in deep sea like this, and it took only minutes for the enormity of what she'd done to sink in. Her limbs felt heavy and weighted—the denim shorts seeming to weigh a ton—and it occurred to her that she had drunk two glasses of wine and that her judgement may have been blunted. But still she kept striking out—and it seemed more as if she was lashing out against life, and fate. Hot tears of fury mingled with the salt of the sea on her face, until she realised that she was in danger of getting completely exhausted, and so she began to tread water.

Turning on her back, she could see that the *Corazón Frío* had stopped, and that a little boat had been lowered and was heading her way—but before it could reach her, something else did. Or rather, someone. A streamlined body which was powering its way through the water towards her and which suddenly emerged from the depths like some golden-wet colossus.

Sleek black hair plastered to his skull, Carlos reached out and caught hold of her, his face contorted with fury. But the relief he felt at having located her was overwhelming and it washed over him in a great wave. *The little fool. The stupid little fool.*

'Let me—' uselessly, Kat wriggled against the formidable strength of his body '—go!'

His mouth was close to her wet ear as he trod water, her breasts flattened against his chest as his hands tightened around her waist and held her closer. 'You are not going *anywhere*, *querida*,' he gasped. 'You will stay right here until the tender reaches us—or you'll have us both damned well drowned!'

The awful thing was that for the first time in her life Kat felt safe. Truly and properly safe. His arms were so strong and powerful and his hold on her so firm that she felt as if nothing or no one could hurt her just as long as this man was holding her. And how crazy was that—in view of the circumstances? If she could place her trust and her confidence in a man who clearly despised her, then surely that really *did* mean her judgement was terminally flawed.

'Damn you,' she whispered shakily.

'No, damn *you*,' he shot back furiously. 'I was warned that you liked running away—but nobody told me you'd be a liability!'

The boat reached them, with Mike at the helm, and Kat was helped aboard—acutely aware that the flat of Carlos's palm was shoving firmly on one sodden denim-covered buttock from behind. Then he levered himself up and into the boat and helped to sit her down. His feet were bare, the black jeans were soaking and the white silk shirt now clung to his chest like a second skin—the fabric so fine that she could see the whorls of black hair through it. Suddenly, Kat felt quite weak as he crouched down beside her, placing one hand at the small of her back to help support her.

A pair of stony black eyes were levelled at her. 'Don't ever try pulling a stunt like that again,' he warned softly. 'Understand?'

Kat was aware that Mike had his back to them as he steered the little boat towards the yacht. Was he diplomatically pretending not to listen, or would it even make any difference if he was? If she started screaming hysterically like one of those women in an old black-and-white movie, was it likely that Mike would turn round to the 'boss' he clearly revered and demand that he return her to shore immediately? No, it was not.

Which meant she was stuck here. Stuck with the only man she'd ever felt a physical connection towards—and still did, if she was honest. Even when she was physically and mentally exhausted.

'Understand?' repeated Carlos.

Staring into eyes which were as emotionless as rock

itself, Kat swallowed down the salt taste of the sea. 'Do I have any choice?' she questioned bitterly.

'No, *querida*, you do not—other than to work your way on this voyage and prove that you can do it. To stand on your own two feet for once…if you think you can.' Black eyes challenged her. 'After that, you can walk away and we need never set eyes on each other again.'

The aftermath of all the emotion suddenly hit her like a roller coaster, along with a dull aching which had now begun to gather at the front of her forehead, and Kat began to shiver uncontrollably.

Carlos frowned, but the arm which was still at her slender back tightened by a fraction. Her face was white—almost translucent—and her lips were turning a faintly blue colour. *Y por Dios*—but she suddenly looked fragile. Like a little doll who might snap in two.

'Hurry up!' he snapped at Mike as the small craft moved alongside the larger vessel. 'She's freezing!'

Kat was vaguely aware of being lifted onto the deck of the *Corazón Frío* and aware too that Carlos had curtly dismissed Mike and the rest of the crew who had appeared to help.

And then, to her astonishment, he picked her up as if he picked up full-grown women every day of the week, and carried her along one of the wood-lined corridors to some sort of cabin. But it wasn't the same poky little cabin which Mike had taken her to earlier.

Dazed by shock and the sensation of being held within his strong arms, she looked around at the unfamiliar luxurious surroundings. 'Th-this isn't m-my c-cabin,' she protested, her teeth chattering uncontrollably as he set her down. Her eyes widened as her heart began an erratic pounding. 'It's n-not *yours*, is it?'

'Mine?' Carlos gave a forbidding smile as he set her back down on her feet. 'Please don't overestimate your appeal, *querida*. I don't take idle little rich girls to my bed.'

His cruel words should have hurt but Kat was now feeling so numb that she could barely move, let alone protest at his rudeness. Disconcertingly, he had started tugging at her top and she could feel the sudden heat of his hand against her frozen skin.

'W-what do you think you're doing?' she breathed.

'What the hell does it look like?' he demanded, but his voice sounded distorted and he hated the sudden urgent escalation of his heart. Damn her, he thought—and damn her sleek and inviting body! 'I'm getting you out of these wet clothes before I have to cable ashore for a doctor.'

Kat expelled a shallow breath because even through her icy confusion she liked the feel of his skin against her skin. She liked it a lot. She felt faint as he peeled off the sodden T-shirt and saw his body tense as he tossed it aside, a look of grim determination etched on his face. Next, he began undoing her bra with lightning-fast dexterity, until that was also cast unceremoniously to the floor. Then, pushing her down on the bed with a touch which was more gentle than she would ever have expected, he tossed a blanket over her. A blanket so warm and so soft that it felt as if she had been enveloped in a cloud. Teeth still chattering, Kat clutched at it with convulsive fingers.

'That's b-bliss,' she stumbled, her eyelids feeling weighted as the temptation to sleep began to steal over her.

'Take off those damned shorts,' he demanded on a snarl, but either she wasn't listening or she hadn't heard him. Or maybe she was in shock. He remembered the scent of wine on her breath and his mouth hardened. Or drunk.

Carlos had been the greatest bullfighter of his generation and the adroitness of his wrist action had caused ecstatic crowds to sigh in admiration. Yet such skilfulness had bizarrely deserted him when it came to removing a tiny pair of soaking denim shorts from the delectable bottom of Miss Kat Balfour. His only saving grace was that she seemed scarcely aware of the exquisite torture she was unknowingly inflicting upon him.

Only when a tiny thong had been tugged down over her goose-bumpy thighs, and she was completely naked beneath the blanket, did he step away—and then very gingerly, for he was more aroused than he had been in a long time. *¡Maldición!*

Picking up another of the cashmere throws, he floated that down over her for good measure and heard her sigh before she snuggled down into its soft folds. Her eyelids had fluttered to a close and rested on her pale cheeks in two dark feathery arcs. Her lips—now restored to a rose-petal hue—were parted and she gave a soft sigh and snuggled into the pillow while he watched her. With her damp hair fanned over the pillow, she looked pure—almost innocent.

But appearances could be deceptive, he reminded himself acidly, forcing himself to remember all the reasons why he disliked her. Predatory, unscrupulous and spoiled—she was antithesis of all the qualities he admired in a woman. Carlos admired hard work and humility far more than privilege, or position.

He had appeared at her family ball with a woman on his arm, but Kat Balfour hadn't cared about that, had she? No. She hadn't cared about a thing except homing in on him like a sex-seeking missile. Why, even when she was half drowned she was somehow managing to send out the instinctive message of the siren.

And just for a moment back then, he had responded, hadn't he? Responded big time.

Carlos's mouth hardened with fury at his own susceptibility. He should have demanded that her father pay him danger money to have taken on this task. Better still, he should have told Oscar Balfour to find someone else. But it was too late to back out now. And surely this snip of an Englishwoman—no matter how flighty or petulant—could never be compared to the challenges he had faced in the bullring?

Her arm had moved back to lie above her head and he stared down at the diamond-encrusted wristwatch which dangled from her fragile wrist—an expensive-looking piece which looked as if it was completely wrecked by sea water. He saw the outline of her luscious curves beneath the fine cashmere and knew he did not dare risk removing the watch. Not unless he planned to wake her up in a way which he could—suddenly and inexplicably—imagine all too vividly….

His throat thickening, Carlos walked over to the door and snapped out the light, knowing that he had to get the hell out of there.

CHAPTER FOUR

KAT awoke to an unfamiliar room and an unfamiliar feeling.

Eyelids fluttering open, she gazed around in confusion as she registered the strange rocking sensation, trying to work out where she was and how she'd got here. The room was luxurious, lined with gleaming wood and Venetian mirrors. Persian rugs lay strewn on the floor and she could see her two bags standing next to the wardrobe. And hanging on the back of the door was that damned apron. She was on Carlos Guerrero's luxury yacht!

Groaning, she propped herself up on the bank of soft pillows. She was lying on top of a huge bed, covered by two enormous cashmere throws. And... Kat froze as the palms of her hands skated down over her body as if to verify her initial fears. Because beneath the blankets she was *completely naked.*

That would explain the unfamiliar feeling. She always slept covered up. Always. Cosy, warm pyjamas in winter and a lightweight cotton-lawn version during the warmer weather. It dated back to childhood—a habit she'd never quite got out of, a habit more deeply engrained by never quite knowing what the night might throw at you….

With a start, she sat up, her eyes automatically straying to her wristwatch and blinking in confusion to see that it was shiny with droplets of water—and that it had stopped completely.

Haphazardly events came flooding back in a disconcerting stream. Being tricked onto the yacht and told that she was to be some sort of servant to Carlos Guerrero. And then… Kat bit her lip as she remembered trying to flee. Diving overboard into the Mediterranean and Carlos coming after her and bringing her back. *Had she really done something that crazy?*

Hanging over the back of the chair were her little denim shorts, T-shirt, her bra and tiny thong—and with a heated rush of blood to her cheeks, Kat recalled Carlos peeling the garments from her body. *And the way that had made her feel.*

Locking the door and picking up one of her bags, she stumbled into the bathroom, shocked at the sight of her white face and the mess of black hair. But a hot shower and an intense toothbrushing session soon had her feeling almost normal as she riffled through her bags for something to wear. But what? The clothes she'd brought had been chosen for the purpose of not doing very much at all—other than lazing around on deck and relaxing in the sun.

Yet since she had been duped into coming here, why should she care that many of the outfits at her disposal were completely inappropriate for her lowly new post? Especially when there was *no way* she was going to take that post on—no matter what her father said!

Defiantly, Kat pulled a slithery silk slip-dress over her head. It was made by that season's hottest new designer and it had sold out weeks before it had even hit the shelves. Only the favoured few had managed to get their hands on it—and Kat had been among them. Falling to mid-thigh, it showed off the even caramel tan of her legs and was an extremely flattering fit—so why *shouldn't* she wear it?

But her heart was pounding with something which felt like trepidation, as she went off to find Carlos Guerrero.

Guided by the strong aroma of coffee which was drifting in from the direction of one of the decks, she stepped out into brilliant light, blinking a little and wondering if she should go back for a hat. Sunlight was dancing in a frenzied light show on the sapphire sea, and the sky was a piercingly clear shade of azure. At any other time and in any other place, Kat might have sighed and simply appreciated the scenic splendour—but now her attention was elsewhere. Diverted to the infinitely more human splendour which was lying just a few short feet away....

Carlos was sprawled on some sort of huge chaise longue—tapping away at some sleek-looking computer, wearing a pair of low-slung white jeans, an open white shirt and a pair of dark shades. Nearby, was a large table on which stood a steaming coffee pot and a basket of different breads. But despite the sudden gnawing hunger at her stomach, Kat paid the food no attention.

For a moment she simply stood there and observed the man whose blue-black hair glinted in the sunlight. Powerful and lean, his body looked indolent and relaxed—the way you sometimes saw those black pumas in wildlife programmes looking when they'd just been fed. Kat's stomach flipped as she registered the broad shoulders, the narrow jut of his hips and the long legs which seemed to go on for ever. And yet coupled with her undeniable attraction towards him was a faint sense of wariness and the reluctant acknowledgement that this was the kind of man whose will could never be bent to the wishes of a woman…

Carlos glanced up as Kat walked out on deck towards him and felt his body tense. He wondered if she realised that the powerful sun was angling on her tiny sundress and outlining her body in eye-popping detail, making it appear as if she wasn't wearing anything at all.

Of course she realised, he told himself cynically. Women like her used their clothes to showcase their sexuality. A sexuality which she seemed to have no qualms about putting out at every opportunity and which he was just going to have to ignore. His mouth hardened as he averted his eyes from her magnificent breasts.

'So you have decided to grace us with your presence at last,' he observed coolly.

And stupidly, despite his disparaging tone, Kat's heart began beating furiously. 'Wh-what time is it?'

'Eleven.'

'In the morning?'

He glanced around at the gold-dappled splendour of the deck. 'We don't usually have sunshine at eleven in the evening,' he answered sardonically. 'Even in the Mediterranean.'

'Eleven!' she exclaimed, ignoring his sarcasm. 'You mean I've slept for…for…'

'Hours,' he agreed tightly. 'Too much burning the candle at both ends, no doubt. Either that or the wine you drank made you sleep.' He lifted the dark shades away from his eyes and stared directly into her face, fixing her with a glittering black gaze. 'And I see that you opened the Pétrus.'

Kat remembered the anger she had felt at being trapped and told she was to work on the Spaniard's yacht. Remembered too the discarded gold bikini top—and once again a stab of something which felt uncomfortably like jealousy unsettled her. So what if she *had* drunk half a bottle of his very expensive wine? 'Sorry. I just couldn't resist it,' she said guilelessly. 'Was it very expensive?'

There was a pause. 'Very.'

'Oh.' She opened her eyes very wide. Maybe if she annoyed him enough he might drive her to the nearest shore himself. 'And did you mind?'

Mind? What he minded more than anything was her

careless attitude and the way those bright blue eyes sparked at him so defiantly. She *wanted* him to mind, he realised, and would have liked to have shown his displeasure in a very primitive way indeed. By upending her on his lap and slapping the palm of his hand against her delectable bottom. 'You have very good taste in wine, *querida*,' he observed.

Kat stared at him suspiciously. This was not the reaction she was expecting. 'I…I have?'

'*Sí. Absolutamente.* There will, of course, have to be some adjustment to your wages as a consequence.' He shrugged as he saw her perfect lips part in a disbelieving circle. 'Though naturally, it will simply be a token gesture, since no galley-hand could ever afford to pay the full price for such a bottle of wine.'

Suspicion turned to frustration. 'You're not still maintaining this fiction about me working on your boat, are you?' she demanded.

Carlos pushed his laptop into a shady corner beneath the lounger and rose effortlessly to his feet. 'I can assure you that it is not a fiction, Kat. It is a done deal and I have given my word to your father that I will employ you—despite the fact that you do not seem to have a single useful qualification to your name.'

'That's none of your business—'

'I'm afraid it is. I have agreed to take you on—and one of the first things you'd better learn is that as a member of my crew you will be expected to be punctual at all times.'

'But I'm not—'

'I am not interested in your objections.' Once again, his clipped words sliced through her stumbled responses. 'All I know is that you've made an appalling start.' His gaze flicked over the mutinous tremble of her lips and he felt an undeniable beat of pleasure. 'However, in view of the *exceptional* circumstances, I'll let you off this time—just don't try it again. In future I want you on deck by seven. The crew can fix themselves breakfast, but I expect you to attend to what I like. Good coffee, a little fruit and some bread. My needs are very simple.' His eyes mocked her. 'You'll make a light lunch for everyone and a rather more elaborate meal for the evening. And you'll be expected to keep the decks and cabins clean, though obviously not the crew's. Understand?'

There was a moment of disbelieving silence while Kat looked at him with shock and dislike as he shot out his list of outrageous demands. 'No, I don't think *you* understand,' she answered furiously. 'You've had your little *joke*, Carlos, but it's gone on for long enough. I don't want to stay here and I don't want to work for you. I…I want to go back to shore.' There was a pause while he looked at her expectantly and she forced herself to say it, even though the word felt as if it might choke her. 'Please.'

Carlos clapped his hands in mock applause. '*¡Bravo!*' he said silkily. 'We make progress! The spoiled Englishwoman—she learns what it is to be polite!'

Kat looked at him hopefully. 'So you'll take me?'

'I cannot,' he snapped. 'Surely your attention span isn't so short that you've already forgotten the letter from your father which you read last night?'

She thought back to that ridiculous set of rules her father had set out—the one Carlos had presented her with when he'd arrived on board. 'Of course I haven't forgotten, but my father has clearly taken leave of his senses!'

'Wrong again.' Carlos's lips flattened into an uncompromising line. 'In fact, I think his intervention is long overdue and it's time you stopped acting like a spoilt little princess. One who snaps her fingers and thinks the world owes her a living. An overindulged rich girl who sees just what she wants and then takes it. I cannot believe that nobody has ever accused you of it before. *Princesa.*'

Kat stood as he taunted her with the word, but now her heart had begun to thunder erratically as ice-cold tentacles of fear began to tiptoe down her spine, in spite of the warmth of the morning sun. Fear that she usually kept battened down, hidden away like a dark secret. Didn't he realise that she, of all people, couldn't cope with the idea of being trapped? That she had witnessed enough violence and horror to last a lifetime—and that sometimes she needed to run from those memories. Quite literally, to run.

Like a dark and acrid poison, reminders of that time rose up in her mind, but she blocked them. The way she'd been blocking them ever since her world had been turned upside down by the death of her stepfather and nothing had ever been the same again. She never talked about it with anyone. *Anyone.* Not all the counsellors or psychologists they'd paid for over the years. Not her mother or her father. *Nobody.* And she certainly wasn't going to start with this arrogant beast of a man who seemed to bring out the very worst in her.

'I am not going to stay here slaving away for an arrogant man who insults me,' she blurted out. 'And what is more, you can't force me to!'

'Oh, but I can. And I will,' he returned implacably as he rose from the table. 'One day you may even thank me for it.'

'The hell I will!'

He gave a short laugh. 'Oh, but I can see that you are in urgent need of subduing, *Princesa.* And if you're planning any more theatrical displays like diving in and swimming to shore, then forget it. I might not be so inclined to jump in and save you next time.'

He saw her bright blue gaze moving distractedly round the deck, as if searching there for some other kind of getaway. 'What's more, if you're thinking you might spirit yourself away on one of my motorboats, I'd better warn you that I'll be keeping all the ignition keys close to me. And the rest of the crew have instructions not to take you ashore, no matter how beguilingly you decide to ask them.' His black eyes glittered a stark warning. 'So don't bother wasting your time trying to escape.'

Kat stared at him. If being trapped with him wasn't

bad enough, his cavalier and *patronising* attitude made it a hundred times worse.

And suddenly, all her feelings of hurt and rage and frustration welled up into an urgent need to make him realise that she meant what she said.

'Let me off this boat at once, you…you…overbearing…*beast*!' she half sobbed, launching herself towards him before she stopped to think about the wisdom of her actions, drumming her fists furiously against the rock-solid wall of his chest. *'Just let me go!'*

For a moment, Carlos didn't react to the warm intoxication of her proximity and the realisation that the soft curve of her hips was only a thrust away. He was known for his restraint, for a steely self-control which had seen him turn down more women than most men would dream of.

And yet now he could feel the first stealthy silken tug of sexual awakening as the coldly analytical side of his brain fought against the escalating clamour of his senses.

His mouth hardened. He didn't even *like* Kat Balfour. So why was his body hardening with unbearable tension, its demands beginning to wash over him in hot, sweet waves?

'Let me *go*!' she repeated, as the drumming of her fists increased.

'No,' he grated, staring down into her bright blue eyes with dislike. 'What a little hypocrite you are, Kat. Women who want men to let them go don't start pressing themselves against them and flaunting their bodies in such a way that shows they're just begging to be kissed. Do they?'

She opened her mouth to deny it but as she stared up into his face she could see that his eyes were no longer like stone. In fact, they blazed like ebony fire as they raked over her. And despite the condemnation in his tone, Kat's words died on her lips as, with a growl of desire and fury, Carlos lowered his head towards hers and began to kiss her.

She swayed as she felt the hard pressure of his mouth driving down on hers, clutching at the silken-clad expanse of his shoulders, her thoughts swirling as their flesh met and melded. This was *bliss*, she thought distractedly, as she clung to him, heart beginning to pound as she felt the first flick of his tongue. Wasn't this how a kiss was *supposed* to feel? What she'd been holding out for all her life? *'Oh,'* she moaned helplessly, as the pressure of his lips increased. 'Oh!'

¡Dios!

Carlos felt her instant capitulation, as sweet and responsive as he had guessed she might be. As he deepened the kiss, he could feel her breasts peaking against him. Sweet, neat breasts—like tender peaches just waiting to be bitten into. He wanted to take one into his hand, to rub his thumb against its ripe nub. And then to delve his fingers beneath the soft silk of her sinful little dress, to discover if she was wearing proper panties this time. Or another of those X-rated G-strings…

For several agonisingly tempting moments, he

imagined plunging into her, imagined her hungry little cries as she urged him on. And then, just as suddenly as the kiss had started, he tore his lips away from hers, stepping back as if she was contaminated, his furious gaze raking over her flushed cheeks and darkened eyes.

Frustrated desire found an outlet in heated accusation as he willed the frantic thudding of his heart to lessen and the fierce aching at his groin to stop throbbing and tormenting him. 'Do you always act like this—like a sex-starved tramp?' he demanded unevenly. 'Are you one of these women who are ruled by the hunger of their bodies, perhaps—who grab at the nearest man whenever he happens to be available?'

The harsh words hurt, but presumably that had been his intention. 'C-can't the same be said about you?' she shot back, stung, because he was so wrong in his character assessment of her that it would have been almost laughable had it not been quite so insulting. Clamping her arms around her still-tender breasts she hid her arousal and confusion behind a shield of sarcasm. 'I mean, obviously you have a fantastic technique—'

'That was never in any doubt, *Princesa.*'

'I'm just appalled at my own reaction to an uncaring brute like you,' she choked. 'Especially since you had another woman in your arms only yesterday!'

Carlos found his gaze drawn irresistibly to the rapid rise and fall of her breasts which she was trying and failing to hide. 'I had another woman in my arms only yesterday,' he repeated slowly.

'The woman in the gold bikini!' she accused, hating the shaft of pure jealousy which shot through her.

'The woman in the gold bikini?'

'Will you stop repeating everything I say?'

'Then would you mind explaining what the hell you're talking about?'

'The gold bikini top,' elaborated Kat bitterly. 'The one I found along with the remains of the meal in the dining room!'

'Ah, yes!' A slow and glittering smile of comprehension began to curve at Carlos's lips as he remembered. 'Tania Stephens…I had forgotten all about that.'

Kat felt sick, appalled at her own behaviour. She had been…been… Well, if she were being absolutely honest, hadn't she been like the softest putty in his hands? Wouldn't she still be writhing pleasurably beneath his practised caresses if he hadn't put a stop to it so abruptly? And yet he'd been doing the same thing to another woman only yesterday and had *forgotten all about it*! Didn't that speak volumes about his attitude to women in general and her in particular? What a lucky escape she had had!

'You make love to a woman and less than twenty-four hours later you've "forgotten all about it"?' she breathed in disbelief.

'I did not make love to her.'

Kat's heart pounded. 'So a woman's gold bikini top just *happens* to be lying discarded on the floor of your dining room, along with evidence of some intimate little meal *à deux*—and yet you claim to know nothing about it?'

'That's not what I said,' he snapped. 'I said that I didn't make love to her.'

'But...but she wanted to?'

There was a pause. 'Of course she did,' he agreed softly. 'All women want me to make love to them. Didn't you demonstrate that yourself only moments ago?'

Kat flinched at the accusation, but she couldn't deny it, could she? 'So who was she?' she questioned.

'A journalist.' Carlos allowed himself a brief, hard smile. 'Who I heard was doing a feature on me—and so I invited her here to find out what angle she was taking, and whether or not I needed to persuade her to adopt a different one.'

'Why would anyone want to do a feature on you?'

Black eyes challenged her. 'Any ideas?'

'Because you're rich? Or because you're unbearable?'

He gave a soft laugh. 'Wealth is hardly an achievement in its own right. You of all people should know that, *Princesa*.'

And then she remembered the photo. That startling photo. The young Carlos wearing the richly ornate jacket of the bullfighter—his face just as proud and as beautiful as it was now, but without the cynicism which time had etched onto the features of his older self.

'Bullfighting,' she said slowly. 'She wanted to talk to you about bullfighting.'

There was the beat of a pause. 'Of course she did,' he said slowly. 'They always want to talk about bullfighting.'

'But why?' Kat stared at him. 'Because it's exciting—or because hardly anyone does it as a career choice?'

'Both those things, but it is a little more complex than that.' He met the question in her eyes. 'It's fifteen years since I left the ring, and she's just digging around because she wants to know why.'

'And why did you leave?'

'You think I want to talk about it with someone like you?' he queried softly. 'A woman whose definition of a hard day's work is painting her own nails because the manicurist happens to be off sick?'

He saw her flinch but Carlos didn't care. Couldn't she take the truth about the kind of woman she was? He had vowed never to talk of those days, to relive the pain and the torture which had raged inside him during his tumultuous years in the ring. A pain which had little to do with the noble bullfight itself, and more to do with the cruel father who had made his life such a torment.

The journalist had tried every trick in the book to get him to talk, and a couple more besides. She had certainly been enterprising, he would say that for her. The editor had probably selected her for her beauty and her sheer ruthlessness. So that when the lunchtime interview had not been progressing as she'd wished, she had suggested sunbathing. And then laughingly stripped off her bikini top as if it had been the most natural thing in the world.

He had been aroused, yes—of course he had. The woman's breasts had been full and pale and her glossy lips had parted as if to demonstrate that she was very accomplished with her mouth. But sex offered to him on a plate had never been his thing.

He looked down into the blue eyes of the Balfour girl. Maybe he should tell *her* that and have done with it—because, in effect, wasn't she doing exactly the same? Trying to twist him round her little finger with her come-to-bed eyes and pouting lips. Perhaps he should tell her that no matter how much she tried to tempt him, she was here to do a job and nothing more. He had given his word to her father that he would teach her something in the way of commitment, and Carlos always kept his word.

So why had he kissed her? And why was the memory of that kiss making him grow hard even now? So hard that he would have liked to have taken hold of her aristocratic hips and thrust right into her.

'You'd better have some breakfast,' he said harshly. 'And then start by clearing away the mess in the dining room.'

Kat met the stony black gaze. 'And if I don't?'

He thought how beautiful she looked when she defied him. 'If you don't? Then, *Princesa*, I will quickly lose patience with you, and I don't think that's such a good idea,' he answered. 'You might do well to remember that the sooner you start fulfilling your obligations, the sooner you can leave—and free us both from this infernal incarceration.'

Shaken, Kat stood watching as he walked away from her, her eyes drawn to the graceful movement of his white-jeaned physique and the way the silk shirt billowed slightly in the breeze. Unthinkingly, she touched her fingertips to her lips—to where the tender flesh still tingled with the heat of his passionate kiss—and she felt the corresponding thunder of her heart as she remembered it. But the kiss meant *nothing,* she reminded herself—and Carlos couldn't have made that clearer.

She wondered if he'd gone off to work in one of the warren of luxurious rooms which lay below the deck, but it wasn't until a few minutes later when she heard the throaty roar of a powerful engine that she realised that he'd gone. Properly gone.

Racing over to the side of the yacht, she saw a flash of silver as a powerful little motorboat cut through the sapphire waters. The wind streamed through the wild black curls of the man who stood at the helm and the sun had illuminated his olive skin into dark gold. He looked, she thought, like some powerful and formidable god of a man.

For one split second, their eyes met—and Kat registered the implacable coldness in his gaze, with barely a flicker of recognition or acknowledgement on his stony features. Was he demonstrating the fact that he was free to come and go as she was not? Or was he silently laughing at her and her lowly predicament?

She turned away and looked around the deck. Either way, she was trapped here—with a list of menial chores to do for a sexy tyrant of a man, and no means by which she could escape.

CHAPTER FIVE

AFTER Carlos had gone, Kat was left with the stinging realisation that she'd never had to clean up after anyone.

At all the different schools she'd attended—before being kicked out of most of them—there had always been someone else to make the beds and do the laundry for the privileged schoolgirls. Even at home, she'd managed to wriggle out of helping with domestic chores—maybe because her kindly and efficient mother had been a bit of a pushover.

When her mother had divorced Oscar and married Victor, it had been a fairly amicable arrangement for all concerned. But even so, Tilly Balfour had been so racked with guilt over the inevitable disruption it had caused that she'd tried to cushion her three daughters against any emotional fallout by spoiling them just a little. And Kat, being the youngest, had been very easy to spoil.

And then when Tilly's new husband had been posted to Sri Lanka, there had been servants galore to run around after the whole family. Until…

Kat blinked back the tears which could still catch her by surprise, even all these years later. But for once the thought was stubbornly refusing to be blocked.

When Victor had been killed—murdered—nobody in their right mind was going to ask Kat to do anything she didn't want to do. And if they did, then she usually turned her back on it and ran away.

But now suddenly that had all changed. Because for the first time in her life—quite literally—there was nowhere for her to run. And she was faced with a man she could not twist around her little finger. A man she still desired, no matter how much she tried to deny it.

She felt the acrid rise of panic in her throat—but with an effort she forced herself to crush it because what good would panicking do? It would paralyse her as much as stubborn defiance, and she could afford to do neither. Because even though she hated to admit it, she could see that if she wanted to get off this boat she was going to have to make some kind of an effort. To *co-operate* with Carlos Guerrero, even though every fibre of her being screamed out in protest.

Kat set off to explore the galley, where she found a cupboard containing an army of brushes, buckets and cloths as well as a confusing array of cleaning products, and she carried a selection of these down into the dining salon and set to work.

The first thing she did was to dispose of the gold bikini top, gingerly picking it up as if it was contaminated and chucking it into a black bin-liner. With a smile of satisfaction on her lips, she threw all the left-over food on top of it and watched the gleaming fabric sink beneath the weight of a banana skin. After that, she piled up all the crockery and china onto a tray and carried the whole lot down into the galley, and left it by the side of the sink before going back upstairs.

With the table now clear, she gave the place a quick wipe and sprayed some furniture polish in the air for added effect because she remembered reading somewhere that this would make the room *smell* clean. And then, her tasks completed and with no sign of Carlos returning from his boat trip, she slipped into a bikini of her own, found a magazine and went to lie by the swimming pool.

It should have been heaven basking there—with the warmth of the sun stealing over her skin and the sound of the waves swishing rhythmically against the boat. But in truth, Kat felt jittery and couldn't concentrate on any of the iconic fashion images which usually held her attention—because a face with glittering black eyes and a mocking stare kept breaking into her thoughts and unsettling her.

She did her best to enjoy the hours which drifted by and eventually fell into a fitful sleep—only jumping into half wakefulness by the sound of a distant drone and then by the certainty that someone was watching her. Her eyes fluttered open to see that her thoughts had become reality and a shadow had fallen over her—its hard, dark outline making her heart leap into an annoyingly dizzy and familiar beat. Kat felt her throat dry. Carlos!

'What the hell do you think you're doing?' came a low and disbelieving voice.

She'd tidied up his salon, hadn't she? Put on that stupid apron and buzzed around like Mrs Mop? Yanking the straps of her bikini back up, she sat up and pushed the hair away from her face. 'What does it look like?'

'It looks,' he gritted out, trying very hard not to let his gaze linger on the miniscule bikini she was wearing, 'as if you're just indulging in a little more of the same of your idle, jet-set lifestyle.'

'I've done what you asked me to do!'

'Oh, really?' he questioned dangerously.

'Yes, really,' she defended. 'I've tidied up the mess left by you and your tame journalist—'

'You think so? Then I must beg to differ, *Princesa.* You've left it only half done,' he corrected coldly. 'The salon is not properly clean and I understand you haven't even bothered to wash up.'

'So?'

'So, you'd better get it into that little air-brain head of yours that I am used to perfection from my staff and you have fallen way short of that. And what about the crew's lunch?'

'What about it?'

'It's almost three o'clock. Didn't it occur to you that they might be hungry?'

Three o' clock? Kat stared at him blankly. 'Is it really *that* time?' she queried. 'I had no idea—and as you know, my watch is broken—'

'Get up when you're talking to me!' he roared, and then when, to his surprise, she shrugged and began effortlessly to rise like some graceful Venus emerging from a shell, he instantly regretted his suggestion.

Because if he'd thought that the little sundress she'd been sashaying around in earlier was sinful, then this bikini was positively X-rated. *¡Madre de Dios!* Two tiny scraps of turquoise material which had been sewn with exquisite care to make a garment which was only this side of decent. Or maybe it was just the way she wore it. Her breasts seemed to be spilling over a woefully inadequate top and the bikini bottoms taunted him with two tantalising bows on either side of her hips. Bows which could be undone with a single tug of a silken piece of fabric....

Bad enough that her kiss had awoken in him an inconvenient hunger he had no intention of satisfying, but to add fuel to the fire which still smouldered within him, he was now forced to confront the stuff of fantasy.

'And for pity's sake, cover yourself up!' he snapped. 'Instead of draping yourself around the deck like some kind of latter-day Mata Hari!'

'Who?'

'It doesn't matter,' he retorted impatiently, tossing her a filmy sarong. 'Put this on?'

With a scowl, Kat folded and weaved the piece of material around herself, pushing her feet into a pair of glittery flip-flops. 'So what do you want me to do now?' she questioned insolently.

To his fury Carlos felt the sudden hot rush of blood to his groin. Thinking that if she'd asked any other man such a question in such circumstances as these, she might find herself being pushed back on that sun lounger and having the turquoise bikini peeled away from her body. And this time he just might not have the self-control to stop….

Carlos swallowed down the dryness in his throat. 'Just go and get dressed,' he ordered tersely. 'And then come back here.'

Infuriated by his peremptory tone, Kat was tempted to disobey him just for the hell of it, but the rebellion had left her by the time she reached her cabin. Because hadn't she already decided that there was no point in fighting him—other than an enduring battle of wills which Carlos would surely win, simply because he was in the dominant position of power? No. Better to co-operate. To make an attempt to do the wretched man's bidding and pray that time passed quickly.

Peeling off her bikini, she changed into a pair of linen trousers and T-shirt. She even twisted the thick fall of her dark hair into a practical knot and pulled on the dreaded apron, regarding her reflection in the mirror with a grimace. Why, she was scarcely recognisable as herself!

He was waiting where she'd left him, talking into a cellphone, his dark features shuttered as he finished his conversation.

'Buy,' he was saying softly. 'But don't go any higher than forty. *No. No. De eso ni hablar. Sí.*'

He glanced up as Kat approached, his black eyes narrowing as he terminated the connection, surprised to see that she had fallen in completely with his wishes and had covered up. The turquoise bikini had been consigned to fevered memory, but although almost every centimetre of her flesh was no longer visible, her outfit did little to deter the heated progression of his thoughts.

She should have looked demure, but somehow she failed on every level because now he knew only too well what lay beneath. He could picture her creamy-caramel flesh beautifully naked, with all its enticing shadows which beckoned a man to the places where nature had intended for him to linger. The firm curve of buttock and breast, and the delicious honey-sweet destination between her thighs.

'Is that better?' asked Kat.

'Marginally better,' he conceded thickly.

'What were you buying on the phone just now?'

'Property.'

'Is that what you do, then?'

'Some of what I do. And stop trying to change the subject. Just go back down to the galley and wash up all the dishes which I'm told you left dumped on the side. And after that, you can make a start on dinner. Do you think you can manage that?'

The fact that he obviously *didn't* think she could rankled, and a long-forgotten streak of pride made Kat nod her head. How difficult could it be to knock up a meal? 'Of course I can manage,' she said haughtily.

But once she'd made her way downstairs, Kat found herself wondering just what she had agreed to. What the hell could she cook for seven hungry men, including one she knew would be exacting and waiting to take her to task if she made the slightest mistake? Especially as she'd never cooked a meal for anyone in her life.

She thought back to all the different restaurants she'd eaten in over the years. Surely one of those could give her a bit of inspiration? What about that amazing, award-winning place in the centre of Paris, where they'd served a whole duck smothered with a delicious, creamy sauce and everyone around the table had sighed in delight? Couldn't she do the same sort of thing with the giant fish which was currently wrapped in newspaper at the back of the fridge and which, according to Mike, had been bought from a passing fishing boat that very morning? Perhaps with some sort of salad to start, leaving room for the elaborate kind of pudding which all men seemed to love?

But events seemed to be conspiring against her, even though she attempted to use the remaining hours as constructively as possible. The oven took some getting used to—and in between all the juggling of ingredients and familiarizing herself with an astonishingly large store cupboard, there was still the table to lay.

'Where does Carlos usually eat?' she asked Mike distractedly.

'It varies,' answered Mike, snapping open a can of cold cola and then swallowing half of it. 'Sometimes with us, sometimes up on deck. Depends if he's working—usually he has some big deal on and rarely comes up for air, and it's best to leave him be. He's...well, he's a bit of a loner.' The engineer shrugged, and smiled. 'But when he eats with the crew—well, he's pretty laid-back.'

Kat didn't respond to that. Personally, she found Carlos Guerrero about as laid-back as a piranha fish. but she was not going to let her own feelings ruin what she was determined was going to be a fantastic meal.

'He seems to want breakfast at the crack of dawn—and my watch is broken,' she said slowly.

'Don't worry,' said Mike. 'I can lend you an alarm clock if it helps. He's dead hot on punctuality.'

Kat grimaced. 'So I gather.'

The evening didn't start very promisingly. All her timings were out so that the fish was cooked before the starter was even ready, the sauce she'd cobbled together had started to curdle and she forgot all about the accompanying vegetables until the last minute. With a grimace she lifted up the lid of the boiling potatoes—only for a cloud of steam to hit her in the face and make her feel as if she'd been thrown into a sauna.

There wasn't even enough time for her to touch up her make-up and brush her hair before the hungry crew arrived. They crowded in a cluster around the table outside, onto which she'd just piled a haphazard collection of crockery and glasses.

And then Carlos appeared, looking infuriatingly cool and sexy. *He* had clearly found time to shower and change because the thick black hair was still damp and Kat thought she could detect the raw clean tang of sandalwood.

For a moment he just stood there, surveying the general air of disarray—and his mouth twisted.

'Has someone trashed the boat while I've been showering, or are you trying to sabotage the meal in order to prove a point, *Princesa*?'

An image of Carlos in the shower was the last thing Kat needed to add to her already-shot nerves, and a renewed waft of sandalwood as he waved a disparaging arm around didn't help. She gritted her teeth in a grim replica of a smile. 'Would...would you like to sit down?'

'Where?' he questioned pointedly.

Kat leant over and cleared a space at the table. 'Right there. Dinner is about to be served.'

'I can hardly wait.'

Horrible, sarcastic *tyrant*! I'll show him, vowed Kat silently, as she went back into the cramped galley to prod at a boiling potato which unfortunately still had the consistency of a rock. She tipped salad onto eight plates and drizzled on some of the dressing she'd made, trying desperately to remember what was supposed to go in it, but afraid to ask for fear of looking stupid.

But she knew the moment that everyone had started eating that something was wrong.

'Is everything...okay?' she questioned.

There was a brief but loaded silence.

'Salad dressing which tastes of washing-up liquid is

an interesting innovation, *querida*, but perhaps it's easy to see why it hasn't yet come to dominate the market,' came Carlos's sarcastic assessment, and Kat felt like hurling a dish at his arrogant face as the rest of the crew burst into relieved laughter and pushed their barely touched plates away.

The main course was no better. The fish was stone-cold, the potatoes still rock-hard and the overambitious sauce had congealed into a horrible mess around the plate. As Carlos pointed out, it was a waste of a perfectly good fish, and once again Kat ended up scraping most of it into the garbage.

She felt hot from the heat of the kitchen when she appeared on deck again after crushing amaretto biscuits and cooking some mixed berries which now resembled roadkill. They looked up at her expectantly. Seven faces in all, but Kat could see only one. It swam before her line of vision with cold ebony eyes that mocked her which made her aware that her face must be flushed and her hair falling down.

'Everyone ready for pudding?'

'What kind of pudding?' questioned Mike.

'I'm calling it "Berry Surprise",' said Kat brightly.

Carlos took a mouthful of wine and put his glass down, a sardonic smile curving the edges of his lips. 'Please, no more surprises—not tonight—I don't think I could take it.' There was an answering peal of laughter from the other men before he fixed her with a cool stare. 'I don't really think you're up to it—at least, not tonight. Perhaps you could bring some cheese and fruit upstairs and I'll eat there instead.'

She wanted to tell him to get it himself. That she wasn't his slave. But in a way, that's exactly what she *was*. And if she threw some sort of tantrum about her treatment, wouldn't that only increase his glaring contempt for her?

And stupidly, his assessment hurt. Really hurt. *I don't really think you're up to it.* With those few wounding words he had made her feel so…so *inferior.* And the trouble was that he had been right. Was he a man who enjoyed wounding, she wondered bitterly, and was that why he had been such a success as a bullfighter?

Determined to salvage something of the evening, Kat put a ridiculous amount of care into arranging a dish for him, washing and drying all the fruit and arranging it in an artful rainbow display. Placing two pieces of cheese at the dish's centre, she added bread and crackers and took it upstairs, to a deck that was washed with moonlight and empty save for a tall figure which dominated the skyline.

Carlos was leaning over the rail, looking out to sea—and there was something so silent and imposing about his frozen stance that, for a moment, Kat just stood in the shadows silently watching him. Seemingly lost in thought, she'd never seen anyone looking quite so *alone* before—nor quite so comfortable with his own sense of solitude.

And despite his wounding words, she found herself realising that she knew little of the man who was now effectively her employer. Not even how old he was. Mid-thirties, perhaps—maybe more, for his handsome face was hard and lined with experience and he carried with him a habitual and faint air of cynicism. Why hadn't he settled down with a wife and a family, she wondered, when women must have been beating a path to his door for most of his adult life? Was it because, as Mike had said, he was a true loner?

He must have heard her, or sensed her presence, because he turned round and Kat forced herself to stir into life, to step out of the shadows and into his private circle of silver moonlight.

'I'll…I'll put this over here,' she said, holding the platter up, her voice suddenly faltering and she wasn't sure why. 'Is that okay?'

'Thanks.'

He watched as she bent over the table, the dark hair falling in untidy strands around her face and the linen she wore now looking crumpled. And yet she looked…*delicious*—more womanly than at any other time he'd seen her, and curiously accessible without her ridiculous high-fashion status symbols and dripping with jewels. Her face was flushed with heat and the effects of probably the only honest day's work she'd ever done.

How ironic that this sexy creature was as unlike the real Kat Balfour as it was possible to imagine.

Kat straightened up to find the ebony eyes fixed on her and, as she stared into the shadowed and shuttered features, her heart began a strange, rhythmical pounding.

Nervously, her tongue flicked over her lips as she looked up into the impenetrable black eyes. 'Will…will there be anything else?'

Oh, what a question, he thought wryly. Innocent or deliberately provocative? Was she doing her best to slip into her role as domestic, or simply acknowledging the silent hunger which was sizzling between them? He felt the thud of his heart. As if sexy Kat Balfour would ever do innocence! 'No. Nothing else.' He shook his head as he read the silent yearning on her face—was she mirroring something of his own, he wondered frustratedly.

She went to walk past him but something made him stop her. Something in the gleam of moonlight which glanced off the thick abundance of her dark hair and arrested his attention as much as the pure lines of her perfect profile and the parted promise of her soft lips.

He stayed her with a touch of his hand to her bare forearm and she looked down at it and then up at him and he could feel her shiver beneath him. Could feel an answering tremor in his own body—the familiar tightening, like a bow being stretched by the sharp point of the arrow.

'Kat,' he murmured, barely aware that he had said her name.

All Kat was aware of was the wild black buccaneer curls which framed the shuttered face. The way that the moonlight cast indigo shadows on the golden-olive skin. The powerful physique and the long, long legs. She swallowed. It was as if he had cast some dark and silken net over her, rendering her incapable of sensible thought and feeling. Making her world telescope down and focus on the vibrant allure of the Spaniard. He had done it unconsciously on the night of the Balfour Ball but now she was certain that he was doing it deliberately. Why? *Why?* Was he simply playing with her—as a cat played with a foolish mouse before it moved in for the careless kill?

'Stop it,' she whispered, hardly realising what she was saying.

'Stop what?' he echoed.

'Making me…' Embarrassed now, her words tailed off—for how could she possibly admit to him what she didn't even want to acknowledge to herself?

Yet it seemed that Carlos had no such similar qualms, for he gave her a mocking smile.

'Stop making you want me?' he taunted softly. 'But I'm not. You're doing that all by yourself. You just can't help yourself, can you, Kat?'

She shook her head, rooted to the spot as if he had turned her into a statue. Where was the wisecracking Kat now? The woman who was left cold by members of the opposite sex? 'Yes, I can,' she whispered, but even to her own ears the denial sounded phony.

'Liar.' His voice dipped to become a verbal caress. 'I can read your desire for me in your eyes—it's so obvious that you might as well be carrying a banner saying so. And I can see it in your lips too—their beautiful pout forgotten. Everything forgotten, in fact—because there's only one thing on your mind and we both know what that is.'

'Please!' Her protest came out like a squeak—and now she even *sounded* like a mouse. Was that because she couldn't bring herself to inject the word with any real conviction? Because despite Carlos's clear disdain for her on so many levels, she stupidly wanted him just as much as she'd always wanted him?

'You're longing for me to kiss you, aren't you, Kat?' he mused. 'To kiss you—only this time, not to stop. To lie you down and part your silken thighs and to thrust into you long and hard and deep until you cry out your pleasure.'

Kat's knees buckled and for a very real moment she was afraid that she might faint, because the graphic words were only increasing her desire. And how shameful was that? Tell him no. Tell him no and then push past him and go back down to the galley. He might be a practised seducer with a cruel tongue which could lash out at her, but she doubted that he would actually pull her into his arms and take her by *force.* Hating herself for the shiver of longing which accompanied this dark fantasy, Kat stayed mute.

'Aren't you?' he prompted silkily.

Her desire became intolerable. Unbearable. She fought and fought it but in the end it was no good. *'Yes!'* she burst out at last. 'Yes, I am!'

Carlos nodded, recognising what it must have cost her to admit it. 'Well, that makes two of us,' he said unsteadily, and leaned forward to kiss her unprotesting lips.

She had expected urgency. A rapid escalation into full-blown desire. An unashamed seduction. But Kat was wrong. Instead, he slowly pushed the fallen strands of hair away from her face as if he had all the time in the world, studying it like a scientist looking through a microscope for some rogue cell. He let his gaze drift from her brow to her eyes, then slowly down until it focused entirely upon her lips, and she felt them automatically part beneath his scrutiny.

'Flawless,' he said slowly, shaking his head a little. 'Absolutely flawless.'

The kiss, when it came, was nothing like she expected. More of a graze than a kiss—a quicksilver brush of his lips against hers. And then again. Back and forth his mouth teased her, light as a butterfly and as tantalising as the first warmth of the morning sun. His breath was warm and she could smell his own particular raw, clean scent. It was a kiss which managed to be both innocent and sensual all at the same time. Nothing more than that, but enough to make Kat sway and weaken.

'Oh!' she breathed, and hungrily she reached for him.

But, using an expertise which he'd employed more than most men—often to literally save his own skin in the bullring—Carlos neatly sidestepped the movement. Putting out his hand he caught and steadied her, though he kept his body at an untouchable distance from hers, his face tight with tension. Because this was, in a way, the ultimate demonstration of his formidable control over his body.

'No. *No.*' There was a moment while he steadied his

breath, and when he spoke he seemed to be speaking to himself as much as to her. 'I can't do it,' he said flatly.

Incredulity made her voice falter even while her body screamed out for the closeness of his. 'C-can't?'

Carlos narrowed his eyes. Did the little witch think he was *incapable* of giving her what she wanted? 'Forgive me if I have not made myself clear, *Princesa.* Sometimes when I speak in English, the subtleties of your language escape me. What I should have said is that I *won't* make love to you.' Her bright blue eyes continued to stare at him in puzzled query. *Maldición*, but she was persistent. And shameless, he reminded himself. For a woman like this was used to getting exactly what she wanted—and she wanted him. Too bad. 'It would be an abuse of my role as your employer,' he finished softly.

The rejection hurt more than it should have done and the telltale pricking of her eyes warned her that she might be about to do something intolerable, like burst into tears. And that Mr Ego might think she was crying over *him*. As if she would ever shed a tear over a man as unfeeling as Carlos Guerrero!

But Kat knew she needed to get away from here—and quickly—before he inflicted any more emotional damage on her.

As she lifted her head with a proud gesture, she was grateful at that moment for all the poise which her years as a Balfour had taught her. All the showy affairs where she had learnt to put on a careless expression.

'You're probably right,' she said, and the surprised narrowing of his eyes gave her the courage to continue, even though her voice was threatening to tremble. 'Affairs in the work place are never a good idea, or so they tell me. So if you've got everything you want, I'll go downstairs and start clearing up.'

Just let him try to stop me, she thought fiercely, as she brushed past him. Just let him *try*.

But he didn't try. Although his shuttered black eyes were watchful, he let her go without a further word.

And frustration only increased her bitter sense of rejection, as Kat half ran from the deck and back downstairs to the galley with tears blinding her eyes.

CHAPTER SIX

THE alarm clock shrilled out like a fire alarm and Kat woke with a start. Fumblingly, she switched it off and made herself get straight out of bed before she fell asleep again, surprised at how deeply she'd slept. And surprised that the restless night she'd anticipated hadn't materialised—despite the fact that Carlos had rejected her for a second time. Maybe because it had been past midnight when she'd finally crept to bed after clearing away the remains of the disastrous meal—and she'd been too tired to do anything but fall into a dreamless sleep.

Quickly, she showered, dressed and was on deck soon after six, determined to salvage something of her pride. She was *not* going to think of Carlos—or his teasing and provocative kisses and the fact that he seemed to like playing with her. As if it gave him some sort of kick to demonstrate his power over her. Kat stared out to sea, her lips set in a line of grim determination. What had happened couldn't be reversed, and this morning she was damned well going to show Señor Guerrero that she was worth something.

And despite the bizarre circumstances in which she found herself and her trepidation of what the day might bring, Kat couldn't deny the beauty of her surroundings as she stood quietly for a moment. The light was soft and milky, the sky tinged with rose and tangerine and the dark blue sea stretched towards the horizon as far as the eye could see.

Even the oven in the galley seemed like an old friend this morning so that she was able to warm the half-baked bread without mishap and assemble it on a tray with fruit and a pot of strong, dark coffee which she carried up just before seven, just as Carlos appeared, laptop under his arm.

Dressed in jeans and a soft silk shirt, his face was shuttered as he walked out onto the sun-washed deck—but the way he carried himself was so full of grace that just for a moment Kat was dazzled. How easily she could imagine him in the bullring—his head held proud and his narrow hips encased in those dark, tight breeches as he weaved a mystifying dance around a huge, quivering bull. *Stop it,* she told herself fiercely. *Stop fantasising about him.*

Hadn't she told herself that from now on she was going to remain immune to his dark beauty? That he had little respect for her as a person and had rejected her as a woman. So why was it that she seemed to be powerless over the thunder of her heart as she carried the tray towards the table?

'Good morning!' she said.

Carlos watched her approach and his eyes narrowed. There was something *different* about her this morning and he couldn't quite work out what it was. *'No me lo creo,'* he observed, his voice silky. 'I don't believe it. The *princesa* is up and working—and what is more… she's on time.'

Kat put the tray down. 'You said breakfast at seven and here it is—I'm simply following your orders, Carlos.'

'But I am impressed, *Princesa.* I was expecting sulky acquiescence.' And hadn't he thought that she might be a touch coquettish this morning, her body silently imploring him to carry on with what he'd so foolishly begun last night? Perhaps he had. But her attitude towards him was merely businesslike as she poured out a cup of coffee. *He* had been the one to suffer an agitated night spent trying to banish the memory of her soft kiss and eager body—and yet here *she* was, looking infuriatingly calm and rested. 'Not such an air of docile servility,' he finished softly.

'Docile servility wasn't what I was aiming for,' Kat returned. 'I'm just trying to do my job to the best of my ability since I seem to be stuck with it.'

'So what's the catch?' he questioned softly.

'Catch? No catch, Carlos. I've decided to accept my fate and do what's required of me.' She pushed the coffee across the table towards him. 'But I wanted to ask you a favour.'

'What kind of favour?'

Kat shrugged. 'Well, I can't possibly provide meals for the crew when I don't really know how to cook.'

'So what are you suggesting?' he drawled. 'That I fly out a trained chef to teach you how to boil an egg?'

'I think that even *I* could manage an egg. Actually, I was thinking of something a little simpler.'

'Such as?'

'Well, access to the Internet would help. I assume you have it on board?'

'Oh, come on.' His hard smile became edged with mockery. 'And have you sending out SOS messages to all the admiring men in your life, asking them to come and rescue you?'

Kat shook her head. The only man she could imagine masterminding some sort of high-seas rescue mission was sitting right in front of her and he was far from admiring. 'I'm not planning to escape. I already told you that. All I want is to find some simple recipes with simple instructions. Recipes that I might actually be able to use—and prevent some sort of mutiny from the crew.'

Carlos studied her thoughtfully. She had a point. There was no way he wanted a repeat of the fiasco they'd been forced to endure last evening. The question was—could he trust her? Should he even try? Staring down into her brilliant blue eyes, he dipped his voice. 'But if I let you, I don't want you wasting time.'

'Of course not.'

'No emails. No browsing unrelated websites.'

What a tyrant he was! 'Maybe you'd like to stand over me and police it?' she challenged.

He met the challenge in her eyes with one of his own. 'Maybe I will.' Or maybe it would be a little crazy to put temptation in his way when he was finding it harder and harder to remain immune to her aristocratic appeal.

Sipping his coffee, he studied her. This morning she'd tied the thick black hair back into a single plump plait which gave her a particularly youthful appearance— emphasised by the simple shorts, T-shirt and deck shoes she wore. But it was something else. Something other than a more casual look than she usually favoured. He frowned. 'You're not wearing any make-up,' he observed slowly.

With something of a shock, Kat lifted her fingertips to her face as she realised that he was right—and that she hadn't even noticed. She who had worn make-up every day since she'd been fifteen years old! 'There wasn't time this morning. To be honest I didn't even think about it. I…I must look a fright.'

A fright? He felt the sudden beating of a pulse at his temple and the flickering throb of awareness as their eyes met. 'On the contrary—I think it suits you,' he said obliquely, pleased when his cellphone began to ring and he could turn his back on the crushed-petal perfection of her lips. 'Speak to Mike about the Internet—tell him I've given you permission to have limited access. And I mean *limited*, *Princesa*.'

He really *was* a control freak, Kat thought, as she heard

him begin to speak rapidly in Spanish, and she hurried down to the galley to make herself a cup of coffee.

But the tiny freedom Carlos had granted her by allowing her access to the Internet somehow shifted the balance of power, if only slightly. Very subtly it changed her attitude towards her enforced captivity. By giving her an element of responsibility, she now felt that she had something to prove to him—and she was determined to do it.

She was allocated use of the desktop computer in Carlos's study which apparently he used mainly in winter or when the weather was inclement. His desk was bare and uncluttered—without a single family photo and barely a keepsake which might have given a clue about the identity of its owner. Only a single oil painting gave some sort of idea about what kind of life Carlos Guerrero might live when he wasn't at sea—and it was not what Kat would have expected. Instead of some sophisticated modern canvas, the painting was of a lovely and rather old-fashioned house set in a beautiful landscape of lemon trees and distant mountains, bounded by a sky which was vast and magnificent.

Kat found herself staring at it more than once and wondering where it was—and if it had been anyone else she might have asked them. But not Carlos. Carlos didn't really invite small talk—and hadn't he made it crystal clear that any kind of personal interaction between the two of them was strictly off the menu?

She found a website for beginner cooks called 'Can't

Boil An Egg?' which was reader-friendly and took her through all the basics. And Kat soon realised that the number-one rule about successful cooking was to keep it simple. Fancy sauces and hundreds of clashing ingredients were passé—fresh and seasonal was the way to go.

She soon found that the stronger she made the coffee, the more everyone liked it—Carlos especially. And that the crew adored warm bread served with every meal, and were just as happy with cheese as a pudding afterwards.

That wasn't to say that there were no more disasters, though none quite as bad as on that first night. She quickly learnt that it was a mistake to make ice cream unless you were a lot more experienced than she was. And Kat soon noticed a direct correlation between hard work and personal satisfaction. That if the crew—and Carlos—were happy with the meals she prepared, then she was too….

Happy? Well, that might not be the best word to choose to describe her feelings, not when she felt a sense of aching awareness every time she saw him. The memory of his kiss lingered just as potently in her mind as it ever had and reminded her how it felt to be held close to that powerful, hard body. And she'd have been a liar if she'd denied her desire to have him pull her into his arms again—only this time, not to stop. To carry on plundering her lips with that hard and hungry kiss…

She was just writing down a recipe for a green sauce to accompany some free-range chickens she'd defrosted when a shadow fell over the desk and she looked up to find Carlos standing there staring down at her, his expression inscrutable.

'How diligently you work, *Princesa*,' he said softly.

Hating herself for noticing that the top three buttons of his shirt were revealing a tantalising triangle of silken olive-gold flesh, Kat attempted an expression of cool efficiency. Not easy when her heart was pounding so loudly beneath her breast that she was surprised he hadn't heard it.

'Is that supposed to be a criticism?'

'Actually, it was supposed to be a compliment.'

'In that case…thank you.'

'You're welcome,' he mocked.

Walking over to a line of leather-bound books, he ran his forefinger over the ornate gold script of an atlas, trying to analyse why he found Kat Balfour's presence here so unsettling. Maybe because a boat was such a confined space and he was not used to being in such close proximity to a woman—not 24/7. It was too close to something Carlos didn't do—and that something was intimacy.

Because Carlos compartmentalised his women, in the same way that he compartmentalised the rest of his life. Work came first—which was why he now owned real estate in most of the major capital cities in Europe. He rarely took a holiday—even his luxury yacht doubled as a temporary office when he was on board. Enforced relaxation made him restless—it always had.

Women were for bedding and occasionally providing a little light relief in his high-powered competitive world. The occasional dinner or breakfast with them he could tolerate, mainly because he knew that was the price you paid for sex. But the moment they started yearning for the impossible—some kind of commitment—then that was the time to kiss them goodbye. With a costly bauble which would cushion some of the pain they felt on parting.

But having Kat here…

He wondered if she knew just how different she looked from the pouting beauty who'd arrived. The absence of make-up seemed to have become a daily habit, just as she'd taken to wearing her clothes looking like she wanted to leave them on, instead of stripping them off to the sound of sultry music. Even her hair was now worn in a functional plait which fell over one shoulder.

The look should have been the antithesis of sexy, and yet ironically it was the very opposite. She looked very sexy indeed. Cinderella in reverse, Carlos thought wryly. And as she peeled off all the different layers of artifice, he thought he could catch a glimpse of the woman beneath.

'We were thinking of taking a couple of boats over to Capraia tonight,' he said suddenly.

'Capraia?' She blinked up at him. 'What's that?'

'A beautiful little island where you can eat fish which has been caught about an hour previously. Want to come? We're all going.'

Kat nodded, not wanting to appear too eager. She told herself it was nothing but a careless query and yet she felt an unmistakable fizz of excitement. Dinner—with

Carlos! Okay, the rest of the crew would be there too, but who cared? Automatically, she tugged at the thick plait which dangled over her shoulder. 'What time?'

'We'll leave at seven.' Black eyes flicked over her as he thought about all the unsuitable little outfits she might choose to send the other diners' blood pressure soaring. And his own. 'Oh, and don't bother getting dressed up and making some sort of fashion statement,' he said curtly. 'It's a casual little place.'

Kat heard the unmistakable censure in his voice as he walked out of the study, leaving her staring blankly at the computer screen, wondering what on earth would win such an exacting man's approval. Then she tried telling herself that she was dressing for herself—and not for anybody else.

But more than anything she wanted to fit in. To just be part of the gang—the way she'd never been before. Later that afternoon, she washed her hair and knotted it into a French plait, then changed into a simple white linen shift dress and a pair of brown leather gladiator sandals. Her face was naturally tanned, glowing from hard work and plenty of sleep and, she realised, didn't actually *need* any make-up.

She was aware of Carlos's eyes on her as she walked out on deck—and of his piercing black scrutiny as she stepped into the first boat. This was crazy, she thought faintly—they were surrounded by Mike and the others and yet she felt as self-conscious as if she were alone on a deserted beach with him.

The tiny island was a stunning pearl of a place, studded into a sea of matchless blue. Lots of different little boats bobbed around in the small harbour and the air was scented with sweet local herbs which perfumed the air the moment they stepped ashore.

Kat found herself praying that she would be seated somewhere—anywhere—as long as it was away from Carlos and his watchful black eyes. Then felt the thrill of unalloyed pleasure when he slid his long-legged form onto the narrow bench opposite her.

'Like it?' he questioned idly.

Drinking in the beauty of his rugged face, Kat smiled. 'What's not to like?' she said softly.

Hidden by the darkness of his sunglasses, Carlos ran his eyes over her, thinking that he had never seen her looking quite so relaxed or so carefree before. The simple dress suited her—it showed off the sleek lines of her limbs. His gaze drifted to her lips, wondering how, without any gloss or colour, they still managed to symbolise a kind of wanton wildness. Especially when they parted like that….

'Let's have some wine,' he said unevenly.

The waitress brought jugs of cold, red local wine to accompany the fish which they ate with rice flavoured with lentisk—an aromatic herb which Carlos told her grew prolifically on the island.

Kat put her fork down. 'My mother would probably have heard of it.'

Black eyes narrowed. 'Because?'

'Well, that's her job. She's a cook.'

He put his fork down. 'Your mother is a *professional cook*?'

'Yes, Carlos, my mother is a cook—she runs a small bakery business. You sound surprised.'

'Maybe that's because I am, *Princesa*.'

'You thought I'd been born with a silver spoon in my mouth?'

Thinking about her mouth again was a distraction he *didn't* need. 'Something like that.' Carlos frowned—because, yes, he'd imagined her to have been descended from a long line of aristocrats on both sides of her family. 'Your mother was Oscar's third wife, right?'

'Second,' said Kat drily. 'He's a much-married man, my father.'

He drank a mouthful of wine. 'And she was a cook when they met?'

'Well, not exactly. My mother was the family nanny. She worked for my father and his first wife, Alexandra, and looked after their three daughters. Then, when Alexandra died, he…well, it was hard for a man in his position to cope with a young family, especially in those days. He decided that he needed to get married again—and quickly. And since my mother already got on so well with his three girls—and with him—it seemed convenient for them to get married.'

'Convenient?' echoed Carlos sardonically as he speared a piece of fish and ate it.

Kat nodded. It wasn't a romantic way to describe a

marriage, but her parents' union had never been a love match—and they had never pretended it had been. Inevitably, the relationship had become a self-fulfilling prophesy which had resulted in divorce. But at least the marital breakdown had been amicable—more amicable than anyone else's she knew. 'And they went on to have three daughters of their own. I'm one of them,' she added helpfully, because people always got thoroughly confused by Oscar's complicated love life.

'But no son?'

'No, no son.' She saw the look in his eyes. 'I suppose you think it's a tragedy not to have an heir?'

He shrugged. 'Well, yes. I would want an heir,' he said simply.

That didn't surprise her. But then, none of his outrageously macho behaviour really surprised her. Kat ate some fish, but the evening was much too balmy to produce an appetite. Plus, she wasn't finding it very easy to concentrate on food, not when Carlos was sitting there with the light breeze billowing at his silk shirt and hinting at the hard torso beneath. She pushed her plate away.

'Not hungry?' he questioned softly.

'Not really, no. It's too hot.'

'Sí.' Carlos leaned back in his chair. It was much too hot, and she was much too distracting. The sun was dipping now—its magnificent light gilding the deep sapphire of the sea, while the faint pinprick of stars were beginning to appear in the darkening sky. He could hear the slick lick of water as it slapped against the sides

of the boats which were moored in the tiny port, and his eyes drank in the distant green hues of the island's mountains. It looked like paradise—and in truth, at that moment, it *felt* like paradise. Good food. Good wine—and a beautiful woman who wanted him. And if it were any other beautiful woman than Kat, he would be sailing urgently back to his yacht to make love to her.

His thoughts were rewarded with the sharp stab of desire and he cursed himself for his stupidity in dwelling on such thoughts. Because this was the real world, he reminded himself—not some soft-focus ad man's version of it.

Okay, so she'd embraced a little domesticity these past few days at sea, had shown that she wasn't completely spoiled. But she was still trouble. Still the kind of idle, rich woman for whom he had no time. The fact that he wanted her was just nature's idea of a joke—and nature could be cruel. Carlos's mouth hardened. Didn't he know that better than anyone?

He hadn't had sex in almost a year, although offers spoken and unspoken came his way pretty much every day of the week. But he was discerning—and increasingly so as time went by. Although creamy, firm flesh still appealed to him on a very base level, his boredom tolerance was at an all-time low. And sometime last year he had decided he couldn't face any more early morning pillow talk with beauties who turned out to be total airheads with nothing but marriage in mind.

Sooner or later he would carefully select for himself

a bride with all the qualities he admired in a woman. Qualities such as humility and compassion. And she would possess a quiet, soft beauty—not the hard-edged glamour of this Balfour heiress.

So get away from her before the moon rises and the wine blurs your senses any more.

'Has everyone finished?' questioned Carlos, pulling a wallet from the back pocket of his jeans.

Deliberately, he sailed back in a different boat to Kat in an attempt to limit temptation to a manageable degree, though the two vessels were close enough for him to see her face as they cut through the indigo waters.

From the distant shore, he heard the crack-crack of some small explosion—was it fireworks?—and his attention was drawn to the small sound of alarm she made in response. Saw the sudden blanching of her face beneath her tan. Was she frightened of fireworks? he wondered.

But Kat Balfour's neuroses were as meaningless to him as was fantasising about her body.

She was there to work, Carlos thought grimly, as he turned his back to the other boat. Not to tempt him into doing something he would bitterly regret.

CHAPTER SEVEN

'No!'

The piercing and blood-curdling scream echoed through the night and Carlos woke instantly. Staring into the pitch darkness, his senses were on instant alert as the reality hit him that it was a woman's scream—and there was only one woman on board. He frowned. Kat? *Screaming?* What the hell was she playing at?

Leaping naked from his bed, he dragged on a pair of jeans and headed for her cabin, his heart pounding frantically in his chest as he pushed open the door.

'No!'

Once more he heard the terrified word torn from her throat as he burst inside—but it was not directed at him, nor at anyone else. For the cabin was empty save for Kat sitting bolt upright in bed. Through the moonlight which flooded in from the porthole he could see that her face was ashen with terror, her eyes glazed as they stared unseeingly in front of her. She looked as if she'd seen a ghost and was clearly having some kind of nightmare.

His movements were soft and stealthy as he moved towards her—remembering reading somewhere that if you startled someone from a nightmare, it could cause them a serious shock to the system.

'No, no, *no*!' she screamed again, now shaking her head wildly from side to side.

Carlos reached the bed and, brushing aside the silken spill of her hair, placed his hands on her shoulders, his voice as soothing as if he were calming down a fractious horse. He could feel the heat of her skin and see the frantic movement of a pulse at her temple. 'Kat,' he urged softly. 'Kat. Wake up. Come on, wake up, *Princesa*—you're having a bad dream.'

'No, *please*,' she whimpered. 'Please don't. Don't…'

He found her helpless whisper curiously affecting and a rush of unwilling protectiveness flared through him. Had someone attacked her in the past? Made her…

'Kat,' he said again, his voice firmer now. 'It's okay. You're here. Nothing's happened. Wake up. You're safe.'

Safe… The single word filtered into her consciousness as Kat awoke, memories which she kept buried deep and out of sight now staining her mind like a dark poison. Convulsively, she shivered as graphic images danced in her mind and sheer horror racked through her body.

But someone was holding her in their arms—and it was the warmest and most comfortable place she had ever been. So that, yes, for a moment, the word had the ring of truth to it and she really *did* feel safe. Safe and protected.

Until past and present merged with horrifying clarity.

It was no nightmare. It *had* happened. Victor *was* dead. Her beloved stepfather gone.

'No,' she whimpered.

'Kat,' came a whisper as strong hands now shook her with surprising gentleness and her eyelids fluttered open. 'Wake *up*. Come on, wake up, *Princesa.*'

Her vision cleared and her heart missed a beat. Because the man holding her was none other than Carlos—sitting in *her* cabin and on *her* bed and wearing nothing but a pair of jeans.

The same man who had made it very clear he didn't want her was holding her in his arms—and Kat knew she should have torn herself away from his embrace and told him to go. What had she told herself about pride and not letting him see her vulnerable again? But she was still scared enough from the aftermath of the dream to want to stay exactly where she was. Here, where she could feel the powerful pound of his heart.

Carlos stroked the silken tumble of her hair, knowing that the rhythmical movement would soothe her, in the same way that frightened animals were always soothed by rhythm. He was aware of her sweetly scented femininity—but at least she wasn't distractingly naked. In fact, he was slightly taken aback by her choice of night attire, because a pair of cotton pyjamas was not what he might have expected the sexy Kat Balfour to sleep in.

'You were having a bad dream,' he stated softly.

Briefly closing her eyes, she shuddered. 'Yes.'

'Well, you're awake now, so forget it. Come on. Let it go. Nightmares don't happen in real life.'

Was it reaction to the shock of having the reoccurring dream that made her want to contradict him? Or was it because, with Carlos holding her like that, she felt as if nothing or no one could ever hurt her again?

'It's...it's n-not a n-nightmare.' Her voice was shaking with fear as she spoke against the silken warmth of his bare shoulder. 'It's t-true.'

Carlos knew about fear. After all, that was one of the simple lures of bullfighting. That's what the spectators paid huge amounts of money to witness. Why poor men would happily forgo half a week's wages to watch the ancient battle between man and bull. It had been a long time since he had encountered real fear outside the ring, but he could sense it now in the slender frame of this woman in his arms, and he stilled. 'What are you talking about?'

Lifting her cheek away from his shoulder, she looked up at him, her heart pounding as she met the gleam of his eyes which was as bright as the light of the moon. 'I told you,' she whispered. 'It's true—all of it!'

Suddenly, she looked vulnerable, dangerously vulnerable. He stared down into the pale blur of her face and saw the way she was biting her lip—no trace of the confident Kat Balfour now, he thought in surprise. 'What's true, Kat?' he questioned softly. 'Tell me what is frightening you so much.'

Kat trembled. It was the first time he had ever really spoken to her as an equal. The first time he'd shown her kindness, or consideration. It shouldn't have mattered but somehow it did—it mattered much more than it should have done. She tried telling herself that she shouldn't trust him—but somehow she couldn't help herself. Was it the protective warmth of his embrace which suddenly loosened her tongue—or the inexplicable understanding in his deep, accented voice which made her want to pour it all out?

'They killed him,' she whispered. 'They killed him and I couldn't stop them.'

'Who did?' he commanded urgently. 'Tell me, *Princesa*.'

'I don't know where to start,' she whispered.

'Start at the beginning,' he said simply.

And then words really started tumbling out—like feathers falling from a pillow which had been ripped wide open by a particularly sharp knife. Words she'd never spoken before. Words which her father had paid counsellors a small fortune to try to extricate from her and which instead she now found herself telling a cold-hearted Spaniard on a luxury yacht in the middle of the Mediterranean.

'I told you my parents didn't marry for love—but for c-convenience,' she stumbled. 'But then my mother met someone else—someone she knew could be special to her. My father felt it was only fair to let her go, and so they divorced, and she married Victor. He was a major in the army and he was lovely. Really lovely. And a good stepfather to me and my sisters.'

For a moment she allowed herself to remember the happy times. Her mother being truly in love with a man for the first time in her life. The sense of being a proper family. The real bond which had existed between her and Victor. She had been the youngest girl and he'd spoiled her, treated her just like his own daughter. She remembered the joy of his promotion and the sense of excitement they all felt at the prospect of an exciting new country to live in. 'When he got posted to Sri Lanka, we all went with him,' she said slowly.

Carlos nodded and continued to stroke her hair, careful not to say anything in case he halted her flow.

'We were happy there. And then my mother had to take my sisters back to England, back to boarding school, the way she always did. And one night…' Her voice began to shake again. 'One night, while I was asleep…b-burglars b-broke into the house. There was nothing much to steal, but Victor challenged them. There was…there was a fight. I woke up and heard voices shouting, and then…then…'

This time he did prompt her even though he could feel the frozen fear in her body. 'Then?'

'I heard a gun go off!' she blurted out. 'I was so frightened that I just lay there. I was terrified that they were going to come upstairs and shoot me.' For a moment she said nothing, her breathing shallow and rapid as she relived that night of violence.

'That's why you don't like fireworks,' said Carlos slowly, as he remembered her brief moment of fear in the boat.

Kat nodded.

'So what happened next?' he questioned softly.

She swallowed. 'I crept downstairs—to see the burglars fleeing. And that's when I found Victor. He'd been shot….' She swallowed, trying and failing to quell the pain of that awful memory. 'There was blood… *everywhere*.'

Carlos stilled. 'And?'

'He…he died.' She sucked in a shuddering breath. 'He died right there, in my arms.'

The hand which was at her back stilled, and instinctively he pulled her closer. Her hair brushed against him and he was fleetingly aware of its softness. 'He *died*?'

'Yes!' she sobbed.

'How old were you?'

'Ten.'

Ten. A child. An innocent, sheltered child. Beneath his breath, Carlos let free a flow of some of the more colourful curses he had learnt during his own chequered upbringing. He felt rage. More than rage—a sudden and unwanted sense of identification with her, because hadn't the trust of his own childhood been destroyed by the greed and violence of adults?

'A long time ago,' he said.

'Thirteen years.'

Was she really twenty-two? Hadn't he somehow

thought that she was a couple of years younger than that? And hadn't it suited him to think that? To add her relative youth to the list of reasons why he shouldn't want her? But now that was forgotten as he found himself wanting to comfort her—she, a woman he had never imagined would need anything as basic as comfort.

'How often do you get this nightmare?' he demanded.

'Depends. When I hear fireworks. Sometimes a film can spark it off. Sometimes often, sometimes not.' She shrugged. 'It's random.'

Carlos nodded, and something about her listless body language made him want to reach out and take something of her pain away. 'You know, we're all products of our past, *Princesa*,' he said softly. 'And yours has been more tainted than most. But there are parts of it you have to let go. You have to, if you're going to live any kind of meaningful life.'

People had said it to her before, many times—but she had stubbornly refused to believe it. Yet when Carlos said it, the oddest sensation began to creep over her and Kat started to think that maybe he was right. That it *was* true. Was that because he'd never spoken anything to her but the stark truth, no matter how painful that could sometimes be? Or just because he seemed so confident and brash about life, so strong and powerful?

'I know I do,' she answered. 'It's just easier said than done.' She forced a note of lightness into her voice, wanting to dispel the heavy mood which seemed to have settled over them. She looked up at him. 'Any tips on how to go about it?'

He wished that the light scent she was wearing would not invade his senses with quite such unerring provocation. Or that her hair didn't feel like liquid silk spilling over his fingers. 'You have to tell yourself that you're more than a product of what happened to you,' he told her fiercely. 'Otherwise, it's like letting the perpetrators of the crime win. Like allowing them to claim two victims, instead of only one. And you have to start believing that, as of now. Right now.' With the tip of one finger he tilted her chin upwards and looked deep into her eyes. 'Do you think you can do that?'

Kat thought how astonishing it was that he could quickly turn from sexy tyrant into a man of rare understanding—and yet didn't that make her want him even more? 'I'll try.'

'Good.'

But despite her tentative word of resolution, he could still feel the faint trembling of her body. Clearly, she was in some kind of reactive shock to the bad dream and had then relived it by telling him about it. And she was still locked in his embrace too. Carlos shifted slightly. It felt almost comfortable to have her leaning on him like that. A little too comfortable.

Suddenly, he let her go, pushing her back gently against the pillows, hardening his heart against the startled question in her eyes even as his body instinctively hardened to the soft promise in hers. 'Get back underneath the blankets,' he informed her tersely. 'You need to sleep.'

Sleep? It seemed as distant a possibility as dry land at that moment. And he had left behind an aching void. All Kat knew was that, without him, she felt cold and frightened again. Once more she bit her lip as a faint memory of the nightmare whispered over her skin and her eyes locked with his in terrified question. 'Where are you going?'

Where the hell did she think he was going? 'Back to bed.'

'Don't…' She swallowed, hardly daring to formulate the question, not wanting to open herself up to rejection once again. But Kat was not asking him to make love to her—she just wanted his presence to reassure her. To stay until the dream became a distant memory. 'Please don't go,' she whispered. 'Not yet. I'm…'

'What?'

'Scared.'

Carlos swallowed. Her slender limbs were splayed like a colt's and the ebony fall of her hair was spilling onto the pillow like dark satin. Reaching out, he clicked on the bedside lamp in the hope that extra light might dispel some of the unbearable intimacy of the setting. But it was a vain hope, because now she was bathed in a soft, apricot light which made her skin look completely edible.

How could he resist such a heartfelt plea—but what the hell was she asking of him? That he endure a temptation which was fast becoming unendurable? Staying close to the enticement of her body when his own was crying out to touch it?

Yet hadn't he always been the master of control in so many areas of his life before now? And surely this could be just another opportunity to prove his own inner strength and determination.

'Okay,' he bit out, and lay down beside her as gingerly as a man might lie beside a snake. 'I will stay, but only for a while. Understand?'

'Yes,' she whispered.

Instinct told him that it was pointless to leave her trembling on the other side of the big bed, and he intended the arm he reluctantly put round her shoulder to be nothing more than comforting as he pulled her close. A cuddle—even though, as a rule, he didn't do cuddling.

And he soon saw why. He had been a damn fool to minimise the sensual impact of her slender body, despite the fact that it was covered with those rather prudish pyjamas. Or maybe that was what added to her allure. He'd never been to bed with a woman wearing pyjamas before. Come to think of it, he'd never been to bed with a woman and just lain there with a chaste arm around her shoulder either.

Kat snuggled against him, loving the way his fingers were now idly playing with her hair. Loving the solid reassurance of his powerful physique and the warmth of his nearness. 'That's nice,' she breathed.

He knew that. Too nice. Carlos didn't know how long he lay there for but it was long enough for his growing desire to stab like a heavy arrow at his groin. And if he didn't do something soon, she was going to pick up on it.

'Better?' he questioned thickly, wondering how soon he could make his escape, even while he silently mocked himself for his own hypocrisy. *Because you don't want to go anywhere, do you, Carlos?*

'Sort of,' she replied softly.

He rolled over, glad to be able to shift his position and to fractionally ease some of the terrible aching. 'Only sort of?'

'Well, like a big weight's been lifted, only I…' Suddenly, Kat felt awkward and wondered how she could ever have bared her soul like that. Especially to *him*—of all people. The man who was only tolerating her because he had to. Because he owed her father a favour. 'Listen, Carlos, maybe I shouldn't have unburdened myself—'

'Forget it,' he said curtly.

'It was crazy to have bottled it up for so long,' she said, half to herself. 'And in a funny sort of way, it feels so much better now that I've said it.'

In the soft glow of the apricot light, his eyes narrowed as he took in the full implication of her words. 'You mean you've never talked about it before? Not to anyone?'

'Never. I'm not really into counsellors—and it's not the greatest subject to bring up at parties, is it?'

'I can't believe that your father didn't tell me any of this himself,' he said, his voice growing bitter.

She stared at him. 'He didn't?'

'Of course he didn't! *Madre de Dios*, Kat! Do you really think I'd have brought you on board like this if

I'd had any idea of the kind of trauma you'd suffered in the past?'

Actually, up until about half an hour ago, if someone had told her that Carlos Guerrero had a tiny pair of diabolical horns growing amidst the tumble of his dark curls, she would have believed them. But as she stared at his angry and shifting features, Kat realised that her feelings for him were undergoing a rapid change. Her physical attraction to him had never been in any doubt, but his surprising protectiveness towards her was forging an even more indelible mark than desire.

She shrugged, trying hard to focus on something else. To protect something of her family's reputation. And in so doing, surely to protect herself. 'Daddy's just a bit insensitive, that's all.'

'Please don't defend the indefensible!' And then something else occurred to him. 'Come to think of it, you must have known that I wouldn't have kept you here if I'd realised what had happened to you as a child. So why the hell didn't *you* tell me, Kat?'

Why indeed? She gave a brief smile. 'Because I can be stubborn,' she admitted. 'And proud'.

'*Sí*, I can imagine,' he commented drily, thinking how that tentative smile lit her face up. And how the apricot light of the lamp threw beguiling shadows over the pristine white of her top, emphasising the soft blue shadows which fell beneath the pert swell of her breasts.

'You know this changes everything?' he said suddenly.

She blinked up at him. 'What does?'

'After what you've told me, there's no way I can keep you on board. Not now.'

Kat stilled. She had rebelled against the lowly duties entrusted to her and being incarcerated on Carlos's luxury yacht, and she had wanted more than anything to escape. But while it was perfectly acceptable for *her* to object to staying, it was quite another for him to tell her she couldn't! She had always rebelled against authority, and she found herself protesting now. 'Why not?'

He wanted to say, *You know damned well why not.* But he didn't. Because once you openly acknowledged sexual attraction, it became almost impossible to resist. He wanted to tell her to stop looking at him as if butter wouldn't melt in those luscious lips of hers—because he knew that was simply an illusion. Yet their soft petal shape was putting him in danger, making him forget the conflict of interests raging within him.

'Because maybe you've learned a lesson after all,' he said. 'That you have to confront your demons in order to get rid of them, and that running away doesn't solve anything.'

Reality hit her with a harsh jerk. 'You're thinking about those rules,' she said slowly.

'*Sí.* The rules—and your father's wish that you learn the importance of commitment. I hope you have.' His voice hardened as he told himself that she was no longer his responsibility. 'But that is up to you, Kat. If you want to spend your life running away, then so be it, but I am no longer willing to be your enforcer. Not any more. I will order the crew to set sail for shore and as soon as we reach dry land in the morning—I can arrange to have you flown back to London.' His eyes narrowed in question. 'Unless there's somewhere else you'd prefer to go? France, maybe? Or perhaps the States?'

Kat swallowed. He was giving her back her liberty—but never had freedom seemed to mock her quite so much. She thought about how nomadic and pointless he made her life seem. The little rich girl with no real place to go—who could just choose where she wanted to flit around the globe, like someone idly stabbing a pin into a map.

She looked into those cold black eyes of his and suddenly a wave of longing washed over her—because didn't the cloak of darkness liberate her from convention? She didn't *want* to go and she didn't want to leave him—it was as simple as that. At least, not before she had sampled some of his magic. A taste of the sensual promise which radiated like an aura from his powerful frame, and which had ensnared her from the beginning.

She knew it was probably wrong and almost certainly foolish—because what if he pushed her away yet again? But Kat couldn't help herself. He had ignited a flame in her and she wanted Carlos Guerrero with a hunger she'd never experienced before. And maybe never would again.

She found herself wondering if a woman could just come out and tell a man that she wanted him. And wasn't it crazy that at the ripe old age of twenty-two, she didn't have a clue?

'Let's not talk about it now,' she whispered, and snuggled into the warmth of his bare torso.

Uncomfortably, Carlos shifted again—because now her appeal was growing by the minute, and acquiring all kinds of different dimensions on the way. Like a neglected kitten that had been brought inside and given food and shelter, she was looking up at him with something in her eyes which looked uncomfortably like trust.

He wanted to tell her not to trust him, that he never gave enough of himself to a woman to warrant such trust. But he knew from experience that even opening up a topic like that made women brighten. It made them think they were getting close to you. And there was only one way he wanted to get close to Kat Balfour… and no way was he going to give into it….

So why was his hand drifting down from her shoulder to her slender waist, the slick movement of his wrist bringing her soft body even closer? Like a drowning man he fought for control—a steely control and self-will which had always come as naturally to him as breathing. And to his fury and despair, he felt it slipping away from him.

'Kat…'

'Mmm?' All she was doing was whispering her lips against the line of his jaw and there wasn't anything so very wrong in that, was there? Not when he felt and smelt so warm and so *vital.*

'Kat.' Carlos swallowed, because the ability to speak coherently seemed suddenly to have deserted him. He felt his body tense with a sudden sense of urgency. 'If

I don't get off this damn bed in a minute, I'm going to do something…something I'll regret.'

'Something like what?'

Just then she lifted her face to his, and the moment he felt her warm breath against his skin, Carlos knew that it was too late. 'Something like…this.'

Feeling the last of his self-control desert him, he pulled her against his hard and hungry body. And with a small, angry curse, he began to plunder her lips with a hunger which now seemed unstoppable.

CHAPTER EIGHT

'OH!' KAT squirmed with pleasure as every fantasy she'd ever had about Carlos began to come true. She was in bed with the black-eyed Spaniard and he was kissing her—kissing her with the kind of passion she had somehow known existed, even if she'd never experienced it before. And somehow it didn't surprise her a bit to realise that she'd found it, with him.

'Oh!' Moaning softly, her body jerked in disbelieving reaction as he captured her breast, his fingers playing with one pert nipple which peaked against her cotton pyjama top. Sharp sensations of pleasure shot across its tightened bud and she could feel it begin to flower beneath his expert caress. Words slipped straight from her mouth and into his. 'Oh. That's...*gorgeous*.'

'You think I don't know that?' he growled.

Now the hand had slipped beneath the thin cotton top and made contact with the naked flesh there and she shuddered at that first intimate contact with her skin. 'C-Carlos!' she gasped.

'You want more?'

Breath drying in her throat, she nodded.

'How much more?'

'I—'

'This much?'

'Yes. Oh, yes.'

Trailing his hand down, he let it skate over the warmth of her belly and down beyond that to the faint fuzz of hair to where she was warmer still. Slicking his fingertips with soft precision to delve into her honeyed heat, he felt her buck beneath his touch.

'Carlos!' she gasped again.

Oh, but she was responsive—instantly and gratifyingly so—yet Carlos was a little taken aback by her unashamed hunger. Hadn't he expected her appetite to be jaded, as befitted a woman who must have enjoyed sex time and time and again? But instead she seemed almost *wondrous...*with a sense of near awe in her bright eyes as she cupped his face and kissed him back so passionately. Who would have thought it?

With the sleight of wrist which had made him so masterful in the ring, Carlos skimmed the little top up over her head and tossed it to the floor. Then he tugged at the matching bottoms, peeling them down over her hips before sliding them off completely. And, oh, she was beautiful—her body a creamy cascade of inviting curves and enticing shadows. *'Mía bella,'* he ground out unsteadily, as he caught hold of her fingers.

Her breath gasped against his neck as he guided her

hand to the hard ridge at his groin, clearly discernable even through the thick denim of his jeans. 'C-Carlos,' she stumbled, her cheeks growing hot at this very physical evidence of how much he wanted her.

'I think I'm a little overdressed, don't you, *Princesa*?' he questioned unsteadily.

'Y-yes.' She should have been scared, but strangely enough fear was the last thing she was feeling as she heard the sound of his zip rasping down.

He moved away from her to remove the jeans from his aching flesh—and then he was naked and so was she, and Carlos could never remember feeling so hard and hot and hungry before. Because this was forbidden? he wondered fleetingly as he stroked his fingertips over her silken skin. He didn't know—and right then, he didn't care.

With one sure, swift movement, he moved on top of her and thought how light and how slender her body felt beneath his. 'Now,' he said huskily. 'Where shall I begin, *mía princesa*?'

'Anywhere,' she whispered, praying that he wouldn't expect her to take some sort of lead. To perform any kind of erotic act with him. The kind she'd heard her more experienced friends talk about. 'Anywhere you like.'

His mouth was at her throat as his hand moved down to the silken surface of her thighs, feeling them part beneath the soft insistence of his touch. He kissed her for an age, tempering his own hunger as he felt her melt into ever more willing compliancy. He touched her in places which made her moan, until he felt the restless urging of her body—and only then did he allow his own hunger to spiral up inside him. Technique and restraint were forgotten as he found himself compelled by a primitive urge to fill this woman, and for a moment he tensed, before driving into her body with what felt like the most powerful thrust of his life.

'Ah!'

A small sound was torn from her lips. A sound he'd never heard before. Feeling her flinch beneath that first exquisite thrust, Carlos lifted his head to see the briefest twist of discomfort cross her beautiful features. He stilled, his heart wrenching as he wrestled to take in the unbelievable implications of her reaction. 'Kat?' he questioned in disbelief.

Her eyes snapped open but she could read nothing in the dark, shuttered features, and suddenly Kat didn't want him to say the words out loud. Didn't want questions or explanations. Didn't want him to do anything but to carry on. The pain had passed now and she wanted it—she wanted *him*—just the way she'd always wanted him.

'Please,' she whispered, her voice slurred with the pleasure of feeling him inside her—and a thought flew into her mind before she could stop it. *That this was what her body had been made for.* To have Carlos Guerrero's joined so intimately with hers. That this was exactly where she was supposed to be—and her heart turned over with longing. 'Make love to me.'

If Carlos hadn't been deep inside her, he might have objected to her choice of words—for what did this have to do with love? If her tight, virginal hotness hadn't been clamped around him in the most delicious way he could ever recall, he might even have had the strength to pull away from her.

But it was too late for that. Her innocence had been taken—unwittingly—by him. He couldn't undo what had already been done, so why not make the most of it?

His own hunger now put on hold, Carlos proceeded to employ every pleasurable technique he had ever learnt in the arms of a woman. And there were plenty of those. He knew that virgins notoriously had a disappointing introduction to sex and rarely orgasmed. Well, not this one. Oh, no. Miss Kat Balfour may have sprung on him the biggest surprise of all, but she would leave his bed knowing real pleasure.

He teased her and played with her. Withdrawing from her so that she gasped aloud with instinctive alarm that he wasn't going to continue. As if he would stop now! First tantalising her with the tip of his manhood as she gave breathless little moans of pleasure, he then drove deep inside her, so that the moans became gasps of pure joy.

He did it to her slow. Then fast. And just about every variation in between. And when he felt her pleasure begin to build to an unstoppable peak, he watched her. Felt her. Enjoyed the exquisite sensation as she spasmed around him. Saw her lips part and her back arch—and the corresponding rosy flush which bloomed all over her breasts. Heard the way she gasped his name.

Only then did he let go, allowing his own orgasm to

wash over him with bittersweet waves which had never seemed quite so intense nor so long-lasting.

His body was still shuddering as he withdrew from her, taking a moment to steady his breath before turning to look at her, where she was lying back against the bank of pillows, her body looking completely relaxed and satiated but her eyes wary, and watchful. But not nearly as wary as him.

Because Kat Balfour had just detonated his image of her as a sexually experienced party animal and blown it clean out of the water. It had thrown him off balance—unsettled him—and Carlos didn't *do* unsettled. After sex he was used to turning over and going to sleep—not lying there as feelings of disbelief and anger began to build up inside him. Propping himself up on one elbow, he surveyed her flushed face and kiss-bruised lips.

'So,' he drawled. 'Am I supposed to be flattered?'

There was an odd, fraught silence as his question echoed round the cabin and Kat found herself feeling lost, the dying waves of her first-ever orgasm now muddied by the mocking tone of his words. A sudden chill iced her skin. His beautiful golden-olive body was sprawled naked amid the rumpled bedclothes and it should have felt perfect. But the expression on his face drove home the cold-blooded nature of his question, leaving her wondering what she could possibly say in response. Because wouldn't a lie or an evasion only sound hollow?

Play it as cool as he is, she told herself, even though her heart felt as raw as her newly awoken senses.

'Flattered?' she answered softly. 'I don't know. You tell me.'

Black eyes iced into her. 'But that's precisely the point, isn't it? If there was any telling to be done, then it should have been you. Telling me.' He gave a short and disbelieving laugh, saying the words aloud in some vain hope that she might deny them. *'That you'd never had sex with a man before.'*

Kat swallowed. He made her virtue sound like a moral offence! But still she was determined to keep calm. She tried for her best light, cocktail-party tone. 'Is that how it's usually done, then—some kind of confession from the woman before it all begins?'

His face darkened. 'I wouldn't know, since you're the first virgin I've ever had.'

She tried to be flip. 'And did you like it?'

'Of course I liked it!' he bit out. 'It just might have been better if you'd warned me.'

Warned him? You *warned* people about ice on the road or about high winds at sea, but surely it was the wrong word to use when talking about the fact that a woman was completely innocent of men. Suddenly, faced by the censure which blazed from his eyes, Kat found the shaming words slipping from her lips, as if trying to offer him some kind of explanation. 'I thought…I thought it might spoil the mood.'

There was a pause. 'Damn right it would have done.'

In fact, it would have spoilt the mood so completely that he would have dragged himself from her cabin—no matter how hot and how aching he'd been—and spent a night in bed alone with his frustration.

But instead… Instead, he had taken the sweet, curvaceous body she had offered him so willingly. Had entered her with a fierce hunger of his own and discovered that he was thrusting into hot virgin tightness. Carlos winced, for he was macho enough and old-fashioned enough to acknowledge virginity as sacred territory. And somehow he felt as if she'd *tricked* him into taking her. The protectiveness he had been feeling towards her after her nightmare had somehow been warped by what had just happened. As if she had cast some dark net over him and dragged him forcibly into her inner life—a place he had no desire to be.

And now… What the hell did he do now?

'*Madre de Dios*, I can scarcely believe it,' he exclaimed softly. 'You always look like you…'

Kat's heart missed a beat. 'Like I *what*, Carlos?'

He shrugged but didn't falter. 'Well, let's face it—you hardly dress or act like an innocent, do you?'

It hurt—and yet it was true, wasn't it? Apart from these past few days, she always dressed in haute couture—and sometimes those clothes were very provocative. Kat now saw that she might be guilty of sending out the wrong message entirely. And coupled with the way she'd come onto him at last year's Balfour Ball, who could blame him for thinking that she was a woman of the world, with many lovers in her past?

'Appearances can be deceptive,' she said quietly.

So could women, he thought bitterly. 'You should have told me.'

'And if I had?'

'I would never have done it, *Princesa*.'

'Maybe that's why I didn't.'

'So why?' His words were soft now. 'I mean, why me?'

She wanted to laugh. Was he *serious*? Possible explanations buzzed around in her head. She could tell him the truth. That he had enchanted her from the moment she'd laid eyes on him—and that on some subliminal level she'd always wanted him. Or would that inflate his already swollen ego? Fill him with fear that she might now demand some kind of commitment from him? Of course it would! Women always wanted Carlos—he had told her that himself—and she was no different from any of the others who had shared his bed. Just because she'd willingly given him her virginity wouldn't—and shouldn't—make a difference.

So she must show him. Show that she wasn't going to become needy or dependent. Wasn't going to fall in love with him. *She wasn't.*

Raking her hand back through her tousled hair, she shrugged, as if she'd given the question some thought. 'Well, you do have a bit of a *reputation*, Carlos.'

'Really?' he questioned silkily. 'Pray, enlighten me, *querida*. What kind of a reputation is that?'

'You're known in certain circles as a lover par excellence. And let's just say that I decided that it was time to lose my innocence.' Deliberately, she injected a nonchalant note into her voice. 'Virginity can become *such* a burden after a while. I wanted a lover and I wanted the best—and you, it seems, fitted the bill very nicely.'

He had never heard anything so outrageous in his life—and for a moment her sheer audacity took his breath away. But then the truth behind her words began to nag at him, like a rogue grain of sand which rubbed insistently at the skin. Because this was a scenario with which he was all too familiar. When he'd been a young matador, born on the wrong side of the tracks, rich and predatory women had made no secret of their desire to be possessed by his hard, powerful body.

And yet, hadn't she now made it easy for him? Easy for him to just give her one more taste of pleasure and then tell her that it wasn't going to happen again.

'Like a common stud, you mean?' he demanded hotly. 'A little bit of rough for the *princesa*?'

The accusation was angry and harsh, and completely at odds with what his hands were doing—for one was cupping her breast and feeling the nipple spring to instant life again beneath his questing fingers. While the other…

Kat gasped.

The other hand was inching its way down over her body once more and this felt like pleasure and punishment all in one. It was lingering provocatively on the swell of her belly and now it was skating down to the soft fuzz and the fork at her thighs—which instantly parted as if she were a puppet and he was jerking her strings. His fingers danced briefly on the warm cushions of her thighs and Kat held her breath…wanting him to touch her—not there, but *there*…where she ached so much that she began to squirm restlessly.

Waiting for an objection which never came, Carlos gave a low and savage laugh as a feather-light fingertip alighted with unerring precision at the hot, hard nub of her femininity. Felt her buck as pleasurable sensations rocketed through her.

'Oh!' she breathed.

'Oh, indeed.' Carlos groaned as he began to rub her sensitised flesh, watching her with almost clinical detachment as he brought her closer and closer to orgasm. He knew that she wanted him again—and he wanted it too—indeed he was hard enough to explode. But something stopped him from entering her body a second time. Something which niggled at the back of his mind and filled him with disquiet. But he carried on with what he was doing as he leaned to whisper in her ear.

'You know that this should never have happened?' he demanded. 'We're too different—we come from different worlds. Do you understand?'

'I…don't…*care*!' she gasped, greedy for him now. Wanting that amazing feeling to wash over her body once more and wanting the hard pressure of his kiss.

His finger still applying its remorseless rhythm, Carlos leaned over her and kissed her at the very moment of her orgasm. His lips quietened her soft squeal of delight and briefly he closed his eyes as she clung to him—her moment of vulnerable trust making him want to melt right into her. But he extricated himself from her arms as soon as it was decently possible. 'Go to sleep now,' he said roughly.

Pulling the sheet over the distraction of her naked body, he hardened his heart to the confusion in her blue eyes and the temptation of her embrace. More out of duty than passion, he lay down beside her, but he did not take her in his arms. Just lay there, listening to the sound of her breathing. At last, its rhythmical heaviness told him that she had drifted off, and his mind was able to focus on the unbelievable truth.

That for the first time in his life, he had neglected to protect himself while making love to a woman.

CHAPTER NINE

IN THE morning, of course, Carlos was gone. It came as no surprise to Kat to discover that there was nothing but an empty space beside her among the tangle of bed-clothes. For hadn't he begun to distance himself from the moment he'd… She bit her lip and blushed with the memory. The moment his big body had shuddered inside hers and he had moaned something soft and fervent in his native tongue.

His very scent seemed to be in the air around her and it clung to her skin like a sensual perfume. Like a starving person who had enjoyed the most delicious meal, Kat found herself reliving every glorious moment in Carlos's arms. He had touched her *everywhere.* She found herself glancing down at her naked body, somehow expecting it to look different after what had happened. But it didn't. It just *felt* different. Or rather, she did. All soft and glowing and aching. Kat swallowed as she got out of bed and stared in the full-length mirror at the bright-eyed and tousled-haired woman who gazed back at her.

She had lost her virginity to Carlos Guerrero—and despite the fact that it had been a rapturous experience for her, on his part he had seemed *furious*. Maybe it was just a myth that men liked virgins, or maybe Carlos was just a rule to himself. But she still had to face him—and she would not crumple with any kind of shame in front of him. She would *not*.

Showering her newly sensitised skin, Kat dressed and went up on deck, though her heart was beating nervously as she walked out into the golden Mediterranean morning and prepared to face her lover.

But as she busied around fixing breakfast, she heard no sound to indicate that Carlos might be awake and ready to start work at the unearthly hour he always chose. In fact, he was nowhere to be seen—and for one awful moment Kat experienced a sensation of panic. What if…?

What if he'd simply gone off on his little motorboat like he had the other day? Left without saying goodbye, feeling unable or unwilling to face her in the cold light of day? Maybe regretting that the seduction had ever happened and trying to work out the most diplomatic way of extricating himself.

Kat cast her mind back to the previous night, remembering that after she'd told him all about her stepfather's death, he'd announced he intended to sail back to shore. And that he would no longer be keeping her on board, against her will. He'd told her, quite kindly, that he would send her on her way, without forcing her to work for him any more.

But that had been before he had taken her virginity, she reminded herself—before bringing herself up short. Because Carlos didn't *take* anything. She had *given* it to him—and what was more, she had given it to him eagerly.

And things had changed. She didn't feel as if she was on board *against her will.* She *wanted* to be here. But there was a reason for that, and Carlos was that reason.

She felt her stomach flip as he walked out on deck at that precise moment, carrying a file of papers in one hand and his laptop in the other. The dark glasses he wore hid his eyes but his face was as enigmatic as it always was. Her heart began to race erratically as her gaze ran over him, trying to conceal the hunger she felt, and the warm aching awareness she felt in his presence.

Was it normal for a woman to feel like this when she had just made love for the first time? she wondered. To experience strong feelings of emotional attachment towards the man who had shown you what real pleasure was? To feel all fluttery in his presence—and for your breath to catch in your throat, making breathing quite a feat?

'Buenos días,' he said, putting the papers and laptop down on the table. 'Did you sleep well?'

'I...well, yes,' she answered awkwardly, wondering what the protocol was—whether he would come over and take her in his arms and start to kiss her.

He didn't. He simply sat down at the table and began to pour a cup of the coffee she'd just made. 'Like some?' he questioned.

Kat swallowed down her disappointment, pride

making her nod her head and force a smile as if the thought of a cup of coffee pleased her more than anything else. But inside she was hurting as the absence of a kiss or a hug told her as clearly as words that he regretted what had happened last night.

She took the cup he slid towards her. In a way, she might have preferred it if he was being angry—at least anger might have indicated that he felt *something* towards her. But this…this cool air of near impartiality was making her feel as if she had no substance at all. As if she hadn't gasped out her pleasure while his powerful body had filled her. And surely such cool indifference meant that he couldn't wait to be rid of her? So tell him you want to leave before you have the indignity of him asking you to go.

'So,' she said, careful to keep her voice steady. 'What time do you estimate we'll reach shore?'

Carlos's eyes narrowed—because this was not the reaction he had been anticipating. Women always clung to him like vines the day after he'd made love to them, pressing their bodies against him and urging him back between their soft thighs. Sometimes he succumbed and sometimes he didn't. But he *always* expected a come-on.

So why were Kat Balfour's bright blue eyes shuttered by the long sweep of her ebony lashes, and the lady herself doing a very good impersonation of an ice queen? And why was she talking to him in that cool and careful way, as if she was a completely different person from the one who had cried out her pleasure in his arms last night? Unexpectedly, he felt irritated.

'What are you talking about?' he questioned.

'You said that we would be sailing for shore today. You offered to fly me back to England—even America. Remember?'

'Yes, I remember,' he said slowly. 'But that was then. Things have changed now, Kat—you must realise that.'

Trying to keep the hope from her voice, Kat quickly put her cup down before she slopped hot coffee all over her lap. 'They have?'

'Of course.' For the first time, he recognised that the reality which had deprived him of sleep for much of the night had not even occurred to her. But then, why would it? This was a whole new territory for her. She was probably still getting used to the way her body felt and had given no thought to the potential bombshell it might now be concealing. He now had to think about the best way to put this. Only there *was* no best way, he realised. Just the bald, blunt truth. He stared at her. 'You do realise you could be pregnant?'

Kat's world stopped as the word spun. Round and round in her head it went. 'Pregnant?' she repeated blankly, as if it was something he had plucked at random from the dictionary.

Carlos's voice roughened. 'That *is* one of the consequences of having unprotected sex,' he said, and saw her mouth open in distress. 'Mea culpa, mea culpa!' he exclaimed bitterly, and slammed his fist on the table so that his cup half jumped out of its saucer. 'I blame myself! *I* was the experienced one. I was the one who should have used something. Who should not have been so overcome by lust that I failed to protect myself. Better still, I should have walked away.'

He was still trying to come to terms with what he had done. That of all the people in the world, it should have been this blue-eyed heiress who had succeeded in making his legendary control dissolve. The kind of woman who epitomised everything he despised. And he had taken her virginity. Her purity lost on the bonfire of his lust. Contrition didn't come easily to a man who rarely considered himself to be in the wrong, but for once in his life Carlos recognised that contrition was due. 'For what it's worth, I'm sorry.'

'If it makes you feel any better, I feel exactly the same,' said Kat quickly, but inside her heart lurched with pain. Because this wasn't how it was supposed to be. She'd waited years and years to have sex—and every fairy-tale hope she'd attached to it was being systematically smashed by the Spaniard.

Oh, the physical expectations had easily been met—in fact, they'd surpassed her wildest dreams. It was this grim aftermath which was threatening to erode that ecstatic recall. She didn't want apologies and regrets that it had ever happened—she longed for him to take her into his arms and comfort her. And maybe kiss her too. Tell her that he adored her, leaving her free to admit that he was already occupying a sizeable place in her heart, despite all her determination not to let him.

Well, it's your own stupid fault, tormented the voice

of her conscience which she had been failing to quieten all morning. *It was you who was hell-bent on having this man to be your lover. And he made it clear that you were the kind of woman he despised, so you have only yourself to blame for the consequences.*

Carlos looked at her, thinking how pale and pinched her face looked this morning. And suddenly, his imagination conjured up an image of his seed—one of the many seeds he had planted in her last night—growing into a baby. A *baby.* Beside his coffee cup, one hand balled into a tight fist as a strange, nameless emotion caught in his throat. 'Our feelings on the subject are irrelevant,' he said unevenly. 'What we have to decide is what to do next.'

'Well, I want to get off this boat as soon as possible,' she put in, determined to beat her own retreat before she was evicted. 'Just the way we'd planned.'

Carlos narrowed his eyes. *You and me both, Princesa,* he thought. And not just because the idea of her working on his yacht now seemed intolerable after everything that had happened. Last night had been a spur of the moment thing—a gesture of comfort which had escalated into something else. Being cooped up on board with her—having once tasted the pleasure of her delicious body—would stretch his resolve to breaking point. *But it wasn't going to happen. Not again. It wouldn't be fair. Certainly not to her.* And in the meantime…

'When will you know?' he demanded.

She stared at him blankly. 'Know?'

His black eyes were fixed on her face. Didn't her rich-girl's education provide basic classes in biology? he wondered bitterly. 'Whether or not you're carrying my child.'

Colour flooded into Kat's cheeks, because this question seemed almost as intimate as what they had done together last night. And bizarrely, the thought of a tiny, black-haired baby with golden-olive skin—a miniature Carlos—did not fill her with the dread and fear she would have expected. Instead, she felt an unbearable sense of longing wash over her and she shook her head in slight disbelief. How crazy was that? Letting her mind do a few swift calculations, she stared at him. 'In about two weeks.'

Carlos didn't react, and neither did he point out the obvious. That they had chosen her most fertile time to make love. 'In that case, I think you should stay here, with me,' he stated flatly.

Kat stared at him, trying desperately to keep the naked hope from her eyes. 'Why?'

He took off his shades then and, for the first time, Kat noticed the dark shadows beneath his ebony eyes and the undeniable strain around his sensual lips. As if he hadn't slept a wink.

'Where else are you going to go?' he questioned.

Had he intended to make her sound like some piece of unwanted luggage which had turned up on his doorstep? Twisting her fingers in her lap, Kat thought about her options. 'My family own a couple of apartments in central London. Or there's always…home…'

But as she thought of her mother's gatehouse or of the magnificent Balfour Manor itself, her voice trailed off unconvincingly. Was that because *nowhere* ever really felt like home and never had, except for that halcyon period in Sri Lanka, before Victor died? She'd never experienced that real sense of *belonging* which other people seemed to take for granted. Of knowing her place in the world, and where she fitted in. But if sleeping with Carlos had succeeded in making her feel even more alienated, she was certainly not going to let *him* know that. Kat lifted a defiant chin. 'I can always go there.'

'No, you can't go there,' he contradicted firmly. He had noticed the unmistakable tremble of vulnerability on her lips—and it suddenly occurred to him that maybe Kat Balfour was not the woman he had thought her to be. 'Not with this preying on your mind. People will notice that you are pale and distracted and they will want to know why.'

'And of course I won't be able to tell them, will I?' she demanded hotly. 'Because that might just compromise the mighty Carlos Guerrero's integrity!'

He flinched, unable to deny her angry accusation. 'It might just create a whole host of unwanted problems for you as well, *Princesa*,' he answered quietly. 'Particularly if it isn't true.'

'And if it *is* true?' she questioned, her voice rising a little. 'What, then? Won't that pose even more problems?'

There was a long pause as he tried to imagine Kat Balfour giving birth to his baby, and when he spoke his voice sounded empty. 'Of course it will, but nothing that can't be worked out. And in the meantime…'

Hesitation was not something she associated with him, and Kat looked at him with a sudden nervous trepidation. 'What?'

Black eyes regarded her and Kat thought how suddenly *cold* they had become.

'I think it would be better for both of us if we viewed what happened last night as a one-off,' he said softly.

Suddenly, despite the blazing heat of the Mediterranean sun, she found herself shivering. Better for *both of us*, he had said—but that was surely a lie. It was better for *him*, that was all. He was obviously the kind of man who could swat away memories of a woman once he'd bedded her. Whereas she…why, she was in terrible danger of concocting fantasies about her Spanish lover, if she wasn't careful. But somehow she nodded, even managed to conjure up a faint smile. Sometimes she had seen her sense of pride as a burden, but now she saw it as her saviour.

'Much better,' she agreed calmly. Two weeks of waiting and wondering if there was a baby on the way—and all the while she and Carlos would be like polite strangers. Could she go through with it? Or would the effort of maintaining such a pretence drive her mad?

Yet the alternative was far more daunting. Stuck in Balfour Manor or one of the London apartments with such a massive secret eating away at her.

'Why not just regard the next couple of weeks as a

kind of holiday while you wait to find out?' he continued coolly. 'The kind of holiday you first envisaged when you were brought here. You can lie around on deck, doing nothing more taxing than sunning yourself by the pool, and reading magazines. I'm sure you can find enough to amuse you.'

The words hung in the air and mocked her. He made her sound like some spoilt little girl who needed to be entertained. But that was how he saw her, wasn't it—even now? How he'd always seen her. Some vacuous little airhead.

Well, damn Carlos Guerrero. She would go crazy if she had to mooch around on deck acting as if there wasn't this great time bomb waiting to go off.

'I don't want to lie by the pool reading magazines, Carlos,' she said slowly.

His eyes narrowed with surprise as he stared at her. 'You don't?'

'No. I'd like to carry on cooking for the crew. That *is* what I'm supposed to be here for.'

'Are you serious?'

'Entirely serious. I was just starting to get into it—and there are plenty more things left for me to learn. So if you'll excuse me, I'd better get on with the preparations for today's meals.' The decision which had clearly surprised him now empowered her enough to give him a serene smile. 'Don't worry. I'll let you know when lunch is ready.'

Carlos stared at her, his eyes narrowing with frustration. What the hell was the matter with her? She hadn't flirted or pouted—and now she was proposing to carry on working!

He felt the sudden leap of desire as she picked up her coffee cup, and he lifted his hand in a silent gesture of command, dampening down the voice of reason which was demanding to be heard.

'I want you eating your lunch up here with me today,' he informed her silkily. 'Understand?'

Kat stared into the shuttered black eyes, convinced that his autocratic statement had more to do with possession than because he actually enjoyed her company. Wasn't it just a demonstration of his power over her—and could she possibly maintain this air of nonchalance if she had long periods of being alone with him?

'As you wish,' she said carelessly. 'You're the boss after all.' And she headed off towards the galley.

Carlos was left looking at the empty space she left behind with a feeling of disbelief, and it was several minutes before he was able to lose himself in his work.

But he wasn't deaf to the sounds of laughter which occasionally drifted upwards from the galley, and as the morning wore on, he found that his mood was growing increasingly sour. So that by the time Kat appeared, bearing a bowl of salad and some sort of pasta dish, his nerves were frayed and he felt the slow and relentless beat of frustration.

'Hungry?' she questioned with a smile which sent his pulse rate soaring.

'I can always eat, *Princesa.*'

Sitting down opposite him, Kat wondered if he knew that her heart was racing erratically or that the desire to touch him felt almost like a physical *pain.* What on earth were they going to talk about, when all she could think of was how it felt to have his warm skin next to hers. Especially when he was behaving as if she was completely invisible. *Pretend you're at some tedious social function and have just been sat next to the guest of honour.*

'Why don't you tell me how you got into bullfighting in the first place?' she enquired politely, doling out a spoonful of pasta onto one of the plates.

There was a pause. 'I thought I told you I don't like talking about it?' he snapped.

'Did you? Okay. Then let's try something else.' She picked up a dish of salad and held it towards him with a polite smile. 'Tell me about your business interests instead, Carlos. How you got started, how you made the jump from bullfighter to international tycoon—that must be quite some story.'

Black eyes were narrowed at her in disbelief. She sounded like one of those women he occasionally ran into at diplomatic parties—the kind who had been schooled in making polite small talk to a variety of guests. And Kat would have grown up learning how to do that too, he recognised. 'I don't want to talk about my damned business either.'

She shrugged. 'Well, we've got to talk about *some-*

thing over the next couple of weeks, haven't we? Otherwise what else are we going to do?'

Carlos stared at the blue-black gleam of her ebony hair and felt all his good intentions dissolving by the second. Her blue-eyed beauty and breezy attitude were shattering his equilibrium and making a mockery of his determination not to touch her—but when he stopped to think about it, why had he insisted on her joining him for lunch unless it was to do precisely that?

'Put the dish down, Kat,' he said slowly.

'What did you think I was going to…?' But her bravado suddenly deserted her as she saw something written on his face—a look which pierced her heart and her body like an erotic arrow. It was desire—raw, undisguised and urgent. 'C-Carlos?' she questioned, her voice and her hand shaking as she put the pasta down. 'What do you think you're doing?'

'I'll give you three guesses.'

He was on his feet now, moving with the lithe grace of some dark panther as he stalked towards her, as if he were the predator and she his prey. Almost roughly, he pulled her into his arms and Kat stared up at him in confusion.

'But you said…' she whispered in confusion.

'To hell with what I said—I've already broken every rule in the book for you, Kat Balfour, so why not break one more and have done with it?' he demanded, as his mouth came down hungrily on hers.

The kiss was hot, breathless. Two mouths meeting and mingling with urgent greed. Kat shuddered as her hands flew to his shoulders while his own snaked possessively around her waist. She tried telling herself that his stark declaration of desire hadn't contained a single word of affection, and surely she shouldn't settle for that. But as his lips continued to sweetly plunder hers, all her doubts just melted away. Sucked into the powerful vortex of newly awoken desire, she found herself wondering just where all this was going to lead. Up here, on deck…surely he wasn't planning to…to…

But abruptly, he terminated the kiss and, catching hold of her hand, wordlessly led her towards his cabin.

Kat hadn't been in Carlos's bedroom since she'd taken that rather resentful tour of the yacht on the day she'd arrived, before he had flown in by helicopter. It seemed a lifetime ago, and yet she could count off the days on one hand. A few days and your life could change for ever….

'Carlos—'

'Do you know what we're going to do for the next two weeks?' he questioned silkily. 'I am going to take you to heaven and back, *Princesa.* I am going to show you a hundred different ways to make love.' His voice dipped. 'And then a hundred more.'

'I…I—'

'Sssh. Just kiss me,' he commanded unsteadily.

An unmistakable note of hunger had now deepened his voice and it was strong enough to make her forget her fears. Strong enough to make her feel his equal again—her, the woefully inexperienced Kat Balfour feeling the equal of this worldly wise and powerful Spaniard. How crazy was that? But she did. In that hot and breathless moment she *did*. 'Oh, Carlos,' she whispered helplessly, as she drifted her mouth against his.

Inexplicably, Carlos's hands were trembling, and for the first time in his life he had difficulty yanking down the zip on a pair of woman's jeans. But Kat proved bold. She slid his silk shirt off as if she had just been taught the most erotic way to remove an article of clothing—and where she laid his flesh bare, her lips followed, anointing tiny butterfly kisses on his skin.

Her soft, sweet seduction almost took his breath away, and Carlos tumbled her down onto the silken counterpane which covered his vast bed, his hands reacquainting themselves with all her soft curves and secret places as if it had been months since he'd last touched her body, instead of hours. Burying his head between the lush warm globes of her breasts, he could feel her squirm with excitement beneath the flickering path of his tongue. His mouth drifted to one rose-peaked nipple and he heard her gasp as it puckered in his mouth.

'Carlos!'

'Sí, Princesa—qué pasa?'

Kat's fingers tangled in his black curls as waves of pure pleasure washed over her. 'K-kiss me.'

'Oh, I will kiss you,' he murmured, with a low growling laugh. 'Don't you worry your beautiful head about that.'

Kat had meant a kiss—a *proper* kiss—but now his

dark head was drifting down towards her belly. And his tongue was sliding into the faint dip there and flicking at her so playfully that she felt quite faint. He was certainly kissing her, but…kissing her *there*? She shuddered as a wave of pleasure racked through her body, accompanied by another wave of disbelief and wonderment. 'C-Carlos.'

'Mmm?' Now his lips were brushing over the soft fuzz of hair between her thighs, hearing her tiny gasp as he parted her legs and began to lick at her honeyed sweetness.

Kat couldn't talk. Couldn't think. She was aware that she was trembling as tiny shimmerings of pure excitement began to build inside her, promising the same pleasure as he'd bestowed on her during the night. Just as she was aware of the sensation of Carlos's mouth kissing her at the focal point of her femininity. It felt almost unbearably intimate and yet—bizarrely—it also felt like the most natural thing in the world.

The shimmerings now became little peaks—a whole range of sensations which began to hum and throb deep inside her, like a heavily laden honeybee about to topple from a flower.

'Oh!' she breathed—and then she clutched his broad shoulders. 'Oh, oh, *oh*!'

Inhaling the distinctive scent of her arousal, Carlos sucked deeply on her throbbing flesh while she orgasmed against his mouth, her sighs of satisfaction sounding like tiny gasps of disbelief.

He moved back up to lie over her, brushing her tousled black hair away from her flushed face. 'You liked that?' he asked eventually, a finger moving to trace the trembling outline of her lips.

Liked it? Kat was so overawed by what had just happened to her—so seduced by the subsequent gentling of his tone—that she couldn't hold back on the way she was feeling. Lifting her hand to one olive cheek, she let it trail deliciously over the dark rasp of his jaw. 'It was…it was wonderful.'

'Then let's make it even more wonderful, shall we?' But this time he reached for the condom he'd laid in readiness by the bedside and he saw her watching him from between slitted blue eyes as he carefully ripped open the wrapping. 'Better not make the same mistake again,' he declared, as he took her into his arms once more, softening her with kiss after kiss until she was ready for that first sweet thrust.

And afterwards, Kat lay there, curled against his hard body, watching the sunlight which was shafting in from the portholes while one word danced around in her mind. *Mistake,* he had said, as he had slid on the protection and moved over her with dark intent in his eyes.

Carefully, she turned her head to look at him, but his eyes were closed—the harsh lines of strain on his face now dissolved by the recuperative power of sleep. In repose, his face seemed softer, but no less formidable for that. The strong line of his jaw and the proud slash of his cheekbones still spoke of a certain arrogance, and strength.

His was the face and the body of the hunter—strong and powerful—with the finest genes and an unmistakable air of dominance. The kind of man that nature had conditioned women to desire. Instinctively, Kat let her hand flutter down to lie on her belly. How flat it felt—and yet, even now, his child might be growing there. Layer upon layer of tiny cells building by the minute, the hour. How big would it be by the end of the week? By the end of two?

Her heart gave a leap of something which felt uncomfortably close to excitement and, with an effort, she forced the thought away. But then, she'd had a lot of practice at pushing away disturbing memories. And it was pointless getting worked up by a pregnancy which probably didn't exist outside her imagination.

What if it did? What if she was carrying the Spaniard's child?

How had Carlos described it? Kat bit her lip, remembering the sudden tightening of his hard features and the words he had used.

Carlos had not viewed the prospect with anything other than a dark foreboding—hadn't he made that clear with the very word he'd used?

A *mistake*, he had said.

CHAPTER TEN

'SO HOW exactly *did* you get into bullfighting?'

Carlos slid the cork from the bottle of wine and slanted her a look of irritation as he poured some into her glass. '*Infierno*, Kat—why won't you give up on that?'

'Because I'm curious, that's all. You know pretty much everything there is to know about me, Carlos, but you always get so tight-lipped about your own past.'

Staring at him across the table, which tonight—like most nights—she'd laid on deck beneath the stars, Kat didn't bother pointing out that they had to talk about *something*. They couldn't spend every spare minute having glorious sex and revelling in its lazy aftermath, as the luxury yacht skimmed the sapphire waters of the Mediterranean and they waited to find out if she was having his baby. It was the elephant in the room. The subject they never touched on.

Yet it was funny how life sometimes adapted to the strangest situations. Or maybe that was the enduring wonder of the human spirit—that you always got on and made the best of things. And with Carlos conducting business deals and Kat cooking up increasingly ambitious meals, sometimes it felt like playing house. Even if deep down she knew that all they were doing was a form of displacement therapy, while they tried to ignore the great question mark which hovered over them.

Sometimes it frightened her—the ease with which she had been able to push the burning issue far from her mind and to concentrate instead on the proud, dark allure of her Spanish lover. Even if she knew that she was storing up danger for the future—because she had started to care for him in a way which would never be reciprocated.

She had become his eager and responsive lover—though time after time she had told herself it was crazy to become emotionally involved with a man whose heart was famously as cold as ice. Why, hadn't he warned her of that himself when he'd recounted with amusement just why his yacht had been given its unusual name of *Corazón Frío*? A Spanish newspaper had nicknamed him 'Cold Heart' because of a particularly ruthless takeover bid he had executed—which had coincided with a starlet selling her story of their doomed relationship. And Carlos had shown complete contempt for the article by adopting the name for his superyacht.

As the days ticked by, Kat found herself in a terrible dilemma—knowing that she should be praying that there *was* no baby. Because Carlos didn't want a baby—he had made that quite clear.

'If you are pregnant, then we will cope,' he had stated

in a flat voice which she had found especially chilling. 'And our child will never want for anything.'

Except two parents who loved each other, Kat realised miserably.

Her troubled thoughts cleared and Kat found Carlos staring at her across the table, his expression curious as he pushed away his plate.

'You were miles away, *Princesa*,' he observed softly.

Grateful for the candle-light which disguised a multitude of emotions, Kat shrugged. 'Well, there's a lot to think about.'

'And it makes you frown?' he prompted.

'Sometimes.' She met the question in his eyes. 'Well, it's not exactly…ideal—this situation we find ourselves in,' she said carefully. 'Is it?'

There was a pause and Carlos gave a ragged sigh, knowing that evasion would be kinder. But ultimately, what could he say—other than the truth? 'No, of course it isn't. But there's no point in discussing it until we know one way or the other, is there? I thought we'd already decided that.'

'Which is why I was asking you about bullfighting.' Kat's voice lowered defensively. 'I'm certainly not trying to invade your precious privacy, Carlos—just trying to make conversation.'

His eyes narrowed as he looked at her. Was he really the tyrant she sometimes hinted at? And if she was expecting his child, then did she not have the right to know something of his past?

But where to begin? He stared at her across the flickering candle-light. 'We were poor,' he said simply. 'And I mean dirt poor. My mother used to work around the clock to provide for us—in fact, I hardly saw her when I was growing up.'

Kat remembered some of the remarks he'd made about spoilt, wealthy women. Was that why he had sounded so caustic—because his own mother had had nothing? 'And…your father? What about him?'

'My father?' He gave a short laugh. 'Oh, my father was too busy chasing his dreams of being Spain's best matador to care about anything or anyone.'

'So he was a bullfighter too?'

He drank a little more wine. 'He was, until a horrific accident in the ring led to the loss of his arm—and the even greater loss of his dreams. For a while he was a broken man, until he realised that he might be able to live out those ambitions through his son. And that is what he set about doing.'

There was an odd, brooding kind of silence. 'So?' she prompted softly.

His mouth twisted. 'So he sat me on my first bull at three.'

'Three?' Kat echoed in horror.

'At five he armed me with my first sword,' continued Carlos implacably. 'And because Spanish law decrees that novice bullfighters must be at least sixteen, at ten he uprooted us all to Central America—where the rules are more…*relaxed*.'

He shrugged and there was another odd kind of silence while Kat watched a series of conflicting emotions chasing across the hard, handsome face of her Spanish lover. 'And did you like it?' she whispered. 'Bullfighting, I mean.'

'I loved it,' he said unexpectedly. 'And I was good at it.' There was a pause, before he gave a brief, hard smile. 'Too good.'

'How can you be too good at something?'

'Because it makes it difficult to walk away, even when you know it's the right thing to do. I left the ring when I was barely twenty—when I was on the brink of a glittering career.' His voice lowered as his mind took him back to that hot and dusty day—remembering the heat and the dust, the strong smell of death. 'I made the kill, dropped my cloak and, as the crowd grew silent, walked away without a backward glance.'

There was a moment as Kat registered the sheer drama of his words. 'But why?' she whispered.

Carlos looked at her, knowing that, like her, he had secrets which at times had proved unbearable—and like her, he had buried them deep. How could a man admit to the humiliation of having been forced to endure cruelty in his own home? The fierce beatings he had suffered at the hands of his father. Because hadn't that cruelty made him the man he was today?

'Because my father beat me,' he said slowly. 'In fact, he spent most of my childhood beating me. It was all about control. To show me who was boss. To get me to do what *he* wanted—which was to be the greatest bull-fighter in the world. And then, when I was a teenager and old enough to stand up for myself, he stopped.' He paused, and his eyes glittered. 'Because by then there was no longer any need to threaten me with physical violence since I stood on the brink of a career he had coveted all his life. Success and riches and fame were all there for the taking.'

Kat stared at him. 'And that's why you walked away from it,' she breathed. 'You took back control of your life—and, in doing so, you were punishing him for all the hardships you'd endured at his hands.'

Carlos nodded, her perception surprising him, even though he found it slightly unnerving. 'Exactly.'

Kat nodded. It made more sense now—or rather, *he* did. He had known brutality and hardship on a scale which few others would identify with—and not only because he had been beaten by his father. Fancy putting a little boy of three on a bull and then two years later presenting him with a real sword. No wonder they called him Cold Heart!

She rose to her feet. The expression on his face expressly told her that he did not want any sympathy. In fact, there was only one thing which she was in a position to give him—and maybe not for much longer. *Because if she wasn't pregnant, what then?* She tried to push the unwelcome thoughts from her mind—but one in particular kept coming back to taunt her. *That if he hadn't taken her virginity, then he would have put her on a plane back to London days ago and it would all be over. She was only here because she had to be.*

But still she went over to him and put her arms around his neck, tenderly nuzzling her lips in the thick dark curls which grew around its nape. And, as if sensing her thoughts, he lifted his head to look at her, but his eyes were shuttered.

'Any day now, you should know?'

'Yes.' The question took her by surprise and she found herself resenting it for all kinds of reasons. It made her feel like some hen sitting on top of an egg, waiting to see if it was going to hatch. Suddenly, she saw the vivid image of her body as a cage, its contents having the potential to trap them both with a baby they'd never planned. And Kat shuddered—for how on earth could she bear to trap a man like Carlos, a man who had spent his childhood trapped by his father's ambition?

In the muted light of stars and candles, Carlos observed her tense reaction to his question and narrowed his eyes. 'You don't want to be pregnant, do you?' he bit out harshly.

She walked away from him, distractedly shaking her head to halt words which seemed intrusive—afraid that she might give herself away, because how could she possibly explain to him all her mixed emotions? Especially when he'd never made any secret of the fact that he didn't want a baby. He hadn't even wanted an affair with her, had he? *We are too different,* he'd said.

But Kat knew that she couldn't dwell on Carlos's

lack of feelings for her. She had to be strong. She would cope with whatever hand fate had dealt her. And if she *was* pregnant, then she would love his baby with a fierce love, but she would not hold Carlos Guerrero ransom to fate. It would not be fair, not after all that he had told her. She shook her head. 'Not now, Carlos,' she whispered. 'I don't want to discuss it. In fact, I'm…I'm tired. I'm going to bed.'

His mouth hardened—angry with himself for having broken a lifetime rule of non-disclosure. Why the hell had he poured out all that poison about his childhood? And angry too at the way his rashness—his *lust*—had the potential to complicate Kat Balfour's life in a way she'd never envisaged. Nor deserved. 'So go,' he said abruptly. 'I'm not stopping you.'

She did—but for once he didn't follow her, though she waited and waited with breathless expectation, until she realised that her wait was in vain. Eventually, she must have fallen asleep because when she awoke in the cold, grey hours of dawn, Carlos was not beside her—and a chill feeling of dread stole over her heart. Creeping from her cabin, she went to look for him, half hoping he might still be out on deck, perhaps having fallen asleep where he sat.

But the deck was empty and, for once, the light there was gloomy, the stars fading into insignificance in the pearly light and the first blush of sunrise not yet visible. In the distance she could see the faint twinkling of lights and Kat blinked her eyes in surprise. Land. Funny how it could just loom up and surprise you—when all you'd seen for days were just different variations of a stunning sea. Yet, all the time, the yacht was moving—taking them back towards France from where they'd started. And Kat realised that Carlos had cleverly timed it to coincide with her finding out whether or not she was pregnant.

Barefooted, she tiptoed to his cabin, and when the door swung quietly open it was to see his sleeping form sprawled on the bed. He had flung the bedclothes away and was lying there—gloriously naked—outlined like a golden statue against the pristine whiteness of the sheet.

His black hair was ruffled and she found herself gazing lovingly at his face—the proud lips and the haughty slash of cheekbones. She remembered what he had told her about his heartbreaking childhood—about his cruel father and a mother who sounded weak and put-upon. Was that why she had not been able to put a stop to her son's beatings? she wondered sadly—and Kat's heart turned over with a love she knew he was not seeking.

As she stood there silently watching him, his dark eyes fluttered open.

'Kat?' But he said it with all the emotion of someone saying *window* or *door*, and for a moment, their gazes locked—until she realised that he seemed to be gazing right through her. As if he hadn't really seen her. Or hadn't really wanted to. And then he turned over and went right back to sleep.

A dull kind of pain cloaked her heart as she crept back to her own cabin—but during the night came a different and very familiar kind of pain. Snapping on the bedside light, she found herself staring down at the crimson flowering of blood with eyes which were inexplicably filled with tears.

And it was a white-faced and trembling Kat who was already dressed and on deck the following morning when Carlos emerged.

'You're up early,' he observed.

'You didn't come to bed last night,' she accused, wondering if she was hiding the trembling hurt in her voice.

Dark eyebrows rose in arrogant query. 'Are you nagging me, Kat?'

'I'm just asking a question.'

He remembered the way she had shuddered when the subject of pregnancy had come up. Her avowal that she had no desire to have a baby. And even though her words made complete sense, something in her statement had filled him with distaste. So that he had been glad to spend the night apart from her—yes, *glad.* For what man would want to make love to a woman when she'd just told him something like that? 'You said you were tired,' he said coldly.

Was that the only reason? Kat wondered—as she registered the sudden iciness in his voice. Or was he regretting everything he'd told her about his tortured childhood? Had he wanted to distance himself after the confidences he'd shared—or simply decided that the affair had now run its course?

Well, in that case, his wish was about to come true.

Biting her lip, she looked up into his hard and handsome face, trying to tell herself that this was all for the best, even if it felt as if her heart was breaking in two. 'Well, anyway—all that's irrelevant now. I've…well, it's good news really,' she said.

'Oh?'

'I think…' She swallowed down the terrible feeling of loss which had washed over her and presented him with a resolute face instead. 'I'd like someone take me ashore please, Carlos.' She met the cool question in his eyes but she didn't flinch, even though the unbearable intimacy of what she was about to say made her cheeks turn hot. 'That is unless you happen to carry sanitary protection on board.'

CHAPTER ELEVEN

AN ATMOSPHERE like a heavy blanket greeted her announcement and Kat insisted on being ferried ashore as quickly as possible. She just wanted to get away from the yacht—and away from the cool indifference with which Carlos had greeted the news that there wasn't going to be a baby.

'I'll take you,' he told her, as she appeared back on deck after packing her bags, her face set and her mouth composed in a thin line.

But Kat shook her head. And have her breaking down and making a complete fool of herself in front of all the jet set milling around the port at Antibes? Risk telling him how empty her life was going to feel without him—or even worse, beg him to let her stay?

'No,' she said, and wobbled him an attempt at a smile. She wasn't going to cry. She *wasn't.* 'It's better this way, Carlos. We're both relieved at the outcome, you know we are.' So why did her heart feel as if someone had taken a dagger to it and driven a gaping great wound into its centre?

'Sí,' he said slowly. 'You are right. It is better this way.'

Her voice was determinedly bright. 'Well, then, there's nothing more to be said, is there?'

He let his eyes drift over her, taking in the soft skin and the beautiful lips—and the eyes which were as blue as a Mediterranean sky. 'Except that it was a pretty amazing affair while it lasted,' he observed softly.

'Yes. Yes, it was.' Was this what he usually said—his farewell line? A whole script prepared to ease the pain of the parting, cleverly couched to sound almost *tender*, but cautious enough not to whip up any false hope. And suddenly Kat knew she couldn't face anything which masqueraded as tenderness, because that would just make this parting even more unbearable. Her fingers clenching into a fist over the handle of her bag, she stared up at him. 'But it's over now.'

Carlos had never been left quite so swiftly nor so efficiently by a woman before. Come to think of it, it was always him that did the leaving. Hadn't he wondered whether Kat might try and drag it out a bit longer, digging in her delectable heels and intimating that she had no desire for their affair to end? Well, she hadn't—and once again she had confounded all his expectations. His eyes narrowed. And maybe she was right. Maybe it really *was* better this way.

Leaning over, he planted the briefest of kisses on her trembling lips just as Mike appeared from the galley.

'Look after her,' said Carlos abruptly, and turned and walked away.

Kat's heart sank as she watched his retreating back, but what had she expected? That he might stand there watching her wave a dinky little hanky as the speedboat put more and more distance between them? Why, he was probably heaving a huge sigh of relief—like a man who had just been relieved of a mighty burden.

She felt slightly ill as she stepped ashore, where Carlos had a car waiting for her, and was startled by a sudden blue flash.

'I think somebody just took my photo,' she said in confusion.

'Oh, there's always paparazzi hanging around here,' said Mike with a shrug, as he hauled out her bags and put them on the quayside. And then, to her surprise, he enveloped her in a brief bear hug. 'We're going to miss you,' he said gruffly. 'You've done good.'

The farewell only added to her highly emotional state and, once Mike had gone, she clambered into the back of the car, directing it to stop at a *pharmacie.* And afterwards she was whisked to a nearby airstrip, where Carlos had arranged for a jet to fly her to London.

As soon as she'd touched down, her cellphone started ringing, with her father on the other end of the line.

'Kat,' he said gruffly. 'Are you okay?'

'I'm…fine,' she answered warily. 'Why?'

'I've just had Carlos Guerrero on the phone.'

For a moment she froze as the Spaniard's dark and

golden features danced provocatively in her mind. 'What…what did he say?'

'Just that he was very pleased with you.'

'He…he did?'

'He certainly did. Said that you seemed to have been cured of your tendency to run away from problems, that you seemed to have learned the meaning of the word *commitment*, and that I should be very pleased with you. Oh, and he also advised me to let you have use of the London flat and start paying your allowance again.'

The breath which she only just realised she had been holding escaped from Kat's lips with a sigh. But really, what had she expected? That Carlos would tell her father that he'd become incredibly close to her during the voyage? Or that he'd realised he didn't want to live without her? As if it was some old-fashioned scenario and he was ringing to ask her father for permission to carry on seeing her!

When the reality was that all Carlos cared about were the stupid rules—which were what the two men had colluded about in the first place. And didn't her father's words reinforce the fact that the Spaniard may have taken her to his bed, but inside he still regarded her as a spoilt little girl who needed her allowance to be doled out?

'Are you still there, Kat?'

'Yes, Daddy,' she said resignedly. 'I'm still here.'

'I just want to say…well done, darling. I'm very proud of you. The flat's all ready and you can access your bank account immediately,' he announced, and then his voice softened. 'And you can treat yourself to something nice, because I'm increasing your allowance!'

It felt a little like being offered a poisoned chalice, and the drive from the airfield left Kat feeling dejected and slightly sick.

Installed in the vast Balfour apartment which overlooked Kensington Gardens, she was soon confronted with a reality which she didn't quite understand. And at first she couldn't quite believe. Because all the signs had been there….

She'd been…

She'd felt…

She'd thought…

It was only after more reasoned consideration and a glance at the calendar that her skin began to ice, as the mixed messages which her body was sending out caused her mind to scream with confusion.

Scanning the phone book for a list of physicians, she made an appointment with a doctor and managed to get someone to see her that afternoon.

Pushing her way past the man who seemed to have been hanging around outside her apartment all week, Kat flagged down a taxi which took her straight to Harley Street and a middle-aged gynaecologist who looked at her with a frown.

'I'm not sure I understand exactly what it is you're asking me, Miss Balfour.'

'I thought I might be pregnant,' she summarised quickly. 'And then my period started. Or, at least, I thought it did. Only it hasn't, not really, not like normal. I'm not sure what's going on.'

'Let's do a couple of tests, shall we?' he questioned.

Twenty minutes later, she was in another cab heading back for the apartment, where—physically and emotionally drained—she fell into a fitful doze, and woke soon after dawn, unable to get back to sleep. She forced herself to shower and dress and spent long minutes putting on her make-up, realising how long it had been since she'd worn it. But grateful now for the mask it provided. The familiar old mask which was now back in place—something for her to hide behind. Because new and scary territory had opened up before her and she was going to have to face it. Alone.

She'd just finished dressing when the silence was broken by the loud jangling of the telephone. It was her sister Sophie, who wasn't usually given to making early morning phone calls.

'Hello, Sophie,' said Kat, trying to sound like her 'normal' self, even though she seemed to have forgotten what that felt like. 'This is a surprise.'

'Have you seen the papers?' her sister demanded.

'No. I've only just got back from…' Suddenly, Kat registered the urgency in her sister's voice. 'Why? What's happened?'

'There's a picture of you on page three of the *Daily View*. Coming out of a *doctor's surgery* in Harley Street.' Sophie's voice dropped to a worried whisper. 'Kat, are you *okay*?'

What would her shy, artistic sister say if she told her the truth? 'I'm fine,' lied Kat, as the doorbell began peeling with a loud and imperious bell. 'Listen, someone's at the door. I'd better go, Soph. I'll ring you.'

Flicking her hair away from her face, she ran to the door, peering at the CCTV image of the man who stood outside the apartment block and then freezing in disbelief.

Carlos!

Kat's knees buckled and she swayed. Thoughts which were already confused now began to go into overdrive.

Carlos?

The doorbell rang again—and it seemed that this time he must have jammed his thumb on the bell and left it there so that she was forced to click on the intercom without giving herself a chance to compose herself. Though maybe that would have been asking too much of anyone.

'Y-yes?'

'Let me in.'

'What the hell are you doing here?'

On the doorstep, Carlos failed to make the obvious response; his mood was too black for that. 'I said…*let me in.*'

Trembling, she pressed the button, dashing into the bathroom to check her appearance—but there was barely any time to brush her teeth before a loud thumping on the door announced his presence. He must have run up the stairs, she found herself thinking inconsequentially, because the ancient elevator took ages.

Opening the door to him, she could see that her assumption had been correct—since he was slightly out of breath and his colour was raised—but most of all she noticed the rage which sparked in dark flames from his ebony eyes. He was carrying a newspaper in one hand and he looked *furious.* Pushing past her, he slammed the door shut behind him and then turned on her.

'*Perra,*' he whispered, his face contorted into a dark mask of anger which automatically made Kat's heart begin a frantic racing. 'You lying little cheat.' He took a deep breath and pushed his face a little closer to hers—but a wave of minty toothpaste hit him and this, with the glossy fall of hair and the carefully made-up face, was enough to make him recoil as if he'd just been bitten by a snake. He stared at the tight, white jeans she wore and the cute silk T-shirt—which was exactly the same colour as the costly aquamarines which glittered at her throat. He found himself looking at the sleek and pampered little rich girl and it was as if the past few weeks simply hadn't happened.

'And there was me thinking that you'd changed,' he raged. 'That you were no longer the girl who ran away at the first opportunity. Who had learned to deal with life and look it in the face. But, no, I was wrong. Very, very wrong. First you lie to me, and then you run—just the way you've always run! Commitment?' he bit out. 'You wouldn't know the word *commitment* if it jumped out and shook you!'

Kat was trembling as the force of his words compounded her own growing sense of realisation, and fear. And with it came the sinking sensation that he was all too eager to think the worst of her. 'You've seen the paper?' she questioned.

Carlos looked as if he was about to explode. 'So you *know* about the paper? Of course I've seen the damned paper!' And then his face darkened with suspicion. 'Is this some kind of elaborate set-up?' he demanded. 'A teaser for some newspaper deal you're setting up? Have you perhaps succeeded where every other journalist has failed in "getting to know" the real Carlos Guerrero and are about to do an exposé on me?'

Kat felt sick. How could she have ever believed he felt for her anything other than contempt? The fact that he hadn't been able to keep his hands off her while she'd been on board his yacht meant nothing. *Nothing,* she reminded herself bitterly.

'We can't have this conversation here,' she said dully—for she was afraid that if she didn't sit down she might do something unforgivable. Like faint. Or be sick—a fear which now felt very real indeed.

Without waiting for his reply she began walking towards the sitting room, aware that he was following her. She turned around as he came into the room, wondering how a man could possibly dwarf a room as huge as the main drawing room of the Balfour apartment—but somehow Carlos managed it quite effortlessly. In his dark suit and snowy shirt, he looked the epitome of crisp elegance. And a complete stranger.

'I haven't seen the paper,' she said.

His eyes narrowed. 'But you knew about it?'

'My sister rang.'

'How convenient.'

'May I see it, please?'

He half threw it onto the coffee table and Kat knelt down and opened it up with hands which were shaking. And there, on page three, was the article Sophie had alerted her to.

It wasn't the first time she had been featured in a national newspaper but it was the first time she had been visibly shocked by what she saw. The Kat who had been photographed leaving the doctor's rooms in Harley Street was barely recognisable as herself. Her face looked bleached, her eyes huge and a pashmina shawl hugged around her shoulders seemed to envelope her.

But it was the headline—and the subsequent article which disturbed her far more.

Guerrero's Society Babe Visits Baby Doc.

Swallowing down her disbelief, Kat read on.

Famous ex-bullfighter Carlos Guerrero is used to playing cloak-and-dagger—and the latest beauty in his life seems to be following in his footsteps. Fresh from a Mediterranean trip on the Spanish billionaire's luxury yacht, stunning Kat Balfour was tight-lipped as she left Dr. Steve

Smith's Harley Street surgery. Dr. Smith is best known for his delivery of last year's Royal Princess and his spokesperson refused to comment on rumours that one of the notorious Balfour Babes is pregnant.

Kat Balfour hails from one of the richest and most scandal-ridden families in the land, but her new beau is more than a match for their colourful history. Playboy tycoon Guerrero was once tipped to be Spain's finest bullfighter before dramatically withdrawing from the ring, fifteen years ago.

Who knows? With capricious Kat Balfour at his side, the man tagged 'Cold Heart' by the Spanish tabloids may have taken on his biggest challenge yet!

Dazed, Kat sat back on her heels and stared up at the forbidding mask of Carlos's face.

'But they didn't ask me to comment!' she protested. 'I didn't even know they had a snapper there!'

Carlos clenched his fists in fury. 'Is that all you care about?' he demanded. 'The fact that you didn't know you were being photographed? Why, would you have applied a little more gloss to those lying lips of yours?'

Her heart began to race as she registered the venom in his voice. 'How dare you speak to me like this?'

'Quite easily,' he snapped. 'And before you start to offer any half-hearted defence, surely the fundamental flaw in your argument is that you lied to me, Kat. But we could spend the whole morning railing against each other and none of it is relevant. In fact, only one thing is.' He fixed her in the piercing spotlight of his ebony eyes. 'Just tell me one thing. Are you or are you not…pregnant?'

There was a horrible pause and the only sound which Kat could register was the uncomfortable irregularity of her own breathing. 'I…'

'*Are* you?'

'Yes! *Yes!*'

He let out a hiss, like the sound of a pressure cooker which has just had its lid removed after many hours of being on the boil. 'So you *did* lie,' he said in a voice which sounded suddenly flat.

Kat shook her head. 'Not exactly.'

Cold black eyes were turned on her. 'Not *exactly*? How many variations of the truth are there? Perhaps you'd care to explain, or did I dream up the fact that you told me you needed to find a chemist because your period had come?'

'I thought…' Stupidly, she was blushing now. 'I got a pain during the night and I started bleeding.' The night he hadn't been there—when his absence had seemed to emphasise that there was nothing between them but an enforced captivity while they waited to discover whether or not they were going to be parents. 'I thought it was my period. It was only when I'd been home for a couple of days that I realised that it wasn't.'

'But you weren't going to bother to tell me about it?'

'Of course I was! I just needed it to be confirmed first.'

'Or was it something more than that?' he demanded, his heart beating now with a slow and steady kind of dread. 'Did you go to the doctor for something other than confirmation?'

It took a moment or two for his meaning to register and, when it did, Kat thought she really *might* be sick. Swallowing down the bile which had risen in her throat, she stared at him. 'How…how *dare* you suggest such a disgusting thing?' she spat out, trying now to rise from her subordinate position on her knees. But her rage was so intense that she half stumbled and Carlos automatically put out his hand to support her. 'Get away from me!' she flared.

He took no notice, just made sure that she was steady once more and then strode over to the window, looking out at the manicured beauty which was Kensington Gardens—seeing the glitter of the Round Pool in the distance, trying desperately to assemble his thoughts into some kind of order.

It was several moments before he had composed himself enough to turn round and, when he did, it was to see that Kat was sitting in the centre of a huge, overstuffed sofa, looking impossibly fragile. And in that moment, he could have kicked himself for the whiplash quality of his words. What kind of a brute was he, he wondered disgustedly, to harangue a woman who was newly pregnant?

'Can I get you something?' he questioned in a hollow voice. 'Something to drink?'

'I feel sick.'

Quickly, he found a bathroom at the end of one of the long corridors and tipped out a pile of rose petals which had been cluttering up a porcelain bowl and then took it to Kat. On further exploration of the apartment, he discovered a high-tech kitchen, where he made a pot of ginger-and-lemon tea, because he remembered reading somewhere that ginger was good for nausea.

She was still sitting where he'd left her, the towel on her lap, the porcelain bowl empty at her side. And suddenly he looked beyond her painted face and saw the vulnerability in her huge eyes.

'I've made you tea,' he said quickly, as he put the tray down.

She looked up, telling herself again that she must be strong. Carlos hadn't broken any promises. He'd never claimed to *feel* anything for her. She certainly couldn't demand love from him because she was carrying his baby. And she must close the floodgates on her love for him. He mustn't know about it. It wouldn't be fair—because then, wouldn't she be burdening him with unnecessary guilt as well as a baby he'd never planned?

'I didn't run away,' she told him tiredly. 'I honestly thought my period had come, so there was no reason to stay. We'd already decided that.' And he had done nothing to stop her leaving, had he? That had been the bottom line. Even now, he was only here because he *had* to be—not because he wanted to. 'But I'd just had some kind of bleeding—apparently, it's not unusual in the early stages of pregnancy.'

'But you're okay?' he demanded urgently.

'I'm okay.'

'And…the baby? The baby is okay?'

'The doctor tells me that everything's fine.'

'Thank *God*,' he breathed.

And for the first time, Carlos began to take in the enormity of what she had just told him. A single fact that had the power to change his life for ever. He was going to be a *father*. Placing a delicate mug of steaming tea into her unprotesting hand, he realised that his baby was growing beneath her heart even now—deep in her belly.

He wanted to reach out and touch her—to place the palm of his hand on her still-flat belly, as if to reassure himself that his child really was in there. But he felt as if he had forfeited the right to do any such thing, his bitter accusations driving a wedge between the two of them. And he wondered now if his father had bequeathed him something of his own cruelty—whether or not he was fit to be a father to her child.

He flinched. 'You know that there were photographers hanging around outside when I arrived and that it's only going to get worse?'

'But *why*?' she wailed, letting her hormones get the better of her. 'Why can't they just leave me alone?'

His body tensed. 'It is the joint legacy we share, *Princesa*. One which is bread and meat to the ever-hungry media,' he said bitterly. 'The ex-matador and his scandalous heiress.'

At that moment the telephone began to shrill and, putting her tea down on the table, Kat leaned over and picked it up. It was her father.

'Would you mind telling me what the hell is going on, Kat?' he began ominously.

Kat opened her mouth to start explaining when it suddenly hit her that she didn't *have to.* She didn't have to do anything. Not any more. Maybe in the past she *had* run away from her responsibilities—and maybe her father's set of Rules had helped her see her life in a different light. Or maybe Carlos had. But she wasn't running now. Even if she wanted to—which she didn't—running was no longer an option. She was going to be a mother. She was going to have Carlos's baby and she was going to have to learn to stand on her own two feet. And that meant that the rest of the Balfours were really going to have to butt out and leave her to get on with it.

Without thinking about it, her fingers of one hand drifted to her stomach and she let them rest there—almost protectively—looking up to see a sudden flare of light in the ebony eyes which were fixed on her.

She turned her lips back to the mouthpiece. 'Actually, I don't really want to talk to anyone at the moment, Daddy,' she said steadily.

'But—'

'No buts. I'm fine.' She listened to her father for a minute, acutely aware of Carlos's intense scrutiny. 'Yes, he's here. With me. No, Daddy. No. I'll talk to you in a couple of days. Yes. I promise.'

Slowly, she replaced the receiver and Carlos saw the wariness in her eyes as she regarded him—as if expecting him to start interrogating her again. His mouth hardened. And maybe she had good reason to think that.

The phone began to ring once more and, seeing her eyes close wearily this time, Carlos snatched up the receiver, his eyes narrowing as he listened. 'Yes?'

'Carlos! It's Tania Stephens here,' came the throaty voice of a woman. 'I'm the one who left my bikini on your yacht and wondered if you'd just like to—'

'No comment,' he snarled, slamming it down again, and when it began to ring again almost immediately he took it off the hook. Was this what it was going to be like? he wondered. With the phone ringing and the press clamouring and Kat getting bigger. Living out her pregnancy in the middle of the city, with that cold and unapproachable air about her while the media-hungry world closed in.

There was a solution to the problem which lay before them, he realised slowly. But only if Kat would agree to it—and that was by no means certain. 'I can find you somewhere safe to stay,' he said slowly. 'Somewhere the press won't bother you.'

She looked up. 'Where?'

'That's up to you, *Princesa*. I can give you several options. I have places pretty much all over the world you can choose from.'

'With you, you mean? You'll be coming with me?' she questioned in a cool voice, as if she didn't care one way or the other. Because the last thing she wanted or needed to feel right now was disappointment when he told her that, no, he'd be leaving her alone to face the coming months.

Carlos expelled a breath. 'Well, that depends,' he said slowly. 'On whether or not you want me there.'

There was a pause while the question hung in the air.

Don't make yourself vulnerable, Kat told herself. Don't open yourself up to yet more pain. 'If you want,' she said, with a shrug. 'I don't really care either way.'

Carlos met the blue of her dazzling eyes which now seemed as cold as a winter sky. She had agreed to leave the spotlight of the city and he was going with her.

His mouth hardened. It may have felt a little like a victory, he thought, but it seemed a very hollow one.

CHAPTER TWELVE

HE TOOK her to a house she recognised, though it took a moment or two for Kat to realise why.

'It's the house in the painting!' she exclaimed, her heart lifting with an unexpected kind of delight. 'The one in your study on the yacht.' The one she used to gaze at when she was transcribing recipes during a time which now seemed like light years ago.

'It is indeed. My hacienda,' said Carlos softly.

Standing in the doorway of the lovingly cared-for old house, surrounded by a shaded veranda decked with flowers and foliage, Kat looked out at the stunning Andalusian countryside. Outside were orchards of Carlos's very own oranges and lemons—which scented the soft, warm air. And in nearby pastures overlooking distant mountain peaks lived his beloved Andalusian horses which people came from all over the world to buy.

Despite her mixed emotions, Kat thought she had never seen anywhere more lovely in her life. It seemed so solid and real—so far away from the hustle and bustle of the city. And it made her feel indescribably wistful for a life she had never known and probably never would. A life with deep roots and the promise of longevity.

'So what do you think of my home?' asked Carlos, as he came out of the house to find her standing there, perfectly still. They'd travelled down earlier that afternoon on the jet he'd hired, and Kat had just drunk tea and eaten from a dish of fruit which his housekeeper had served to them.

She turned to face him. 'I think it's beautiful.'

'So why the troubled look?'

Was he completely dense, Kat wondered, or did he just have the ability to completely switch off? Maybe with men it was different—or maybe it was just different for Carlos. Beneath her outwardly calm exterior she could feel the riot of emotions which were as tangled as an old ball of string, but presumably he suffered no similar disquiet as he contemplated their uncertain future.

'Oh, it's all been a lot to take in,' she said evasively. 'The news about the baby, the journey here—wondering just what we're going to tell people.' She bit her lip. Plus the mind-boggling adjustment of having to redefine herself as a single mother. 'And when.'

Staring down into her bright blue eyes, Carlos saw the unmistakable strain which shadowed them. And wondered whether the brittleness she seemed to have acquired might melt away again. So that once again she became that soft, smiling Kat who used to tease him. The woman who used to welcome him into her arms and into her bed every night.

'We're not going to do anything until you've relaxed,' he said softly. 'That was one of my reasons for bringing you here.'

Not quite daring to ask him what any of the others were, Kat returned his stare. 'And what about you, Carlos—what will you be doing? Relaxing—or tapping away on your damned computer as usual?'

He heard something which sounded close to accusation in her voice and Carlos nodded. 'I think I might try a little relaxation therapy myself,' he agreed softly. 'There happens to be a pool here which I haven't swum in this year.'

There was indeed a pool—and Kat blinked with disbelief when she first saw it. A vast infinity pool overlooking an enormous mountain range, the clear blue waters seeming to go on for ever.

After breakfast the following morning, he suggested she change into a swimsuit and meet him there. And although it was a sensible enough suggestion for such a sunny day it seemed a curiously *intimate* thing to say. Lazing by a swimming pool was the sort of thing which couples did and they were most definitely not a couple—a state of affairs which had been reinforced by the fact that they'd spent their first night at the hacienda sleeping in separate rooms.

Well, of *course they had.* Carlos wasn't interested in her any more, was he? Not in that way.

Because he hadn't touched her. Not once. Not a tight, comforting hug when she'd told him about the baby. Not a squeeze of her fingers during the flight over here, nor even a protective hand held at the small of her back as he guided her through the doors of his beloved hacienda for the first time.

Nothing.

And didn't that send out the clearest message of all—that the sexual side of their relationship was over? That really, everything between them was over—other than the mechanics of working out how to manage their shared parenthood. She guessed that at some point they were going to have to sit down and discuss what the future was going to bring, but she knew without him having to tell her that it was not going to include coupledom.

Kat went to her room and changed into a bikini which seemed too skimpy for comfort—though, logically, she knew that her body had not yet begun to alter. Just that now it felt more vulnerable than it used to. More exposed. Just like she did. Pulling on a silken robe and carrying a book she had little enthusiasm for, she went downstairs to find Carlos was already by the pool.

He looked up as she approached, and frowned. 'You need a hat.'

'I haven't brought one with me.'

'Well, there are plenty around the place. Here. Have this.'

Fishing out a battered old panama from underneath one of the loungers, he tossed it to her, and she caught it.

'Thanks.' Her throat was dry as she slipped off her silken robe and lay down beside him. It was still early and the air was fresh and sweet. Unknown birds were making distant calls and she could smell the heavy fragrance of jasmine.

For a while she felt brittle, unsure of what to do or say to the man whose golden-olive body was so near—and yet which might as well have been on a distant planet for all the closeness which existed between them. There were a million things she felt she should ask him, but she was too weary to begin, and the sun sinking into her skin was so very distracting…and gradually it made her relax a little. She drank some cool water and picked up her book. Put it down again, and dozed.

Deep, accented words floated into her dreamless state and she looked up to find that Carlos was leaning over her, his black eyes gleaming with concern. 'You'll burn if you're not careful,' he said softly. 'Want me to rub some cream on for you?'

'I…' What could she say? That she was afraid if he touched her she might not be able to control her emotions, or her body's response to him? She would risk burning her skin because she was so vulnerable around him? How pathetic was that? Kat nodded, tongue flicking out over suddenly bone-dry lips. 'If you don't mind.'

Mind? Carlos's mouth hardened. 'Turn over.' He squeezed lotion onto the firm flesh between her shoulder blades and then began to rub it in, expelling a slow rush of air as he felt the silken texture of her skin beneath his fingers. How long had it been since he had touched her like this? Pushing aside the straps of her bikini he began to massage her tight muscles, feeling some of the tension begin to melt beneath his questing fingers.

'Carlos…'

'Is that good, *Princesa*?'

Squeezing her eyes tightly shut, Kat couldn't make up her mind whether she wanted to laugh or cry. 'Well, yes…yes, it's good.' Of course it was good.

'Then lie back and enjoy it.'

Was he *mad*? Didn't he realise that, with his hands edging down to the wide band of flesh which lay above her bikini bottom, she just wanted to wriggle and squirm and pull him down against her rapidly warming body? Against her and into her. To feel his hard flesh united with hers once again. Kat swallowed. Now his fingers were kneading at the tops of her thighs—and this was really dangerous territory because what else would account for her almost strangled little gulp and the terrible sexual hunger which had begun to bubble up inside her?

'Carlos!' she said urgently.

'What? What is it, *Princesa*?'

'I…I…'

And suddenly Carlos couldn't bear it for a second longer, knowing that he was about to fall into a snare of his own making. Knowing full well that he could seduce her in an instant, exactly where she was. He wouldn't even have to meet the expression in her cold, hurt eyes. Could thrust into her from behind for a wordless and blissful coupling, knowing that they would both gasp out their relieved fulfilment and then it would be over. Their frustration forgotten and their bodies satisfied. And suddenly registering the certainty that it was no longer enough. Not nearly enough. Not any more.

Yes, it would be as easy as breathing to take her, but where would that leave them? Hadn't he used the power of his sexual expertise to shield him from life for too long, seeking the heady power of sex as a substitute for emotion, time after time? And didn't he owe this woman the truth, no matter how hard it was for him to admit it?

Turning her over, he stared down into her face—at the dark dilation of her blue eyes and the flare of colour which washed across her cheekbones—and felt a strange rush of something like pain in his heart. He had faced death and danger many times during his life, but he had never known such a feeling of trepidation. How was it possible to face the mighty wrath of a thirteen-hundred-pound animal in the bullring with a degree of steadfastness and resolve…and yet be rendered weak by the blaze in a woman's beautiful blue eyes?

'I'm sorry,' he said simply.

Kat frowned. What was he saying—that he'd changed his mind about making love to her when it had obviously been on his mind only seconds ago? 'Sorry?' she echoed. 'What for?'

He gave a bitter laugh. 'How long have you got? For doubting you. For being a victim of my own prejudice. For not realising that the woman I saw on my boat was the real you, not the poor little rich girl I was determined to see. That once you'd peeled away the layers you'd used to protect yourself from the tough blows that life had dealt you, I caught a glimpse of the woman you really were. The real Kat. That beneath all the finery was something much more precious.' For a moment his voice sounded shaken. 'And that something was you.'

Kat stared at him, confusion tempered with the frantic clamour of her mind telling her not to raise her hopes. Not to let him hurt her. Not any more. 'Are you saying all this because I'm having a baby?' she whispered.

He shook his head. 'I'm saying it because I mean it. Because I've been a fool, Kat. A stupid fool.' Taking a deep breath, he forced himself to admit why. 'Resenting you for the fact that, for the first time in my life, I lost control when I was around you. Without realising that sometimes a man needs to lose control, because that is what makes him human. What enables him to grab at the things which make life worth living.'

Suddenly, Kat could see how Carlos's steely self-will had protected *him* in exactly the same way as the armoury of her clothes and rebellious attitude had protected *her.* The two of them had a lot more in common than she'd ever realised. They'd both witnessed violence and pain. Had both deployed their own methods of coping with them.

And now?

They could, she realised, put all their demons in the past—but only if he wanted to. Because she realised something else too. That time after time she had given herself to Carlos, only to have him push her away. She understood why he had done it—but she couldn't keep on doing it. Giving was a two-way street—or there could be no true equality. No real relationship. Her voice was gentle. 'Carlos, what exactly are you saying?'

He was intelligent enough to know that this was one of life's big questions, the sort that your entire future would depend on. And even as she asked it, the answer came to him instantly, with a kind of blinding certainty he'd never before realised he was capable of.

He stared straight into her face. 'That I love you,' he said simply.

They were words she never thought she'd hear—never from Carlos—but it didn't occur to Kat to doubt them. Not for a minute. Perhaps because she sensed how much it had taken for him to say them—and because although his words could sometimes wound, they were always truthful. And perhaps because she knew that he had missed out on love for so much of his life, it didn't occur to her to hesitate. Nor to hold back in any way. In fact, she couldn't have done—for the joy in her heart was too insistent to be silenced.

'Oh, Carlos. My sweet, darling Carlos. I love you too,' she whispered. 'So much.'

He took her face in his hands, cupping its heart shape between both palms. 'I want to marry you, Kat,' he said unsteadily. 'I want us to make a life for ourselves together. A new life. A proper life.'

And now she *did* hesitate. For Kat hadn't grown up

with the best role models in the world where marriage was concerned. Her family was littered with divorces and their complicated consequences.

'And I want to be a good father,' he continued fiercely, before she had spoken. 'The best father in the world to our child. He—or she—will have their own destiny and never will I try to live my life through them.'

She heard the resolve which had deepened his voice and knew that Carlos was determined never to replicate the cruelty practised by his father. And that determination of his spurred her on. Because wasn't marriage a leap of faith for everyone? In a way, she and Carlos were lucky. They had witnessed the mistakes that other people could make with their lives—and they could do their best to ensure they didn't repeat them.'

She drew back a little as she looked up into his face. 'Oh, Carlos—of course I'll marry you. I want to marry you more than anything else on earth.'

He nodded, and for a moment there was a lump in his throat so big that he had difficulty in speaking. 'Then seal it with a kiss, *Princesa*,' he commanded at last.

Something in his eyes made her tremble and something in the sweet restorative power of his lips made her tremble even more. She sighed when he lifted her off the sunbed and carried her to the nearby cabana, where he peeled off her little lemon bikini with a quiet and urgent hunger which was underpinned with an unmistakable sense of awe.

A shaft of pure love shot through her as he positioned

his powerful naked body over hers and when he filled her with one slick, long thrust, she cried out her pleasure. As sunlight and birdsong drifted in to mingle with the sound of their muffled moans of pleasure, Kat thought she had never known happiness like it.

Please make it last, she prayed silently, as she held him, both still shuddering from the sweet onslaught of their passion. But somehow she knew that they would *make* it last. The two of them—and then, one day in the coming months, three. They would do everything in their power to ensure that life would be good.

Snuggling against him, Kat felt the slowing of his heart and she nuzzled against his neck, wanting to shower him with tiny kisses which demonstrated all the love she was bursting to give him.

Funny, really—her father had sent her away to learn commitment and she had found it. It had been a tough lesson but she knuckled down to it—and Carlos had helped show her how. So really, it made sense for him to reap the benefits.

For wasn't marriage the biggest and most wonderful commitment of all?

Coming Next Month

in **Harlequin Presents® EXTRA.** Available September 14, 2010.

#117 ONE NIGHT PREGNANCY
Lindsay Armstrong
Unexpected Babies

#118 SENSIBLE HOUSEKEEPER, SCANDALOUSLY PREGNANT
Jennie Lucas
Unexpected Babies

#119 FIRED WAITRESS, HIRED MISTRESS
Robyn Grady
Jet Set Billionaires

#120 PROPOSITIONED BY THE BILLIONAIRE
Lucy King
Jet Set Billionaires

Coming Next Month

in **Harlequin Presents®.** Available September 28, 2010.

#2945 PUBLIC MARRIAGE, PRIVATE SECRETS
Helen Bianchin

#2946 EMILY AND THE NOTORIOUS PRINCE
India Grey
The Balfour Brides

#2947 INNOCENT SECRETARY... ACCIDENTALLY PREGNANT
Carol Marinelli

#2948 BRIDE IN A GILDED CAGE
Abby Green
Bride on Approval

#2949 HIS VIRGIN ACQUISITION
Maisey Yates

#2950 MAJESTY, MISTRESS...MISSING HEIR
Caitlin Crews

HPCNM0910

Spotlight on

Inspirational

Wholesome romances
that touch the heart and soul.

See the next page
to enjoy a sneak peek from
the Love Inspired® inspirational series.

CATINSPLI10

See below for a sneak peek at
our inspirational line, Love Inspired®.
Introducing HIS HOLIDAY BRIDE
by bestselling author Jillian Hart

Autumn Granger gave her horse rein to slide toward the town's new sheriff.

"Hey, there." The man in a brand-new Stetson, black T-shirt, jeans and riding boots held up a hand in greeting. He stepped away from his four-wheel drive with "Sheriff" in black on the doors and waded through the grasses. "I'm new around here."

"I'm Autumn Granger."

"Nice to meet you, Miss Granger. I'm Ford Sherman, from Chicago." He knuckled back his hat, revealing the most handsome face she'd ever seen. Big blue eyes contrasted with his sun-tanned complexion.

"I'm guessing you haven't seen much open land. Out here, you've got to keep an eye on cows or they're going to tear your vehicle apart."

"What?" He whipped around. Sure enough, mammoth black-and-white creatures had started to gnaw on his four-wheel drive. They clustered like a mob, mouths and tongues and teeth bent on destruction. One cow tried to pry the wiper off the windshield, another chewed on the side mirror. Several leaned through the open window, licking the seats.

"Move along, little dogie." He didn't know the first thing about cattle.

The entire herd swiveled their heads to study him curiously. Not a single hoof shifted. The animals soon returned to chewing, licking, digging through his possessions.

Autumn laughed, a warm and wonderful sound. "Thanks,

I needed that." She then pulled a bag from behind her saddle and waved it at the cows. "Look what I have, guys. Cookies."

Cows swung in her direction, and dozens of liquid brown eyes brightened with cookie hopes. As she circled the car, the cattle bounded after her. The earth shook with the force of their powerful hooves.

"Next time, you're on your own, city boy." She tipped her hat. The cowgirl stayed on his mind, the sweetest thing he had ever seen.

Will Ford be able to stick it out in the country
to find out more about Autumn?
Find out in HIS HOLIDAY BRIDE
by bestselling author Jillian Hart,
available in October 2010
only from Love Inspired®.

SHLIEXP1010